ZAPATA

JOHN STEINBECK was born in 1902 in Salinas, California, a town a few miles from the Pacific Coast and near the fertile Salinas Valley—an area that was to be the background of much of his fiction. He studied at Stanford University but left without earning a degree and, after a series of laboring jobs, began to write. An attempt at a freelance literary career in New York City failed and he returned to California, continuing to write in a lonely cottage. Popular success came to him only in 1935 with *Tortilla Flat*. That book's promise was confirmed by succeeding works: *In Dubious Battle*, *Of Mice and Men*, and especially *The Grapes of Wrath*, a novel so powerful that it remains among the archetypes of American culture. Steinbeck's later books, most of them set in California, include *Cannery Row*, *The Wayward Bus*, *East of Eden*, *The Short Reign of Pippin IV*, and *Travels with Charley*. He died in 1968, having won a Nobel Prize in 1962.

ROBERT E. MORSBERGER taught in Africa for two years and is now professor of English at California State Polytechnic University in Pomona. He has published over 150 articles, eight short stories, and nine books, including *James Thurber*, *Lew Wallace: Militant Romantic* (in collaboration with Katherine M. Morsberger), *Swordplay on the Elizabethan and Jacobean Stage*, and two volumes on American screenwriters that he co-edited for *The Dictionary of Literary Biography*. He also edited the original publication of John Steinbeck's screenplay *Viva Zapata!* and is head of the editorial board of the *Steinbeck Quarterly*.

EMILIANO ZAPATA.

ZAPATA

John Steinbeck

edited and with commentary by

Robert E. Morsberger

penguin books

PENGUIN BOOKS
Published by the Penguin Group
Penguin Books USA Inc., 375 Hudson Street,
New York, New York 10014, U.S.A.
Penguin Books Ltd, 27 Wrights Lane, London W8 5TZ, England
Penguin Books Australia Ltd, Ringwood, Victoria, Australia
Penguin Books Canada Ltd, 10 Alcorn Avenue,
Toronto, Ontario, Canada M4V 3B2
Penguin Books (N.Z.) Ltd, 182–190 Wairau Road,
Auckland 10, New Zealand

Penguin Books Ltd, Registered Offices:
Harmondsworth, Middlesex, England

Viva Zapata! first published in the United States of America
in a Viking Compass Edition 1975
Zapata first published in a limited edition by
The Yolla Bolly Press 1991
Published in Penguin Books 1993

7 9 10 8

Copyright © Elaine A. Steinbeck, 1975, 1991
Copyright © The Viking Press, Inc., 1975
Copyright © Viking Penguin, a division of Penguin Books USA Inc., 1991
All rights reserved

Elaine A. Steinbeck acknowledges the courtesy of
Twentieth Century-Fox Film Corporation, producer of the 1952 film,
in making the manuscript available.

Photographs courtesy of Photofest.

LIBRARY OF CONGRESS CATALOGING IN PUBLICATION DATA
Steinbeck, John, 1902–1968.
Zapata/John Steinbeck; edited and with commentary by Robert E.
Morsberger.
p.   cm.
Includes bibliographical references.
ISBN 0 14 01.7322 6
1. Zapata, Emiliano, 1879–1919—Drama.   I. Morsberger, Robert
Eustis, 1929–   . II. Title.
PN1997.V56   1993
812'.52—dc20   92–35434

Printed in the United States of America
Set in Bodoni Book
Designed by Cheryl L. Cipriani

¡STEINBECK VIVE!

Preface

John Steinbeck's original version of the drama of Emiliano Zapata differs substantially from the screenplay for *Viva Zapata!*, released by Twentieth Century-Fox in 1952, which earned Steinbeck an Academy Award nomination. The original, which forms the first part of this volume, is not a shooting script but a long narrative that provides extensive historical and cultural background, along with a more detailed life of Zapata than the one that appears in the streamlined and austere screenplay. Parts of the complicated history of the Mexican revolution, between its beginning in 1910 and the assassination of Zapata in 1919, are given in straightforward narrative, others are in dramatic format, and yet others are not dramatized at all but summarized in notes that include suggestions as to how they might be filmed. Only a few scenes correspond to the final shooting script, which follows it here, and even these were changed, usually condensed in the interest of cinematic brevity. Thus the original manuscript, which Steinbeck titled *Zapata, the Little Tiger*, is essentially a different document from the screenplay. Almost two-thirds of it takes place before the scene with which the film begins.

In transforming *Zapata, the Little Tiger* into *Viva Zapata!*,

Steinbeck reworked the material extensively, making changes in emphasis and focus. Although the original narrative is less cinematic, it is valuable for its wealth of research, including oral history not recorded elsewhere, and it contains many episodes that do not appear in the final shooting script. Thus the two versions of *Zapata* do not duplicate but complement each other; together, they give a more colorful and extensive picture of Emiliano Zapata and the Mexican revolution than either does alone.

The shooting final of *Viva Zapata!*, published in 1975 as a Viking Compass book, has long been out of print and has become a collector's item. The original 337-page typescript of *Zapata, the Little Tiger* was never published and was for some time considered lost. It turned up in the film archives at UCLA and was published for the first time in 1991 by the Yolla Bolly Press in a deluxe limited edition. Now for the first time, both versions of Steinbeck's *Zapata* are published together in one volume.

Acknowledgments

I should like to express my gratitude to Elaine Steinbeck, Elia Kazan, John Womack, Jr., Herbert Kline, and Richard Astro for generously providing correspondence and taking the time to answer questions about John Steinbeck and *Viva Zapata!* Katherine Lambert, Frances C. Richardson, and Kenneth Kenyon of the Research Department at Twentieth Century-Fox made the resources of the studio files available. A slightly different version of "Steinbeck's Zapata: Rebel versus Revolutionary" was published in 1971 by the Oregon State University Press in *Steinbeck: The Man and His Works*, edited by Richard Astro and Tetsumaro Hayashi, copyright © 1974 by Richard Astro and Tetsumaro Hayashi; the essay is reprinted here, with slight modifications, by permission of the Oregon State University Press. "Steinbeck's Screenplays and Productions" originally appeared in a slightly different form in *A Study Guide to Steinbeck*, edited by Tetsumaro Hayashi, copyright © 1974 by Tetsumaro Hayashi, published by the Scarecrow Press, Inc. "Zapata: The Man, the Myth, and the Mexican Revolution," copyright © by Robert E. Morsberger, originally accompanied a deluxe limited edition of *Zapata* (a.k.a. *Zapata, the Little Tiger*) published in 1991 by the Yolla Bolly Press, and it is reprinted with thanks to James and Carolyn Robertson, proprietors of the Yolla Bolly Press. I also wish to thank Denis Halliwell of the Viking Press and Dawn Ann Drzal of Viking Penguin for editorial assistance and Julie Fallowfield of McIntosh and Otis and James Dourgarian, bookman, for their support and encouragement. Thanks are inadequate for the suggestions and moral support provided by my wife during all stages of this project, from its inception to the final proofreading.

Contents

Part One

ZAPATA

A narrative,
in dramatic form,
of the life of
Emiliano Zapata

EMILIANO ZAPATA

The Man, the Myth,

and the Mexican Revolution

An Introductory Essay by Robert E. Morsberger

In 1867 Benito Juárez overthrew the empire set up in Mexico by French emperor Napoleon III, executed the Hapsburg puppet Maximilian, and established a democracy with himself as the president. Juárez died in 1872, during an attempted insurrection by Porfirio Díaz, a former ally. Díaz took over leadership of the opposition, refused to acknowledge his defeat in the election of 1876, and overthrew the victor. Proclaiming himself president, he allied his government with the great land monopolists and perverted the presidency into a dictatorship. After thirty-four years of increasing oppression, the dispossessed peasants revolted in 1910. Their nominal leader was Francisco J. Madero, but the effectual leader on the battlefield, who continued the struggle for freedom and land reform after a counterrevolution by General Huerta and the murder of Madero in 1913, was a farmer from Morelos named Emiliano Zapata, a born leader and military genius. After the defeat of Huerta in 1914, Zapata's former ally Venustiano Carranza seized power and was resisted by Zapata and Pancho Villa. Betrayed by an emissary of Carranza, Zapata was assassinated in 1919 at the age of forty.

The story of Emiliano Zapata and the Mexican revolution has everything: battle, murder and sudden death, a man of the people who becomes a great general and revolutionary hero, the temptations of power, a compelling love story, betrayal, martyrdom, and myth. The story of Zapata's fellow general, *Viva Villa!* was one of the most popular movies of 1934, but Zapata is a far more admirable, complex, and appealing figure, and it is surprising that no one thought to make a film about him before 1952, when *Viva Zapata!* was released by Twentieth Century-Fox, with a screenplay by John Steinbeck. Director Elia Kazan claims that the proposal for a screen treatment of Emiliano Zapata came from him. It was the first film that he made without using a professional screenwriter. He told Michel Ciment, "I began to go to authors like Steinbeck, Budd Schulberg [*On the Waterfront, A Face in the Crowd*], Inge [*Splendor in the Grass*] who were not screenwriters. . . . What I needed most was someone who saw in Zapata what I saw in Zapata."[1] He and Steinbeck were friends and neighbors, so when he began to think about the project, he asked Steinbeck "if he'd be interested in working on it with me. He said he'd been thinking about Z for years."[2] Almost twenty years, in fact, for Steinbeck first became interested in Zapata and the Mexican revolution around 1930 after conversations with Reina Dunn, whose father, Hearst journalist H. H. Dunn, later wrote the book *The Crimson Jester, Zapata of Mexico.*[3] Dunn's book, published in 1934, is a sensationalist narrative that repeats uncritically the tabloid tales of anti-Zapata newspapers like the far from impartial *Imparcial*, which called him "the modern Attila" and characterized his followers not as rebels against oppression but as *bandito* anarchists wallowing in plunder, arson, and debauchery. Steinbeck discounted the lurid coloring of Dunn's work and did his own research in quest of the

1 Michel Ciment, *Kazan on Kazan* (New York: Viking, 1974), p. 97.

2 Elia Kazan, letter to Robert E. Morsberger, March 29, 1973.

3 Richard Astro, letter to Robert E. Morsberger, September 29, 1971.

real Zapata. Much of it was in the form of oral history, for beginning in the early 1930s, Steinbeck made a great many trips to Mexico, where he interviewed veterans of the revolution and other survivors of Zapata's time. Fluent in Spanish, Steinbeck traveled extensively through the areas where Zapata fought, and the oral history that he compiled was invaluable both for the immediacy of its eyewitness recollections and for the fact that it was not available in any other written record. In addition, Steinbeck saw with his own eyes the struggles of the dispossessed and landless poor farm workers, whose problems were all too much like those of their counterparts in the United States, whom Steinbeck wrote about in *In Dubious Battle*, *The Harvest Gypsies*, *Of Mice and Men*, and *The Grapes of Wrath*.

His research moved into high gear when he returned to Mexico in 1940 to write his first screenplay, the narrative for a documentary film to be made in collaboration with director Herbert Kline, who had made several antifascist documentaries. Steinbeck had originally intended to write a script about the Mexican fascists' attempts to overthrow the liberal government of President Cardenas. But when he joined the production crew on location in Chalco, Mexico, Steinbeck became intrigued by material Kline had discovered about the resistance of Indian villagers to the efforts of rural doctors to eradicate epidemic disease; he wrote a new script, *The Forgotten Village*, documenting this conflict. Despite his attack on the forgotten village's superstitious fear of scientific medicine, Steinbeck learned to respect the villagers' character and culture. Such people were the core of Zapata's following. The wealthy landowners who tried to sabotage the film and prevent the peasants from being paid fair wages gave Steinbeck personal knowledge of the reactionary forces that Zapata had fought to overthrow. By coincidence, the village was celebrating a commemoration of Zapata. In a local *pulqueria*, some of the old-timers spoke "of Zapata still being alive in the mountains nearby, riding his horse . . . and looking after the peons he came from and loved." Kline believes that the experience in Chalco gave Steinbeck an authentic sense of life among the Zapatistas and provided him with the background for *Viva Zapata!*[4]

It was at this time that Steinbeck began concentrated research on Zapata and the Mexican revolution. Rejecting Dunn's distortions in *The Crimson Jester*, he turned to *Zapata the Unconquerable* (1941), a narrative by Edgcumb Pinchon whose *Viva Villa!* was the source for the 1934 movie of that title. Pinchon's was the most recent study in English on Zapata until John Womack, Jr.'s definitive biography was published in 1969. Though he inserted some fictional elements, Pinchon spent a year doing research in Mexico, and Womack credits his work as being "a good popular biography."[5] But Steinbeck used Pinchon only for the broad historical outline; he omitted most of Pinchon's treatment and borrowed only a few scenes (the opening audience with Diaz, Pablo's return from Texas, the procession accompanying Zapata when he is taken prisoner, the audience with Madero, and a dialogue between Villa and Zapata), all of which he trimmed down and made more dramatic. The material that he added is more significant, especially the role of Zapata's brother Eufemio (whom Pinchon barely mentions), Zapata's courtship of and marriage to the aristocratic Josefa Espejo, and the death of Eufemio. For the final shooting script, he added the execution of Pablo, a major new character named Fernando, Zapata's need to relinquish power, and much of the film's political philosophy. Supplementing Pinchon with his own research in Mexico, Steinbeck not only collected oral history but got a first-hand sense of people and places. His personal involvement contributed to *Viva Zapata!*'s authenticity and helped make it more compelling than the melodramatic, sentimental, or textbookish 1930s film biographies of assorted statesmen, inventors, composers, and artists.

In 1947 Steinbeck returned to Mexico to observe the filming of *The Pearl,* for which he'd written the screenplay, in collaboration with Jack Wagner and Emilio Fernandez. Directed by Fernandez,

---

4 Herbert Kline, letter to Robert E. Morsberger, June 5, 1973.

5 John Womack, Jr., *Zapata and the Mexican Revolution* (New York: Alfred A. Knopf, 1969), p. 422.

The Pearl was produced in Mexico, with Mexican players acting in English. When it was released the next year, it was the first Mexican movie to be generally distributed in the United States. Its sympathy for the poor and its anger at their exploitation by the arrogantly and unjustly wealthy anticipate Steinbeck's next work, *Viva Zapata!*

Steinbeck spent most of the summer of 1948 in Mexico doing research on Zapata, but he observed that it was difficult to get reliable information, since Zapata had become such a legendary figure. In November he went to Mexico City and then to Cuernavaca with Elia Kazan to search out more material on Zapata, but the trip was unsatisfactory. Even so, he wrote to his friend Bo Beskow on November 19, "My material for the Zapata script is all collected now and next Monday I will go to work on it with great energy, for I have great energy again. Whether there is any talent left I do not know nor care very much."[6] Still traumatized by the breakup of his second marriage, Steinbeck was having trouble concentrating on his work; his energy came and went in a manic-depressive fashion. Late in January 1949, he went once again to Mexico, determined to stay until he had finished the screenplay. "I need the country and the language in my eyes and ears," he wrote to Pascal Covici, his editor at the Viking Press.[7] But he found himself depressed and lonely in Mexico and came home after only two weeks. Still, something had freed him momentarily from writer's block, for he wrote to Covici a few weeks later that "the dams are burst."[8] By March he had managed to pull some of the raw material together, writing to Kazan that "there are some great scenes in the Zapata script. I don't know whether they will ever get on film but they are there."[9] To Covici he confided, "I think this script must

---

6 Elaine Steinbeck and Robert Wallsten, eds., *Steinbeck: A Life in Letters* (New York: The Viking Press, 1975), p. 342.

7 Jackson J. Benson, *The True Adventures of John Steinbeck, Writer* (New York: The Viking Press, 1984), p. 630.

8 Ibid.

9 *A Life in Letters*, p. 632.

be excellent. The dialogue has a good sound to me . . . the speech sounds like talk."[10] Meanwhile Steinbeck's agent and publisher were getting frustrated, for they wanted him to complete his next novel, a work in progress called "The Salinas Valley" that eventually became *East of Eden*, which Steinbeck had put on hold; he was spending several years without payment working on the screenplay, with the end nowhere in sight. According to his biographer Jackson Benson, Steinbeck "seemed to feel that completion of the script was somehow connected to his personal and artistic survival."[11] In the fall of 1949, Steinbeck sent the material on Zapata to Darryl F. Zanuck, the head producer at Twentieth Century-Fox, which had made Steinbeck's *The Grapes of Wrath* (1940), *The Moon Is Down* (1943), and *Lifeboat* (1944), as well as Kazan's *A Tree Grows in Brooklyn* (1945), *Boomerang* (1947), *Gentleman's Agreement* (1947), and *Pinky* (1949). Zanuck in turn had his assistant, Jules Buck, see if he could help Steinbeck whip it into shape. Kazan observed, "You could tell a hundred different stories with that material."[12] After examining Steinbeck's text, Buck called it "a very definitive breakdown of the revolution, the causes—it was magnificent—and of Zapata, the history. A master's degree is what he had, together with a Ph.D. Except it wasn't a screenplay."[13] Zanuck demanded a screenplay within four weeks, so Buck and Steinbeck got together first in Hollywood and then in Pacific Grove. Buck would make suggestions about form and structure that Steinbeck would accept or reject. Finally Buck said, " 'Okay, John, today's the day,' and then I said, 'Give me the words,' and by God, he gave me the words. No problem in copy, none."[14] While Steinbeck dictated, Buck typed; Steinbeck would occasionally rewrite a passage in pencil and try it out on Buck, and sometimes he would

---

10 Benson, p. 630.

11 Ibid., p. 651.

12 Ciment, p. 87.

13 Benson, p. 651.

14 Ibid., p. 652.

actually diagram a scene on paper. Thus prodded, Steinbeck managed to condense and telescope his material, with such concentration that he averaged twelve pages a day and finished a draft in eleven days. Buck declined any co-authorial credit, insisting that the words were Steinbeck's and that he had functioned only in the role of producer.

When Buck left, Steinbeck turned to another project and quickly knocked out the first draft of his play/novel *Burning Bright*. He was not entirely satisfied with *Zapata*, however, and continued working on the screenplay well into 1950. From February through April, he spent much of his time in New York, conferring with Kazan about the script, on which he was putting what he hoped was the final polish. Kazan would help frame the action for a scene, then type Steinbeck's dialogue for it.[15] Thinking he was finally finished, Steinbeck then wrote a lengthy sketch of his late friend Ed Ricketts as a preface to *The Log from the Sea of Cortez*, then polished the script even more, until in the late summer he was able to write to Kazan:[16]

Dear Gadg:

Last night Elaine read me parts of the script. She liked it very much and I must say I did too. It is a little double action jewel of a script. But I was glad to hear it again because before it is mouthed by actors, I want to go over the dialogue once more for very small changes. Things like—"For that matter." "As a matter of fact"—in other words all filler wants to come out. There isn't much but there is some. I'll want no word in dialogue that has not some definite reference to the story. You said once that you would like this to be a kind of monument. By the same token I would like it to be as tight and terse as possible.

---

15 Elia Kazan, *A Life* (New York: Alfred A. Knopf, 1988), pp. 396–397.

16 *A Life in Letters*, p. 407.

It is awfully good but it can be better. Just dialogue—I
heard a dozen places where I can clean it up and sharpen
it. But outside of that I am very much pleased with it. I
truly believe it is a classic example of good film writing.
So we'll make it perfect.

This "jewel of a script" that he is talking about is the shooting
final, which differs substantially from the original treatment that
Jules Buck compared to a Ph.D. dissertation. That first version,
which Steinbeck called *Zapata, the Little Tiger*, is published here
for the first time (excepting a deluxe limited edition brought out
by the Yolla Bolla Press in 1991). It is not a shooting script but
a preliminary treatment that opens with a good deal of historical
background and local color—almost a third of the text—after which
some scenes are written out dramatically while other parts of the
complicated history of the Mexican revolution are not dramatized
at all but merely summarized, with some sketchy suggestions as
to how they might be filmed. Almost two-thirds of the preliminary
treatment takes place before the scene where the actual filmscript
begins. Only a few parts roughly correspond to scenes in the final
shooting script, and even they were changed, usually shortened in
the interests of cinematic brevity, sometimes moved to a different
context.

The preliminary treatment is valuable on several counts. It
incorporates a vast amount of research, done over a space of nearly
twenty years, much of it oral history that is not in any of the
published biographies of Zapata or histories of the revolution, and
it is here presented for the first time. A later Zapata biographer,
Harvard historian John Womack, Jr., credits Steinbeck with dis-
covering documentation of Zapata's hitherto secret marriage to Josefa Espejo.

The final shooting script eliminates or condenses much of the
history in the preliminary treatment: It opens, for example, with a
delegation of farmers from Morelos, who protest to the dictator Díaz

that their land has been stolen by an anonymous "they," whereas the original version tells in vivid and angry detail the manner in which Díaz, in collaboration with the great landed families, subverted the democratic legacy of Benito Juárez by consolidating power into absolutism, systematically subjugating the peasant farmers and stealing their land. It also dramatizes many events, real or imagined, that are not in the final shooting script: It opens before Zapata is born, gives dramatic vignettes (probably fictitious) of his boyhood and adolescence, tells a great deal more about Zapata's roisterous brother Eufemio, and provides different or longer dialogue for the few scenes that roughly correspond in both versions. Not only are these omitted passages compelling in their own right, but they enable us to follow a work in progress, study the process of revision, and see how Steinbeck shaped his final screenplay from the fuller but less cinematic early narrative. Sometimes he is trying out ideas that he later dropped; sometimes he picks up a footnote and fleshes it out into a fully dramatized scene. Finally, the early treatment contains notes to the director about the problems involved in filming in Mexico, with suggestions for casting, costuming, and photographing some episodes, taking us behind the scenes and into the writer's mind—much as the *Journal of a Novel*, a collection of Steinbeck's letters to his editor, Pascal Covici, illuminates the writing of *East of Eden*.

The focus changes between the first and final version. The first not only contains more history but is also more mythic, showing Zapata as a man of destiny, his birth and greatness predicted by the oracular *curandera*, his childhood a preparation for the role of revolutionary leader awaiting him. We follow him as a boyhood bandit stealing weapons from the *rurales* that will later be used to arm insurrectionists, and we see him as the ideal *charro*, the most magnificent horseman in Mexico. At the same time, we are made aware of his womanizing and extramarital affairs—there is even a scene showing Zapata and Villa in a brothel—whereas the shooting final omits any mention of these and presents Zapata as a loyal and devoted husband. Steinbeck incorporates a good deal of local color and folklore into the tapestry of the original treatment, making it more sprawling than the tightly knit filmscript, but also giving it a richer texture than the more austere final script.

In the latter, Zapata is a more modest man. Far from believing himself destined to be the hero of his country, he shuns power and accepts it reluctantly when it is thrust upon him. He wants to live a private life, marry Josefa Espejo, and settle down into respectable anonymity. But he cannot stand by and do nothing when he observes acts of oppression, and his decisive actions to counter them cause the people to make him their leader. Steinbeck and Kazan noted that one thing that fascinated them about Zapata was that unlike most revolutionaries, who too often turned totalitarian, Zapata not only did not seek power but relinquished it rather than let it corrupt him. As a foil to Zapata, the shooting final introduces the ruthless revolutionary Fernando, who is a friend to no one and believes in nothing but the necessity of killing and the elimination of all opposition. When Zapata thwarts him by leaving the presidential palace to go home and restore power to the people, Fernando proposes the plan that leads to Zapata's betrayal and death. Fernando is a fictitious character, a composite of all those who have betrayed democratic revolutions and replaced them with repression.

A historian might object that Steinbeck's screenplay vastly oversimplifies the actual events. The film gives no sense of a ten-year time span, nor do any of its characters age perceptibly. But it is possible to get at the essence of events better through drama than documentation, and John Womack, Jr., Zapata's biographer, has called the film "a distinguished achievement," which, despite inevitable distortions that result from condensing the revolution into a taut tragedy, "quickly and vividly develops a portrayal of Zapata, the villagers, and the nature of their relations and movement that I find still subtle, powerful, and true."[17] Carlos Fuentes,

---

17 Womack, p. 420.

Mexico's leading novelist, has also spoken highly of *Viva Zapata!* as a powerful and accurate portrayal.[18]

Steinbeck's technique is like that of Shakespeare in his history plays. A complexity of events sprawling over a great deal of time and space is telescoped into a compelling drama:[19]

Carry them here and there, jumping o'er times,
Turning th' accomplishment of many years
Into an hourglass. . . .

Kazan was aware of this quality and commented that "Shakespeare is more contemporary than the plays that are being written today. He leaps from here to there, he goes to climaxes, and the figures are big-sized."[20]

Steinbeck and Kazan had hoped to make *Viva Zapata!* in Mexico on authentic locations. The preliminary treatment includes a running dialogue with director Kazan ("Gadg") on how to take advantage of local color, how to get things done effectively in Mexico, how to take advantage of Steinbeck's experience with the film crews of *The Forgotten Village* and *The Pearl*. But according to Kazan, the Mexican authorities were committed to a dogmatic Marxist view of Zapata and refused to cooperate. The film was made instead in Roma, Texas, a small town of fewer than 2,000 inhabitants just across the border on the north side of the Rio Grande, in Zapata County, about ninety miles south and east of Laredo. To play Zapata, Steinbeck said only one actor would do: Pedro Armendariz, who had starred in *The Pearl* and played the pursuing policeman in John Ford's adaptation (*The Fugitive*) of Graham Greene's *The Power and the Glory*. Armendariz bore a remarkable resemblance to Zapata and could certainly have played the role convincingly, but Zanuck wanted a bigger star. Kazan

---

18 Carlos Fuentes in conversation with Robert E. Morsberger, spring 1986.

19 William Shakespeare, *Henry V*, Prologue: 29–31.

20 Ciment, p. 176.

proposed Marlon Brando, whom he had just directed on stage and screen in *A Streetcar Named Desire*, but Zanuck at first wanted no part of Brando, who had made only one film prior to *Streetcar*, and proposed Fox's favorite leading man, Tyrone Power. Power had played Spaniards and Mexicans convincingly in *The Mark of Zorro*, *Blood and Sand*, and *Captain from Castile* and doubtless could have handled the part. But he was preparing to go on stage in *John Brown's Body*, and after Brando won an Oscar nomination for his sensational performance as Stanley Kowalski, Zanuck withdrew his objections. Power's leading lady in *Captain from Castile*, Jean Peters, was cast as Josefa, and the half-Irish, half-Mexican Anthony Quinn was cast as Zapata's brother Eufemio. The Zapata brothers' mustaches were trimmed to a less extreme length in the movie, but otherwise all the players were made up to have a remarkable resemblance to their historical counterparts. The scene of the victorious generals Villa and Zapata posing for their photograph was duplicated exactly by Kazan; the source was a photograph in *Historia Gráfica de la Revolución* in the Mexican archives. At one point in the development of the script, Steinbeck proposed having *corridos*, a running commentary of traditional Mexican songs, "to be written by a wandering poet named John Steinbeck to music by Alex North" and performed by one of Zapata's men, or else "to be accompanied by either guitar music solo or music from our conception of a typical five-piece Mexican Country band."[21] Unfortunately, this device interrupted the narrative and was dropped, but, striving for authenticity, Kazan got together a group of old-time Mexican musicians with period instruments and had them play traditional Mexican songs and songs of the revolution, which he taped and which became the basis for Alex North's Oscar-nominated score. Instead of creating the customary symphonic background music, North made most of his music function as a natural part of the action—as mariachi bands, military parades, serenades, religious chants, songs, and celebrations—all in in-

---

21 John Steinbeck, "Note to the Reader," Twentieth Century-Fox, July 31, 1950.

digenous Mexican modes, to accentuate both the realism and the ballad-like quality of the film.

Released in 1952, *Viva Zapata!* earned Steinbeck an Academy Award nomination for best story and screenplay. It was Steinbeck's third Oscar nomination; he had been nominated for the best original story of 1944 for *Lifeboat* and (with Jack Wagner) the best original story of 1945 for *A Medal for Benny*. Marlon Brando received an Oscar nomination for best actor as Emiliano Zapata. Only twenty-eight years old at the time, Brando gave one of his most subtle and durable performances. He lost to Gary Cooper in *High Noon*, but John Womack, Jr., writes that "Brando captured wonderfully" the character of Zapata, his "integrity, his suspicion of all outsiders, his absolute sense of responsibility."[22] Anthony Quinn did win an Oscar as best supporting actor for his dynamic portrayal of Eufemio Zapata. Together with *High Noon*, *Singin' in the Rain*, and *The Quiet Man*, *Viva Zapata!* remains one of the four most memorable films of 1952, and the screenplay is arguably Steinbeck's best work since *Cannery Row* (1944).

R. M.

---

22 John Womack, Jr., letter to Robert E. Morsberger, April 28, 1973.

ZAPATA

A Narrative, in Dramatic Form,

of the life of

Emiliano Zapata

by *John Steinbeck*

Introduction

I

Mexican history is thought by most Americans to be a series of banditries and of small revolutions and revolts led by venal and self-interested men. The outbreaks and explosions are considered as comic opera movements of an inferior people. While it is true that there have been Mexican leaders who turned dishonest and who have sold their own people, even these leaders have been the products of a mass desire and a mass movement of the Mexican people. Because there is such a misconception of the forces in back of Mexican outbursts, it might be well to put in this introduction a short résumé of what has actually happened in Mexico.

When the Spanish conquerors under Cortez came to Mexico, they found tribes and communities more or less like the Greek city-states, each one highly integrated, and each one possessing to a certain extent its own culture. Some of these states were tied together in larger leagues. There was nothing like the nation as we understand it today.

The Aztec group, a small and conquering people, had brought

a great number of these cities and leagues and small groups under its sway, but the Aztec group was not a nation, in the sense that it had no intention of making the conquered peoples a part of itself. Indeed, the conquered peoples were simply tributary groups which paid the Aztecs to keep out of war, and failure to pay brought immediate reprisals—slaughter and slavery and the sacrifice to the gods of the best and most perfect individuals of the revolting people. But, since the domination of the Aztecs was harsh, and since its sole purpose was that of tribute, some of its subject states were in continual revolt against it.

It was only because of this hatred by the subject peoples of the Aztecs that Cortez was able to take Mexico. Had he been alone, and had he not had the help of Indian allies, he would never have been able to conquer the Mexican lands so easily; but every dominated people came to him because he spearheaded the revolt against the hated Aztec empire.

Cortez had three great weapons. He had firearms, he had smallpox, and he had the church, and of the three, the latter two were his greatest weapons, for the early authorities of the Spanish church, far from being cruel and rapacious, actually brought to Mexico a new sense of the dignity of men and brought, also, a concept of the importance of the individual soul—a thing which was completely foreign to Indian thinking. Indeed, the early members of the Spanish church allied themselves quite often with the Indians against the Spanish conquerors.

The cruelties and the slaveries of the Spanish domination were condemned equally by the Spanish throne and by the Spanish church. The villain here, as everywhere, and in all times, was greed.

A large part of the land was cut up into great holdings which were delivered over to those men who had fought in the conquest. Large numbers of career men came over from Spain to take what they could get out of the newly conquered country, and although slavery was not countenanced, something which was actual slavery was introduced—the Indians came with the land, and they were used with the land. They were worked in the mines and in the fields.

It is usual now, for ill-informed people, to say that the indigenous social and economic system of the original Indians of Mexico, and, indeed, of all America, was communistic. This is an oversimplification. Communal it was in a pre-Marxian sense, but communistic it was not. The system it most closely resembled was the early Greek city-state, or city group.

Land was not owned by individual men, in the sense that it could not be inherited by a man's son, but it surely was owned in the sense that he maintained it during his lifetime. Government was by village elders and by town elders. Groups of the older men held permanent positions in governing the communities. Land was allotted by the elders. In the long run, the land was actually owned by the community and was let out during the lifetime of a man to an individual for as long as he should make it produce. This was true of the producing lands. There were, in addition, the common lands, such as were in existence in England—grazing lands, woodlands, and so forth, but these came under other categories and were common to the use of all.

The laws were very definite and were largely traditional, like British Common Law. They were strictly enforced by the village elders. The laws were strangely general throughout the whole country and jumped even racial and tribal boundaries. They governed nearly all phases of human conduct. Thus, there was a law in the Aztec league, strictly enforced, that any man under fifty who got drunk was automatically executed, whereas after fifty he could get as drunk as he wanted to. The reason for this, of course, was that in a warlike nation the younger men must be ready for war and must be in good physical condition. After their time of military value was over, the state had little interest in what they did with their bodies.

The laws covered the most minute things, such as who owned an animal wounded by one arrow and who owned an animal wounded by two arrows when the animal was finally tracked down.

It is necessary to put in these details so that it can be realized how deeply ingrained in the Mexican people are their traditional laws, for many of those unwritten laws are still in force.

The Spanish conquerors, while they did break up the land to a large extent, had a healthy respect for the village lands, and it must be admitted that the church was one of the strong factors in maintaining the system of landholding, the economic and social systems they found there. The church had absolutely no patience with the indigenous religious system, but it went along very freely with the other forms it found there. The fact that certain religious practices, beliefs, and customs of the original people crept into the church could not be helped, because these things were so deeply ingrained in the people that they managed to maintain themselves against other customs. However, this has been the invariable practice of the church all over the world. What it cannot destroy, it must incorporate. For instance, it is true that certain hill peoples come still to the chapel of the Virgin of Guadalupe on December 12, and they not only dance before the altar but make symbols in colored sands on the church floor just as they did to another goddess who had had a temple in that same place before the Spaniards ever came; but now it is in the name of Christianity instead of in the name of the goddess Atlitl.

It must be remembered that the primary drive of the Spanish throne was one of conversion of the world to Christianity, its kind of Christianity and its form, and only secondarily was it interested in profits. The fact that this changed later does not in any way lessen the original and initial drive. It was a profoundly religious time. The monarchy and the Spanish church truly believed that their first mission was to convert the world. That this project required money and soldiers and arms and ships is self-evident, and this money had to come from some place since Spain was a very poor nation.

When the Spaniards had fastened themselves upon Mexico, a gradual change took place. There was an immediate and quite general mixing of bloods. If the Spaniards had been content to accept the product of these bloods, they might still be holding Mexico, but the contrary was true. The Indian was not even a citizen. He was a native animal. The product of a marriage between a Spaniard and an Indian, while he had a slightly better social position, still held no office and was given no political preference of any kind. Officers were sent out from Spain. The Spanish colonies were the thriving ground for native Spaniards, practically never for either the intermixtures of Indian and Spanish, or even of the pure Spanish born in Mexico. Only a man born in Spain, of good blood, had any chance in the government of Mexico.

This was not true in the case of education. Very early, Indians entered the priesthood, and many of the first records, not only of the conquest but of the time that followed it, are the work of those first Indian Christian priests. It may be that they could not aspire to the highest ranks of the church nobility, but certainly they were used all over the country.

As far as the economy of Mexico went, it was a conquered and occupied country, and all of its products were considered to be the property of Spain and of people of Spanish blood, with the exception of the village lands, which were left and were protected.

Over the hundreds of years of the occupation of Mexico—and it was a true occupation—the great group of the mixed bloods increased, but their increase in numbers did not give them more preferment than they had had, political or social. They did not become the great middle class. They became the scholars, priests, the small storekeepers, but the threshold of advancement was very, very low. After a great number of years, they had become, in numbers at least and probably in intelligence, the dominant group in Mexico.

Then came two events which had a profound effect on this large group of Mexicans of mixed blood and native-born men of pure Spanish blood. The first of these great events was the American Revolution, and the second was the French Revolution.

A change had come over both the monarchy and the church, and in Spain at this time the two were more or less one. They had ceased to be missionary powers and had become economic systems whose purpose was the gathering of taxes, or tithes, and the accumulation of money and lands. These powers ignored the pressure of the growing group of intelligent Mestizos of Mexico. This group, stimulated by the two revolutions which had given them hope, broke into revolt, and, oddly enough, the leader of the revolt against the Spanish monarchy was a priest named Father Hidalgo. It was an extremely popular revolt. Parts of the local church broke off from the parent church, and only in the hierarchy, in the highest groups, did the church side with the Spanish monarchy. In addition, the revolution of Mexico against Spain was backed by the great mass of the indigenous Indians, a faceless, nameless people who had never been recognized even as humans by any group except the church, and by them only more or less as humans who would assume their rightful stature in heaven after their death.

In addition, there was great sympathy for the Mexican Revolution against Spain from those two nations which had given them their initial hope, the new United States and the French Republic.

This was a revolution geographic in scope, but once it was accomplished another and perpetual revolt took its place, and this was not geographical. It was the revolt of the dispossessed against the group which held the resources of Mexico, and that revolt has continued during all Mexican history and still continues.

The revolutionary intent of the Mexican people, now as then, has not changed. It is a desire for the distribution of the land and resources of Mexico among the Mexican people. This hunger for land was the cause of the revolt of Morelos, another priest incidentally, for the revolt of Benito Juárez against the reign of Maximilian, against Porfirio Díaz by Madero, and it continues into the present time.

Mexico, during all of its history, has had to contend against foreign domination, first Spain, then France, and then, in 1910, against a combination of Germany, France, the United States, and England. In every single case the revolts of the Mexican people have been aimed at land and, through land, at food.

In many cases the leaders of revolt have gone over to the other side and have become the dominant class against which a new revolt must be formed.

In this connection an interesting story was told me by Lincoln Steffens. He was a reporter at the time that Carranza was in a state of revolt, and he was on the train with Carranza after the final battles which put Carranza in power. The general said to him, "I know the pressures that will be put on me. How can I remain honest?" To which Mr. Steffens replied, "Why don't you leave the rifles with your men?"

"Why that?" Carranza asked.

"So they can kill you if you become dishonest," Steffens said.

Carranza nodded and said, "Yes, that might be a good way," but he didn't do it.

We come now to the time and the condition out of which our story grows, the story of Emiliano Zapata.

II

Benito Juárez was a pure Indian from the state of Oaxaca. His great admiration was for the American Constitution, and he attempted to build for Mexico a constitution like it. He was a friend of Abraham Lincoln and admired Lincoln above all other men. As a matter of fact, it was during Juárez administrations that Mexico grew conscious of constitutional law. But, as always, where it has been started, constitutional law runs afoul of those forces which, through possessions or positions, consider themselves outside the law.

The development of the Mexican constitution has been no different than that of any other. Although Juárez was able to get a constitution written, he was not able to get it enforced, and, after ensuing difficulties, another man—again an Indian—took over, and his name was Porfirio Díaz. He soon became known as the Strong Man of Mexico.

He realized that Mexico was weak internally, and that she was surrounded by very strong and rich neighbors; and so he worked out a system for not only placating those rich neighbors but for buying them off, and trading with them. In the process he ignored his own country almost completely.

He established a system which is still called "Porfirismo," and his system was very simple. He collected a group of strong and intelligent men about him. He paid Mexico's debts to foreign nations; he distributed concessions of all kinds to foreigners, always for a price, but he delivered.

It is natural that the governments of Japan, Germany, France, England, and the United States admired him very much, for he had pacified the country. *How* he did it is another story, but people could go at will about Mexico without danger of being injured or robbed.

The interest on Mexico's debts to foreign nations was paid on time, and it was of little interest to those foreign governments how he got the money.

Foreign capital admired him very much, for it was able to invest its money in Mexico with some feeling that the properties bought would not be taken away. There was no interest in how Díaz got the property and the concessions to sell.

He was considered a great, strong, gifted man. He was given every decoration known, and nobody thought to investigate what his own people were going through, nor what was happening to them.

His methods were quiet and effective. If anyone disagreed with him in any matter, he first tried to buy that man, and if he did not succeed, the man disappeared and was not heard of again. It was clean and neat, and there was little publicity in any of it. There is on record a telegram he sent to one of his field officers which gave a long list of names, and his final sentence was "Catch and kill instantly."

He established a rural police, highly paid, made up mostly of criminals. These horsemen dispensed his justice and kept order, and their method of keeping order was by summary execution of anyone who interfered with their ways. They patrolled the roads, they acted as the private police for the large landholders, they carried out the secret orders of President Díaz, and they executed his opponents, usually far in the desert—and only the buzzards had any record of what had happened.

Meanwhile, for a price, Porfirio Díaz distributed to foreign capital the oil, the minerals, and the land.

Mexico had abolished slavery twenty years before the American nation did, but soon a new slavery took its place, which was just as effective but was not called slavery. This was the slavery of debt. A man who owed money could not leave the land until it was repaid, and by a process of charging more for food and clothing than a man could possibly make, the probability that he could ever escape debt was very remote.

The rural police backed up these debts, so that if a man who owed a company store, or hacienda store, tried to leave that part of the country, to leave his work or his land and go somewhere else, he was instantly brought back and kept where he belonged, near the store. If he tried to escape too many times, the buzzards circled in the desert and that was that.

The pay and wages were exactly pegged to the point where a man could not possibly *ever*, in his whole life, get out of debt. It was not called slavery, but it was a most effective kind of slavery.

There was peace in Mexico. It was the peace of the rifle and the machete, but still there was peace, and it was said that you could ride along a lonesome road and never be robbed, and this was probably true.

By the use of his methods Porfirio Díaz stayed in office for eight administrations. There was no question of re-election or election; he was simply declared president after a kind of token vote which meant nothing. But since all the foreign powers agreed that he was the best and strongest and wisest man, and since the vote was not widely distributed in Mexico, there was little doubt as to who was always going to be the next president.

His own people grew poorer and poorer, and fewer and fewer owned any land, and more and more of the Mexican land was distributed, for a price, to the large landholders. There were fewer little privately owned fields. Food supplies and minerals got into fewer hands, and those hands raised the prices, and wages never raised, and the food standard of Mexicans went down and down. What little educational standard there was disappeared completely, except among the very rich and among foreigners.

All of this was bad enough for the average Mexican, but Porfirio Díaz went even further. He began distributing the traditional village lands to the great landholders, and this was a crime so deep in the eyes of the village people that it cannot even be conceived. This was a violation of something that had been true for two thousand years. Not only were the village lands taken away, but in many cases the villages themselves were torn down and scattered to make room for more land for the landholders.

The tough and active rural police enforced these distributions and kept order, and there was peace, although many people had to die because of that peace.

Now, since this script is to be written in microcosm, and since nearly all of its action takes place in a very small area, we shall move down to the state of Morelos, south of Mexico City, just over the range from the Valley of Mexico. It is a state which lies on a slope, and its temperatures go from cool-temperate into the tropics in a very short distance. It is a rich state, rich agriculturally and rich in silver. There is no oil there.

It is inhabited by a gentle, soft-spoken people of a tribe slightly different from the Aztec tribe. The men are great horsemen and great workers. They are filled with energy, but there's a gentleness about them that is unusual. Their faces are delicate, both those of the men and the women.

Their land—or rather the land of the state of Morelos—is well watered and rich, but in the time of Porfirio Díaz they did not own the land anymore. It had been discovered that sugar cane could be raised on these lands and that refined sugar brought a price which made it an easy competitor to silver mining and even to oil for profits. With such riches to be taken out of the raising and refining of sugar, the large landholders were not content that the village lands should remain in the hands of the Indians. And so, through the work of Porfirio Díaz, the haciendas, the great landholdings, spread out from their boundaries. In many cases the villages were burned and sugar cane was planted where the houses had stood, and the people who were evicted from their village lands had to go to work for the large landholders or run away and become fugitives.

The people of the state of Morelos are gentle and patient people, but their lives gradually became impossible under the system which was put in place by Porfirio Díaz and enforced by his troops and by his rural police.

Even the grazing land was in many cases taken away from the villages, so that the cows, upon which the Indians depended for their livelihood, had no place to feed. The slightest sign of rebellion or revolt was put down with a ferocity that was incredible. The Indians were treated like animals, they were driven like animals.

The events of this time are documented and quite provable. It is not propaganda in any sense.

In every town of even small size in Mexico there is a bandstand in the middle of the central plaza, and on several nights a week, usually on Thursday and on Sunday, a band plays in this stand. In the time of Porfirio Díaz the upper classes paraded around the bandstand, but the Indians were not permitted, except on the *outside* of the plaza; and if anyone, even while drunk, blundered in, he was bodily thrown out by the police who were constantly in attendance.

Any disagreement between the Indians and the owners of the land was instantly solved by the rural police, who were also the police of the landholders, and the Indians were never, never right. There were only three punishments for a recalcitrant man: he was put in the army, he was put in the rural police, or he was killed.

The haciendas became larger and larger. They actually were like medieval baronies. They had great houses, their sugar mills were usually on the property, they had slaves (or the slaves of debt), they had power for holding their slaves, and they actually had the power of life and death over the working people. No one ever questioned them.

I myself have seen records of this time on one of the great haciendas, or what is left of it. I remember a man's name on the record and his value. Against his name was put "zero." He was not worth anything, whereas the others were rated in what they were worth to the hacienda.

As this reign of Porfirio Díaz grew longer and longer and the people became hungrier and hungrier, and their sense of outrage greater, more and more pressure from the rural police had to be applied, and the punishments had to be more drastic and the killings more often.

Meanwhile, the outrage and the pressure and the simmering grew greater. This does not seem to have been realized by the men in power at that time. They felt that they had made a system which could survive indefinitely as long as they could get money from Germany and Japan and the United States. They completely ignored the explosive qualities in their own people; and why shouldn't they have so ignored them, for the people were disarmed, they had no weapons, they had no organization, they had no learning. The middle class was destroyed, the schoolteachers were dominated. The priests, those who favored the people, had little power—and there were many priests who favored the people. But the pressure of unrest grew and had to be kept down with more and more harsh methods all the time.

These were the conditions which brought about Emiliano Zapata and which brought about our story. This is the political and economic background of this introduction.

█ █ █

It seems valuable to put down a number of customs, habits, costumes, appearances of the people who will be used in this story, for the information of *both* the director and the producer.

The people of Morelos, at the time this story occurs, dressed as they still do, in white cotton pajamas of the coarsest cloth, tied at the ankle, tied around the waist. There is a shirt which buttons to the throat, and in front the shirttails are usually tied in a knot.

The hats worn by the common people at the time of this story were larger than those that are worn now. In fact, when these country people became a part of the revolutionary army they were known as "White Cigars" because of their white clothing and because the huge straw hats they wore looked like puffs of smoke. They were a very simple and highly religious people, and it was customary for many of them to wear on the front of their turned-up hats a figure of the Virgin of Guadalupe, the patron saint of Mexico. On their feet they wore sandals, if they could afford them, although many of them went barefoot. It was rare for a woman to have shoes or sandals.

The women wore long, gathered skirts, loose shirtwaists, and rebozos—long head scarves which had many uses. They carried babies in them, they carried wood in them, they wrapped themselves in them at night—it was their only bedclothing. They were married in them, and they were buried in them. They wound them and put them over their heads at midday to protect themselves from the sun. A new rebozo to a woman was a sign that something very great had happened; either she was being married, or she was being buried. It was seldom that a woman had more than one in her whole lifetime.

The climate in the state of Morelos is very gentle. The houses of poor people are made of straw, thatched, both sides and roof; or of wattles, mud packed between sticks, and with a thatched roof; or of stone in the volcanic area, again with a thatched roof.

Their tools were, and are, very primitive. Every man has a short, curved machete, or knife, with which he does nearly everything—cuts wood, cuts cane, fights, grubs out roots. In fact, it is his only tool, his only personal tool. In addition, there is a sharp, pointed hoe, pointed stick, and these are just about all. The plows that are still used in the country districts of Morelos are little more than pointed sticks mounted on handles and without an iron point.

Oxen are now, as they were then, the draft animals, the means of doing every bit of work that is done. Burros were used for transport, except by the great transport trains, which used high-wheeled carts drawn by oxen.

Nearly every beauty that came into the lives of these people centered around the church. Here they heard the only music, except for the singers of ballads. Here they saw the only color. All of their celebrations, in some way, had something to do with the church. Even the market days, even the fairs (and every small town had at least one big fair a year), centered around a religious ceremony. I shall go into the fairs again, because they are very necessary to this story.

There was a relatively small class of landowning Mestizos, people of part Indian and part Spanish blood, but as the reign of Porfirio Díaz went along, even they were becoming dispossessed through debt or through actual removal of their lands. When a man's land was removed by a hacienda, the burden of proof was on himself to show that it was his. Since records were badly kept, and in many cases were only by word of mouth, it was impossible for him to show his ownership of the land.

We have, then, at the time of our story, the explosive quality which destroys, eventually, all systems: property accumulated in very few hands and the great mass of the people dispossessed and hungry. In a land that was full of fruit, the people had no fruit. In a place that produced sugar, the people had no sugar—it was all sold outside. In a country capable of producing abundant food, the people were in a state of semistarvation all the time. In addition, they were constantly outraged and pushed and whipped and beaten and driven by the rural police of Porfirio Díaz.

IV

It will be necessary to set down some of the customs and some of the personalities of a small Mexican town in the early 1900s.

In some cases these customs and habits and persons have disappeared, due to the coming of roads and electricity, and, in other cases, they simply are not known in the United States. The ones I will describe are extremely pertinent to the script which will follow.

Very little of the script will happen in Mexico City, but most of it will take place in the tiny towns of the state of Morelos; the towns which are cut off from the outside world and which live a life more or less of their own.

The first thing to be described is the fair, the yearly fair of a small town in the state of Morelos in the back country. The fairs were nearly all alike. They happened once a year, on the day of the patron saint of the village; at least the fair was centered around that day. It was the most important social, religious, and economic time of the whole year for the community in question.

Most of these were alike. They were commercial, they were religious, and the fewer the means of communication with the village where they were held, the greater splendor they acquired. Barter was the system of trading used.

All the feasts and the entertainments took on great animation, and even the religious ceremonies, dedicated usually to the patron saint of the village, were animated and splendid.

The costumes, usually kept in the church, were brought out. Sometimes dances were performed which had been performed in the same village since long before the Spaniards came to Mexico.

I shall abandon the word "Aztec" from now on and substitute the name "Nahuatl." The reason for this substitution is that, while the Aztec group is a small group, the Nahuatl group is a larger group, taking in all the people who speak the language which the Aztecs also spoke. These were the people of Morelos, as well as of the Valley of Mexico.

Now, the Nahuatl people had a curious feeling about villages. They had an idea, in common with the ancient Greeks, that a city or a town was an actual personality, and with them it went further than it did with the Greeks, for there were father villages and mother villages. A very tiny town, which was an original town and from which another district was colonized, quite often remained small while its colony became very large; but if it was a father village, it maintained its prestige and its importance above the larger town.

An example of this is Anenecuilco, a tiny little hamlet in the state of Morelos. It is a father village. It is also near the village where Emiliano Zapata was born. Its child is Cuautla, which is a very large town, but in spite of the fact that Cuautla soon outgrew its parent and became what amounts to a city, Anenecuilco still maintained its prestige, just as the father of a family retains his prestige when he becomes old and weak. It is the strong paternal feeling of the Mexican Indian, the distinct feeling of a tribe, group, and family.

Thus, when Emiliano Zapata's father died, his older brother became the head of the house, and although his older brother was a drunk, a bum, a sadist, and literally no good, nevertheless it never occurred to Emiliano, who was a very great man, to enter a room where his older brother was without kissing his hand, for his brother was the head of the family.

These strong relationships are very important to the Mexican, and I intend to make them very important in this script.

But to get back to the little fairs, they usually continued for a week, beginning a week before the religious festival of the patron saint of the village, and continuing in a gradually rising crescendo until there was a huge explosion on the Sunday which celebrated the feast day of the patron.

How the outside people know and remember these feast days is not known, but they are generally known, and people from sometimes hundreds of miles around come in to the great fairs of even the little towns. The people who come do not come empty-handed, for one village makes one kind of pottery, another weaves straw mats, a third cures leather, a fourth makes saddles, a fifth weaves the woolen blankets which are worn by men, a sixth makes the rebozos which are worn by women. Each village has its specialty and, in some cases, has more than one specialty. Cuautla is a leather center; Iguala makes fine pieces of silver. Tepac burns a curious kind of black pottery from which little whistles and figures of birds are made, and this is the only place such pottery is made. From the mountains comes the resinous incense which is burned in the church.

For a week or ten days before the fair, people are seen on the mountain trails with great headloads of the goods they are bringing into these fairs to sell. They will stay there all week until their loads are sold.

They will bring more than just goods to be sold. They bring the news of the whole countryside; they are the living newspapers, these bearers of burdens, sometimes a man, sometimes a man and wife, and sometimes a whole family, but usually they come on foot with their great loads of produce. It is not unusual for a family to walk two hundred miles to one of the more famous festivals, and it must be borne in mind that the size of a town has nothing to do with the importance of a festival. Sometimes they are drawn by a miraculous Christ, sometimes by an ancient dance, and sometimes by a quality which is not even known, except that certain villages have an aura of some kind of importance and that certain fairs are very renowned.

Nearly all small Mexican towns are built on the same pattern. In the center of the community there is a plaza, and in the center of the plaza a little bandstand. On one side is the church, and on the other whatever small mud government building there is. If there are hotels they usually front on this plaza too. When the fairs start, the sellers of goods all congregate in this central square, and they put up some cloth to protect themselves and their wares from the sun, until the whole plaza is covered with white cloth and people squatting among the things they have to sell—fruits and vegetables, chickens and turkeys, pottery, saddles, and little dolls. From this position, squatting in the plaza, they are able to see nearly everything that happens during the fiesta, everything except the violent sports with horses and cattle, which usually take place just on the edge of the village.

These events, which are very good for this film—the events with horses and bulls—will be described in the future, because they are not only interesting, but they are characteristic; and, also, because the chief character in this script was the greatest horseman of his time in his state and was famous as a rider of wild horses by the Mexican method, and this, as far as I know, has never been put on film.

Through these fairs wander the musicians who make the *corridos*, which are really the folk songs of the nation. They are made about every important thing that happens in the country, so that when any historic event happens, within a very short time one of these songs is written about it. I myself remember one time when a Mexican flier, who had made a goodwill tour to the United States, crashed on the way back to Mexico City, and within twenty-four hours, even among the hill people, the folk songs were being sung about him.

This custom still continues. Mexico had one fighter squadron of airplanes in the Pacific. It was the 201st, and all over Mexico the *corridos* are sung concerning exploits of this squadron. Some of them are probably not true.

Now, the people who come in with wares from the whole countryside not only bring news to the village where the fiesta is taking place, but they learn all the news of the great radius in all directions and carry it back to their own villages. They are the news gatherers and the news bearers. This is very important to this script, for, when the rebellion happened, these were the people who carried the messages, these were the people who made possible the movement of the rebel armies. They were the bearers of messages, they were the bringers of news, they were the spies. They were the communications system of the ragged peasant army. They travel very rapidly at a shuffling trot and cover great distances.

I shall use an account of the fairs given to me by Licenciado Arturo Torres, who was born in a little town in Morelos, and who attended many of these fairs in the nineteenth century, when he was a child.

He says the fairs usually lasted about a week, generally starting on Monday or Tuesday and finishing on Saturday or Sunday. On Sunday all of the faithful congregated, and still do, he says, in the church to give thanks and to make offerings and to venerate Christ. The church was never large enough to accommodate all the believers, who, on finishing their prayers, would file in Indian fashion, turning always to the right before the image of the crucified Christ.

In his village the Christ reclined horizontally upon the cross, with his head facing toward the east and his feet toward the nave of the church, and he rested at the head of the altar steps.

After kissing the feet of the image, they would move slowly out of the church, along the left side.

On Friday, and sometimes with two or three days of anticipation, groups of Indian dancers, including those from the high mountains, arrived at the portico of the church to begin their dances very early in the morning, at daybreak. They accompanied themselves with singing and, sometimes, with a music called *chirimia*. This is a curious music, made by flutes and little drums—an almost elfin music. I have heard this playing on the mountains at night, and it's a strange and magic music. It sounds like something that might be played by little people.

To go back to Arturo Torres, he says that after dancing almost without interruption from the beginning to the end of their dances, and dancing all day, they stop at last only when the night has fallen. This monotonous dance and the monotonous music will make a very fine background for such a fiesta.

The Indians are dressed in a very original and picturesque style, depending on the village from which they come. Your director will be able to find any number of these costumes when he goes to Mexico.

In many cases the hair was dressed with huge tufts of feathers in varying colors, red and green predominating. The plumes were held in place by a narrow band that encircled the head from the forehead to the nape of the neck. The band was adorned with encrustations and embroideries of tiny, round mirrors.

Their bodies were clothed in a kind of tunic in color, in brilliant color, or sometimes in white, which was also adorned with tiny mirrors, or sequins, in different colors. They wore sandals on their feet.

They sang, and some of the songs I have. One of them, I remember, goes, "Heavenly Father of the village, I have come to see You. A year ago I did not come, because my wife gave birth to a child that day."

With the great influx of people, there are vendors of every kind of food and drink—dried fruits, coconut milk, sugar-covered sweets, enchiladas, *molotes*, tamales, *atole*, which is a powdered corn in water or milk; and there were many sellers of drugs and of herbs.

Near the entrance door of the church were installed the vendors of wax candles, rosaries, pictures of various saints, sheeps' eyes to ward off the evil eye, and many other amulets and charms, whose doubtful efficacy nevertheless carried some comfort or hope to the spirit of the simple people who attended the fairs.

On one side of the square were the liquor shops and the liquor stands, where *pulque* and beer and *aguardiente* and tequila and the rough, harsh sugar alcohol were sold. These usually opened about midday and didn't close until dawn, when they were left without customers, not because of the wishes of these latter, but because by that time the buyers were either passed out or got in trouble and were put into the little local jail. These latter, usually accompanied by one or two uniformed police, were herded in and booked on the police register on the most charming charge, *borrachos cansados*, which means "tired drunks."

Now, it is the custom among Mexican Indians, when they feel particularly fine, in liquor or in an emotion, to lay back their heads and give what is called a *carcajada*. This is a high, screaming, piercing laugh, and it, with the *chirimia*, will make a very fine background for pictures of such a fiesta.

On another part of the square were installed the wheels of fortune, the little handmade merry-go-rounds, and flying chairs, where from six in the afternoon until late at night grown persons, as well as children, rode on the strange little contraptions.

Nor were there lacking sideshows and tent shows, which exhibited freaks, such as the Spider Woman and the Eagle Woman, who could be seen later, calmly dining on enchiladas and drinking glasses of watermelon and other fruit juices, with their enchantment taken off. This enchantment was believed to be magic that they were able to apply. There were also those who pointed to these people as examples of God's punishment for having failed their parents.

There was usually, also, a large tent where a company of traveling actors performed dramas and comedies, and there were acrobats and all kinds of little vaudeville entertainers, who went from fair to fair and performed in the tents; and there was usually a small circus with trained animals.

On each day of the fair, outside the town, there were rodeos and cockfights and a bullfight. The bulls that were run in these fights were native to the region, usually coming from the hills (the names of the towns I can put in if they are necessary). There was one town, Huichila, which produced bulls that generally turned out to be the angriest. The bulls were brought to the plaza in the center of the city through one of the principal streets, between eleven and twelve o'clock, noon, herded by a group of *charros*, or cowboys, at whose head rode the keeper of the bulls, who was usually their owner or somebody trusted. Immediately behind the *charros* came a band, playing ceaselessly and mostly out of tune. Ahead of the bulls, and alongside the *charros*, went others, throwing firecrackers and skyrockets and giving out programs. Mixed in among all of these, and sometimes among the bulls themselves, there went four or five drunks, dancing and leaping to the rhythms of the discordant band, which usually played "Los Huehuenches." At the bullring, on the edge of the town, one or two barrels of punch had been prepared, with the harsh alcohol, and was distributed freely to everybody who wanted it.

The bulls were immediately placed in the bull pen, and then two or three were brought out to fight. This is what has been called the *toro de once*, the eleven o'clock bull.

In the afternoon in the bullring usually some kind of rodeo took place, and some very amusing things happened, and some quite sad things, for in the long run a number of people were bound to be killed by the bulls, some gored, some trampled. The drunks usually fought the bulls and were hurt.

Sometimes one man mounted a bull while another fought him. These feats began with the release of the bull that was to be ridden. Awaiting him there was a huge crowd of men on horseback who were constantly trampling each other, all of them slightly intoxicated, all trying at once to lasso the hind legs of the bull. When they managed to subdue the bull by his feet and overthrow him, so as to put on him a *pretal*—that's a halter or a truss—there was already in the ring a veritable skein of lariats, all tangled up, and it took sometimes a long time for each man to untangle his lariat. But once the bull was bridled, the rider was called, to the shouting of "*e una novia*" ("that's a bride"). Once the rider was astride the bull's back, he was loosed, and the brute was fought by the whole crowd on foot, not only with capes, but with blankets and serapes or any common, ordinary cloak.

The riders of the bulls, as well as the toreadors, were just simple villagers, or countrymen, untrained, who had been drinking more than they should. Many of the riders did not wear shoes, so that they were sometimes given shoes by a horseman, or loaned shoes by one of the spectators.

As many of the bulls were run in as daylight permitted, and frequently they held *rondas* at these festivals. These *rondas* consisted of the following procedure: Once the bull was lassoed and thrown by his feet, the *charro* who had thrown him would tighten his lariat and, keeping it long and tensed, would begin to run around the ring, circling the animal on his horse; and without giving the animal time to escape or surprise him, he would begin to confuse and abuse him, either with his horse or his lariat tensed. This was the common practice and invariably ended in one or more people injured by the tight lariat.

The people of the state of Morelos are extremely clean people, and while their field clothes may be dirty and ragged, when they went to the great fairs they usually carried little bundles in which were the clean white *calzones* and *camisas* to be worn at the fair (these are the loose pajamas which were described earlier). They carried them rolled up, and when they got to the little town they put them on. And also for the fairs they sometimes wore colored handkerchiefs around their necks, knotted at the throat or held together by a ring at the hollow of the throat. They wore the usual wide-brimmed hats of palm straw, called *trestellas*, and the wealthier ones wore hats of felt. The white cotton pajama was the costume of the peasant. Slightly above him, and usually of Mestizo blood —and of these was Emiliano Zapata—were the *charros*, or the cowboys. They were the men who worked with horses, sometimes hired out to the owners of the haciendas and sometimes had little bits of land of their own. They usually saved all of their money and put it into clothes, and this clothing is the traditional *charro* costume: a great hat of felt, peaked and huge; tight trousers that fitted the leg and that sometimes had a fin down the outer seam, which was ornamented with silver and silver thread; a white shirt, sometimes even of silk, if the man had saved long enough; and a tight vest, ornamented, again, in silver. Later the ornamentation even went on the back, but it was said in the time of Zapata that only a woman would wear decoration on her back, the indication being, of course, that no one would turn his back who was not a coward.

The costume of the *charro* was one of his dearest possessions, that and his saddle and his horse. He may have got his horse by theft, or he may have saved a life to buy a likely colt, but his horse was first, his saddle was second, and his clothing was third. Some of these saddles were highly ornamented, and there was usually a machete hung on one side of the saddle. The whips were sometimes made of silver, that is, with silver handles, and the body of the whip was made of a bull's penis, dried and twisted until it became rawhide, with a great spring in it like whalebone.

The fiesta, as it has been said, usually lasted for a week, and its dispersal is something I've never been able to understand. On Sunday night, sometime in the dark, the whole thing melts away and disappears, the people are gone, and on a Monday morning there is nothing left in the plaza but a tired little tiny village, completely uninhabited by strangers; the visitors have all drifted away in the dark, and they are on their way home. It may take until the following Wednesday for all of the effects of the celebration to wear off the male population. The dead are buried and the wounded are patched up, and the village gradually resumes its old life.

During the fiesta the priest has a very definite place. He is the controller, not only of the church festival itself, but he hears confessions of people who have been in the mountains. Sometimes men and women who have been living together a long time use this time to be married, children become legitimate, names are placed in the church registry. There are mass baptisms and mass confirmations. Little girls in white, with pink ribbons in their hair, go up for their first communion. It seems to me that the Mexicans, above all people, love children. Everything a man has goes into dressing his child and taking care of him.

There are a number of public characters invariable to a Mexican village, who should be noted.

There is the public letter writer, who usually has an old Oliver typewriter. He sits in the plaza and writes letters for people who cannot read or write, and he reads the letters that have arrived to people who cannot read or write. Then the Indians come and tell him what they want to say, and he couches it in the glorious language that is common to his trade. Through his ears and through his typewriter go all the little tragedies and all of the joys of a Mexican village.

I remember one time asking a public letter writer what his charges were. These men have all the government forms and all the petition forms; they do a great deal of legal work. He told me that for a document having to do with the government, he usually charged one peso. In the earlier days it may have been twenty-five centavos. For news of families he charged fifty centavos, but for love letters, he said, there is no charge. "How can one charge for a love letter? The man gives me what the letter is worth. A love letter," he said, "is art, and there can be no price on art. Art is only what a man feels it is worth." I should imagine, too, that his pay had a great deal to do with how the man felt about the dame at that particular moment.

There is another official, or semi-official, in every little Mexican town, about whom very little is known here. It is usually a woman, and she is called a *curandera*, and since we are going to use her in this script, her profession and herself must be described with some care. There are male *curanderos*, but ordinarily it is a woman, an old woman.

In Mexico there are still very few doctors. In the early twentieth century, in the hill districts, there were none at all, except in the large towns, and they were half-trained quacks.

The *curandera* does all of the village healing. She does it with herbs, and she does it with magic, and some of the magic is very, very old. These women have great authority. They are a combination of psychoanalyst, hypnotist, magician; they are the midwives. In some parts of the country their practices for forcing birth are so savage that deaths in childbirth increase.

Their treatment of wounds is barbarous and sometimes causes blood poisoning, but they are masters at curing fever, and they are masters at the suggestion which makes nervous disorders disappear.

They are wild-looking women. They carry in their bags the strangest articles—herbs and snake skins and the skulls of animals, certain sea shells, and magic things, like the eyes of lizards—truly a magic bag. There is the owl's skin, there are the little hummingbirds of good luck which take many, many days to make. It is a real hummingbird wrapped in colored silk thread, and inside the silk, in the stomach of the hummingbird, is a piece of tiger heart and a bit of semen from a goat, and scrapings from the dried eye of an owl, and the claw of an ocelot, which is a spotted wildcat, and a piece of dried orchid from the jungle, and a piece of lily bulb, and a little bit of ground semiprecious stone, a little gold dust and a little silver dust and a little mother-of-pearl dust. The symbolism here is obvious; it is just imitative magic.

Some of these *curanderas* become very rich. I recall one with whom I worked one time, who was so rich that she had four chairs, real chairs, but she didn't put them on the floor—they were hung on nails, on her walls, so that they would not be lightly used, and they were only taken down for great dignitaries.

These women usually braid their hair around their brows, and in their hair there are little bits of colored string and ribbons, all parts of their trade.

They are great professionals, and, except in matters of infection, they are probably very good doctors. We lost a helper one time who had a cut healed by a *curandera*. His leg swelled up, and he died of blood poisoning.

These women sell magics to get love and magics to repel love. It is said that some of them will kill at a distance, but I have not known any who followed that practice.

The church does not fight them, because they use the patter

of the church, but their magic is the magic of old Nahuatl people, and the language they speak in their spells is the Nahuatl language. The people fear them because of their powers and need them because of their abilities.

Some of them are clairvoyant and go into trances and make prophecies. Some of them, it is suspected, take the drug peyote, which is a button of cactus and acts as an hypnotic. It causes a semiconsciousness. Under the influence of this drug all sorts of prophecies are made, and, surprisingly enough, a number of them come true. It's probable that the ones that come true are those which are the result of unconscious judgment on the part of the practitioner.

The *curandera* officiates at all births. In different parts of the country she has different magical methods and different physiologic methods of inducing a quick birth, which seems to be desirable to these people. She uses, always, incense, but then, also, she uses many sorts of sympathetic magic. Since we will be using one, I think it's necessary to know about these things.

The people who have been treated by a *curandera* recently are almost invariably recognizable by a sign that they wear. The *curandera*'s method of drawing pain is to use a symbol through which the pain can pass, and the most common of these symbols is a white band around the temples, and protruding from the edges of the band, a little pointed leaf over each temple. This leaf is said to draw fever and pain even from the stomach. The leaves and the bands are worn for many days, so that one can always tell a person who has been sick in the village because of this unusual headdress. The leaf is about an inch and a half long and quite pointed. I do not know what it is, but it is an herb that is sold all over Mexico.

The usual method of the *curandera* for mixing various herbs and making an infusion is to chew them and to spit the resulting infusion onto a wound, even, sometimes, an open cut. This quite often causes blood poisoning. Some of the herb cures, the teas and the poultices, are very effective.

Curanderas use herbs which have some remarkable qualities. Consider, for instance, a small, curious bush, which grows from California clear down to the jungle in the south, which is called *yerba* or *vibara*, rattlesnake herb. An infusion of this herb is highly efficacious in taking down the swelling from a rattlesnake bite. They have found that the *yerba saponica*, which is a lilylike root, makes the most wonderful soapsuds for washing the hair. They know that certain sea shells, ground and taken internally, will stop hemorrhages, and this is also true. They are masters of the hot bath and the massage. They are great appliers of heat, heating stones and placing hot stones against injured muscles.

Last, but far from least important, particularly to our story, they take up where the priest leaves off in confession. They are psychoanalysts of the first order. Many of them are also natural hypnotists.

The result of this is that the *curandera* knows everything that goes on in the village, knows everything that goes on in people's lives. She knows a sterile woman, because the woman comes to her for cure; she knows a man when he has disease; she knows the troubles of children; and she goes further, she knows political trends. Not having the moralistic background of the church, she is even likely to hear of secret murders and conspiracies that not even the priest would hear.

She tries at once to inspire both terror and confidence, and among her clientele terror and confidence are the same thing, for anything that is not frightening or a little painful is not efficacious.

She is a professional, highly trained, extremely educated in her business. She may know as many as 50,000 different charms in the ancient language; and it is surprising that even now, at the present time, many Mexicans, well-educated, and who should have lost every vestige of magic, will still go to the *curandera* for certain diseases which are not treated by doctors any more successfully than by the *curanderas*.

I have put so much in about the *curandera* because I intend to use one of them throughout the script as a kind of prophetic character. Indeed, it is attested in the town where Emiliano Zapata was born that a year before his birth, the *curandera* in the plaza, under stress of emotion, forecast his birth. Another, or the same, *curandera* brought him into the world, and just before he was killed, a third, or maybe the same one, climbed to the top of the mountain where his position was and warned him not to go to his death.

I have said that there was a rodeo practice which might be very good for film, particularly since it is known that Emiliano Zapata was the greatest performer at this particular sport of his time, or probably ever since. The method is this: Into the corral, or bullring, on the edge of town, is driven a completely wild horse, without saddle, bridle, surcingle, or anything. He is herded in by a dozen or so men on horseback. The man who is to do the riding is mounted on his own very well-trained horse. The wild horse progresses around and around the arena, and, at a given time, the man who is to ride him rides up on his own horse, leaps from his horse to this wild horse, and rides him with nothing to hold onto, with *nothing* except his sense of balance. It is a vicious sport, and very few people have been known to stay on such a horse, but Zapata himself was able to ride in this manner. It must be understood that there is no mane and absolutely nothing to grip, except balance and the pressure of knees. They are great horsemen, these Morelos people.

There is a third, very spectacular sport which is never used in this country, which might be very good for film. In this case, a young, very active bull, or steer, is driven out, and the rider rides alongside the steer, which is going very fast (they can run like rabbits). He leans over, grabs the tail of the steer, wraps it around his leg, and rides his horse off at an angle. This requires great strength and dexterity. The moment he has pulled the hindquarters of the bull, or steer, crosswise, naturally the animal collapses and rolls over on the ground. He must then leap from his horse and, before the animal can struggle to its feet, throw a loop around its hind legs. I've seen this performed in the United States. It does not hurt the animal, even as much as the bulldogging we use, and

I'm rather surprised that none of our rodeos have tried it. It is called "tailing the bull," or *coleando*.

I'm putting these things, which amount to footnotes, first in this for several reasons. One, to get them down; two, so the reader will have some idea of the background of the script when he comes to its actual dramatic succession; and, third, to stimulate, or at least to give some background of imagination, to the director concerning these rather specialized things.

For a moment I want to put in a footnote about Zapata's birthmark. It was on his chest, it was a true birthmark, and it was in the shape of a little hand.

Now, the people of Morelos do not believe that Zapata is dead. They think that he is living back in the hills and will one day come to them again, and one of the reasons they give for this is that when he was killed and his body was exposed, in the plaza, there was no *manito*, or "little hand," on his chest. I have found that there is one kind of birthmark that disappears at death. This must be remembered, because I intend to use this disappearance of the birthmark in the script.

The mark itself, the little cherry-colored hand on his chest, gave him, even as a child, a kind of importance, for the *curandera* who officiated at his birth recognized in it the hand of God. And he became eminent, even as a child, because of this birthmark. Indeed, I suppose, some psychologist might find that part of his sense of destiny came from the fact that he bore this birthmark on his body.

In Mexico, at the time of our script, social strata were very closely defined and very strictly adhered to. Thus a peon was looked down on by a *ranchero* who owned a little land, although the two of them were very close together; and a person who owned a little store was infinitely above the *ranchero*. This must be borne in mind, because a part of our script deals with the marriage of Zapata, who wanted to marry into the family of a little storekeeper, and who was refused because he was a *ranchero* and did not belong to the elevated class of storekeepers. He was refused, indeed, until he became a general, at which time he married her, but she would only accept him then. As a matter of fact, her own acceptance had nothing to do with it. It was her father who accepted him.

I want to do a sequence on the Mexican marriage at that time, the courting under the vicious eye of the women of the family. I think it would be very charming. And finally the marriage, for it must be remembered that Zapata was married in the church, and that his wedding was the traditional wedding of the Mexican of his time.

v

The story of Emiliano Zapata is one of the strangest I have ever come across. It is strange in that, even as it was lived, it has the qualities of literature and of folklore.

His life had beginning, middle, and end, and this is very rare in the world.

He had his Cassandra and his Homer.

Even his death had meaning, and he understood that meaning, according to his own words. His life lies very heavily on the southern part of Mexico. He is still alive and still a force all through the states of Morelos, Puebla, Michoacán, and the south.

There are still many people alive who knew him and served with him, and it is fortunate that this research took place now instead of some years later, when they will all be dead, because I was able to get a number of physical characteristics that will be lost once his friends and his enemies are all gone. He was as much hated on one side as he was loved on the other, but as time goes on the hatred dies out, and the love for the man increases all the time. Even those who hated him, and their children, find the hatred dying out and the admiration of the man increasing. It is more than probable that with more time Emiliano Zapata will emerge as the great and pure man of Mexico and will take a parallel position to the Virgin of Guadalupe, as the human patron of the freedom of Mexico.

Although he has been dead a very short time, his life has already taken on the qualities of folklore. You can get an argument about nearly everything in his life. His life has not shaken down into that concrete thing which is folklore, but every facet is rapidly becoming just that. Zapata is becoming a combination of father, symbol, spokesman, and actual projection of his people. A simplification of his life is already taking place. The Indians do not believe him dead. They think that he, physically, is alive, and anyone who goes into the country where he operated, and where his force is still strong, can see in a moment that some part of him is still alive and powerful.

Now, since this is true, and since he will become in time even more a thing of folklore than he is now, it occurs to me that this script should have the quality of folklore from the beginning. It should have a quality of simplicity and simplification, which is the quality of folklore.

I should like to make him a real and a living man, and to have his relationships warm; but at the same time, I should like to lift him above the real and the exact, since that is the way he is considered in his own country now. While he is the "Little Man," he rose through pure ability above everyone else and brought everyone else up with him. Since he is in truth the symbol of the best there is in the Indian, there is no reason why we should not make him so in this film.

We know that, in fact, he was a man of great courage. According to his own words, he never felt fear. He was better at the principal sports than anyone around him; he *was* a better fighter than anyone else; he was a clearer thinker than the people of his time; he was stronger and more virile. In fact, he carried the virtues of the Indians to their peak, and therefore he became the epitome of the Indian.

I think this film should be made in that spirit. But there is another reason for simplifying and making this picture a matter of folklore.

There are still living in Mexico many people who were involved in his murder, and some of them are still powerful in the government. There are many people who were despoiled, and whose property was ruined, by the forces of the revolution which he led, and these people are still filled with anger at Emiliano Zapata, as well they might be. The grandchildren of the *haciendados* are still angry because of their burned sugar mills and houses and their ruined properties.

Those people involved with his defeat and final murder still feel a sense of guilt which makes them fierce toward this story, so that they describe Emiliano as a murderer and a bandit.

There is no question that he was a violent man, but he was no more violent than his enemies, and he fought a war only on the terms that it was already being fought. He did not invent the cruelties that were carried out. He simply followed along a pattern of the fighting as it was going on when he came into power.

There were vicious cruelties on both sides. There were violent tortures on both sides. I do not see any reason for putting these in the film, except in so far as they show emotional violence of the times.

But Zapata was a greater man than his people. He belongs to the whole world, and his symbol of piracy and violence, and of resistance against oppression, is a world symbol. Because this is so, I propose to write this script, taking it out of the exact place of Mexico, taking it out of exact people.

It occurs to me that I could solve many problems if I used no names. The president, who was Porfirio Díaz, will simply in my script be the *Presidente*. Zapata himself will be, in his early youth, Emiliano, and later he will be *El Jefe*, or the Chief, and later he will be known as the General, and his name will not be used, except possibly once in the very last of the film. The people who fought against him, I think, can be named simply by their military titles, the General, the Colonel, the Sergeant, etc.

There is a custom in Mexico which makes this very easy to do. It is the custom of using the full name, so that a man does not mention Zapata; he mentions Emiliano Zapata, or 'Miliano Zapata; using both the first and the last names, so that it is quite easy to use only the first name and be well understood in that nation and, indeed, in all Latin America. I think, by the use of this method, the script can be lifted out of the costume-timeliness, which it might have, into a more generalized and world significance; and I am sure that this will alleviate any quarrel with the people who were involved in some of the unfortunate circumstances of the time. If their names are not used, they will have no weapon to use against this film, and, of course, everyone knows who they are in Mexico. Still, not putting their names in will make a great difference.

I want also to give a certain terseness to this story. Emiliano has been described to me, by his friends, as a man not given to speeches. His ordinary speech was short, curt, and to the point. Unlike many Mexicans, he made no long and flowery speeches. He spoke like a cowboy, which he was. His grandeur was in his simplicity.

For example, I have been told that when his own troops refused him permission to go personally into battle at the siege of Cuernavaca, he spent his time cutting limbs of trees to make stretchers for the wounded. *His soldiers had toward the last to keep him behind the lines for fear that they might lose him when they needed him very badly.* His impulse was to fight in the front lines. But he obeyed them on several occasions and did stay back of the lines.

While this story must be told on film with a simple, direct, almost childlike quality, it must also have a quality which indicates that it is a world story and a semi-mystical story, for its meaning is exact. It seems to me that its meaning has a direct application to the present time. Collectivization can come from both directions—from the extreme left and from the extreme right—and the life of Emiliano Zapata is a symbol of the individual standing out against collectivization from either side. He is the strong, self-contained individual, which the whole world needs right now.

We come now to the last part of this perhaps overlong introduction, but I have felt that the introduction was necessary. The last part deals with suggestions for production.

To my mind there is no necessity of jumping a company all over Mexico. Within, say, thirty kilometers of Cuernavaca, nearly every kind of countryside required for this film can be found. Indeed, there are little villages within a half-hour's drive of the town of Cuernavaca which can be used for nearly all the small-town sequences. Such a village is Xochitepec, which is about twenty minutes' drive from the city. Another is [word omitted], which has fantastic background, almost mystical background; it can hardly be believed if it is not seen. In all of these towns Zapata operated. Some of them, if you get a little off the highway, have not changed one little bit since the time Zapata lived. By moving the camera thirty degrees, you could have a whole new set.

I think that, wherever possible, the people of the countryside could be used. They are good actors, they take direction well if they are approached properly.

I cannot recommend too strongly that, wherever possible, Mexican personnel should be used. It will make it much easier for the film to be completed.

The film crews are excellent. They work as units, and with a little enthusiasm they are the best crews I have ever seen. One in particular, with which I have worked, gets things done more quickly and with more imagination than any group I've seen.

It must never be forgotten that the hatred and suspicion of the gringo is very strong in Mexico, and wherever there can be used the cushion of a Mexican between an American company and the people, it should be used. This is true of all films made by an American company in Mexico, but with this particular film it is absolutely necessary, because here we are dealing with a man so deeply beloved by the Mexican people that any hint that he was being run down, or in any way made ridiculous, would cause a riot, and you would probably have the picture destroyed. It is true that even those people who hate him would, nevertheless, defend him against a gringo.

Elia Kazan feels as I do, that there is no reason for jumping about. I showed him a number of the small villages, and he feels that in one or two he can get all of the sets he needs, ready-built and without any change whatever.

The only modernization in Mexico, since the time of Zapata, is along the paved highways where the power lines go. Otherwise, it is exactly as it was.

I think that this film should be begun, probably, from the end of August on. This will give the best time in Mexico, for in the end of August the rains are still occurring, but they are lightening up. The country is green and beautiful, the crops are strong, and if the shooting time verges over into the dry season, we'll have probably the most beautiful film that has ever been taken. At that period the whole countryside is a mass of flowers, of flowering trees and flowering grasses. The corn then is coming up strong, and the fields are rich. The sugar cane and the rice are brilliant green, and the simple color contrasts are very beautiful.

It is my further recommendation that the studio employ a Mexican production man as a front. He need not be coproducer, but he can in many ways make it easier to work. The history of *Captain from Castile* would indicate that this would be a good policy. I have followed in the footsteps of *Captain from Castile*, and the history of waste, and of lost time, and of general confusion is fantastic.

There are ways of getting things done in Mexico, and they are not the same as our ways. Any American company which goes into Mexico and tries to use our methods is going to find itself very royally taken.

I should like to recommend, for this position of "front" production man, Oscar Danziger, who is the president of Aquila Films. He is a man of great integrity, enormous experience, and honesty. I have worked with him very successfully before, and I cannot think of anyone better fitted to do this job of "fronting" for an American company. He knows how to do everything in Mexico. He knows not only Mexican law, but the laws of the unions, which are equally important, and a violation of any of them will bring your production to a standstill.

He knows, further, how to keep costs to a minimum. His background was in French pictures. He has been now for a number of years in Mexico in production. I myself worked with him in the production of *The Pearl*, which, while it is not a very good moving picture, at least got by and also did not cost very much to make.

In conversation with Elia Kazan, we agreed that great numbers of people should not be used. It is much easier and more effective to indicate numbers, rather than to use them. The camera can only receive so much.

Nearly every American production company gets into trouble in Mexico because of a lack of knowledge of local courtesies and local practices. There are certain people to whom presents must be given. There are some kinds of words that must be said, and if they are neglected, a deep insult is established, which is bad not only for the relationships of the company, but also is bad for the finished picture. It is very possible for an angry group in Mexico to sabotage any picture that is made if it wants to, and it is quite easy to avoid such sabotage. This is only one more reason for the employment of a Mexican production man, to give advice and to help out.

Finally, Kazan and I see eye to eye on this picture, in both its production methods and in the handling of the story itself. We get along very well on this. He has been a student of the life of Zapata for a number of years, as have I. Both of us feel that it is an important job and could be an extremely important picture.

Both of us feel that by providing an intricate script, before production starts, and by planning very carefully, the cost of the film could be kept down.

Finally, and I do think that this is the final matter in this introduction, I know only one actor who could play the part of

Emiliano Zapata with veracity and integrity and believableness, and that is Pedro Armendariz.

Compare a photograph of Armendariz with one of Zapata, and you'll see the same face, the same fierceness, the same vitality. In addition, Pedro is a good horseman, and he is believable in all ways. In physical structure he is taller and a little broader than Emiliano was, but his face is the same, and his race is the same.

There are certain liberties that must be taken with Zapata. We cannot leave the ultra-long mustaches that he wore, and which were popular in his day, but we can bring them in and shorten them a little bit. I am afraid that if we left them as long as he actually wore them, it would be a matter for laughter in our theaters, but they can be slightly changed, so that the mustaches are still there and are not ridiculous to a present-day audience.

This, I think, is the end of this extra long introduction. I am sorry that it is so long, but I think it was necessary.

I shall start the script with very full descriptions of all scenes, which, I think, will give your production people a better idea of cost. It will be a very full script.

SCENE

A small village in the state of Morelos, in the late sixties or early seventies of the last century. The yearly fair is in preparation. This is a village like all villages in Mexico. It has a central plaza; a church stands high on one side, the municipal building on the other. Around the other side of the square are small stores. In the center of the plaza, among beat-up little plants, dwarfed trees, there is a small bandstand built of cement and ornamental iron. The whole square is poor and light-bitten. It is the small town of all Mexico.

The fiesta is the yearly celebration of its saint's birthday. The church is being decorated with flowers. Foot-weary peddlers of all manner of goods are coming into the plaza and setting up their stands. Small squares of cloth are tied with string on poles to protect the sellers and their goods from the sun.

NOTE: See any Mexican market day of the present time where nothing has changed. The wares have not changed. Nothing has changed.

The priest is distributing the costumes for the religious dance of the Moors and Christians. These consist of masks, feathered turbans, wooden swords. We have scenes of excitement and preparation for the yearly party, but formalized because it has been repeated for centuries just as it is today, and just as it is in our scene. There is a little quarreling for places, but not fierce quarreling. The people from different districts wear slightly different costumes. And from the mountains have come some Indians who look very foreign to this place, who stay together silently in groups because they are strangers. There are all kinds of mixed musics: guitars and pipes, the drums and fifes of the *chirimia*. There are wooden xylophones; there are sellers of sweets and of colored rings, of *pulque* and *aguardiente*.

This is a celebration in every sense—religious, drinking, musical, economic. There are scenes of color and confusion, building, and mounting. Probably, here our commentary describing the process might be written against the scene so that the words can take on the rhythm of the film. The excitement must be inherent in the scene, but it is a kind of formal excitement. This fiesta has happened every year for many hundreds, and perhaps even thousands, of years. Burros laden with goods; men carrying great headloads of pots; horsemen from the hills; bulls for the fighting, and the conglomerate produce of the country have been brought in and dumped in the marketplace. This is the time of marriage, and christening, of courting, of rutting, buying, selling, acquiring, losing, winning, fighting, and loving. This is the process of a fiesta: a new dress, a new love, a new sin, and a new confession. So in the little town new lives start in the fiesta. Some sense of plodding destiny should be in this scene.

A mud house and a small hill ranch not far from the town. The house has one room. It is surrounded by a growing cactus fence, chickens, turkeys, two pigs, a cow, and a few burros. There is a horse, too, a symbol of some slight gentility. The family is poor, but not Indian poor. The persons involved are: the father, a fierce man, a *charro*; the mother, soft, but made of iron; the grandmother, wrinkled and already consigned to death; two small girls, perhaps twelve and ten years old; and a small boy about five years old.

This family is preparing for the fiesta. There is washing of faces, getting out the party clothes from wooden chests. The father is polishing his *charro* spurs and cleaning his saddle. The daughters, like small grown-up versions of their mother, are getting their clothes on. The small boy is quite proud and fierce, even as a child. He wears a little *charro* suit that is embroidered, a costume only used for fiestas, obviously. (Mexicans dress their children for occasions, especially the boys.) Eufemio, the little boy, has his whip, his tight pants, and short jacket, his spurs, his version of his father's big hat. The family is in a slow hurry, chattering and excited.

MOTHER (*To the small girls*): And you must make your duty to Saint
Anthony and to Our Lady of Guadalupe.

THE GIRLS (*In chorus*): Yes, Mama.

MOTHER: And you must stay close by and not go wandering away
or the big man will get you.

THE GIRLS (*Formally*): Yes, Mama. (*And they giggle silently under
their rebozos. And then they turn up serious faces.*)

Eufemio is dressed and ready. He wanders to his father's
saddle, and from its scabbard on the side, he partly draws out the
charro machete, but secretly, as though this were an untouchable
instrument. The father looks up and sees what he is doing. Eufemio
drives the machete back into its scabbard and looks guilty and
uninterested. He whistles a guilty whistle.

FATHER: Yes, it's time, Eufemio, it's time. We will see if we can
find one.

EUFEMIO (*Excitedly*): But not a hooked one of the fields. Like this?
Like yours?

FATHER (*Regards the boy with pride*): You think you're a horseman?
You think you are big enough?

EUFEMIO: I will be.

He draws his father's machete. He goes into a pantomime of
swinging and cutting with a big blade. He picks a small serape
from the floor and balls it around his left arm. The little girls edge
back into the corner to be out of the way. Eufemio slashes and
parries and guards as though he were really fighting with the
machete.

EUFEMIO: There, and there, and there, and so.

And he kills his fancy opponent. He sees it in his head, and
he looks down on his fallen enemy and wipes the blade of the
machete on his balled serape. He has been, in his own mind, in
a real fight, and has really killed a man and has taken a fierce
pleasure in it, and it has even convinced his little sisters. His
mother smiles a little. Father looks at him with interest.

FATHER: You learned this where, Eufemio?

EUFEMIO (*Coming out of his dream*): With a stick, Papa.

FATHER: And you fought *who?*

EUFEMIO: A shock of corn, Papa, but I will kill.

FATHER (*With solemnity*): Oh, I'm sure of that. (*He takes the blade from Eufemio's hand, looks at it, bends it, puts his thumb along its edge, and then he puts it back into its scabbard.*)

FATHER (*Softly*): Who will you kill, Eufemio?

EUFEMIO: The big ones who took the land.

FATHER (*Lifting his saddle and starting for the entrance*): They are very big, Eufemio, and you are very little. (*He looks at his son; there is a kind of a defeat in his eyes, and there is some fear.*)

EUFEMIO (*He whips his wrist as though the machete were still in his hand.*): One at a time, Papa, and quietly. (*He speaks like a man.*)

FATHER (*Smiles*): Oh, very quietly.

SCENE

One of the great haciendas in Morelos. Since sugar has come to the state, these have become vastly rich, and as they grow richer, they grow more greedy. The lands reach out. Titles to the village lands are bought from a dishonest government. The walled principalities, which are called haciendas, enclose orchards, sugar mills, stables, and very large and rich houses. The owners and their guests live like medieval nobles. There are servants for every little duty. The rooms are decorated with furniture and pictures from France. The children are educated in Europe, and the people of the haciendas insulate themselves from countryside. They have their own church, their theaters, everything. They entertain lavishly. Guests come from Europe as to a principality, and they are entertained like princelings. The contrast of the inside of this hacienda with the outside world of poverty and despair is fantastic. It is medievalism transplanted from Europe after it has disappeared from Europe. The whole life is anachronistic, but it is lived, never-

theless. It is France before the revolution. As this scene opens,
Don Carlos is showing his new guests over the hacienda: the stables,
the mill, all of the riches and ease. A footman follows. A coach
is being prepared in the courtyard. The guests are a young Frenchwoman and her mother, both of a regime that is dead. Don Carlos
is about sixty, strong of face, a greedy, furious man. His son has
become soft in a soft life. What they cannot bribe, buy, or steal,
they hope to get from women, position, and wealth. There is a
young daughter of the hacienda, also, and, perhaps this is why the
guests were invited, and perhaps everyone knows it. Don Carlos
is trading for a title for his son. Another guest is a young Frenchman
of position who hopes to cash in his position for wealth. And the
daughter of the house is intended for him. He is aloof, as though
he didn't care, but in fact, he cares very much. The guests are
coming back to a little terrace, where coffee and brandy are waiting
for them. The young Frenchman speaks.

THE YOUNG FRENCHMAN: It's a rich country. Your gold is sugar.

DON CARLOS (*Laughs loudly, a little too loudly*): You put the exact
   words to it, monsieur, exact words. (*He repeats in an attempt
   to get the other's exact explanation. One knows that he will
   quote this many times.*) Our gold is sugar. (*He looks happily
   about.*)
   And our sugar is gold! (*He has made a mot; he is delighted.*)
   Our sugar is gold!
   (*And he repeats it so that no one will miss his poor saying.*)

THE FRENCHWOMAN (*The last of the ancien régime*): I am told that
   outside the walls it is not safe, nor so beautiful, nor even so
   rich.

DON CARLOS: You are right, madame. (*He speaks with a kind of
   passionate unctuousness one hears so often in Mexico.*) My poor
   country; my poor, poor country. She has two faces; one civilized, and the other, well, you will see.

MADAME'S DAUGHTER: Is it true, sir, that the natives still practice
   their savage rites, and maintain the old god right in the shadow
   of the church?

DON CARLOS (*He was raised and educated in France, and it is probable that he has never seen his own country save from a coach window.*): That is, to a certain extent, true, ma'm'selle. It is a harsh and stubborn people, and a secret people. There is no way to know what they are thinking. But you will see. (*Ten* rurales, *heavily armed, ride into the gate of the courtyard and dismount, standing by their horses.*)

MADAME: And what are these, Don Carlos, your private army?

DON CARLOS (*Smiles a little thinly*): No, they are rural troops, but they are assigned to these centers of civilization to keep, uh—well, order. We think of ourselves as islands of culture, rather, madame, like rocks standing against the sea.

THE YOUNG FRENCHMAN: Surely, there's no danger from these primitives. They are unarmed, and the ones I have seen are docile, well, they're even polite.

DON CARLOS (*Rubs his chin*): We take our little precautions, m'sieur. Tonight we are going to see a little local fair, a fiesta, at a nearby town. The Indians will be there for their yearly festival—half religious, and half, well, whatever it is. You will see more than I can tell you.

MADAME'S DAUGHTER: Is it safe?

DON CARLOS (*He flicks his fingers toward the* rurales *in the courtyard.*): It will be safe. We have learned from France, you see. If France had acted instantly against the violence of the mob instead of trying to make a treaty with the so-called people, the terror might never have come; France might still be France, instead of . . . (*He waves his hand wearily, and his guests become gloomy. He changes his tone.*) Now, madame, may I suggest one of our better customs, a little sleep in the afternoon. (*And as the party rise to move away, Monsieur comes close to Don Carlos.*)

THE YOUNG FRENCHMAN: You are sure it will be safe to go. I should not like to endanger my mother for a sensation.

DON CARLOS: It will be safe enough for us. If you wish, I can let you have a pistol or a sword. But our soldiers are iron men;

they will not let any evil come to us, believe me. You know, sir, there is a stretch of land near that village—what they call village land—that cries for sugar cane. I want to look at it again before I go to Mexico City to see the President.

THE FRENCHMAN: Ah, what do they do with it now?

DON CARLOS (*With contempt*): They pasture cattle. They will not learn, they will not change. (*Almost in a rage*) They will not change and so we enlighten men with scientific minds; we must, well, we must even force them.

THE FRENCHMAN (*Cynically*): You mean that you are going to take their land from them, Don Carlos?

DON CARLOS (*He looks suddenly at the young Frenchman with an expression of a Republican manufacturer on hearing the word "Roosevelt." He seems to be digging into the young man's brain. His face is red and angry, and only gradually does he control himself. And then the cold comes down over him, and he speaks with restraint.*): There are things a stranger does not know, m'sieur. A harsh name cannot change the course of history. (*He becomes confidential. The ladies have gone, leaving the two together. He puts his hand on the young man's shoulder.*) Mexico is a backward country. For hundreds of years we have had wars, revolts, fighting, *anarchy*. Now we have a president, a strong man. Now we will have order, discipline, progress. Now we will be governed, not by the worst, the most violent, the unpredictable, but by the thoughtful, the scientific, the best. Those men who, in the long run, love this country, not their own bellies.

THE FRENCHMAN (*He glances at the luxury of the hacienda with a small, satiric smile.*): And meanwhile, the Indians lose their land. (*He speaks softly.*)

DON CARLOS (*Shouts*): Meanwhile, we will establish something towards which they can rise, a goal. We will have a nation among the nations. A Mexico respected, and not a black brew of witchcraft and squalor. You foreigners do not understand our problems. We would take care of our own affairs. (*He thinks he has gone too far with his proposed son-in-law. His voice changes.*) What are we arguing about? Your pardon, m'sieur. You were testing me. You were making a joke. (*Seriously*) But if you were not, what you will see tonight will convince you, I think, that we are taking the only way.

THE FRENCHMAN (*With tenacious French logic*): What will they do when they have no land?

DON CARLOS: What will who do?

THE FRENCHMAN: Why, these Indians.

DON CARLOS: Why—what the others have done. They will come to work on land that is well worked. They will learn the scientific method of agriculture.

THE FRENCHMAN: And how will that help if they have no land to apply it to?

DON CARLOS (*Not to be trapped again*): Ah, you are making intellectual riddles, my friend. Reality, that's what you intellectuals need, a sense of reality. Your head is in the clouds, my boy. Go, sleep, and you will see the problem, but in terms of men and animals, not in the blue clouds of your philosophy.

SCENE

Again, the plaza of the little town, but it is night now, and the band is playing in the bandstand—bad but enthusiastic music. The little stalls are lighted with candles which throw flickering lights on the produce under them. Perhaps the camera can walk around the square, into the church, where the rosary is going on. Hundreds of candles in front of the shrine, and hundreds of dark figures on their knees on the bare floor. The gruesome, bloody pageant of the Mexican church. Another scene, an open doorway, dimly lit. A casket is in the room, and a dead man is lying, receiving his friends for the last time. And a candle to right and to left to light his face, and his wife in the background, her rebozo drawn about her face.

And another series of scenes: the various commodities and markets, the meat, the goats' heads, the poor strips of pork and beef to be bought, the booths with the colored sugar water, and the children buying it. The *pulqueria*, with the drunks beginning to get on their evening heat.

NOTE: Study this, Gadg [Elia Kazan], because a Mexican Indian drunk is something quite unique. The chained devils really come out of him. His balance and his fears disappear; his anger is released. He is practically never gay, and he drinks until he falls unconscious.

Out of the church come the dancers in their violent costumes, the Moors and Christians, celebrating a way everyone has forgotten, fighting formally with wooden swords, and dying symbolically; Christians always winning. (You can get real dancers in Cuernavaca to do this. They do it every year.)

Out into the plaza itself, another scene among the poor sellers of produce: the little cups of corn, for corn is the medium of exchange here. One buys and sells with these small cups of corn as a measure. Then to the leather stalls, the saddles, bridles, whips, and harnesses, all lighted with little flickering candles. They use kerosene now, in tin lanterns, but then, that is fairly recent. We come to a stall where knives and machetes are sold, and here we pick up our family we have seen earlier. The father, Eufemio, the mother, and the daughters. The women are all dressed in their rebozos, and skirts, and little shirtwaists, and they're barefooted. They hold their rebozos over their noses to keep out the night air, and also in a curious gesture of modesty, an indefinable thing. The father and son are inspecting the machetes, testing and balancing. It is a slow process. They have a long time. One buys only one machete in his lifetime, perhaps. Now we notice that they are not father and son, but two men conferring on a man's business.

EUFEMIO (*Balancing a blade in his hand, and weighing it against its handle*): This is blade-heavy. (*He lays it over his fingers to show.*)

FATHER (*Hands him another*): Try this, Eufemio.

NOTE: There is a kind of machete blade made in Oaxaca, and it is very famous, which can be bent double and the blade even tied in a knot. Eufemio would naturally know about this blade; if one could be found, it would be his ideal.

EUFEMIO (*Balances, strikes, feels the edge, bends the blade*): It's too thick here.

PUESTERO (*Hands him a machete blade*): Try this.

EUFEMIO (*He takes the blade. His face changes. Just handling it, he knows the quality.*): This is right, this is good. (*He regards it with love. There's no testing here. It has a bone or a horn handle carved like an eagle's head. He hands it to his father carefully, handle first. His father looks close at the blade, and then questioningly at the* puesto *keeper.*)

PUESTERO: It is beyond price. How can I say what it is worth? It is worth a mountain or a star, or a man's life.

FATHER (*Ironically*): If you will come to a mountain, or fall from a star like an angel, perhaps we can begin to discuss this diamond, this mountain.

PUESTERO: Twenty pesos.

FATHER (*Shrugs*): Eufemio, we are not a family to support a mountain or a star. If I had known that this ill-looking thing was made from the metal of the crown of heaven, I should not have inquired.

PUESTERO (*A light of joy is in his eyes, for he knows a fine session of bargaining is coming, a thing most Mexicans love.*): May I ask what my lord would suggest a reasonable price?

FATHER: Four pesos.

We move to the next stall. Behind we can hear the bargaining continue against the shrill music, the voices, the cries, the general noise of the fiesta, but the camera is on a *curandera* and her stock of goods, and her customers.

The *curandera* in our picture is a powerful woman, with a face full of power, full of strength. Her stock is piled about her on the ground. She has the half-mad eyes of a priestess, and the wile of a witch. She is half charlatan and half Cassandra. Now she is treating sickness, selling herbs, charms, reading fortunes, disposing of amulets. She takes two small pointed leaves from a little pile, wets them with her tongue, and sticks them on the temples of an old woman. Then, with a strip of white cloth, she binds them in place so that the points of the leaves show below the bandage. As she does this, she chants a phrase in Aztec. I don't know the words, but I can get them. I have heard them. We see that her former customers are standing about, the children, other women with bandages of leaves. This is a cure for headache, or for nervousness, or even sometimes for an upset stomach, or for an upset soul. The leaves draw the poison to the temples, and, this being the thinnest part of the body, the poison is able to escape and the patient recovers. And, incidentally, it really works on the Indians, just as the psychoanalytic couch works on our people. Actually, I suppose, it is the same thing.

CURANDERA: Thus the pain goes. It is gone. Does it feel better?
> (*The old woman nods enthusiastically and moves aside. A young girl takes her place. She whispers to the* curandera.)

CURANDERA: No need to tell me. I know. I know how it is, but it is not cheap. It will be a silver peso. (*The girl bows her head and holds out a poor piece of silver jewelry. The* curandera *looks at it disparagingly. She will take anything, but she always pretends she will not.*)

CURANDERA: It's a poor thing, not worth half a peso.

She appears to be about to throw it back to the girl. It must be remembered that the rules of witchcraft and the conduct of a witch are just as formalized as the actions of any pitchmen in the carnival or of most doctors. In the midst of her refusal, the *curandera* seems to change her mind.

CURANDERA (*Softly*): Your need is very great, pretty one. It would be a crime for me to refuse. It shall be from my heart to your heart. (*She puts the silver trinket in her pocket, and from a bag made of plaited grass, she takes a little soft sack with a drawstring. Leaning forward, she ties the little bag around the girl's neck and arranges it against her breast.*) There. What woman's heart could refuse a woman's heart?

GIRL (*Anxiously*): When will he come back?

CURANDERA (*She seems to study, throws back her head, looks at the sky. Her eyes rolled back in her head, her voice changes; she is an actress.*): Soon, now soon. Before the moon is full, he will come.

GIRL (*Her face is flooded with joy.*): Thank you, my mother.

From behind, we hear the voice of the father.

FATHER: When I have said six pesos, I have said all.

PUESTERO: And my mention of fifteen was a period. The weapon of a horseman, a gentleman, is not to be sold for dirt. (*There is joy of battle in both voices and a promise of much arguing, since both know it will eventually be sold for ten pesos.*)

There is a cry. We turn with the others to a silent, furious fight; two Indians, very drunk, are locked in a quiet, deadly grip. Each one holds grimly to the other's knife hand, and we see that their faces are crazy with drink.

Shift now to a country road approaching a small town. These roads are very rough and full of rocks and mud. It's a night scene lighted only by half moon and by the coach lights. It is a big old-fashioned coach. (You can find many of them still in some of the stables of Mexico.) It is drawn by six horses, matched and beautifully harnessed. The *haciendados* took great pride in their horses and their equipment, almost as much as a present-day man takes in his automobile. The horses are ridden. There is a rider on the rear horse of each pair. The *rurales*, their equipment polished and jingling, ride five ahead and five behind the coach. The coach lamps throw a little light inside the coach. There we see Don Carlos, Madame, Young Monsieur, the French daughter, and the son of Don Carlos. The road is very rough. They hold to the side straps to keep from being tossed about in the coach. They are dressed for traveling, long capes and gloves. (See costumes of the period.) Inside the coach there are pistols and holsters, and the two men on the box carry rifles across their knees.

DON CARLOS: And that, all of that land, perfect for sugar cane, is used to pasture thin cattle. Even the town back there could be in sugar, and could raise—how do you say it?—gold, rather than filth.

MADAME: The country seems deserted.

DON CARLOS: Oh, everyone is at the fiesta. They will stay there until it is over, that's all they have to do. Church and fiestas. And they won't be any good for a week afterward. You've never seen drunken men until you've seen drunken Indians.

YOUNG FRENCHMAN: Might not despair have something to do with that?

DON CARLOS: We are nearly there. You will judge for yourself.

The coach is winding into the streets of the little town. The mud houses are on either side. The steel-banded wheels sound on the rough cobbles. We move ahead to the plaza, which we have just left. The jingle of the harness and the sound of the coach come to us above the sound of the fiesta. And then the coach comes in sight. The *rurales* have now distributed themselves on either side to protect the coach. The people make way, crowding back to get out of the way. Only the two Indians, locked in their deadly quarrel, do not move.

The next set of scenes must be shot with such a mounting intensity that it becomes a kind of a dream. A *rurale* rides up to the locked Indians. He swings with the flat of his machete against the white-cloth-clothed back. The Indians break apart. One finally gets his knife free. He leaps drunkenly at the *rurale*, his knife flashing, and receives the full cut of the machete across the shoulder, and he drops, bleeding. Inside the coach, Don Carlos draws a pistol from a holster. The lead horses rear and pitch, dragging the other team sideways. Their riders try desperately to hold them down. The frightened horses heave and pitch, dragging the coach over to the side and in among the *puestos* with their little piles of goods. There's a tangling of ropes and cloth, and rearing and fighting of the maddened horses. We see *puesteros* trying to get out of the way. There is a cry of anger from the people. Now the *rurales* fight their way in among the *puestos*, trying to protect the coach.

Now we see Eufemio and his father. The boy still holds the fine machete in his hand, and his face is full of rage. He raises the blade and runs toward the plunging horses. His father follows him. The boy cuts at a *rurale* with the machete. The father catches him and drags him back out of the way and receives the blade of a *rurale*'s machete in the face, and bleeding, he carries the struggling boy back.

Now a gun is fired from some place, and we see the *rurales* tugging the carbines from the scabbards on their saddles. The *rurales* open fire indiscriminately. The market is a shambles.

We see the father, bleeding, but holding the hysterical Eufemio close, and holding his wrists down, for the boy still has the machete in his hand.

EUFEMIO (*Shouting*): Let me go! I will kill!

We see the *curandera* standing in the midst of her wares, her face like that of a Fury. She stands her ground. The coach drives over her. She is thrown aside by the horse of a *rurale*.

This is the director's scene: the destruction, the fury, and the fear. The trampling horses cutting through the market. A thrown knife cuts a *rurale* from his horse, and a furious crowd closes over him. We see his agonized face under their feet, and his released horse dragging his way through pots and fruits and piles of produce. A candle lights a cloth, and a flame climbs the cloth for a moment, flares, catches another, so that there is a light, and then the light dies down and the flame goes out. The coach exits from the plaza, leaving wreckage. The remaining *rurales* are firing into the crowd. Inside the coach we see Madame and her daughter pushed to the floor. Don Carlos, his face in a rage, is firing into the crowd with his pistol. We can hear his pistol—and then the coach is gone. We hear it rattling over the heavy cobblestones.

And now we see the wrecked plaza. Some people have been hit; some slightly, and some badly hurt. Some are down, groups standing above them. The father is still there, holding the struggling boy, who seems a small demon. The blood from the father's cheek is falling on the boy. The *curandera* is getting up from the ground where she has been thrown, and she has grown in size, and there is something terrible about her. Her face is covered with dirt, and her clothing is torn, but her eyes are ferocious. She raises her arms and gives the fearful laughter called the *carcajada*, the animal laugh. A kind of silence made up of murmurs is in the square. The *curandera* must now be like a figure of fate. Her head goes back as we have seen it do before. Her face is wild. Her eyes roll up in her head in the induced trance so many of them practice. She raises both her fists, and when her voice comes, it is like the pained grunting of a fighting animal.

CURANDERA: Listen to me, listen! I tell you, all of you, listen. There will be borned here, *here*, a man, a soldier, an avenging tiger, and he will tear this fang from our throats. Listen. He will be borned here of our blood, and he will destroy this evil sickness from the land. He will be the tiger of his people, the beloved tiger, and the hand of God will be on him, and we will know him by the hand of God. Listen. He will drive through the land, he will clean out this sickness. Listen. He will be ours, our tiger, our dear tiger and beloved tiger. He will come soon. (*She sways on her feet. Her trance and her voice have hypnotized the people standing around. They watch, wide-eyed. The rolled up eyes of the* curandera *close suddenly. She falls to the ground and rolls on her back, her mouth is open and her lips make the movements of words, but only an animal growl comes from her lips.*)

We see the father still holding the boy, but Eufemio is not

fighting to get free anymore. His eyes are bright. He lies very quietly in his father's arms.

EUFEMIO: I will fight by the side of that tiger. (*He raises his new machete and looks at it. Along the long blade there runs a little stream of his father's blood.*)

Scene

It is the time of birth in the little mud house of the Zapata family. Birth in Mexico among the Indians is a time of magic. I do not know any people who feel more strongly about children. It is even thought by some ethnologists that there was a powerful, religious baby cult among the pre-Hispanic people. Delivery is usually done by the *curandera* in the country. The same one we have seen in the previous scene will be used here. She would be likely to serve the families in the whole area. Sometimes a good *curandera* covers an area of fifty miles. I don't know how much of the birth technique you will want to use. It varies slightly in different places. It is usual to force the birth by massage. For a completely authentic birth technique of the plateau people, see *The Forgotten Village*, which I made a number of years ago. The father of the family usually helps with the birth, even to the point of taking some of the pain to himself by holding the mother, who bears the child in a sitting position. Rather, the mother is in a sitting position. The kid is upside down, I imagine. It is common for the woman to bite one of her thick braids, both to keep from crying out in pain and to keep from biting her tongue. The *curandera* uses incense, *copalli*, which is a kind of magical disinfectant; actually, it is a gum made from resinous pine wood from the mountains. The chants and the words of magic are usually in Aztec and are very ancient. The relationship between man and woman is close during birth. All of this I can give, if necessary, or if you want to use any of it.

And since Emiliano Zapata is a mythical person, whose birth

was forecast, one of the great mystical births, it is possible that some of this magic background might be valuable to the film. It is my personal belief that Emiliano Zapata knew that he was fated, from the first, to be a great man. This must have put him above, or aside, from other people. This, of course, is subject to discussion, but he seems to have known that he was to take a large place in history.

The birth takes place at dawn. This is not by accident. Every effort is made to hurry the births before the dawn. As the night is evil, and the darkness is confused with pain, so the sun and child should be born together. It is a good sign, among other things. These people live by symbols. One other thing. In time of trouble or joy, Mexican people become communal. Neighbors gather from long distances for a birth, a sickness, or a death.

One other thing must be borne in mind. Mexican children are much more an inner part of the family than our children are. Nothing is kept from them. They are not segregated. They eat and sleep with the family. At about five years, they become adult in responsibility; they have beautiful manners because they have never heard anything else. They are regarded as people, not as dolls. Therefore, in the birth, they will have seen everything, and will be required even to help. If we open this scene just before daylight, the girls will be keeping the fire going in the yard, with the little pots of unguents steaming. They will also be preparing breakfast, patting tortillas, and cooking them on the *comales*. I think it will be good to play the ordinary against the unusual. Neighbors, men and women, will be in the yard waiting for the birth, and a number of them will be crowded in the small room where the birth is taking place. Eufemio will be bringing wood and brush and keeping up the fire. This scene should be played against animals, too, for these families live very close to their chickens and their turkeys, and their burros, and their horses. In some cases, a new baby is shown to the animals; introduced to the animals, just as is done in some parts of Europe, in Finland, and in Scandinavia, particularly.

If a birthing technique is required, I will tell the director. I have notes on all of the techniques of birth. However, I do not think very much of it is necessary, and it just causes trouble with censors, and elderly women who have never had children but find them somehow dirty.

Now, as the pains grow closer and closer, so the tempo of the people speeds up in the yard. The whole scene thickens. Finally, in the dawn, there is a great birth cry, and a slap (they use it, too). And then the little cry.

Now, if not before, we can move into the house, and the crowd of neighbors, too, and the girls of the house, and Eufemio. The mother is lying back on her sleeping mat, covered with a serape. The incense pot is smoking; the *curandera* is bent over the baby, tying the umbilical cord, and washing it. This can be done in pantomime, shooting from behind, if you wish. It will be easy for an audience to see just what she is doing without seeing it at all. This against the watching faces of the neighbors. The *curandera* wraps the baby and then she bends close to it, staring at his chest. And then she raises her hand, and we see that even she is frightened by what she sees. She looks again. We see the neighbors peering down. And now we see the baby for the first time. And on its chest is a birthmark in the shape of a little hand. The *curandera* speaks in wonder.

CURANDERA: Why, it is the little hand! (*She becomes excited.*) It is the little hand of God, and this is he. It's the tiger!

Eufemio plows through and squeezes near to the baby. He is still carrying his machete. We have a sense that it will never leave his hand. He puts out a grubby forefinger and traces the birthmark.

EUFEMIO (*Very softly*): My little brother. (*His face grows very fierce, and he says:*) My little tiger. (*And now we know he is remembering the night of the plaza. And we know little Eufemio will never forgive or forget anything.*)

Now the *curandera* wraps the baby and hands him to the father. This is stylized and ritualistic. The father takes the baby, and, kneeling down, places it on the breast of the mother. She makes room for it, raising her arm. She settles herself, and her big eyes have a look of pride and humility. In the yard outside, the *cohetes* (skyrockets for celebration) start to descend and explode above the house. The neighbors go into the yard. Drinking is now in order, for the birth is accomplished. The *curandera* comes out into the yard, her equipment slung in bags over her shoulder. The father stops her.

FATHER: Is this the one, the one you foretold?

These are professional women; they take advantage of every accident, every bit of luck; they are the ad-libbers of fate. Sometimes they believe, and sometimes they are scoundrels. This birth is a surprise. A surprise to the *curandera* as much as anyone, but she will use it.

CURANDERA: This is the one. Guard him well. He will cut a hole in the wall.

FATHER: Will you say more, little mother? Will you say more?

CURANDERA (*She is flushed with success; she can't stop now.*): This child will change the world; his name will be a sun over the land. And when he goes out of the world, he will remain. What will you name him?

FATHER: He shall be called "Emiliano."

CURANDERA: He shall be called "Chief."

NOTE: One of the strange and beautiful things in the life of Emiliano Zapata was his relationship to his brother. There was a close tie, very close. Eufemio knew his brother to be a great man; on the other hand, after the death of his father, Eufemio became the head of the house. So it was, when even Emiliano was grown and was general of all the armies of the south, and was worshiped by the people, Eufemio was still head of the house. Emiliano never entered a room without kissing his brother's hand, as a child does his father's hand in Mexico. Eufemio became a drunkard, a beast, a boaster, but the tie continued, he was still the head of the house, and Emiliano still loved him. And when he was finally killed, Zapata was filled with rage and sadness. He would not permit him, however, to be buried with the soldiers, but his mourning was no less for that. Eufemio embarrassed Emiliano, bothered him, got in his way, did not follow orders; but Emiliano always loved him, and there is no doubt that Eufemio was a man without fear.

The reason for this note is that we must now begin to develop the relationship between the two brothers. Their dependence on one another made a great difference between them. Next, it must be understood that the Zapatas were horsemen; they lived with, and by, horses. Emiliano was, perhaps, the greatest horseman in his time in Mexico.

SCENE

It is the horse corral of the little ranch of the Zapata family. Emiliano is about two years old. Eufemio, about seven. Eufemio is taking care of his brother. They enter the corral where a horse is tied to a fence. Eufemio speaks like a man, like his father.

EUFEMIO: Well, it is time to start.

He grabs his brother and boosts him up on the back of the tied horse. The horse shies sideways, and Emiliano falls into the dirt of the corral. We see the horse striking the ground about him. He does not cry. Mexican children rarely cry, except from hunger. Eufemio leaps around the horse and drags his brother clear. He goes up to the horse, soothes it until it is quiet, and then boosts his brother back on him.

EUFEMIO (*Savagely*): Now, hold on, and don't fall again.

Emiliano grips tight. His face is concentrated with his effort, but as he sees that he will not fall, he breaks into a smile. Eufemio unties the horse and leads it around the corral and the animal skitters, but the baby is seated now, holding tight to the mane, and he is very proud.

EUFEMIO (*Gives orders*): Now let go with your hands. (*We see the hands slowly release the grip on the mane and the little boy has balance. His confidence has returned.*)

EUFEMIO (*Looking over his shoulder, back toward the house*): Now, hold your hands up over your head.

(*Emiliano complies. Eufemio continues to lead the horse.*)

THREE YEARS LATER

We see the brothers, ten and five. They are creeping through the sugar cane toward a tree where five handsome horses are tied. The horses are saddled and bridled, and you can see by their equipment, machetes, rifles, and scabbards, that they are owned by a squad of *rurales*. In a small declivity not far away, we see the five men around the fire. They are cooking chunks of meat cut from the carcass of a sheep, or rather a goat, probably. They are drinking and boasting as soldiers do. Then we hear them. The first *rurale* follows his story with his hands.

FIRST RURALE: Then I rode in—took the regular position to the right, machete for front cut, and, of course, he prepared. Now, I'm a two-handed man. I heard about it from my father. (*He describes it with his body and hands so that we almost see it happening.*) Just before we left and engaged, I swung my horse right, shifted reins to right hand, machete to left; he could not change; I got him here. (*The* rurale *chops his right shoulder with the edge of his hand.*) You must be a two-handed man to do that, but it never fails. My father told me about that stroke as soon as he knew I was two-handed.

SECOND RURALE: I know a guard against it. When you turn right, then I turn right, and swing about.

FIRST RURALE: That's if you expect it, but they never do.

We go back to the two boys. They clear the cane field and creep near the horses, taking advantage of every bit of cover, keeping the tree between themselves and the soldiers. They move silently, like little foxes, near to the ground, and wary as animals.

EUFEMIO (*Whispers*): I will take the bay there; he looks fast. You take the roan.

One of the horses snorts, and the boys fall to the ground and lie very still. It is midday and the sun is hot. The soldiers look around at the snorting horse, but a little rise of ground conceals the boys. The soldiers go back to their cooking and their stories. And now we see that the boys are already horsemen. They slide in among the horses; they speak very softly and very slowly, touching the horses to reassure them. They have the horses to cover against being seen. And very slowly they untie the hackamore lines of the two chosen horses.

EUFEMIO (*Whispers*): Ride low so they cannot make you out. Are you ready, Emiliano?

EMILIANO: One moment. Look, Eufemio. When we get over that little hill, pull out the rifle and the machete and throw them into the cane. We'll come back for them a little later.

Eufemio smiles. He looks wistful because he did not think of it. He turns the horse, puts his foot in the stirrup; he leaps into the saddle and is away. Emiliano's horse rears and plunges, and Emiliano's foot slips from the stirrup. The horse races on. Emiliano is dragged, holding to the horn of the saddle. And then his back arches and his feet go forward and touch the ground and throw him into a flying mount. He is in the saddle, bending low, and right after his brother. There are pistol shots behind. We see the *rurales* rush to their horses. Three of them mount and give chase. The boys top the little rise and disappear over it. We see the boys riding hard, tugging the carbines from the scabbards. They throw them into the brush, and after them, the machetes.

EMILIANO (*Cries*): Now stop, Eufemio, before they see us.

They pull down the horses, they leap to the ground and scurry for cover into the cane, while the riderless horses go galloping on. We see the boys lying hidden when the soldiers tear by after the horses. Eufemio is all smiles.

EUFEMIO (*He rolls over on his back among the cane stalks.*): We will hide these guns. Now we are getting some place. (*He sees that his brother is not gay.*) What is the matter, Emiliano?

EMILIANO: We should have taken the *reatas* too.

EUFEMIO: Well, another time. Now we know how, sometime we will steal a whole *rurale* too. Be patient, my brother.

EMILIANO (*He is silent for a while and then he speaks.*): Eufemio, you saw the soldier cut my father before I was born?

EUFEMIO: I was there. I told you, I tried to kill him.

EMILIANO (*Fiercely*): But you don't remember what soldier. Would you know him if you ever saw him now?

EUFEMIO: It was very dark, and they all looked alike. I would not know him. You asked me before, Emiliano. No, I would not know him. Don't ask me anymore.

EMILIANO (*Quietly*): I will kill him one day, even if I do not know it is the one.

Eufemio does not answer him. The soldiers ride by at a fast trot, leading the stolen horses. The boys flatten themselves close to the ground.

NOTE: In the seventies, the profits from sugar in the state of Morelos became so great that they overshadowed even those from silver mining. Then, although the process had been going on a long time, the large landholders began greedily invading every bit of land capable of raising sugar cane. Lands that had been guaranteed to the Indians, even by the Spanish conquistadores, were taken by the rapidly growing power of the *hacendados*. The process of taking the land was this: The landowner paid a large amount of money to the President and to his group, who were called the *Científicos*. A land title was then given to them, or they were given tacit permission to occupy the land of the Indians. When the Indians protested, they were told to show their titles to the land. Some of them had lost their titles, which had been given hundreds of years before, and only a few of the towns had titles to produce. Then they were told to sue in the courts, and then their suits were kept in litigation year after year. But the *hacendados*, heavily protected by the rural troops, moved in, fenced the land, and planted it to cane. The troops patrolled the boundaries, and in a number of cases, villages were burned and the people driven out to make more room for more cane planting.

Zapata, as a boy, saw this happening. He stood with his father and brother, and watched the soldiers burn the village and drive off the people, and it seemed to have left a mark of rage in him that he never got over. He spoke of it many times in his life, saying that the fire still burned in his brain, and his eyes always glowed when he spoke of it.

SCENE

It is the house of the Zapatas; the father and mother are older now. The scar on the father's face still shows from the machete slash he got on the plaza. Emiliano is about fourteen. The family is having its little supper of tortillas, and beans, and tacos. The chickens are going to roost in the lean-to beside the house. One of the daughters, now grown, is milking a goat on the flat rock. Eufemio bolts his food and drinks deeply from the *pulque jarro*; Emiliano eats slowly and lightly.

EUFEMIO: And what did they say, exactly, my father?

FATHER: Well, I don't know how much they knew. They came down over the mountains from Toluca with pottery. They said the word was out all through the country. They said a whole regiment of cavalry was moving down, skirting the mountains by Tepoztlán. They did not even pass through Cuernavaca. They passed to the east, through the little Pedregal, and headed in the direction of Cuautla. Something was wrong. I do not know what.

EMILIANO (*Speaks calmly*): I talked with our cousin the newspaper man at the hacienda. He has heard them laughing and talking there. They say that they are going to take all of the town lands to the north. Yes, and our cousin said they are going to pull down the village. (*His eyes are brooding.*)

FATHER (*Speaks with relief*): Well, you see how rumors go. When stories get too big, they fall down of their own weight. (*He speaks bravely, as though he gave a lesson.*) The town men are protected. The lands have been the property of the town people for five thousand years. When Cortez came in, even he did not disturb the town land. No, the story is too big. Burn down the buildings? How can that be? What would be the purpose?

EMILIANO: Why, then, do the soldiers come, my father?

FATHER: Perhaps they are at practice. I remember that quite often the soldiers go out on practice trips to keep the men in condition. They play that they are at war. They divide up and they play a game of fighting, everyone knows that. I'm glad the story grew too big.

EMILIANO: The people at the hacienda just got in new plows, new bullocks; all new, all waiting.

FATHER: Well, things wear out and bullocks die. Maybe they're replacing them.

Eufemio stares sullenly away into space. Even as a boy his face is brutal and angry.

EMILIANO (*Speaks softly*): You do not believe what you are saying, my father.

The father looks at him quietly for a moment, his eyes crinkling a little at the corners. And then the Indian shade draws down over them and he speaks acidly.

FATHER: Even the second son can, if he tries, be disgraced.

EMILIANO (*He gets up quickly, walks to his father and kisses his hand.*): And with your permission. (*He goes out of the house and leans on the fence. It is said of him that he is never young and never old.*)

In the distance we see several men in the white dress of fieldworkers coming toward the Zapata house. They are running, a slow, untiring, jogging run with which these people travel. They come up in front of the house yard, and we see that they are old men, or men past middle age. It is, in fact, a delegation of elders from the village.

FIRST OLD MAN: Is your father here, Emiliano?

Apparently hearing the voices, the father comes out of the door followed by Eufemio, and as always, as in a Mexican house, the women stay inside but look out the doorway.

FATHER: My friends . . . (*He leaves the sentence open for a moment; then he continues:*) Will you do me the honor to enter my house?

It must be remembered that this is not a stilted speech in Mexico. This is the way that people talk to one another. The forms of courtesy are never violated.

OLD MAN: Don Gabriel, the troops are surrounding the village. We do not know what they want; they do not speak to us. But there are engineers with glasses on sticks and the men are looking through them.

NOTE: It must be understood that in moments of stress, except when they are drinking, these people are likely to draw into themselves and to appear noncommittal, even uninterested. Particularly when they are most deeply moved or affected.

FATHER (*Sighs*): What do you wish, my friend?

EUFEMIO (*Excitedly*): They are going to take the town lands.

The father holds up his hand with only the slightest acknowledgment. The old men hiss softly. This is the way a crowd of elders always shames children, with a slight hiss. Eufemio is silent. He has been punished.

FATHER: I have not wanted to think so, but I am afraid he is right. Are there many soldiers?

FIRST OLD MAN: Very many.

FATHER: When they took the southern land of our village, we protested to the government. We were told to take action to the courts. I was a delegate. (*He pauses.*) The action is still in the courts. The hacienda still has the land.

FIRST OLD MAN: Don Gabriel, will you dress in your best, and mount a horse and come and ask them what they are doing? They will not even answer us. But you, in the dress of a *charro*, and on horseback, they could not refuse to answer you.

FATHER (*Slowly*): It is late. It will soon be night. (*He waits.*)

The delegation stares impassively at him, and between them, as seems to happen too often, some unspoken conversation must take place.

FATHER (*Still looking at them, says softly*): Eufemio, Emiliano, saddle the horses.

The two boys run quickly away toward the corral. We next see the little group in the deepening dusk. The father and two boys are on horseback. They are all three dressed in the tight pants, short jackets, and big felt sombreros of the *charros*.

NOTE: There must be no embroidery on the backs of the jackets. This is important. In the present day, the back is embroidered, but in the time of which we are speaking, it was said that there was no need since no one would ever see a brave man's back.

The delegation of old men moves along, in their endless, shuffling, trotting. The night is coming, and ahead we see the light of the fire, a very large fire. The faces of the men are hard. Please remember, for directorial purposes, that when most deeply affected, and even when most dangerous (except in drink), these people get an almost impersonal expression on their faces. I think this could be very effective on film.

SCENE

On the top of a small hill, a group of horsemen—they are the commanders of the Federal troops. And behind them standing— their faces lit by fire—are many people, some with bundles of clothing, with babies, and with the curious things people save in a holocaust; pigs and chickens. Remember how they lead pigs with a rope tied to one hind leg, and the squeals of the animals, and the braying of the donkeys, and the crying of the children. The old men fall back, but the father and the two sons ride to the officers. A cavalryman rides his horse in front of them to cut them off in case they are going to attack. All the faces are lighted by the fire.

FATHER (*With patient courtesy*): May I ask what we have here, my Colonel?

COLONEL (*Turns his head slowly; looks the father up and down*): Who are you?

FATHER (*Very patiently*): A landholder, and a *charro*, my Colonel.

COLONEL (*Shortly*): Then you can see. I do not explain. I have my orders.

FATHER (*His voice has become very soft, very quiet.*): May one inquire on whose orders you burn the towns of the people?

COLONEL (*He does not answer. He waves his hand.*)

Five more cavalrymen ride in, their hands rip the carbines from the scabbards. Their horses form a barrier, and they force the horses of the father and the two sons back and away. The shadows are heavy and concealing. I should like to show that the town is burning without showing too much of it. I don't want the usual three-alarm fire sequence—a quick flash, perhaps, but try to show the tragedy in the faces of the people watching.

The father, mounted, on one side of him, Eufemio, and on the other, Emiliano. They are looking at the fire, their faces impassive, but the burning is reflected in their eyes. We stop on Emiliano's face. Reflected in his eyes we can see the leaping flame, and even some of the details of the burning town. Establish this clearly, because later in the film, in times of rage and anger, we will use these flames in the eyes as an indication of the thought, the drive, the impetus of the man.

EMILIANO (*He speaks quietly, as his father did to the Colonel.*): I will stop these things, my father. (*His lips tighten over his teeth.*) I will not let these things happen. This I promise.

EUFEMIO (*Harshly*): Kill them! Kill them all. (*He raises his hand, the fingers flexed, but not closed.*)

EMILIANO (*Still quietly, and we see the fire in his eyes.*): I will stop these things, my father. (*His hand rises, and he touches his breast over the heart delicately with five fingers in a gesture he might make to a lady. His voice turns cold and metallic and penetrating, although it does not rise in volume.*) I, Emiliano, will stop this. This I swear!

SCENE

A hot, dusty, freshet-torn road—the sun is at midday. We see a little funeral procession. Marching first, one of those horrible beat-up village bands of about twelve pieces, mostly brass, and a bass drum. They play dreadfully off-key, but in a slow rhythm, so that even their bad music has a kind of dignity. Next, a few old men, walking, stopping occasionally to light little skyrockets that zip into the air and explode.

NOTE: This is almost invariable at funerals. The *cohetes* are in some ways supposed to be prayers that enter heaven to give notice that a soul is coming. They are used on saints' days, too, as prayers, and besides, people like skyrockets.

Next in the procession is the coffin borne on two poles. The two sons are ahead carrying it, and other men are on the rear of the poles. The coffin is open, and the father is in it. The roughness of the way and swaying of the poles make the body tremble and move in the coffin. On the right hand are the mother and two daughters, their rebozos drawn tight against their faces. They carry small lighted candles, and they shield the flame from possible breeze with their cupped palms. And following the coffin, a crowd of people, each one with a candle. The father was an influential man, and he had many friends. The children (in Mexico, they are little adults) are on the fringe of the crowd. Even some of them have candles, and some, little beat-up bunches of wild flowers. The scene is hot and blinding with light, and very dry. At the graveside: The band is still playing and the sons are shoveling dirt into the grave. One man drives into the ground a board which has roughly carved on it—Gabriel Zapata. The grave is half-filled. The mother takes Emiliano's arm.

MOTHER: That will do now. (*Her face is inexpressibly tired.*)

Emiliano looks at her in question.

MOTHER (*Continues*): Leave it that way. I will be needing it.

NOTE: This is quite often done where there is great love between a man and a woman. They request that they may be buried in one grave.

Now it is the same scene, the same band, the same people. But it is raining. (To indicate a change of season: actually, about six months. They died about that far apart.) The countryside is wet and the light strained through the clouds. Emiliano and Eufemio are filling in the last of the grave, patting the wet earth with their shovels, and a man is writing on the headboard with a piece of chalk or crayon or pencil: "His wife, Cleofas Salazar."

With this scene, I think, there is established not only the background, but also the reasons why Emiliano must spend his whole life in his war. Eufemio is a brave, headstrong man, likely to run in all directions, sure to follow any quick impulse, while Emiliano is now a devoted man. And with the last scene, they are men. They are no longer little boys. We must see now the kind of life that these young men lead.

SCENE

A *pulqueria* in a small town. It is a simple mud room, a dirt floor, a thatched roof. A few benches and crude tables; a counter along one wall, and behind it a pitiful few bottles of good liquor which are never bought because they are too expensive; and there's the colored alcohol, *aguardiente, pulque,* tequila, which all come in jugs of clay. The cups, in that day, are usually gourds, which are sometimes molded while they are growing. A common method is to place the growing gourd inside a bottle until it takes the bottle's shape and then to break the bottle off it. Another is simply to tie a string around the gourd so that it has a handle when it ripens. You still see these tied to the saddles of the Indians. In the bar are the inevitable mariachis, and one in particular sings very loudly and very beautifully. There are no women in the bar but quite a few men, some in the white *calzones* of the field hands, and a few, a very few, in poor suits. These are the pitiful middle class which is either bought or destroyed by the growing hacienda system. The *pelados* are quite drunk as they are likely to get very easily, and on very little liquor. The scene is lit with the candles, but not very many of them. There are a few colored pictures on the wall, the sickeningly sentimental pictures of all Latin countries—arch girls in high combs and mantillas, peeking around fans. A dark-eyed lady is holding a pigeon on her finger. The things haven't changed much, they're still there. A *pulqueria* in a small town is almost exactly now what it was then. They are not gay places. There is no door. People pass in front and are lighted for a moment by the candles. One of the players sings a long dull *corrido* about some forgotten hero.

Eufemio and Emiliano enter. They are men now. And they are well dressed. This was always true. The brothers took great pride in their clothing. A place is made for them at the bar. The bartender, without asking, pours out little glasses of *aguardiente.* Eufemio, without a word, tosses his glass off, has it refilled, tosses that, and has it refilled. We see by the shine in his eyes that it is not his first port of call. Emiliano drinks half of his glass, sets it down and smacks his lips, studies his glass, picks it up, drinks it slowly. The bartender matches his pace with Emiliano. He slowly fills the little glass.

BARTENDER: I haven't seen you two for a while.

EMILIANO (*Shortly*): We've been away. We've been traveling.

BARTENDER (*Curiously*): North?

EMILIANO: No.

BARTENDER (*He is put in his place. He covers up the reproof.*): There was a great scandal a week ago. Nacio Gonzales had trouble with three men. It was here. (*The bartender's eyes glow with pleasure. He pats a place on the bar, a great scoop cut in the wood.*) That might have been Nacio, but he stepped back.

EMILIANO: I heard. Two of the men died. Nacio went away for a while.

BARTENDER: Did you see him?

EMILIANO: Yes.

BARTENDER: Did he tell you they were officials?

EMILIANO: Yes.

EUFEMIO (*Quite drunk, scowling at the bartender*): Oh, shut up. You talk too much. (*He looks to his brother for approval of this move. Emiliano stares, unmoved, straight ahead.*)

BARTENDER: Will you ride at the fiesta?

EMILIANO: Of course.

NOTE: Eufemio's temper was always treacherous. He was often in the most deadly quarrels over nothing at all, a most violent man. He was subject to instant change in disposition and temper.

EUFEMIO (*In a bellicose voice*): What made you think my brother would not ride? Do you think he is afraid? (*He moves close, scowling.*) Do you think he is not the best *charro* in the state of Morelos? Will you say he is not the best *charro* in Mexico? (*His hand moves to his belt.*)

The bartender edges away. He knows this temper that is being whipped into a rage. Two women come in and go to a corner at one of the little rough tables. Eufemio rolls his back around on the bar and looks at them. Their faces are so closely covered by their rebozos that their features cannot be seen. The bartender takes the jug and two glasses and goes over to the table where the women are sitting. Emiliano touches Eufemio's arm and Eufemio whirls on him, his eyes blazing, and then he sees it is his brother who has touched him, and his eyes soften.

EMILIANO: I want to talk to you.

EUFEMIO (*He motions with his hand toward the women.*): Later.

EMILIANO: No, now.

EUFEMIO (*He draws himself up, half in mock dignity.*): Who is the head of the house?

EMILIANO (*He takes his brother's hand and kisses it submissively.*): You are, Eufemio.

EUFEMIO (*He loves his brother, and he is mollified.*): What do you want to talk about, Emiliano?

Emiliano leads his brother to a table at the end of the room away from the women. The bartender brings his bottle and their glasses and fills them. Eufemio drinks his down. His eyes are glazing a little.

EUFEMIO: Talk fast. I have business.

EMILIANO: This is business. Look, the hacienda needs horse trainers.

EUFEMIO (*Hoarsely*): I wouldn't work for the dirty bastards.

EMILIANO: Easy, easy. Look, Eufemio. You know how I feel. But we must think, and to think we must learn.

EUFEMIO: Don't you remember?

EMILIANO: I remember everything. I remember. Look, Eufemio, you are a fighter. Isn't it better to know your enemy? How he strikes? How he parries? How quickly he moves, what is his strength, and what are his weaknesses?

EUFEMIO: What's that got to do?

EMILIANO (*He drinks his little glass.*): We must learn. This is the only way. I think we can get the job. Will you go with me, Eufemio?

EUFEMIO (*He gets a look of screaming subtlety. His face shouts conspiracy.*): I will go, Emiliano. (*He winks broadly.*) I understand—we must spy on the enemy. (*Harshly*) I want a drink.

When Eufemio is drunk, he is a devil. His nature is treacherous, volatile. He can become cruel, lustful, murderous, or infantile, all of a sudden and without any warning. He is overbearing, boastful, and fearless. It is as though a curtain came down over his mind and cut him off from everyone. Only one thing is able to get through, and that is a great deep respect and love for his brother. With women, he is hard and contemptuous. They are only for his pleasure. He has no contact with them except a physical one. This attitude seems to be attractive to some women. He has a great contempt for women and a great lust for them, which is set off by drink. Emiliano, on the other hand, is rather shy with women. He is gentle and seems to be a little afraid of them. And there is in him a curious respect for all women. These things are attested by everyone who knew the brothers.

EMILIANO (*Stands up*): I'll get a bottle, Eufemio. (*He goes to the bar. The bartender leans toward him.*)

EMILIANO: A little bottle—just a small one.

BARTENDER (*Indicating Eufemio with his eyes*): Don't let him get angry, Emiliano.

EMILIANO (*Harshly*): He doesn't mean harm, and if he does harm he pays for it.

BARTENDER: He broke all my tables once.

EMILIANO: And he paid for them.

BARTENDER: You did that. You made him.

EMILIANO (*Tersely*): He paid for them.

BARTENDER (*Uneasily*): Yes, yes. I know. It's all right. (*He leans close and speaks conspiratorially.*) I saw Josefa Espejo today.

EMILIANO (*His face becomes hard and jealous. He strokes his mustache and looks coldly at the bartender.*)

BARTENDER (*Uneasily*): She was walking with her aunt. (*Emiliano continues to stare at him.*)

There is a crashing noise behind. A regular cat fight. Eufemio has one of the women by the arm; he is pulling and yanking her by the arm, trying to pull her out the door, while she fights and spits, and tries to get away from him. It is like the love fight of two animals. Eufemio's face is inflamed and his eyes are very drunken. He pulls and wrestles silently, and a table is tipped over. The woman is more amazed than frightened. She is like a chicken pulled out of a coop, squawking and crying.

WOMAN: Let go, you animal, you pig, you drunken pig. Let me go.

She bites at his hand and is struck in the face by his free hand. He wrestles and pulls her toward the open door. This is a real animal fight, fierce, silent, vicious. There isn't any question about what Eufemio wants, nor that he intends to get it. On the other hand, there is some question about the woman. Here is no outraged virtue. It may be that she even enjoys this fierceness, that after Eufemio has been bitten, kicked, his shirt torn and his face scratched, that she will capitulate with an enthusiasm equal to her resistance. There is a kind of joyousness about this fight. Some time can be devoted to it because it is a fine thing. The attitude of the others in the bar is interesting too. This is a kind of animal interest. No one would think of interfering. It is a kind of sporting event. The other woman, her head and face closely hooded with her rebozo, looks on, completely impassively. She makes only one move. When the fight comes too close to her, she picks up her glass and holds it close so that it won't be knocked over if the table should be struck. The audience is like a prizefight audience. The director can make this a real battle, brutal and happy. Everyone is enjoying it. Emiliano watches—a faint smile on his face, of slight admiration and enjoyment. He lifts his glass to his lips and sips it. He lights a cigarette, but slowly and thoughtfully, the way a man does whose interest is caught with something else. Now the woman sets her feet. Eufemio has both of her wrists and tries to drag her. When he is pulling hardest, she tricks him. She leaps forward, and Eufemio is thrown backward by his own force and weight; he falls over a table, landing flat on his back. He releases the woman's wrists. She (panting) looks about, runs to the bar, picks up a bottle, breaks it so that she has a jagged weapon of pointed razor-sharp glass. Then, instead of defending herself, she attacks. Eufemio is just struggling to his feet; he is very happy. His eyes are bleary. He sees her coming with her terrible weapon, and now we see what a hell of a good fighter he is. His eyes clear. The woman charges at him. He dodges sideways, and the sharp glass only rips through his shoulder, cutting coat and flesh. Eufemio stands casually. The woman recovers and rushes in again. Eufemio is looking right in her face, holding her attention. Just before she reaches him, he kicks a stool in front of her without even looking down. She trips and falls over it and her bottle flies out of her hand. Now Eufemio leaps. Bending down, he grabs her around the waist and lifts her. He tries to throw her over his shoulder and, failing, he simply lugs her out of the door, her arms and legs flailing. And from outside, we hear his wild laughing cry of triumph. Everyone in the bar laughs in appreciation. Even the other woman smiles.

NOTE: This is not particularly overdrawn. From all sources, this was actually Eufemio's nature. A really brutal man who took joy in his brutality and who (until the last of his life) was not disliked for it. In motion pictures it has become popular to have at least one animal fight. This takes the stink off a bad story. I propose in this picture to have a fight between the most vicious animals of all—man and woman. The obvious result is romance, of course. But aside from this scene as a sporting event, I want to establish the essential difference between the two brothers.

From outside we hear the wild laughter of the woman. Emiliano still stands at the bar. There is a kind of affectionate smile on his lips. It might be that Eufemio's way might be the way he would like to be.

BARTENDER (*Shaking his head with a kind of wonder*): What a man is your brother; what a wild man.

EMILIANO (*Smiles*): Sometimes I worry a little that sometime he may not duck in time.

BARTENDER: He will always duck.

EMILIANO: He will always try. When you do, you are the same. The first time you do not, you are different.

BARTENDER (*Crosses himself instinctively as one does when the dead are mentioned*): God will that he always does.

EMILIANO (*Musing*): He is not afraid of anything. He has no caution.

BARTENDER: He is a fighter. A fighter always has caution.

EMILIANO: My father told that when Eufemio was only a little boy, he went after a *rurale* with a machete. He has luck.

BARTENDER (*Piously*): It is well known that the man who attacks has more luck than he who defends.

Emiliano studies him for a moment. He seems to make up his mind. He takes the bottle and the glass and moves over to the table where the other woman is sitting. She looks at him for only a second, then lowers her eyes in a kind of modesty. Perhaps Emiliano thought he could do what his brother had. He would like to, but it is not his nature. And even while contemplating it, he cannot do it and knows he can't. He glances down at the table. The moment his eyes are off her, the woman glances up at him. She knows instantly all about him. His lips smile very faintly. She knows that she will probably have to make all the moves. She has a sense of power.

EMILIANO (*Gently*): Will you like a drink?

WOMAN (*She becomes delicate and feminine.*) Well, a little, maybe. It goes to my head. (*She touches her forehead.*)

With Eufemio she would be a whore; with Emiliano she has suddenly become a lady. Emiliano pours her glass just as full as though it did not go to her head. We see that his shyness is overcoming him. He drinks his glass, fills it, and drinks it again just as Eufemio did earlier. He looks up at her, and her eyes slide away.

EMILIANO (*Uneasily*): You are pretty.

WOMAN (*Her hand rises to her cheek and arranges the hang of the rebozo against her face.*): Well, I have not been very well, and so I think I have lost what little looks I had.

EMILIANO (*Tries again*): Well, you, you are pretty.

WOMAN (*Now she knows she has the situation in charge. Her con-*

fidence grows large. She begins saying dichos.): But her prettiness is mostly in a lover's eyes.

EMILIANO (*Searching for a* dicho *to say back*): Ah, the eyes are the windows of the soul.

NOTE: *Dichos* are sayings. Mexicans know very many of them, and it is a kind of social play to answer one with another. This serves a good purpose—it is a game, and also, because the sayings are all traditional and all tested by time, one never goes out on any limb if he only sticks to *dichos*. The traditional approach is maintained and no dangerous originality can creep in. In all social pursuits, Mexicans are complete traditionalists. Thus the courting of a man and woman can be, and mostly is, carried out completely in *dichos*. We will make use of this later.

WOMAN: I saw you ride in the fiesta last year. I was afraid you might be killed.

EMILIANO (*Still in* dichos, *although the woman has moved out of them.*): Still, death is always preferable to dishonor.

WOMAN (*Archly*): It seemed to me that your eyes were aimed like a rifle at a pretty quarry.

EMILIANO (*His eyes change. He looks at her speculatively. He studies her. Suddenly she is not a woman to whom he is trying to make vague love. She is a person, and he is the clever man he is. Even his voice changes.*): You saw so much?

WOMAN: Yes.

EMILIANO: Did others notice?

WOMAN: How do I know?

EMILIANO (*He is impatient. He is dealing now with an opponent, and he is very good at this, not clumsy at all.*): Perhaps this is a game you play. It is an easy one. We will not mention any name. But you will tell me the initials of . . .

WOMAN: J.E. And the father is a merchant and very rich, and they live in V.A. (*She smiles at him in victory.*)

Emiliano is satisfied that she does know. His love affair with

this woman is now over. We see this in his eyes. But she does not
quite realize it yet. She arranges her rebozo in a nicer frame for
her face. He is looking at her, but his mind is not on her as a
woman now.

WOMAN: I have seen her, of course. You were serious, then, and
the looks meant something?

EMILIANO: Would it be possible for you to approach this lady—
perhaps give her a message?

WOMAN (*She changes. If it is going to be this way, then she must
have something for her trouble. She looks keenly at him, and
she is no longer either coquettish or a lady. She has become a
conspirator, and for this, Emiliano will have to pay. She is
playing poker with him now.*): It would be next to impossible.
She is very closely attended. I have never seen her alone,
never.

EMILIANO: But women have ways of doing these things.

WOMAN: It's possible, but . . .

EMILIANO (*Nervously*): But what?

WOMAN (*Now she has given him up entirely. She has her living to
make; also, now she is his equal.*): Look, my friend. I need
not tell you that her father is the richest man in Villa Agalla.

EMILIANO (*Quickly*): Hush.

WOMAN: In V.A., then. And you will also know that. (*Lowers her
voice*) Josefa is protected. If you have tried, even you, a *charro*,
would not be found acceptable as a husband. And as a lover?
She is very devout and dutiful. I think you will get nowhere,
my friend.

EMILIANO: But could you get a message to her?

WOMAN: I don't know. Have you ever spoken to her?

EMILIANO: No.

WOMAN: Does she know who you are?

EMILIANO: She has looked back at me just for a blinding second.

WOMAN (*Seems to consider*): Well, but no, it would be silly, and I
might be caught. And then, well, her father is very powerful,
and I'm a poor woman.

EMILIANO (*Pleading*): But will you try? (*He pours her another glass. His face is animated now.*)

WOMAN: Well . . .

EMILIANO (*He reaches into his pocket and brings out a handful of coins. There are coppers and small pieces of silver, but among them shines a great and beautiful golden fifty-peso piece.*): I would like to give you a little present if you would try. (*He places the coins on the table.*)

WOMAN (*She looks at the gold piece. Her fingers move over and rest on the gold piece, and she slides it toward herself. She repeats.*): Well, maybe I could try.

EMILIANO (*He watches the golden coin slide away with some sadness. He knows he has been had, and there is nothing he can do about it.*): You will take her a message?

WOMAN: I will try. What do you want me to say?

EMILIANO (*Now that she will, he doesn't have any idea what to say.*): Tell her, let's see. Tell her, well, say that one, who adores her, waits beneath her window.

WOMAN: Yes?

EMILIANO (*Struggling*): Like a fallen angel . . . on the steps of Heaven.

WOMAN: Any more?

EMILIANO: What else should I tell her?

WOMAN (*Amused that she has to coach him*): Well, shall I ask whether she will meet you?

EMILIANO (*Hurriedly*): Yes, yes, ask her that.

WOMAN (*Cynically*): And shall I say things like you are dying for love of her and your heavy eyes are fountains of tears?

EMILIANO: Yes, say things like that.

WOMAN: It may take time. I will have to plan. She is never alone, you see.

EMILIANO: I know. But you will do it.

WOMAN (*With her hand in her lap, she caresses the gold coin. Her fingernail traces the great eagle whose figure is on it.*): You will ride in the fiesta?

EMILIANO (*Jerked out of his silken dream*): Yes, of course. Why?

WOMAN: I will tell her. (*Bitchily*) Perhaps she will give you some encouragement then.

Eufemio comes staggering in the door alone. He barely makes the table. Emiliano kisses the back of Eufemio's hand.

EUFEMIO: Come on, Emiliano. I am sleepy. (*He sits down and rests his head on his hands.*) Very sleepy, Emiliano, very sleepy.

SCENE

Every little village in Mexico has its horse arena and bullring where sports are celebrated. Sometimes it is nothing but a round corral with a high fence, and sometimes it is more elaborate, with seats for the more eminent of the guests. Here, as part of every fiesta, there are sports. There are country bullfights which are usually very bad, and then, in the parts of the country where cattle are plentiful, there are the sports of the *charro*. For descriptions of these sports, see the introduction. I would suggest the wild, crazy, mixed-up bullfight—some of the *calcando*, or tailing, which is a pretty sport, requiring the greatest of judgment and horse-manship—and finally, the riding of the wild horse. This is the sport at which Emiliano is famous. He was also good at *calcando*. Depending on how the director feels, some of each can be used, but it should culminate with the wild horse.

The *charros* put every penny they could get into clothes. Thus, while Emiliano and Eufemio were quite poor, at a fiesta their clothing would be immaculate, decorative, and expensive. Also, they always managed to have fine horses. These *charros* have great dignity and an enormous flair. They ride like princelings in their big hats, and their clothing is ornamented with silver.

Our scene, then, is a little ring on the edge of a small town. In the beginning we have seen what a fiesta is like in the center of the plaza; this is what it is like at the ring. It is a round stockade with cattle chutes on one side and a small bank of seats for the *gente.* These *gente* are of the middle class. They are as stuffy and formal as any middle class. They are the merchants, the traders, the small government officials, the lawyers, the doctor, the priest. They are not to be confused with the great people, the *hacendados*, who are as much above them as they are above the common people who make up most of Mexico. The great ones rarely sit in the seats. Rather, in that day, they drove their coaches near to the ring and watched the sports from their own vehicles.

The women of the great ones would be dressed in the fashions of Paris, and they would carry parasols to keep the sun from their skins. But the *gente* who sat on the seats would be dressed in iron clothing. (There are many photographs in existence to show both kinds of dress.) Meanwhile, the white-clad peons would sit on the fence and the barricade itself. As they got drunker they would be all over the ring.

The three classes kept pretty much to themselves—the peons, the *gente* and the *hacendados*. But the *charros* mingled easily with all of them, and they were held in admiration by all. They were, in a way, the knights errant of their day. Our nearest analogy is the American cowboy on a western ranch, who is as good as the ranch owner and is acceptable to all classes.

NOTE: In the matter of the courtship of Emiliano for Josefa, her family did not so much reject his suit because of his family but mainly because he was poor. This daughter of the *gente* was presumed to bring added wealth to her family. Once Zapata had become a general (and generals, unlike Zapata, almost invariably became rich), he was completely acceptable to her family.

It is the bullring on the edge of the town. It is the drunken end of the melee, which here is called the eleven o'clock bull. The seats are full of *gente.* A few coaches of the very rich are drawn up near the fence, and on their tops are sitting beautifully dressed ladies and gentlemen while deployed about the coaches are their armed and mounted riders there to protect them. In the wooden stands sit the *gente.* They sit very stiffly; some of the women carry black umbrellas, for it is considered silly to a dark-skinned people not to remain as white as they can. We see the family of Josefa: her father, full of importance and growing wealth, her mother, her aunts, her brothers, and Josefa herself. Contemporary pictures do not show Josefa to have been a very pretty woman, but Zapata loved her very deeply, and she, him. He was one of the handsomest men of his time. I do not believe it completely out of order to make her a little prettier than she actually was. She must have at least seemed beautiful to Emiliano.

Josefa is a modest, perfectly trained girl of her class, shy, protected, obedient. Her eyes flick up with interest and down again in modesty. She is shielded from any contact from the outside world. Her angular aunt sits beside her, holding an umbrella over her head. The whole family is dressed in the height of middle-class fashion of the period: heavy gold jewelry, large crucifixes, modest, hot, and uncomfortable clothing. These people were intensely religious, while the *haciendados* used the church and were used by it, as witness the motto of the great silver master, Borda, which was "God gives to Borda and Borda gives to God." But the *gente* were the moral background and the buttress of the church. There is no formality like the *gente* of Mexico; indeed, they are sometimes called "*correctos.*"

JOSEFA (*There is a great sweetness about her, and it later develops that there is also a great strength and loyalty in her.*): Mama.

Her mother turns quickly to this apple of her eye. Her father, fat-jowled and big-mustached, turns. Her aunt, a slab-sided maiden of fifty, turns. Her brother, a kind of small business lout, turns.

They all look at her. Then her mother seems to know what she wants. She reaches into her purse, takes out a lace handkerchief, opens a small bottle, probably scented smelling salts, dampens the handkerchief. She hands it to Josefa. Josefa holds the handkerchief to her nose and sneezes. Her other hand is concealed under the edge of her skirt, and we see it move slightly up. She has a piece of *bisnaga*, a sticky, sweet candy made of cactus boiled in sugar. Under the protection of the handkerchief, Josefa pops the candy into her mouth and drops the handkerchief to her lap. In the next series of scenes when she finds it necessary to chew a little bit or to swallow, she holds the handkerchief up in front of her face.

Emiliano and Eufemio, mounted on beautiful horses, and dressed in silver and black, are outside the barricade. They sit with great and disdaining dignity, like the lords of the world. Their hats are huge and their jackets are covered with silver embroidery. Their reins are dotted with silver. Even their saddles and *tapaderos* are pecked out with silver studs. Their eagle-handled machetes hang from the left side of the saddle with the scabbard back under the leg. These machetes are drawn by the right hand reaching across the broad white saddle horn. Eufemio is a little drunk; Emiliano, not at all. And Emiliano is watching Josefa across the ring. When his brother looks at him his eyes grow noncommittal. He is easily the best-looking, best-equipped man there, and we must see that Josefa is watching him as eagerly, although secretly, as he watches her.

There is a small disturbance at one of the coaches from the hacienda. A very drunk Indian has fallen off the fence and one of the armed guards has ridden in to prevent any possible contact between the man and the coach. Emiliano looks around. His eyes grow fine, and here I think we can use this device: We see his eyes very close up, and in the pupil we see the leaping flames of the burning village, which we have seen in his eyes when he sat with his father. Now his hand moves unconsciously toward the handle of his machete. Eufemio has seen all of this. He sees the hardness in his brother's face, and he looks down at the hand which is moving toward the machete. Eufemio smiles crookedly, and then, to break the spell, he reaches into the *bolsa* which hangs behind his saddle and pulls out a bottle. He holds it so that Emiliano's hand can't help moving away from the machete to take it, and now we see Emiliano's eyes again. The flame goes out, and he drinks shortly from the bottle.

NOTE: For interest, and for something that hasn't been seen in this country, I suggest that the bull tailing start in the ring. (The introduction gives a description of what it is like. It is a game of strength, precision, and horsemanship.) Eufemio was very good at it. And this was a sport that was good for an outlaw to know. For a man could throw a steer or a cow, be off his horse, kill it with his knife before it could get up again, cut off a leg, and be gone before the cowhands could do anything about it. But it was a very difficult sport.

After the bull tailing, we come to the wild horse riding. It is the greatest of all feats of horsemanship. The director may have to fake it, because very few people can do it. (For God's sake, don't let your star try it, you may lose him!) Zapata was famous for his riding. Well done, it looks easy, so it might be a good thing to show what can happen when it fails.

The man who is to ride enters the ring on horseback. Our first pigeon has stripped himself to essentials, he wears a cotton shirt and trousers, he wears no shoes and no hat. He takes his position in the middle of the ring. The chute door opens and a wild horse runs into the ring. His mane is roached, so there is nothing to hang on to. He has been starved until he is angry and crazy. A group of horsemen begin driving him around and around the ring, going faster and faster. When the horse is going at maximum speed, the ring president fires a pistol in the air. The horsemen who are driving the wild horse drop back a little, then the man who has to do the riding comes in at an angle, and when close enough, he leaps from his horse to the back of the wild horse, which immediately breaks into a pitching, twisting buck. The man is soon thrown, falls to the ground, and the other horsemen ride over him. Their horses do leap to try to avoid hitting him. We see him carried out bleeding. Mexicans, and I suppose all people, do not really enjoy a sport unless there is some possibility of death or injury.

Now there is a little pause. In the stands and on the fence a cry starts among the Indians. One man starts it:

INDIAN (*Shouting*): 'Miliano! 'Miliano!

> Little by little the cry is taken up by all the fence sitters and then by some of the *gente*. We see Josefa, her eyes dipped, the handkerchief in front of her face, and her own mouth making the name " 'Miliano."

NOTE: This is true. Emiliano was usually called by acclaim, since it was known all over southern Mexico what a good horseman he was. But all Mexicans are hams, and Emiliano was no exception. So let him ham it.

> Eufemio is back beside his brother. Emiliano sits very straight, looking ahead as though he did not hear the cries. Everyone is looking at him now. Eufemio speaks satirically.

EUFEMIO: Are you not going to ride?

EMILIANO (*He smiles. It is a game they play together.*): Well, I don't know.

EUFEMIO: Have you forgotten who is the head of the house? (*He holds out his hand, knuckles up, and Emiliano makes the gesture of kissing his hand.*)

EMILIANO: You are, my brother.

EUFEMIO: Then I order you to ride even if you are afraid.

EMILIANO (*Laughs with a quick gaiety*): I am frightened.

EUFEMIO: You may not dishonor your brother, even if you have no feeling for your own honor.

EMILIANO: Well, if you will not let me refuse, I suppose I will have to ride. (*He looks across the ring to Josefa, and for once she is looking straight back at him.*)

> Now Emiliano really hams it, and who wouldn't? With majesty he rides to the gate which is opened to him. There is a great burst of applause. Not only does he not take off his jacket, but he doesn't even remove his hat or the great roweled spurs which might catch during his leap. He moves on his beautiful horse and takes his place in the center of the ring where he sits very quietly. Where the first man had been trying too hard, Emiliano seems perfectly relaxed. But we see his eyes flicker again and again toward Josefa

to see if she is watching. And she is. Her handkerchief is in her lap and her eyes are bugged. Even her mouth is open a little.

We see the horse he is to ride in the chute, a great wild stallion, crazy with rage and fright, its eyes rolled, its nose and mouth dripping, its shoulders scarred and torn from old fights. The chute opens and the stallion plunges free. The horsemen cluster behind him and the circling begins.

Now, great athletes seem always to do very easily what is most difficult. The stallion plunges around the circle, the president fires his pistol, and even then Emiliano does not move. He waits like a prizefighter who comes late into the ring. His face is at complete rest, almost sleepy. Then, almost casually, he presses the shoulders of his horse with his knees, lifts it first to a trot, then a slow canter. He glances at the plunging stallion, and then rides not at him, but ahead of him, like a hunter leading a duck with a shotgun. He comes in at an angle and he leaps, and he is astride. The stallion fights and sunfishes. We see the crazy eyes, the stiff legs. Emiliano rides with nothing but balance and the pressure of his knees. His hands are in the air. The stallion finishes his flurry and breaks into a wild run. He rears at the fence, striking at the men on the fence with his hoofs. By some accident, Emiliano's hat flies off through the air, and by some other accident it lands very close to Josefa. Her father picks it up and holds it. He is breathing hard as he watches Emiliano. Again the stallion plunges at the fence and the fence gives way. Emiliano jumps from the horse to the fence as casually as though he were stepping from a streetcar. The whole thing is ham; it always is.

Now a man leads Emiliano's horse to him, and he steps from the fence to his own horse. Now he seems to look all around for his hat. Josefa's father stands up and holds it so that he can see it. Emiliano looks every place else first and only at the very last does he see where his hat is. He rides slowly across the ring. The father has his moment of glory too. He steps down and hands the hat over the fence. Emiliano bows to him, the bearer, and then to the mother, to the aunt, and finally, to Josefa. She stares back at him. Now the aunt's hand moves to Josefa's hand in a kind of protection from Emiliano, and the girl almost guiltily puts her handkerchief up to her face again, while her mother gets the little bottle from her purse and holds it out to her. The father looks closely at his daughter. He is a little worried now, and the loss of the hat does not seem quite an accident anymore.

FATHER: She is tired. Come, we will take her home.

> The family stands up stiffly and moves down from the grand-stand. Where Josefa has sat there is a sticky screw of paper with one piece of *bisnaga* still remaining in it.

SCENE

The bar we have seen in a preceding scene, but now, because it is a fiesta night, it is very full of men. There are even some women. The two women we have seen before are sitting at the same table as in the preceding scene. But now each one of them has a man sitting with her. Everyone in the bar is drinking. The music is loud, the talk is loud, the air is full of smoke. Emiliano and Eufemio enter, dressed as we last saw them. Their large spurs jingle as they walk. They stand in the doorway, trying to see through the smoke. For just a moment the talk stops as the drinkers look at them. Then they pass a greeting and the noise resumes. Emiliano has seen the woman he is looking for. He moves over to the table and leans close to her.

EMILIANO: Did you see her?

WOMAN: Yes. (*The man who is sitting with her speaks.*)

MAN: Sir. Perhaps you did not notice that this lady is not alone.
> (*He is drunkenly courtly.*)

> Emiliano looks at him for a moment as though to see him for the first time, and then forgets him. He speaks to the woman.

EMILIANO: What did she say?

WOMAN (*Smiling*): She said that she knew you were a gentleman.

She said she knew you would tear your heart out rather than
embarrass her.

EMILIANO (*His eyes soften.*): She is correct.

MAN: Sir, perhaps you failed to notice . . .

EMILIANO (*Quite annoyed*): Oh, be still!

The drunk struggles to his feet. His hands strike the table
and knock over his drink. Emiliano is very strong. He puts his
hand almost affectionately upon the drunk's shoulder, bears down,
and the drunk collapses into his seat.

EMILIANO (*To the woman*): Did she say what I must do?

WOMAN: She said there are procedures. She begs you not to embarrass her.

EMILIANO (*Smiles weakly*): Then she did not seem displeased?

WOMAN: No woman who ever lived can possibly be displeased by
admiration, no matter what she might say.

EMILIANO (*Proudly*): I will call on her father.

WOMAN (*Smiles cynically*): Yes, that might be a good thing to do.

EMILIANO (*Formally*): Thank you.

He turns, looking for Eufemio, sees him with his arms around
a stout woman. He is dancing with her, the little hippity dance of
the *burras*. But he has his own version. He beats out the time on
her well-padded buttocks with his open palms.

MAN (*Mumbling to himself*): Perhaps you may not, did you notice
that . . .

Emiliano, with a smug look of pleasure on his face, leans
against the bar, and his eyes are sleepy.

SCENE

One of the little beat-up roads of Mexico, all mud holes and lumps.
Nothing moves over these roads but the high-wheeled ox-driven
carts, men on foot, and men on horseback. The sugar cane grows
close to the road and the cane sticks are very high and thick, so

that the road seems a long slot cut through the greenness. Eufemio
and Emiliano are riding down this road.

EUFEMIO: Well, it's your business, of course. And suppose her
father says no. What will you do then? Why don't you steal
her? You might as well steal her now as later and save the
trouble.

EMILIANO (*Stiffly*): No. I will not embarrass her.

EUFEMIO (*Speaks with cynicism*): This is not like you, Emiliano.
You have always been able to take a girl and forget her.

EMILIANO: This is a very different thing.

EUFEMIO (*Ingenuously*): How?

EMILIANO: My brother, I do not want to talk about her.

EUFEMIO: Well, that's different, anyway. (*He shrugs.*)

Along the road coming toward them there is a sad little procession. First, a rural policeman such as we have seen before. He is
mounted and heavily armed, but almost asleep on his horse. The
hot sun beats down on him, and behind him trudges a completely
ragged, completely exhausted man, dressed in torn and dirty field
clothes. He has no hat. The sun falls on his matted filthy hair. He
is barefoot. As they come closer we see that his hands and elbows
are tightly tied behind him, and that a rawhide noose is around
his neck, and the *reata* is fastened to the horn of the saddle of the
soldier. The man must keep up or the noose tightens around his
neck. His exhaustion and despair are in every line of his body and
face. Moreover, there are whip marks in the dirt of his face. The
soldier dozes on his horse, and as he comes near to Emiliano and
Eufemio, he straightens up and yawns. He attempts to pass the
brothers, but they have put their horses in his way, and his horse
stops.

EMILIANO (*Coldly*): Good day.

SOLDIER: I guess so. I haven't had any dinner. Have you got a
cigarette?

Emiliano reaches into his pocket, takes out a cornhusk cigarette, and hands it to him. The soldier puts it in his mouth and

waits for Emiliano to light it, which he does. The soldier puffs, inhales, then yawns again.

EMILIANO (*Casually*): What animal have you got there?

SOLDIER: Oh, one of the usual. He ran away from the hacienda.

EMILIANO (*His sarcasm misses the soldier.*): You can't trust them for a minute, can you? Why did he run away?

SOLDIER (*He raises his shoulders and breathes deeply on the cigarette.*): Who knows why they run away? He had some story or other—I forget what. They usually say it is a sick mother or something like that.

EMILIANO (*Stiffly*): Why do you bring him back?

SOLDIER (*He laughs.*): Are you playing games, sir? You know perfectly well why I bring him back. He owes money to the hacienda; they all do. He can't run away.

EUFEMIO: How much?

SOLDIER: Oh, I don't know. Twenty or thirty pesos. He bought a blanket a year or so ago. That's what they said. But he's not so important. If you let one get away, they'd all go.

Eufemio is looking at the bedraggled man who stands without movement, with his head down. Eufemio speaks to him very softly in the Nahuatl language. The man's glazed, tired eyes turn upward for a moment, and then he looks down again. Emiliano smiles very courteously, and speaks softly to the soldier.

EMILIANO: Why don't you let him go?

SOLDIER (*Laughs*): You make jokes, don't you?

EMILIANO (*Even more softly*): Let him go.

The soldier slowly realizes that he means it. He glances uneasily to Eufemio behind him and at Emiliano in front. Very slowly his hand creeps toward the butt of his carbine which sticks out from under his left leg.

NOTE: Throughout his life Zapata had the quality of moving quickly without warning or hesitation. This trait is mentioned by everyone who knew him.

Emiliano, all in one motion, strikes the soldier across the

eyes with his whip and rides in to him. The soldier rolls to the ground, his horse jumps forward, pulling the bound man from his feet and dragging him, strangling, in the dust. Eufemio's machete whips out and cuts the *reata*. The man lies on his face in the dirt. Now Eufemio turns on the fallen soldier, swinging down with his machete mercilessly. The soldier in a panic rolls clear, then leaps to his feet and plunges into the tall cane. Eufemio rides in after him, and we see him striking and striking, the way a man strikes at a moving snake in the brush. Eufemio disappears into the tall cane. We see Emiliano dismount. He cuts the bonds from the hands and elbows of the fallen man and helps him to his feet. He rubs the distorted arms from which the circulation has long been cut off. He takes the gourd from his saddle. The man tries to hold it but it falls from his deadened fingers. Emiliano holds it to his lips while the man drinks thirstily. Eufemio comes back from the cane. He is disgusted.

EUFEMIO: I lost him. He got away. Quick as a weasel he is. I couldn't find him in the cane. Emiliano, you should have killed him while he was in the saddle.

EMILIANO (*Impatiently*): Let him go.

EUFEMIO: Well, he'll report it, and we will be in trouble. It's better to kill him.

EMILIANO: But we didn't. Catch his horse.

Eufemio rides after the horse of the soldier. Emiliano speaks to the man. He speaks crisply, like an officer issuing orders.

EMILIANO: Take his horse into the cane, lie still until dark. Ride only at night. Ride south. At the end of five nights go on on foot and don't try to sell the horse. Just turn it loose.

Emiliano reaches into his pocket and takes out a few copper coins. The man looks at him. There is little or no expression on his face. He offers no thanks. He rubs the backs of his numb hands.

Eufemio leads back the soldier's horse, and without a word and without a look backward, the Indian leads the horse into the cane, on the opposite side of the road from that where the soldier disappeared. For a moment we see the cane whipping about, showing his progress. And then it is still.

EUFEMIO: I wish we had killed that *rurale*.

EMILIANO: Oh, let him go. The two are the same man with different lucks.

SCENE

The family of Josefa Espejo has been described: the father, fattening, smug, correct—a small-town caricature of the 400; the mother, stern, correct, religious; the aunts, like black crows. The business and wealth of the family was at this time increasing rapidly. Not only did the father operate a cattle ranch but he had also a freighting business, bringing needed supplies into the country in bullock carts. Also, he operated a store and a warehouse. His office was like all Mexican offices in small towns—small, very dark, with barred windows and a huge old-fashioned safe. Espejo was also a moneylender.

At his desk, probably a rolltop affair, he sat like a little king in the community. He dressed uncomfortably in black clothing, and wore a high, tight collar. As he got older he became increasingly fatter and more smug; in his old age he became more religious. And this was the man whom Emiliano must ask for Josefa. It is such a dark little office with dusty files. Frail little men with thick glasses write in carefully drawn characters in huge account books, working so slowly and dipping their pens so carefully that they seem to be in slow motion. Espejo's fingers drum on the desk. He purses his lips. His breath is noisy in his nostrils, and his blood pressure, normally high, has jumped.

ESPEJO: Sir, I am sensitive of the honor you do me. I regret that I must refuse it.

EMILIANO: But why? I am not a peon. I have some land of my own and I will have more. You know my family. We have always been landowners. I hold your daughter in esteem and love and I wish to marry her.

ESPEJO (*He fancies himself a philosopher.*): I know that, I know that. I will not say that some of your exploits are unknown to me. I might say unfavorably. There is no question about your . . . legitimacy. But consider, young man, you have no fortune. By your own admission your family lands have shrunk to practically nothing. My daughter is much more than a potential wife. She is a daughter, a granddaughter, a niece, and a cousin. You see, she has responsibilities to her family which she must take into consideration. Or I must, if she does not. She must support and build the family, not help it to deteriorate. And you see you are asking something else. You are asking not only to be her husband, but a son-in-law to me and a grandson to my father. (*He crosses himself piously.*) Oh, no, young man.

EMILIANO (*Speaks sullenly*): In other words, it is because I am poor.

ESPEJO (*Nervously*): Well, not entirely. There are other considerations.

EMILIANO (*Suddenly angry*): And with me, sir, there are other considerations also. It would have been very easy, sir, to tear out a bar from a window and take your daughter. Because of my feeling for her, I did not do that. Rather, I submit myself to insult.

ESPEJO (*Anxiously*): Now, please. Let us be men of the world.

EMILIANO: What world, yours or mine? Don't be afraid. I will not steal your daughter. I have too much regard for her. (*He is furious and boastful in his anger.*) No, I won't steal her. But you will come to me and you will ask me to be your son-in-law. (*Suddenly he slaps the desk with his open palm, a quick, whiplike stroke that cracks like a pistol shot. Espejo dodges back. Emiliano's voice grows very soft.*) Remember that, sir, remember that.

He looks down proudly into the eyes of the fat little man until the lids fall. Then Emiliano turns and walks through the door of the office. We follow him, and as he emerges into the street, four men close in on him, two on each side. They pinion his arms. For a second he stiffens, and then, seeing that he cannot resist, he relaxes completely. One man takes a pistol from under Emiliano's jacket, another, a knife from its sheath on his belt.

EMILIANO (*With relaxed courtesy*): Well, my friends. What dinner are you inviting me to? See, I do not try to escape; there is no need to be frightened.

MAN: Emiliano, we do not want to do it. But they say you took a prisoner from a *rurale*. They say you stole his horse and his equipment and nearly killed him. I don't know anything about it. (*And then he speaks with fright.*) Don't hurt me, Emiliano.

EMILIANO (*Quietly*): What will they do with me?

MAN: Send you to Cuernavaca under guard to the Police Headquarters, I guess.

EMILIANO: And shoot me on the way for trying to escape?

MAN: God willing, no, Emiliano. I am your friend.

EMILIANO (*Quietly*): If you are my friend, after you have taken me to the jail, will you find my brother and tell him where I am?

MAN: I will, Emiliano. Unless the Chief orders me not to.

EMILIANO: If you do not mention it, perhaps the Chief will not think of it. (*He looks at the other three men and they smile back at him.*) Come along, now. Take me in.

(*And again he speaks like an officer in command. The five walk away. The guards are very much on guard, for although they like Emiliano, they are also afraid of him.*)

SCENE

A street in the little town at night. And there is nothing darker than a Mexican village at night. A little light comes from some of the doorways—not really a light, but a kind of glow. Only starlight makes the plastered-white, boxlike houses visible at all. A figure is moving through the town, leading three horses, two saddled, the third with a packsaddle loaded. This man does not creep; the sound of his horses' hooves ring on the road. At the plaza, there are trees, and he ties the horses to one of them. He carries a carbine under his arm. This is Eufemio.

Now, Eufemio had a great and quick talent for homespun psychology. He walks carefully across the open space to the tiny jail. Now he taps on the door gently with his fingers, first tapping with his fingernails, and then he drags his nails down the wood in a kind of caress.

We see the inside of the jail. We see the officer sitting in a chair, with a candle burning near him. His uniform is unbuttoned. He hears the caressing tap on the door, the tapping and dragging of fingernail. The officer smiles. We know very well what he is thinking. He is quite sure that it is a girl knocking; he thinks he knows what girl it is. He wets his finger and smooths down his mustaches. He buttons his collar, pats the wrinkles out of his tunic. Now the little tapping comes again, with the little scratch after it. With a beautiful sweet smile of welcome, the officer goes to the door, unlocks it and unchains it, and a carbine pokes through into his stomach. Eufemio enters quickly and closes the door behind him. The officer looks at Eufemio, and there is resignation in his face. He keeps his hands well out from his sides.

OFFICER: He is down there.

EUFEMIO (*Quickly*): Lead the way.

OFFICER (*Hesitates*): Eufemio, if you should ever be asked, would you please say that you were five men and I resisted?

EUFEMIO: Oh, surely. Why, you fought like a tiger. I'll mark you if you like. I'll give you some sign that you resisted.

OFFICER (*Nervously*): Oh, no, no. I can do that myself.

There is only one cell in the jail. The bars are thick oak, crossed so that there are little square holes between them, and the edges are bound with iron. A small lamp is burning smokily in the corridor, and we can see Emiliano's face through the bars. The

jailer unlocks the door, Emiliano steps out. He kisses Eufemio's
hand in a filial gesture. They turn and walk out, and as they go,
Eufemio says:

EUFEMIO: We were ten men. This hero resisted us almost to the
    death.

EMILIANO (*Laughs softly*): He is a lion.

EUFEMIO: I think he wounded me.

The jailer watches them go out the door. We hear the sound
of horses' hoofs trotting over cobbles. The jailer begins to tear and
maul his tunic. He disarranges his mustache, tousles his hair, and
finally, he scratches his face a little with his fingernails.

NOTE: After the escape from jail, the brothers wander for a
while. They work on wagon trains, they range south of Puebla and
even in the state of Veracruz. They work at herding horses. Eufemio
even establishes a wagon train of his own. It was several years
before they returned to their own country.

It was a transition time. When Emiliano went away he was
still a boy; when he returned, he was a man. I could quite easily
work out a series of transition scenes to carry from one to another,
but it seems wise to me to leave it this way. This script is, after
all, only a framework for which a film will be made after a going
over by the director and myself. This life is so incredibly full of
dramatic detail that ten pictures could be made of it. Therefore,
this is an editing job. I have chosen to go into the politics of the
time as little as possible, and then only when they have a direct
impact on Emiliano Zapata himself. There is no question that he
loved Josefa very deeply, since he remained married to her all of
his life. And there is no doubt that she loved him. This, however,
did not keep him from having a very full extramarital life. But this
is a part of the Mexican way of living. Sexual fidelity on the part
of the male is just so much nonsense to a Mexican.

During the time of Emiliano's exile, the process of absorption
of the land by the haciendas increased in scope and speed. The
greed of the *haciendados* knew no limits. And because they made

a great deal of money from the sugar, it was supposed by the rest of the world that Mexico had come into a time of prosperity unique in its history. Meanwhile, the common people were stripped clean, their land taken, and they themselves put in peonage by the method of debt. A virtual slavery was spreading over the nation. A man and his family were in debt all of their lives. And by debt they were bound to the land; they could not leave their jobs while they owed money to the hacienda, and their small wages made it impossible for them ever to get out of debt. Meanwhile, a spendthrift and profligate government, which needed money badly, made it by selling the lands of the people to the haciendas.

Emiliano came quietly back to his own country, and he was not picked up for his old crime. Perhaps a change of commanders of the *rurales* made his defection forgotten. Or perhaps, as is still true in Mexico, if you stay under cover for a while, things are forgotten.

SCENE

Emiliano went to work for Don Ignacio de la Torre (called Nacio), who owned the largest and most important hacienda in Morelos. De la Torre was married to the daughter of Porfirio Díaz, dictator and perpetual President of Mexico. That de la Torre did not like his father-in-law is not important to this story. This hacienda was at once the most luxurious and rich establishment in the whole state. Don Nacio really liked and admired Emiliano. He was insane on the subject of horses, and Emiliano was a great expert in this field.

In the hacienda, Don Nacio, for all his following of the distinctive process of the haciendas, was a good man and a good friend. But what he did not ever understand was that you can never really be liked by a man whose people you have robbed and injured. We see the magnificent stables of the hacienda. Emiliano is overseeing the grooming of Don Nacio's thoroughbreds. Emiliano looks

older, but he has always been very serious. A *mozo* is sponging
and washing the coat of a beautiful thoroughbred filly. Don Nacio
looks on.

DON NACIO: There's a real princess, Emiliano.

EMILIANO (*Nods*): She will be the finest. Her colts will be the finest.
   (*He speaks to the* mozo.) Dry her! Dry her, man! Rub!

The *mozo*, with a fine white cloth, rubs the shoulders of the
mare. There is a bucket of eggs on the ground, and in a bowl,
some beaten egg. The *mozo* dips his sponge into the egg and rubs
the shiny coat with it. The hair gleams in the sunlight, and Emiliano's eyes glow with pleasure. There is a gentleness in his face
that is rarely there.

DON NACIO: Yes, Emiliano, she is a real princess, more than a
   human princess. Do you know, Emiliano, that there's no human family as old as hers? There's no human blood line as
   pure as hers. For a thousand years her ancestors are known,
   recorded, and the records preserved. In all of that time, no
   bad blood has crept in, no disease made the mark. Think of
   that, Emiliano. There's no human with royal blood like that.
   This is the greatest of all princesses. No off-blood stallion
   ever sang under her window, or held a secret rendezvous in
   the cane field. Now, in my family, I know who my grandfather
   and my great-grandfather and my great-great-grandfather were
   supposed to be, but this lady can be sure. She has the look
   of it, too, hasn't she?

Emiliano's dark eyes, for a moment, become very fierce, and
then he conceals his feeling. And we see the leaping flames of the
burning village reflected in his pupils.

EMILIANO (*He speaks shortly.*): She is a fine filly.

DON NACIO (*He is a kind of a small-town philosopher, and he cannot
   let his subject alone.*): You have the look and bearing of an
   aristocrat, Emiliano, somewhere in your blood line. Was it a
   Nahuatl prince or the iron blood of Cortez or Alvarado? (*He
   laughs.*) But we will never know. We can only guess.

EMILIANO (*Speaks harshly to the* mozo.): Now the brush, man, now the brush, before the egg dries!

DON NACIO (*It is the conceit of Don Nacio to dress like a* charro, *but his clothes are fabulously embroidered. He whips his leg gently with his quirt.*): I am buying some horses, Emiliano. My father-in-law has some Arabs recently come in. I thought I would make a back cross with the English. Have you ever been to the Capital, Emiliano?

EMILIANO: No, patron.

DON NACIO: We have a seat there. I want you to go with me and look at these horses. I trust your instinct about horses. (*He laughs shortly.*) I don't quite trust my father-in-law. When he wants to sell something, I look for flaws. We will go up to Mexico, Emiliano.

SCENE

The de la Torre house in Mexico City is like the hacienda. It is on the edge of the city, has a great courtyard and fields around it. (The splendor of these places is unbelievable.) An irrigation ditch runs through the courtyard, and in the fields we can see the hovels of the workers—poor shelters built of sticks, with tattered blankets to keep out the cold. These people live in complete squalor, and right up against the luxury of the palace. There is no transition between wealth and starvation.

In the stable yard, washed and spotless, paved with small, round, clean cobblestones, five Arabian horses are being led in a circle. And on the edge of the courtyard, looking in but not daring to come close, are the people—dirty, their bodies barely covered with torn cotton clothes, barefooted, and crippled. These were then the poor people of Mexico, twisted, sick and hungry, neglected and broken. Don Nacio and Emiliano stand inside the circle, looking at the horses.

DON NACIO: My father-in-law shod them with silver. It's a pretty idea, but it's not as good for shoes as iron.

EMILIANO (*He has been looking past the horses at the ragged people. He speaks suddenly.*): Stop!

The *mozos* halt the circling horses. One young stallion rears impatiently. Emiliano goes to the mare. His hands explore the shoulder muscles, the flanks, the neck. Very gently, he rolls back an eyelid and looks at the eyeball. He raises a lip to look at the gums. He stands back, regards the mare, his eyes half-closed. He speaks curtly.

EMILIANO: That one.

The *mozo* leads the mare into the stone stable.

DON NACIO (*He points to the stallion which has reared.*): I like that boy there.

EMILIANO (*Impatiently*): For colts, maybe, yes. But the hock is too flat. No endurance there on our rocks. Why don't you buy them all?

DON NACIO: No. I want two mares and a stallion.

EMILIANO: Then take that stallion there. See the chest, the big nostrils, the thin lips. See how well-ribbed, and the feet, small, a little long. That's the one.

Don Nacio nods to the boy, and the boy leads the stallion into the stable.

EMILIANO: Now, those two are equal; take your choice, either one. Unless it is a matter of temperament, there is no difference. To me, they seem equal.

Don Nacio squints his eyes the way Emiliano has done in unconscious imitation. .

DON NACIO: Well, that one.

And the second mare is led into the stable. The two men follow.

These stables are still in existence. They were built like palaces. The feed mangers were of marble. The bars of the box stalls were gilded, and the floors were of tiny cobblestones laid in patterns, and since there was unlimited labor, the horses were tended as very rich ladies are served. The carriages against the wall were luxurious to the extent of looking like units of a pageant. The seats of the closed carriages were of tapestry and sometimes of quilted silk. The wheels gleamed with paint. Borda, a little earlier, not only shod his horses with silver but he made the tires of his carriage of the same metal. This is a scene of the most profligate and wasteful luxury.

Emiliano turns. His hand is on a marble manger. He looks out the wide door, past the carriages at the line of ragged people. His face becomes set, and the fire burns in his eyes. His whole posture is one of anger; his lips curl away from his teeth, and his face becomes cruel.

DON NACIO: Emiliano! (*Emiliano doesn't answer. He repeats:*) Emiliano! (*There is still no answer.*) Emiliano! What is the matter with you! I am speaking to you. (*His friendliness is slipping, and a little arrogance creeps into his voice.*)

We are looking toward Emiliano, and his back is toward Don Nacio. He finally hears, and we see his anger is instantly controlled. His expression changes, his eyelids drop, his face relaxes, and the tautness goes out of his body. It is the control of iron over his emotions. He turns slowly.

EMILIANO: Yes, patron?

DON NACIO: You must have gone to sleep; you did not answer.

EMILIANO: I'm sorry, patron. I was thinking; maybe I was dreaming.

DON NACIO: Do you think I should take these horses down to Morelos? (*He considers.*) What were you dreaming, Emiliano? Some girl? (*He chuckles.*)

EMILIANO (*Slowly*): No, patron. I was thinking how beautifully your horses live. I was thinking it might be a nice thing to be a horse.

DON NACIO (*Laughs with delight*): Well, maybe you are right. Maybe you are. (*He looks appreciatively at the stable.*) But it is hard these days to get people to care for things. It seems to me that people don't have a sense of responsibility anymore. You have to watch them every minute. Now, in my father's time . . .

SCENE

A pasturage, with a new fence across it. Emiliano and a group of villagers are walking along the fence. A village elder walks beside Emiliano.

ELDER: They just put it up. No questions, no nothing. Then our bullocks broke through, and we cannot get them back. We have to pay. The foreman says the bullocks were trespassing. He wants two pesos a head for our own cattle. And they were just trying to pasture on our own land. (*There is anger in his voice—anger that has been in him so long that it is part of him.*)

ANOTHER VILLAGER: Last year it was the fields to the south. Now, this. We have no pastures anymore. Two years ago they took our sister village. Next year, it will be ours.

YOUNG MAN (*He is not so controlled as the others—his anger is newer and fresher.*): What are we going to do, Emiliano? Tell us. What can we do? We can't fight. They send the troops. (*He beats his hand on Emiliano's chest.*) What can we do? We have no land anymore. We can't live anymore!

ELDER: We can work for them.

YOUNG MAN (*In fury*): We can't! They have enough! They don't want us! Must we kill ourselves to make room?

EMILIANO (*He looks from one to the other as they speak. His face is calm. He is in the process of becoming a leader.*): Did they bring troops to guard the fence?

ELDER: No. They didn't even do that. They know now that we are helpless. They didn't even bring troops. They just built the fence with the usual guards with rifles. We could have killed them easily, Emiliano.

EMILIANO: And then there would have been troops.

SECOND OLD MAN: Your father was always with us, Emiliano. You are one of us. Do you know what we should do?

EMILIANO (*He looks at his hands. His fingers jerk and tremble.*): I don't know. The President is one of our blood. He speaks of it all the time, I am told. You know, he asks people to come to him personally with complaints. He is the father of his people, he says. He is looking after our welfare. (*Emiliano's lips twitch.*)

YOUNG MAN: We sent a petition, written out and signed by the village council.

EMILIANO: And?

YOUNG MAN: There was an answer. "I will look into it personally," the answer said, and there was nothing more.

EMILIANO (*Dreamily*): Sooner or later, I think we will have to fight. But we have nothing to fight with. I think we had better try everything else first.

YOUNG MAN (*Fiercely*): What else is there to try?

EMILIANO (*Still speaks dreamily*): I think we should send a delegation to the President himself to tell him how it is, and (*He leans forward.*) to look at his eyes when he answers.

ELDER: Do you think a delegation could even get in to see him?

EMILIANO: I don't know.

YOUNG MAN: You don't really think it will work, do you?

EMILIANO: I don't know. But we must try it. We must try everything.

ELDER (*Quietly*): Would you go, Emiliano?

EMILIANO (*For a moment he is startled. And then his eyes turn inward as he imagines how it would be. And he answers.*): Yes. I will go.

YOUNG MAN: Who is to pay for the delegation?

EMILIANO (*Now that he has made up his mind, Emiliano is decisive. The leadership inherent in the man breaks out into the open.*

He speaks curtly.): I will pay for myself. The council must elect the delegates. The village people must each contribute what they can. Every record of the village must be taken with us in proof that the land is ours.

YOUNG MAN (*Speaks very quietly*): You don't believe in this delegation, Emiliano. You know in your deepest heart it will come to fighting. You know that. This President cries for us and sells our land. You don't really believe this, Emiliano.

EMILIANO (*Angrily*): Don't put my thoughts on your tongue! It must be tried if only for the people, so they will know. If this fails, we will try something else. (*He speaks softly.*) We are babies at these things. We must learn to walk before we can run.

YOUNG MAN (*It is a new thought to him.*): Why, of course. Of course that's it. So the people will know.

EMILIANO: And it might work, you know. We must think to ourselves that it might work.

The following scenes are concerned with the delegation from the little town in Morelos to the President of Mexico. In actual fact, the delegation was fairly large. There are some differences of opinion, but about seventeen people went up to Mexico. Everyone wanted to go, for such delegations—and they still exist—are a combination trip and sightseeing affair, as well as the business at hand. In the actual delegation which went up at this time there were too many for our purposes. I am limiting the number to five.

These men wouldn't have had city clothes, but they would feel that city clothes were necessary. And so they would probably either borrow them or unearth clothes they may have used for an occasion years before. I have seen pictures of Emiliano Zapata dressed in city clothes that were much too small for him, with a high, stiff collar that was too tight. He looked very uncomfortable. But perhaps these people thought that they had to be uncomfortable to be correct. Many people think so. It must also be remembered that, with the exception of Emiliano, probably none of these men had ever been to the Capital before, or to any city of size. They must have been stunned by its greatness and overwhelmed at its magnificence.

Our delegates are Emiliano, the angry young man, the two village elders we have seen, and one middle-aged man, of a little better financial standing. He has a small store and he has been included in the delegation because he can read and write, and he knows some of the laws. In that day the ability to read gave a man a certain eminence; lawyers and priests and the upper classes were the only ones who could.

The five delegates, in their ill-fitting clothing and wearing the kind of hats that they are not used to, make a curious and slightly ridiculous appearance. We see them climbing the road to the castle of Chapultepec, staring in wonder up at the big, ugly building. On the road there is a guard post, heavily defended. We see the five men challenged by soldiers. We do not hear the words. We see the soldiers quickly search for weapons; they search their hats, coats, up the sleeves, stomachs, belts, and finally, the lower leg where a man can carry a gun or a knife. It is an efficient job, done by men who are quite used to the duty. Finally we see that the five are allowed to pass.

SCENE

Next we see them in the great presidential chamber. It has not changed at all since that day. It is a huge, long, formal room. The presidential chair is a throne covered with a canopy of velvet. Several little chairs are arranged side by side along the walls. There are great crystal chandeliers and a floor of parquetry. On the walls are huge oil paintings of heroes of Mexican history. It is all still there, still ugly, and still like all the other audience rooms in the world—stiff, formal, noncommittal and political—whether it is the Soviet chamber in the Kremlin or the rooms at Potsdam, it is always the same and it always smells the same.

The delegates walk slowly and with studious dignity around the room, as stiff and self-contained as children at a zoo. They carry their hats in their hands now. They gaze at the huge oil paintings and whisper to one another. They are much too polite to point.

At last they come to the presidential throne. It is a carved and noble piece of furniture, made perhaps for Maximilian's poor, silly behind. All of a sudden, like children who have sat still too long, a change comes over the delegates. They laugh, first self-consciously, then with pleasure, and the spell of their ordeal is broken.

YOUNG MAN (*He speaks to one of the elders.*): Sit in it. Let us see what a President looks like.

OLD MAN (*He is pleased and almost girlish in his embarrassment.*): Oh, no! I wouldn't dare!

YOUNG MAN: You sit in it, Emiliano. The youngest President.

It is obvious that he wants them to ask him to sit in it, and he will, if he is asked. But since he brought up the subject, he can't very well do it.

EMILIANO (*Shortly*): No!

YOUNG MAN (*Playfully*): Sometimes, Emiliano, I have heard that the office seeks the man, whether he wants it or not.

EMILIANO (*Scowling*): No. I will not sit.

YOUNG MAN (*Suddenly*): Help me.

He grabs Emiliano by the arm and forces him toward the chair. The merchant joins in the fun, takes Emiliano's other arm, and together they wrestle him back. They are laughing. The old men smile broadly. Caught off balance, Emiliano is forced back and then suddenly, as he is about to be pushed into the chair, he seems to realize what they are doing. His arms stiffen against the arms of the throne. He is overcome with rage, and he is a very strong man. He throws them back and away from him, and he speaks with a harsh bitterness we have never seen in him before.

EMILIANO: That's enough! Not even in play. Do you know what that chair does to men? Think back, think back! (*He points to the dark, carved throne.*) That's the end, not the beginning!

The four men stand speechless. He has taken it too seriously. They can see no reason for it.

YOUNG MAN: It was only a little joke, Emiliano.

EMILIANO (*The rage goes out of his face. He is a little ashamed of himself.*): I know, but it didn't seem funny to me. It seemed horrible!

YOUNG MAN: I didn't mean any harm.

EMILIANO: I know. I know. I am sorry I was angry.

A voice at the end of the room speaks in an echoing, sepulchral tone.

VOICE: This way, this way. The President will see you now.

We look around and see the official announcer who has spoken. And these are always alike wherever they are found, woodenfaced, bandy-legged, aching for dignity. I do not know how this official would have been dressed at this period, but that is easy to find out. The delegates troop toward him like little boys caught in a reprehensible act. He leads them through several rooms and leaves them finally in an anteroom. He himself steps into the presidential office.

The President is seated behind his desk. Any picture will show what he looked like. He is the perpetual President—Don Porfirio Díaz. When he is in uniform, his chest is covered with all the decorations of all the rulers of the world. He is Mexico's strong man; he keeps the peace and pays his debts and borrows money at suitable interest and grants concessions and land for a consideration. You can trust such a man, and no foreigner ever sees the vultures circling over the desert.

Now he wears what used to be called a claw-hammer coat, striped trousers, patent leather shoes, and spats. His vest has white piping on it. A pince-nez on a black ribbon dangles on his chest. He wears the rosette of a Commander of the French Legion of Honor and no other decoration. His complexion is very dark; there is no doubt about his being an Indian. His hair and huge mustache are startlingly white. His collar is high and stiff and his jowls hang over it. His chin is extremely firm. He is really a strong, unscrupulous man. But he is getting old. He has been President for many years. His eyes are tired. But he is also a consummate actor. One moment he can be fierce, the next, gentle and pleading, the next naive, the next almost stupid. He can cry at will, great, real tears.

In the desk in front of him there is a small shallow drawer and in it, his notes, and beside the notes a pad and a gold pencil, with which he can make notes without seeming to. He has a trick of holding his brow and seeming to close his eyes in thought, when actually he is reading the notes in the drawer. The pince-nez is a fake; he does not need glasses.

As the functionary comes in, he is reading the notes in the shallow drawer. His large desk is completely clear and highly polished. And the room is stern and not luxurious. For it is the President's pose that he prefers simplicity. Also, there are no chairs except his own. He has found that most people do not stay so long if they cannot sit down or squat. If his friends are with him, they go to another office which is quite different. Now this President has dignity and repose. He has been President a long time and perhaps it isn't a pose anymore. The functionary enters.

FUNCTIONARY: Mr. President.

PRESIDENT: The ones from Morelos?

FUNCTIONARY: Yes, sir.

PRESIDENT: How many?

FUNCTIONARY: Five, sir.

PRESIDENT: Seven are listed.

FUNCTIONARY: Five are here, sir. Will you see them now, sir?

PRESIDENT (*He gets up, smooths his coat and moves toward a side door which leads to his private office.*): Let them in.

As he goes through, we look in after him. There are deep, comfortable chairs and sofas. It is the exact opposite of the large, stern room we have left. He seats himself and lights a cigar. The functionary quietly closes the door and then goes to the door leading to the anteroom and opens it.

FUNCTIONARY: You can come in now.

The five delegates enter timidly. They look around the bare room for the President. No one is there. The functionary goes out and closes the door. The room is very still. The delegates look at one another and smile shyly. They are afraid in this bare quiet room. They move their feet nervously. One of the old men coughs, putting his hand politely in front of his mouth. Emiliano stares at the polished bare desk. The young man clears his throat. The merchant puts his hand behind his back and raises his chin as though he is bored. Emiliano finally breaks the silence.

EMILIANO: Someone's been smoking a very good cigar.

The young man reaches in his pocket for a cigar, pulls it out, and sees the old men looking at him with disapproval. He puts it back.

YOUNG MAN: Excuse me.

MERCHANT: Well, the President doesn't have much folderol about him, I will say that. I have heard that he lives as simply as anyone, and this proves it. (*He glances around for approval. The old men nod in agreement.*)

EMILIANO (*He repeats his first sentence, but in a flat, meaningful tone.*): Someone has been smoking a very fine cigar. I wish I had its brother.

YOUNG MAN: Emiliano, when you are President, you will have its brother. (*He chuckles.*)

EMILIANO (*He still doesn't think it's a joke. He speaks soberly.*): I will never be President.

YOUNG MAN (*With mock disbelief*): You don't mean it!

EMILIANO (*He doesn't know that he is saying something ridiculous.*): I do mean it. *I will never be President.*

YOUNG MAN (*Looks at him as though he were crazy, and then humors him*): Well, I guess a lot of people want to be President.

ONE OF THE ELDERS (*Laughs to himself*): Yes, and I am one of them.

The whole group giggles, all except Emiliano, who is edging around to try to get a look at the other side of the desk. And this is difficult, for the desk is set across a corner. This is usually considered wise by a President of Mexico; it makes it impossible for anyone to stand behind him. Suddenly the door opens quickly, and the President enters as though he had just rushed in from another appointment. Emiliano sniffs the air that he brings in with him, and then he exhales slowly, with pleasure.

PRESIDENT: Good morning, my children.

NOTE: This is a term he used with country people. He liked to be thought of as father of his country.

The President goes briskly behind his desk, sits down, arranges his cuffs. It is obvious that he is very busy but of course a very patient man. He looks up with a birdlike and bird-brained interest, a slight smile of encouragement on his lips. But his eyes are watchful, and his right hand secretly opens the little flat drawer. Now he is ready.

PRESIDENT: Now, my children, what is the problem you have brought me to solve for you?

The delegates shuffle their feet and look away from him, the way hayseeds always do in the city. Then all at once they look at the merchant. After all, he is somewhat of the great world; he can read and write. He is, if anything, more uncomfortable than they are. Emiliano in the background is merely watchful. He doesn't seem in the least embarrassed. The merchant sees that they are depending on him to speak, but the President forces him.

PRESIDENT (*Cheerily*): Well, one of us has to tell. *You.* (*He points to the merchant.*) You tell me.

MERCHANT (*He doesn't like limbs, and he is being pushed out on one. He wanted to come for the eminence, but he doesn't want to be saddled with it if they are found wrong.*): Well, there's been, there's been some talk and, well, there's been some, some little unrest in the country, about, well, about the village lands.

PRESIDENT (*Brightly. He is being purposely stupid.*): Perhaps you will explain it to me. I love Morelos, but haven't been able to go there for a long while.

MERCHANT (*He is definitely uncomfortable.*): Well, maybe we just don't understand it, and maybe it's all right, but it seems, well, it seems that, that the hacienda has put up a new fence and some of the people, well some of them, they are a little uneasy about it.

During this recital the others have looked at him in amazement and dismay. Now the young man breaks in angrily.

YOUNG MAN: It's not that at all, sir. They are taking our lands that we have had since the beginning of time. They're just taking them. And when our cattle go to feed on our own land, they make us pay to get them back, or they keep them.

PRESIDENT (*Very softly*): Who is this "they" you speak of?

YOUNG MAN: Why, the owner of the hacienda and the soldiers and the guards. (*As though it just dawns on him*) But they are your soldiers, sir.

PRESIDENT (*With a look of weary pain on his face*): So many things happen. I don't know how I can look after them all. Now you say that they have fenced your land. Can you prove that your village has title to this land?

ONE OF THE ELDERS: Why, yes, sir, we can. Some of the villages have lost their titles or had them destroyed one way or another, but we are lucky. We have the grant issued originally by the Spanish Crown and verified later. We have it.

PRESIDENT: I see. Well, if what you say is true and you can prove title, I can't see where you have any problem at all. It's just a matter of submitting proof to the proper authority, and there you are. (*He speaks as though the thing were already accomplished.*)

EMILIANO (*Speaks gently, but with authority*): Meanwhile, sir, the fences are up and the guards are there. The land is being planted to cane and some rice, and our people are starving. We have not much time, sir. Our people cannot live on air.

The President scowls quickly at Emiliano. He does not like people who argue successfully against him. For a moment his eyes dwell on Emiliano, with a look of hatred, and Emiliano looks back directly into his eyes. The President puts his head down on his hand and closes his eyes nearly all the way, as though in thought. His hand is in the drawer, and we see what he writes: "This man is dangerous—he must be watched." And when he looks up his eyes are weary, and there is a hint of tears in his voice.

PRESIDENT: Oh, my children, if you could only know. Everyone brings problems to me personally, as though I were a king or a dictator. People forget that our country is a democracy, that the President is simply put in office to carry out the laws. I cannot make the laws. I cannot judge in the law courts. I cannot do anything except carry out the direction of the laws. Sometimes I almost wish I did have the power, but then I think, no, the slow way of democracy is the best in the long run.

EMILIANO (*With a deadly repetitiousness*): Meanwhile, sir, the fence is completed and the land is taken.

He is not a bit taken in by this playacting as the others in the delegation. They have been nodding and clucking in sympathy for this poor driven man. The poor driven man uses a treatment on Emiliano that is often effective. He juts his chin out and stares into Emiliano's eyes, trying to frighten him. Emiliano stares back, and it becomes a battle. Finally the President puts his head down again, and we see him writing on his pad: "It might be well to remove him." He raises his head again.

PRESIDENT: My children, I am going to help you. I belong to your race, as you know. Your blood runs in my veins. I wish I could personally go and take back the land for you. But if I did, I should be removed from office by a justly outraged people.

EMILIANO (*Stiffly*): Meanwhile, sir—

PRESIDENT (*Angrily holds up his hand to make him stop*): I will help you in every way I am permitted by the law. The courts must settle this, and I will send you to my own personal attorney. Meanwhile, (*He glares at Emiliano.*) I suggest you get all of your titles, your surveys together, and we will fight this through together, you and I.

EMILIANO (*Quietly*): One such suit has been under consideration for eight years, and a sugar mill has gone up on the land.

PRESIDENT (*Controls himself*): I will expedite the suit. I offer my own attorney. I will suggest to any of the judges who happen to be my friends that it must be done quickly. (*He turns to the merchant and looks at him meaningfully.*) You say there's been unrest in Morelos. What form has this unrest taken?

MERCHANT (*Nervously. He is caught between the two now.*): Well, you know, nothing much, meetings of little protests, talks. Nothing more. (*He throws in for the others.*) But the people are nervous and afraid. They don't know what is going to happen next.

PRESIDENT: I am always glad to be told when there are difficulties. Even a letter is appreciated very deeply by my office. (*Under the eyes of his friends, the President is creating a spy, and they know it.*)

EMILIANO (*Quietly, still*): Then you advise, my President, that we sue for the return of our lands?

PRESIDENT: That is correct.

EMILIANO: And that we gather every scrap of evidence that the lands have from time unknown belonged to the village?

PRESIDENT (*He knows this is leading somewhere. He speaks uneasily.*): That is also correct.

EMILIANO (*Casually*): And that we verify and establish the boundaries?

PRESIDENT (*Very uneasy*): Yes.

EMILIANO (*Very casually*): And we may use your name and title as our authority?

PRESIDENT (*He finally sees where this is leading.*): Well, only as an adviser. I do not have any more power than that.

EMILIANO: But we may say that you advised it?

The President knows he is being trapped now. A look of fear comes into his eyes. It's usually he who does the trapping, and he doesn't like the reverse role. This man, with his clear thinking, his directness, and his lack of fear, is one quite unique in Díaz's experience. He is afraid of him, and it follows that he hates him.

PRESIDENT: In my capacity as President, I do not even have the power to advise. But as a Mexican, one of your own blood, I would think it wise—yes, as a private citizen. (*He stands up to indicate that the interview is over. The eyes of Emiliano challenge him. He wants to avoid them, but he doesn't dare. For he remembers himself when he was lean and hungry.*) I hope we have solved something to your satisfaction, my children.

DELEGATES (*All murmur their thanks.*): Many thanks, my President. Our felicities. You are kind.

Emiliano says nothing. He knows what has happened. He knows what Díaz's next move will be, and the President knows he knows it. They are enemies from the very first. The delegates leave the room. The President sinks back into his chair, and the functionary shows his face.

FUNCTIONARY: His eminence, the Archbishop.

PRESIDENT (*Abstractedly*): Let him wait, let him wait. I want to see the General. You know where to find him, and hurry, hurry along.

FUNCTIONARY: Your permission, sir. (*And he goes.*)

The President takes his note pad from his little drawer and begins to make more notes, and we see him write: "Send word to Morelos. Increase the garrisons of all towns. Let maneuvers of cavalry start for training. Send two companies of *rurales*. Let squads stay on the haciendas for their protection. Watch that man every minute."

The door opens unceremoniously and an old general enters, buttoning his tunic as he comes. He runs his fingers down the buttons to make sure they're all fastened.

GENERAL: At your orders, my President.

PRESIDENT: I don't know how serious it is, but there seems to be some defection in the south. Now with this trouble with the crazy man, Madero, in the north, I'm a little worried. Even if it isn't serious, we lose nothing by being careful. Now I have prepared some orders for you.

GENERAL: Yes, my President.

SCENE

From Mexico City a little railroad runs over the mountains and to the south. It winds up through the shoulder of Mt. Ahusco. It has probably changed some, but not very much. If the engineer blows his whistle too long or too vehemently, the train has to stop and get up more steam. The equipment is outlandish, and the wonder is that it runs at all. It is as bad as the train to Oaxaca, which is estimated at the present time to be five months late, a condition it has accumulated in not too many years. The line from Ahusco into the state of Morelos goes as far as Iguala in the state of Guerrero, in the hot country. Of this train a fine story is told. It started one day for Iguala and somewhere along the line it was stolen. No one ever found it. Engine and five coaches and a flat car. This is impossible, but it is sworn that it happened.

The train—a beat-up little affair with a humorous engine, one first-class coach that would smother anyone if anyone ever rode in it, and three open carriages—is supposed to take off every day from either end of the line, and sometimes it does. The open carriages in the time we are speaking of were little more than flat cars.

The people who ride in the open coaches bring turkeys, pigs, and goats. The amount of food consumed is fantastic. At every little station there are sellers of colored sugar drinks, alcohol, *pulque*, and all of the little catch-penny produce that can be brought out for tourists. And on these trains always some group is singing. Musical instruments show up from nowhere. I once rode this train when it carried a thirteen-piece band which never stopped playing during the whole distance. They were learning a piece and at the end of eight hours they weren't getting anywhere with it. Furthermore, I was holding the aft end of a trussed pig in my lap. The owner graciously took the front end because, as he explained, that end bit. The train is a festive thing, and families sometimes save their pennies for months to ride on it.

It is on this train that our delegation went up to Mexico and now they are on it again, going back home. But they look very different than when we saw them last. Their collars are open, their neckties are loose, their hats are off, and their coats hang over the backs of the benches. The old men are taking off their shoes and are wiggling their emancipated toes happily on the boards of the floor. They have food and drink with them—tacos, tamales, and a gourd of *pulque*, and also a little bottle of *aguardiente*. In addition they buy fruit at every station, oranges, peanuts, and sticky candy. Mexicans are no different from any other tourists; they eat constantly from the time they leave home until they return.

One of the old men is asleep. The merchant is uneasy. He knows he plans to be a spy for the President, and he is not quite sure whether the others know it or not. He picks constantly at a hangnail. Emiliano sits quietly in that state of Indian repose that is so foreign to us. The young man of the delegation has been vastly impressed with Emiliano. He wouldn't think of joking with him now, for he feels the greatness and leadership in him.

YOUNG MAN (*Breaks in on Emiliano's thought*): How will we report to the village, Emiliano, success or failure?

EMILIANO (*Shortly*): Failure. Didn't you know?

YOUNG MAN: But he said he would give it his attention, his personal attention.

Emiliano looks steadily at the young man and then bursts into laughter. The merchant is still picking at his fingernail. He is desperately trying to play both sides.

MERCHANT: Well, I wouldn't be too sure. I thought he was encouraging. You must admit that he has the interest of the people at heart. Why, as he says, he comes from the people. He fought his way up from poverty to his high office.

EMILIANO: And his daughter is married to the son of the biggest hacienda in the whole state of Morelos. And her husband just took over eight hundred hectares of village land.

MERCHANT: Well, maybe the President didn't know about it. He said himself that there were many things he did not know until public-spirited people like us come in to tell him. And you must admit he thanked us for coming.

EMILIANO (*Sarcastically*): He is a darling.

MERCHANT: Perhaps you are too harsh. After all, he has been President a long time, and you cannot do that unless you are gifted.

EMILIANO (*Still with sarcasm*): Never for one moment would I suggest that he is not gifted.

MERCHANT (*Seriously*): What did you want him to do, disobey the law?

EMILIANO: Oh, I would not for one moment have him disobey the law.

MERCHANT: Well, I think we should leave it in his hands.

EMILIANO (*Leans forward and puts his hand on the merchant's knee*): It is already in his hands.

The train pulls into a little town. Emiliano and the young man get off to buy oranges.

EMILIANO (*To the young man*): I think we must be careful with him.

YOUNG MAN: I know. But what are we going to do, Emiliano?

EMILIANO (*Speaks very carefully*): Just what the President suggested. In his name, we are going to survey the boundaries and set up markers. Not just we, the whole village, with flags and a band. We will make a fiesta. If anyone interferes we will say that we are simply following the wishes of the President.

YOUNG MAN: But what will that accomplish? You know that will not be permitted.

EMILIANO: It will do this, either it will work or it will convince the people that their cause is hopeless. It will draw the poison to the head of the carbuncle. Then it will be that the people will either give up and be slaves or they will fight. If they fight, they will either be beaten or they will win. But at least they will know. That's all I can say.

YOUNG MAN: Then you have no hope in the courts?

EMILIANO: Have you?

YOUNG MAN: No.

EMILIANO: I have wanted to tell you this. I walked around the city and listened to the talk. It isn't just our state, the whole country is simmering. In the north there have been uprisings already. There is a great man named Madero there, and the people are flocking to him.

YOUNG MAN: I've heard something of him.

EMILIANO: I think the time has come to have another organization. We must start in secret with only those we can trust. I think we should send a representative to the north to see this Madero. If there is to be a revolt it would be better if it all happened at once. You must not believe that the President is silly. He knows what he is doing, and we do not.

YOUNG MAN: And how will this end?

EMILIANO: I don't know. For us, probably badly. For the future, there is a chance. But I can tell you now what the President is doing. He will soon be sending troops to Morelos. Maneuvers, they may call it, and he won't know anything about it. Before we can get organized we will be surrounded. You will see.

YOUNG MAN: How do you know that?

EMILIANO: Because that is what I should do, up to a certain point, but not quite.

YOUNG MAN (*The train whistles shrilly, and the two move toward it.*): Then what must we do?

EMILIANO: I am not the commander.

YOUNG MAN: But if you were?

EMILIANO: I should never do what they expected me to do. I should work out what they expected and then do something else. I think that right now you would see that.

His voice trails off, and we see a squadron of cavalry on the line. A bugle blows and the men mount and swing into a column. We see a gun crew riding on caisson and a piece of light artillery. We see a machine gun crew packing a water-cooled Lewis gun on the back of a mule. We see a group of rural police riding into the great door in the wall of a hacienda. And through this, we see the face of Emiliano. His eyes are bright and the flames we know are burning in his pupils. His shirt is open. We look down on his chest and see the little hand, the *manito*. It is inflamed and bright. His eyes look at us, and his face is stolid and Indian, with no expression.

SCENE

This scene moves like a pageant, but how much is seen and how much is indicated, I cannot tell.

It is the stretch of land that has recently been fenced. In the distance coming from the village, we see a procession of people. They are dressed in their best clothes, as they would be for a fiesta. At the head of the procession marches one of the oldest men of the village, carrying the Mexican flag. The children are dressed almost as for confirmation. The little girls in clean, starched dresses. On the edges of the procession there are horsemen—men of Emiliano's class who are yet identified with the people. Emiliano is there, and Eufemio, and a number of the men we have seen at the fiesta. Behind the flag bearer marches the same village band we have seen at the funeral. And it is playing, just as horribly as ever.

This column of people moves slowly. Families trudge along together—fathers and mothers, grandmothers and children. Here and there in the procession men are setting off small skyrockets which hiss up into the air and explode. (This, incidentally, is an old, old signal that a fiesta or a saint's day or any celebration is in progress. If you see a skyrocket and go to the place it was sent up you will find some kind of a party going on. Mexicans take their ceremonies very seriously.) There is no laughter in this parade, and no smiles. It is as though this column had the feeling that they are making history.

Now the procession comes to the new fence, and very carefully the men and women and children climb over it. It is apparent that they have been thoroughly coached in what they are to do. Once inside the fence, each one picks up a stone, some little rock, a piece of flint, and carries it in his hand.

A second old man, carrying an ancient piece of paper, is now marching ahead. He looks at his paper, and then sights at the hills and surrounding countryside. He carries a long staff in his hand. On this paper are the boundaries of the land which belongs to the village, and the little rocks are to make the boundary markers. (In all primitive cultures boundaries have become mystical. The Romans and the Chinese, in fact, most cultures, regarded boundaries as so important that they created special gods to watch them.) So in this scene we have a ritual verification of an ancient line. The old man moves on, making his sights until finally he plants his staff firmly in the ground. Then the procession moves past, and each person deposits his stone around the marker until a little mound is made. The old man removes his staff and proceeds, studying his paper again. The band plays, and the people pick up new stones for the next marker.

We see Emiliano directing the horsemen. He is deploying them as scouts. He knows there will be an attack, and he sends the riders out to cover the procession. With Emiliano, tactics are as natural as breathing, as was discovered when he began to command in the field.

Now we see a squad of *rurales* mounted and riding down the lane between fields of sugar. Their carbines are not in the scabbards, but are held in their hands. Next, we see a machine gun crew with its mules. They are mounted, and the mules carry the dismounted gun and ammunition. We see a squad of regular cavalry in squadron formation traveling in a fast trot. We see Emiliano's scouts on places of slight eminence—one in a tree, one on a little hill. We see one of the scouts suddenly wheel his horse and ride at full speed toward the level where the procession is moving. And now we see other scouts riding in. The scouts are talking to Emiliano. He wheels and rides to the procession. We see him shouting.

EMILIANO (*His voice is sharp with command.*): The soldiers are coming. If there is shooting, everyone is to lie down close to the ground. When the shooting stops, go quietly toward the village. Do not run. Remember, lie down if there is shooting. (*We see the frightened faces of the unarmed villagers.*) We are not to fight nor to run.

Now he wheels his horse again and follows the scout. He takes up his position where the little road through the cane terminates in the pasture land. Over his shoulder we can see the approach of the troops. Emiliano is flanked by Eufemio and a *charro*. The column halts and the officer rides forward.

OFFICER: What are those people doing on this land?

EMILIANO (*Quite formally*): On the advice of the President of the Republic we are surveying our ancient lands and setting up the boundaries.

OFFICER: Are you crazy?

EMILIANO: We are following the instructions of the President.

OFFICER: Where are your instructions?

EMILIANO: We are acting on verbal instructions given by the President himself to a delegation from this village.

There is a sharp sound to the left. Emiliano glances sideways. The machine gun crew has emerged from the cane and is setting up its gun in a position to sweep the procession.

OFFICER (*Laughs shortly*): You have no written order?

EMILIANO (*Woodenly*): We have verbal instructions.

OFFICER: That is not good enough.

He signals with his left hand the order for the squadron to advance, and at just this moment the machine gun opens fire.

NOTE: It is attested again and again that Zapata was able to make instant decisions and to act on them.

Now a panic sets up in the procession. The people try to run. Emiliano instantly whirls his horse and rides directly at the machine gun. His machete is out, and Eufemio is riding immediately behind him, also with an unshielded machete. The belt feeder sees them coming. The firer tries to swing his gun to fire at the horsemen, but the third man is in his way, and there isn't time. The riders are upon them, slicing at them with their machetes. The mules in panic run into the cane. Two of the men are killed, and the others bolt.

Now we see Emiliano lean down from his saddle and pick up the heavy gun bodily. We see him riding swiftly away, taking advantage of every bit of cover. We see the people of the village scattering while the cavalry charges at them. We see the old man lying dead, his staff and papers half under him and an unfinished pyramid of stones beside him. And for detail, we see a beat-up trombone and the Mexican flag which has been carried at the head of the procession.

SCENE

A small, utterly plain room. It is equipped with the poor things a Mexican village house has. The windows are shuttered, and the door is closed. There are a few stools, a bench, a rough table, a candle. Three men are in the room: the young man who was a delegate, Eufemio, and Emiliano. They have been eating. The remains of their lunch is on the table—some fruit, tortillas, a *jarro* of beans, and a little dish of chili. It is obvious that they are in hiding.

YOUNG MAN: Well, there it is. They are looking for you. Twelve people killed and the fence is still up. They say a fine will be placed against the village. Is this what you expected from your scheme, Emiliano?

EMILIANO: Yes.

YOUNG MAN: You still think it was worth doing?

EMILIANO: Yes.

YOUNG MAN: Can you tell me why?

EMILIANO: I told you before. Now there is no doubt. It was no accident. Now even our friend who thinks the President is a fine man, even he can have no doubt now.

YOUNG MAN: And now what?

EMILIANO: Now we will build from a new basis, without any confusion.

YOUNG MAN: And what is that basis?

EMILIANO: Only this, that there can be no peace with your enemies. One must survive. The important thing to establish is that they really are enemies. That is now established. And the people are not confused anymore. They know.

YOUNG MAN: What will you do?

EMILIANO: I will get into the mountains tonight, and from there we will try to establish some kind of force and begin the long fight.

YOUNG MAN: Don't you think there is some way without fighting?

EMILIANO: Do you?

YOUNG MAN: Well, I would hate to say that there isn't.

EMILIANO: That is what you want to believe, but you don't believe it.

YOUNG MAN (*Laughs suddenly*): I guess you're right, only . . .

EMILIANO: I know.

EUFEMIO (*Stands up and stretches*): Well, I'm not going to sit like a rat in a hole. I'm going out.

EMILIANO (*Anxiously*): Be very careful, my brother.

EUFEMIO (*Grins*): Where I'm going they will not look.

EMILIANO (*Smiles at him and repeats*): Be careful.

Eufemio and the young man go out. Emiliano lies down on the floor and props his head on his wrist. Only a little light comes through the cracks in the shutters.

SCENE: It is another room, but one more comfortable than the one we have seen. The merchant is speaking to an officer of the rural police.

MERCHANT (*Fearfully*): Then you will never tell where you got the information?

OFFICER (*Cruelly*): Of course not. Then we would lose you, and we need you.

MERCHANT (*Hopefully*): And you will draw my service to the attention of the President?

OFFICER: I do not walk into Chapultepec unannounced. I will speak to my superior and eventually it will come to the attention of the President. Everything does. He knows everything.

MERCHANT: Let me go now. And please do not come out before you make sure you are not seen. You understand I am doing this for my country.

OFFICER (*Cynically*): Of course. That is understood. Everything on all sides is for the country.

MERCHANT: But I mean it.

OFFICER: So do I.

SCENE: We have now rural police moving up streets and through alleys. They are surrounding a small mud house in the town. It is a carefully arranged job. A man trying to get through is stopped and told to go another way. Finally we see six men with cocked carbines move slowly into the house. The door closes behind them and remains closed.

SCENE: We see the merchant sitting in a *pulqueria*. He is drinking mescal and the bottle is on the counter in front of him. He has apparently been drinking heavily.

SCENE: The door of the little mud house we have seen opens and six men come out. They have Emiliano, his arms and elbows are tied behind him. There is a slip noose around his neck, and even then the men carry their cocked carbines, and three of the guns are pointed at Emiliano's back. The police are leading Emiliano through the plaza. A crowd has collected. There are a few boos and catcalls, but done behind hands so no one could be identified.

VOICE: What will you do with him, Mr. Commandant?

COMMANDANT (*Very pleased with himself; he addresses the standing people.*): I have orders to take him to Cuernavaca for trial.

ANOTHER VOICE (*Satirically*): And on the way he will try to escape?

COMMANDANT (*Nonchalantly*): I do not know what he will do. I will deliver him alive if I can.

THIRD VOICE: He will try to escape. They always do.

We see Emiliano's face. He is hatless. His face is bruised and in his eyes fires are burning brightly. The *reata* around his neck tightens, pulling him forward. We see that he cannot walk fast because his legs are tied together with a kind of hobble.

SCENE: It is night in the town, and the motion we want to get is of scurrying among the people, of the carrying and delivering of messages and great busyness, quiet, secret busyness.

SCENE: We see Emiliano in his cell, the same in which he was held before. He is sitting on the floor. His arms are still tied behind his back and his legs are tied. Two men with rifles sit in the cell with him, and they keep their rifles in their hands. Outside the cell door are three more armed men, and even in front of the building are armed police to prevent a raid.

SCENE

It is morning. The convoy which is to take Emiliano to Cuernavaca, or more likely to shoot him on the way, is a fairly large force. It moves out of the town. Emiliano, bound and on foot, is in its midst. As the column moves we see that there is a mass of townspeople who are going along too. They move about fifty yards behind the squadron. Then, as we watch, we see another group come out of

the cane and march fifty yards ahead. The commandant is very
nervous.

COMMANDANT (*To a lieutenant*): Go and ask them what they think
they are doing.

The lieutenant rides back. Emiliano is striding out now. There
is a little smile on his face. The lieutenant comes back and salutes
his officer.

LIEUTENANT: They say they are going along to make sure he does
not escape or try to.

COMMANDANT (*Savagely*): I wonder who thought of this. We will
catch them all, every one, sooner or later. We will have a big
cleanup now. Are these people armed?

LIEUTENANT: They don't seem to be.

The column has now come into open country, and we see that
it is completely surrounded. There are groups of people at the sides
of the column also. We see very far and high in the air a number
of buzzards, but they are not circling. Emiliano raises his head
and sees the buzzards. He smiles slightly and shakes his head.

SCENE: We see the merchant still in the bar. His eyes are
glazed with drink, and he is alone except for the bartender. There
is a shadow in the doorway. The bartender looks up, and then
swiftly moves toward the end of the bar. The merchant looks up
too. His eyes widen for a moment, and then he puts his head down
on his arms. There are three shots and the merchant falls like a
sack beside the bar. His arm sweeps the bottle with him and on
its side it lies beside him, the mescal running out on the floor.

NOTE: By now, the great difficulty of this picture will be apparent. The life of Zapata has some things in common with Joan
of Arc and Jesus Christ, in that his life is an idea. I think I know
as much about him from all angles as anyone living. I have heard
three witnesses describe the same scene which they all saw, and
no two saw the same thing. Zapata was a superman, there's no
doubt about that. And this is very good, but it's unbelievable. We
know that the story of Joan is true, but we really do not believe it

deeply, because we cannot find that strength and devotion to a single idea in ourselves. Most people are not motivated by thought at all, but by a series of small emotions set in action by stomach, heart, liver, or trivial experience—want or discomfort. But Zapata's life was devotion to an idea that never changed. And this makes him unbelievable. Character on stage is usually a balance of weaknesses and strengths, but this man had practically no weaknesses. Therefore, he has practically no character dramatically. For drama is a resolution within one's self during the play. The resolution in Zapata seems to have been born in him. That is the way it really was, and if I make it anything else I will be lying about him. Even the people who hated him agree that he was devoted, incorruptible, and fearless always. There was no internal struggle in the man, no uncertainty, no barrier of fear to overcome. The only real softness in his life was toward women. And even women did not warp his original strength one little bit. In a word, Zapata is *too* literary. Compared to him, Eufemio, with his weaknesses, his violence, his drunkenness and lechery, becomes rather dear.

There is one other thing to say in this note. Just as people see different things in the same event, so no two people saw Zapata in the same way. He is an "owned" man by scholars. The fights about him are continual. No matter what is said about him, an opposition will arise. There are factions still in existence which fight each other bitterly about every phase of his life. And there are as many Zapatas as there are people interested in him. To one, he was cruel; to another, kind; to another, wise; and to another, wily. In this story I am trying to take an Indian's eye view of him, for there are more of them, and to them he could do no wrong. But I must say that, even with the enormous amount of research I have made, the task is extremely difficult.

SCENE

It is a small cup high in the mountains, a place lonely and with great beauty—a lost place. Under the shelter of a cliff, a small fire is burning, throwing the silhouettes of two figures against the cliff. We see that Emiliano and Eufemio are seated by a campfire. Their horses are feeding nearby. Emiliano is dirty and tattered. His shirt is torn open so that we can see the *manito* on his chest. His eyes are very tired. Eufemio sits near him, playing mumblety-peg with a vicious heavy knife. He throws the knife into the turf with great dexterity.

EUFEMIO (*Speaks seriously*): I mean it, Emiliano. That is your last chance. You must never be taken again, for they will never bother to take you alive. They are afraid of you now. They will shoot first.

EMILIANO: I know that, and I will not be taken again. I am grateful, this time. No, I will never be taken again. Now, does that satisfy you?

EUFEMIO (*With a look of affection*): It's the best you can offer. I thought it was over. I thought you were finished.

EMILIANO (*His face tightens.*): Now, the messengers have gone to the Cuautla fiesta?

EUFEMIO: They have been there since the first day.

EMILIANO: And the leaders of the villages have been instructed to come singly?

EUFEMIO: It is all being done. They will be here.

EMILIANO: Is there any word from the north?

EUFEMIO: The north is rising. I hear they are sending trainloads of troops to the north.

EMILIANO (*Anxiously*): But are they drawing any troops from here to send north?

EUFEMIO: Well, no. That I have not heard.

EMILIANO: We must be very careful of treachery.

EUFEMIO: We are doing everything we can. We learned our lesson. There are some who thought there could be peace. I don't think they still believe it. The troops have been going through the villages like weasels through a hen house. Listen! (*They hear the sound of a horse's hooves.*) It's all right. If he got this far, he's all right.

But nevertheless both brothers move back into the darkness away from the fire, their rifles in their hands.

A rider comes near to the fire, dismounts and comes into the light so that his face can be seen. He takes off his hat. The brothers come back and embrace the man.

EMILIANO: Any trouble? Any patrols?

MAN: I did not come by a way that patrols know.

Now we see men riding through the mountains, men riding in the high brush, an indication of the secret gathering of the chieftains in the high cup in the mountains. At the entrance to the little valley we see them challenged, one by one.

And now we see the gathering of the country chieftains around the little fire, a scene only dimly realized. The faces are partly in shadow, but the eyes catch the light. Most of the men are in the dress of field peons—white pajamas and big hats. A few are in the clothing of rancheros. All of the men are armed, and some have bandoliers of cartridges across their chests. Their faces are serious.

Emiliano has been speaking, but he does not use the sonorous phrases of speechmakers. He talks exactness. His voice is as short and harsh as a man reading lists.

EMILIANO (*He is giving orders.*): You understand now that we cannot fight from the front. Always strike from the side or in back. Attack nothing unless it has weapons, horses, or food. Permit no man to join unless he has weapons and a horse. Fight secretly. Always kill the man, never the horse. Pick up every gun, knife, tool. We must arm ourselves with the weapons of our enemies. Now, I think we understand that.

VOICE (*One of the chieftains*): How about the villages?

EMILIANO: Do not attack a town unless you can take it, and then only if it has something you need. A defeat would be very bad at first. Strike and disappear. And above all, keep the communications open. Use the people, the field Indians, the women, the children, sellers of goods in the markets. Use them all for messengers and keep in communication. Let your meetings be under cover of the village fairs. Is this all understood? (*There is a murmur of assent.*) Now, my friends. I hope you know what you have done. Now you can only win or die. There are no other choices. Do not believe for one moment that you will ever be forgiven. We have asked for land and liberty. We must now take them or be killed.

A VOICE (*Wavering*): Chief, do you think we can win?

EMILIANO (*With utter certainty*): I *know* we *can* win. Whether we will win is up to you. That is all.

The men disperse quietly, going different directions, leaving Emiliano sitting on the ground by the little dying fire. He looks depressed and tired.

EUFEMIO: Are you worried, my brother?

EMILIANO: Worried? No. I have just given away my life. (*He pauses for a moment.*) But maybe the men who have it will do better with it than I would have done.

NOTE: The fighting itself is not so important to this story as the people are. But it was a war. I want to show quickly that that war developed from small raids to major warfare, and I want to show the development of Emiliano as a field general. I will perhaps show three fights or parts of three. The first: A raid on a hacienda. And I will use a real one, with an eyewitness account, and the director can make what he wants of it. (The account given by Soto y Gama in an interview. He was one of Zapata's closest friends and advisers.) Second: An account of the attack on a small town defended by Federal troops. Third: An attack that went through the walls of a whole village, the attackers cutting holes like gophers in the mud walls and fighting room by room.

Madero appointed Zapata a general. During the campaign just mentioned, we have seen that in leadership and tactical ability, he has deserved it. I am purposely leaving out his political and economic ideas and pronouncements, not because they were bad but because they do not have dramatic impact.

We want to see what has happened to Emiliano. He has become leaner, his cheeks leathery, his eyes slightly tired, but with a weariness of many weeks in the field and years of planning.

There is one story about him told that is perhaps true which might be used. It is said that at the siege of one of the larger towns the advance was held up by a well-placed Federal machine gun. Now, a number of small boys traveled with the Army, and they were very useful in carrying messages and in spying. Some little girls even served the rebel cause. In this incident, a small boy crept out from the brush in the night, carrying a *reata*. It took him a long time to get there, but once in position, he dropped a noose gently over the barrel of the machine gun and ran like hell, dragging the gun out of the hands of the gunner. He dragged it clear into his own camp and up to Emiliano. Emiliano said, "You were a brave boy. What would you like as a reward?" And the boy said without hesitating, "Your horse, my Chief." Emiliano had a very beautiful horse, and with hesitation he said, "It is yours." And the boy mounted and rode out of the camp. It is just a story that is told that is part of the folklore.

Now when Emiliano had become a general, the father of Josefa sent friendly word to him indicating that he was now acceptable as a son-in-law. And since there are very few really human things about Zapata, I think it would be well to spend some time on his courtship and marriage. Such courtships are sufficiently gruesome, and we can use this one in detail. It is carried out with complete ceremoniousness.

SCENE

The headquarters of Emiliano in the town, let's say, Cuautla. The father of Josefa is standing in front of the table at which Emiliano sits. In drawing and in design, make this as much as possible like the earlier scene, only let the roles be reversed. Now it is Emiliano who is seated and Espejo who is the petitioner. Emiliano, as usual, wears the black clothes of the *charro*. His hat is enormous and very beautiful. He looks at Espejo with a faint dislike, for he doesn't forget that this man once insulted him.

ESPEJO (*Trying to be impressive and jovial but with the disadvantage*): And so, my General, it gives me great pleasure to bring you the invitation of my daughter to call. I might say that her invitation has the full consent of her family.

EMILIANO (*Looks at Espejo insultingly and with such insolence that his words are a complete surprise*): Please say to Señorita Espejo that I shall be honored to obey.

NOTE: The courtships are really this way.

ESPEJO: (*Smiles with his face but not with his eyes. He observes everything—the staff, the troops, even the richly ornamented saddle on the floor. It is impossible that he can like Emiliano as much as he may admire him and want him for a son-in-law.*) I shall carry your message with the greatest of pleasure. And may I say I consider my family honored? (*He bows stiffly.*) Emiliano does not rise. And this in itself is an insult, just as Espejo offered it to him.

EMILIANO: May I suggest eight o'clock as a time?

ESPEJO: I shall inform my daughter. (*And he backs out of the room. And the guards who know the story grin at him.*)

SCENE: The stark little mud room of Emiliano. He has been shaving and dressing, and making a great thing of it. His basin is held up by a soldier. The care given to his mustache and hair, the careful knotting of his scarf, the criticism of his boot polish should be taken into account. The only mirror in the room is a tiny cracked one, and this can be held in all positions so that the general can see himself. (Emiliano, like most *charros*, was very proud and conscious of his clothes and so he would make a great to-do about dressing.) When he is finally ready, even his posture is different, and the men smile a little as he goes out.

Scene

The parlor of the Espejo home. The director can throw the book at this. It is ugly, uncomfortable, over-decorated, stiff, and ceremonious. The chairs are rigid and comfortless. No living has ever gone on in this room. There are religious pictures on the wall, and paper flowers. It's the social pitch of the Espejos, probably the hottest room socially in the whole district. And it is a perfect example of how much bad taste can be crowded into one room.

There are four people in the room—Emiliano, Josefa, the angular aunt we have seen, and the mother. The mother works at a small embroidery frame, while the aunt reads from a small book which might be a breviary. But neither is interested in what she is doing. They are there not only as guardians of their daughter and niece but also more or less as referees of the match.

Josefa is dressed in her very formal best. (We can see the picture of the costume she would wear at this time.) The conversation would have the stiff quality of recitation, for it would be composed entirely of *dichos*, or sayings. These are matched one against the other, and they are what makes up a kind of social game. Emiliano says a *dicho*, and Josefa answers with another one, while the chaperones listen and approve. It is the conversation of a nice young lady. I shall not put all the *dichos* in now, but they would go something like this:

EMILIANO: It is true that birds of a feather flock together.

JOSEFA: Yes, and also, a monkey in any other clothes is still a monkey.

This can go on for hours, and there are millions of them. I shall accumulate a series of the most popular *dichos* of this period for this scene.

There is no comfort in the room and no romance in the scene. Now and then Josefa raises her eyes only for a moment to look at Emiliano, and then drops them virtuously again. For his part, Emiliano is enormously at his ease. (Which, of course, indicates that he is not at all.) The scene comes to a close with the precision of a play. Emiliano stands.

EMILIANO: I hope I may promise myself the honor of calling again?

The chaperones look up. They approve of him. He is playing the game properly. (And, honest to God, people really talk this way.)

JOSEFA (*Demurely*): The honor will be mine, my General.

Emiliano cannot touch her, but he can and does kiss the hand of the mother and then of the aunt.

NOTE: Next in sequence and invariable in procedure would be the serenade. This would take place outside the window of Josefa. Since he is a general, Emiliano might have as many as ten guitars and singers; and while they sing to her, Emiliano, and probably Eufemio with him, would stand under the barred window of her room. It would be customary for Josefa to open her shutters just a little, not enough so that she could be fully seen. And since she is receptive to his suit, she would possibly throw out to him some kind of a memento. It might be a flower or a handkerchief. This he must take and press to his lips, then carefully and ostentatiously place it under his jacket over his heart.

The next move is the *mañanita*, or little morning song. The singers and principals, after the serenade, would go out and get drunk, really drunk. This would take them nearly all night, and they would return about five in the morning to sing the *mañanita* under the same window. But now they are very drunk. Some have lost their instruments, and all have lost their voices. Emiliano will be a little tipsy and very gay; Eufemio, drunk as a boiled owl. The liquor has been free, and the musicians have made the most of it. All of this may seem corny, but it was done and still is.

Scene

We come now to the wedding, and I will indicate only that it is the most formal kind of church wedding, with every fixing. According to pictures taken on his wedding day, Emiliano wore a civilian suit, with a gold watch chain and a high, stiff collar. The length of the scene depends entirely on what the director wants to do with it. A man who was there has this to say of this wedding: "At the entrance to the church, which had been profusely decorated with palm leaves and a multitude of white tropical flowers, the priest awaited the group. Before the altar, Señor Espejo gave his daughter to the groom, who took her by the arm and kneeled down with her on especially prepared low stools, covered with white satin. The filmy veil of the bride covered also the shoulders of the groom as they listened to the service. When it was over, there was a great crowd waiting in front of the church—the whole population of the town was present."

In the Espejo home, a large table had been made of planks, and this was covered with food and flowers. A large but select group had been invited, and the street in front of the house was crowded with people who had not been invited. And now there was music and eating and drinking of toasts.

A formal photograph of Emiliano and his bride shows him sitting and her standing, and from the look on Emiliano's face he, although controlled and formal, had had a great deal to drink. After a long time of celebration, the bride and groom discreetly disappear. This is the end of the eyewitness account of the wedding. But one cannot trust these accounts too closely, for this last quoted person says of the dress: "The bride, dressed in white, with a long train, and carrying a bouquet of orange blossoms, entered the church on the arm of her father. Behind came Emiliano, dressed in a handsome black *charro* costume, embroidered in silver." But a picture taken that day shows him dressed in an ill-fitting and uncomfortable black business suit. And this is the basic trouble with all eyewitness accounts.

NOTE: We come now to the difficult part, which must be well discussed. What happened is highly complicated and must be simplified for film. The Revolution in the north broke through. Porfirio Díaz fled the country, and Madero, the little man from the north, entered the Capital. Soon after he did, the ragged peasant forces of Zapata entered the capital city from the south.

It was a nondescript army, weaponed with anything it could pick up. Some of the soldiers wore five or six belts of ammunition, draped on themselves. But the ordinary costume was the white field clothes of Morelos. Because they had been looting a little, some of the men wore ridiculous combinations of clothing they had picked up along the way. Some even wore pieces of women's clothing. But nearly all wore the gigantic hat curled at the edge, which is indigenous of the state of Morelos. It was popular to wear the medallion of the Virgin of Guadalupe on the front of the hat. Note this well, because it might serve some of your church problems, and it is true that the rebel army had taken the sign of the Virgin as its own.

Now the city of Mexico was in their hands and they were heavily armed men. People who were there say that they wandered about like tourist children, staring at the tall buildings, stricken with awe at the monuments. And when they got hungry, instead of stealing or looting, they took off their hats and begged for pennies. They had been dreadful and cruel in the field, but in the city they were children, and it appears from the records that they did not cause any trouble at all. I think this is not only particularly interesting, but very good for film.

Madero, the triumphant leader of the Revolution, was not, as Zapata was, a man of the people. He was the son of an enormously rich family of landowners in the north, a black sheep. He had been touched to fury by the condition of the people even on his own family's land. It seemed almost instinctive of him, however, and it became a matter of his downfall, to trust the men of his own class.

The account of the meeting of Madero and Zapata is given by Magana, who was there.

Emiliano and Eufemio and staff and guards went to the station in Mexico City to meet the train bringing Madero from the north. There was a huge crowd and a great celebration, and when Madero was driven to the National Palace, Zapata walked beside his carriage.

The first interview between Madero and Zapata is very interesting. They met in a private house. Madero was a little man with light eyes, a blond; Emiliano, very dark, an Indian. Madero was a nervous man, jittery and restless, and already his position and his greatness seemed to have become too much for him.

In the following dialogue, I have cut out the names of people, as always in this script, and have shortened and simplified it a little bit. But the dialogue is essentially as reported by Magana.

SCENE

A room in a fairly wealthy house in Mexico City. Madero is pacing the floor, Zapata sitting quietly with his carbine leaning against his knee.

MADERO: You have done a great work, General.

EMILIANO: It was hard fighting, but my men are fighters.

MADERO (*Nervously, as though he didn't want to say it*): I am told that you have some difficulties with one of the generals I have appointed.

EMILIANO (*With brutal directness*): I do not trust him.

MADERO (*Pauses, and then speaks coldly*): Indeed? He is a loyal soldier.

EMILIANO: That, he is not. He tried to sell us to the dictator. Only the speed of the campaign saved us.

MADERO (*Speaks very carefully*): I think you are wrong, General. I think he is loyal.

EMILIANO: That is your privilege. But keep him with you. Do not let him come into my country that we have won so bitterly.

MADERO: I wish you would make it up with him. I am convinced that malicious tongues have done this harm.

EMILIANO: Well, only time will tell that. But, sir, that is not our first problem. The land must be given back. That is what we have been fighting for.

MADERO: Of course, of course. And it will be done in due time and within the law. These are delicate matters, General. Such things have to be studied if they are to be done properly.

EMILIANO (*Angrily*): I can see nothing delicate about them. Our land has been stolen—we want it back. We do not want to study. We have seen study for twenty years. No, let us have our land back now.

MADERO: Now what is really important is to begin to disband the troops. Since we have won there is no reason to keep so many soldiers. That is expensive.

EMILIANO: If we disband, who will enforce the laws?

MADERO: Why, the regular army, of course.

EMILIANO (*In despair*): But those are the ones we have been fighting!

MADERO (*As though he were explaining to a child*): Listen to me, my General. We can't have peace with a nation in arms.

EMILIANO: We (*Taps his chest*) do not seem to be able to have peace any other way.

MADERO: But can't you understand? We have won. The Revolution is accomplished. It will be different now.

EMILIANO: With the same men holding the guns? Do you believe it?

MADERO: The time when we needed arms is past. Now we must use peaceful means. We must have no more violence.

NOTE: Emiliano took his carbine with him everywhere. It never left his hand unless it stood by his chair. He even had it with him at this conference.

EMILIANO (*He advances near to Madero, points at his gold watch chain*): Look. If I have this (*And he holds up his carbine.*) and I take your watch and keep it, and later you meet me and you have a gun, would you have the right to take your watch back?

MADERO: Why, why yes, I think so.

EMILIANO: Well, that is our story. A few men took our land by force. Now we are armed, and we want it back. If we lay down our weapons, what guarantee have we that we will get any of the land back? Armed, we are sure. Disarmed, we are reduced to a trust that has never been any good to us. With great respect, I tell you, sir, we want our land back now. We do not have it.

MADERO: You have my assurance that it will be done. Have you trust in me?

EMILIANO: Yes, sir, I have. But it's the others with you.

MADERO: You must trust me. I will see that all is done, but it must be done without violence. Now, will you begin to disband your troops, General?

EMILIANO (*Reluctantly*): I will try. But they will be afraid and they must be persuaded.

MADERO: I personally will go through your state and study the problem with full justice. (*He pats Emiliano on the shoulder and speaks jocularly.*) And you, General, I will see that it is made possible for you to acquire a fine ranch, hey?

EMILIANO (*His whole body changes, his face becomes tight. All of his reluctantly allayed suspicions come back to him. He speaks with disgust. He even strikes the floor with the butt of his carbine in rhythm with his words. And these were really his words.*): Sir, I did not enter the Revolution to become a landowner, nor to become rich. If I am worth anything it is because the people trust me. And they trust me because they believe I will give them the land that was stolen from them. If I should not keep my promise, I deserve to be killed.

MADERO (*Smiles, but he is upset by Emiliano's anger.*): General, try to understand me. The promise will be kept, but, also, those who have given valuable service should be rewarded. Don't you agree with that?

EMILIANO (*Speaks coldly and precisely*): The only thing we want is that the stolen land be returned.

MADERO (*Repetitiously*): That will be done, General! That will be done!

EMILIANO: I respectfully suggest, sir, that the same arms which won for you can . . . (*He draws his finger slowly across his own throat.*)

SCENE

The disbanding of troops in Morelos. Actually it was in Cuernavaca. Three tables are set up outside. The men are lined up. They march slowly past the tables. At the first, they deposit their rifles and ammunition. The men are apprehensive about giving up their weapons. They have a crazy kind of assortment. The stack of weapons grows on the ground. At the second table, after their weapons are stacked, they are questioned about their place of origin and given receipts for their weapons. Now since most of the weapons were acquired in action, the men feel that they belong to them, and some are highly reluctant to give them up. At the third table sits Emiliano and a treasurer. Ten pesos is given to each man who lives nearby and twenty pesos to those who live farther away. Emiliano thanks each man for his service.

A number of widows in mourning stand nearby, and when the men have passed and have been paid, Emiliano asks about the widows, and being told that they are the women of men killed in action, he treats them exactly like the soldiers, thanks them, and gives them money to go home.

(Throughout this scene there is a real apprehension. There is very little trust in the situation. Not that Madero was thought to be crooked, but by now they knew him to be weak. And the soldiers were genuinely afraid to give up their guns.)

NOTE: Madero was an idealistic man and his idealism had caught fire and swept him into power in Mexico. But the opposition to him was strong, rich, subtle, and clever. It was composed of all the men of money and property. The representatives of foreign powers headed, unfortunately, by the United States Ambassador Wilson were dead set against him and against his proposed reforms. It had seemed easy and clear to Madero during the Revolution to carry out these reforms, but once in power, pressure was exerted on him from all directions—from his family, from the friends of his life, from all of the rich, from the professional army and the professional politicians. The people of the country were not very vocal; the opposition was extremely so. They talked at him all of the time, and Madero became more and more confused. He took refuge in the reiterated statement of confused men: "This will require study; this is not as simple as it sounds."

The yammering of financially interested men was bad enough, but there was a force even more dangerous to him. In his own revolution, among his own generals, were men of ambition who thoroughly intended to use all of the force and trust of the people for their own advantage. Chief among these was a general with a cold eye and a face like an iron fish. His name was Huerta. He was an excellent general, and he once described himself, saying, "I never say what I mean or mean what I say." This man was starving for power, and he came into power through the idealism of Madero; and once in, even weak opposition to his plans made him furious. Almost immediately following the conclusion of the Revolution he began to make alliances both with the dissidents and others like himself who planned to ride into power and wealth on the Revolution. He plotted with foreign capital and with the ambassadors of nations which had financial stakes in Mexico.

Although he did not know it, Madero was already condemned to death, for only two people really stood in the way of Huerta— Madero and Zapata. Madero was confused, but Zapata was not.

Huerta began his plot by convincing Madero that Zapata stood in the way of peace. Meanwhile Huerta's agents assassinated a number of Zapata's trusted men, men beloved by the people of Morelos. And the poor people of Morelos rose in arms again because they were afraid. For a little time Madero half-heartedly supported Zapata, but he was too weak by now to prevent Huerta from sending troops to catch and kill Zapata.

Zapata had almost expected this. He mobilized his men and retreated, fighting the whole way. The split between Zapata and Madero was permanent. Finally Madero ordered Federal troops to remove Zapata. A number of attempts were made to catch and to kill him, but he escaped always, and the countryside rallied to him. A most cruel warfare broke out. Zapata called a meeting in the same little cup in the mountains that we saw before, and there he put forward his plan for the Revolution which is called the "Plan Agalla." It had to do with return of the land and with a number of social changes for the good of the people. It was greatly applauded and became the form of the new revolt. This plan spread all over Mexico, and Mexico now knew that its first fight had been in vain and that the Revolution would have to be fought all over again. Revolts broke out all over the country. It became a bitter, bloody affair with no quarter given on either side. Federal troops even went to the extent of killing thousands of Indians simply because they "might be Zapatistas."

The murder of Madero is one of the most cold-blooded and cynical affairs in history. Everyone knew it was going to happen, even Madero. Madero was arrested on Huerta's orders, "in the interest of public order." Madero's wife appealed to Ambassador Wilson for the protection of her husband, whom she knew would be murdered. Wilson refused to protect him. But meanwhile Wilson was sending false reports to Washington, which even the State Department later denounced. Madero's wife again appealed to Wilson and was not even admitted in to see him.

Madero was then taken from house arrest to the penitentiary "for safety." In the penitentiary yard he was pushed from the automobile and shot in the back "trying to escape." The next day, when Madero's wife was permitted to see his corpse, she killed herself with a knife on the body of her husband. Wilson instantly backed the de facto government set up by Huerta, the murderer of Madero. It is one of the blackest things our foreign service ever did. (This is not necessary to the picture, but the background must be sketched in.)

Huerta, a man with lust for power, a man of no principles, a traitor to his Chief and his cause, was now in power. And there was only one man in all Mexico who stood in his way, and that man was Emiliano Zapata.

Even before his death, the whole country seemed to know that Madero did not have the strength to keep his promises to the people. The *hacendados* were back in power, Huerta was provisional president and dictator, and Huerta was the worst kind of ambitious man—cruel, cynical, grasping, and clever. The fighting became general again and of an incredible cruelty. Federal troops burned everything in their paths, and since the fighters under Zapata were peasants, all peasants were attacked by Huerta's troops. For example, in Morelos Huerta's commander ordered the country people to leave their homes and villages and to congregate in the cities under penalty of death. This was, of course, because it was known that many of them were secret soldiers. But once he had them in the cities, the commander drafted them into his army; those who could even reasonably become soldiers.

Huerta began also a general practice of murder. Since he could not defeat Zapata in the field, he began to murder all of his friends, in fact, anyone who had known him. And Zapata's wife was constantly moving. She lived like a fleeing animal. The Federal forces wanted to catch her and hold her against Zapata's surrender. Josefa's mother was captured and put into prison.

Now gradually the Revolutionary forces began to gain ground. Carranza in the north, with Villa's help, began to win. Zapatistas in a series of quick and tricky attacks overran more and more territory. It had become a war of small, bloody raids, and it was now that Emiliano showed himself to be a master and inventor of a new kind of guerrilla warfare. He improvised the quick raid, the disappearance and reassembly of troops.

At this time Huerta called for a free election, and when he lost it, he destroyed the ballots, claimed that he had won and became permanent dictator. At this time there was a change in our current administration. President Wilson refused to recognize the Huerta government and cashiered Ambassador Wilson for his open backing of the Huerta government. So at last Huerta was in trouble.

Federal forces were drafted with men caught in the parks and in the fields, and pressing squads acted after the manner of English press gangs of an earlier period. But this, of course, did not work because in every engagement the draftees deserted to the enemy, sometimes shooting their officers first.

As can be seen, this is a very complicated period and I shall have to have some help from the director in putting some scenes of it on film. The preceding is a time so full of incident as to be dizzying. And it is a sad time. A thing once won is sold and has to be won all over again.

Gradually the liberal forces of the north—Carranza and Villa—became dominant and moved toward the Capital. Zapata, with his simple plan and his simple war cry of "Land and Liberty," never changed. The confused people who had depended on Madero and his Revolution went through their period of disillusion and realized that only Zapata in the south kept both his principles and his promises.

Eufemio was Zapata's Chief of Staff, and he won some very fierce battles. But he drank and quarreled increasingly. Sometimes he even forgot to carry out orders, and his cruelty when he was drunk was a constant source of embarrassment to Emiliano.

Scene

We see Emiliano with a few horsemen around him. He is on a small hill that is overlooking an attack that is going on below him. He is on the ground, helping to make crude stretchers out of poles for the wounded. His hands work restlessly tying the cross pieces to the poles. (This he often did.) Now and again he looks down into the valley where the firing is going on. He is restless and nervous.

EMILIANO: Where is Eufemio? I told him to attack from that ravine. What is keeping him? (*He stares at one of the horsemen, who looks back at him with a wooden expression. But when Emiliano looks away, this rider looks helplessly at another horseman and raises his shoulders slightly. Emiliano peers again into the valley. He is like a man who lifts his leg at a track meet to try to help a high jumper over the bar. He says softly:*) Come through! Come through! (*His face lights up.*) That's it! There, that's it, that's a darling! Now go on through, go on through to the left. (*In his mind he is directing the fighting.*) Oh! Good! There's an officer! There's a good officer! But where's Eufemio, where's he?

The horsemen smile secretly. They know where Eufemio is, just as Emiliano knows.

EMILIANO (*Turns, speaks to one of the riders*): Go, circle that way and see what is stopping Eufemio. (*He looks back into the valley.*) No, don't go, don't go. We're coming through. We're coming through without him. (*He shakes his head. He goes back to tying the stretchers.*)

Scene

Emiliano rides into a small camp. A sentry stops him, sees who he is, and salutes.

EMILIANO (*Curtly*): Where is my brother? (*The sentry's face freezes.*)
     Come on, where is he?

     The sentry motions to a poor shelter of cloth and twigs, using
the butt of his rifle to point, but he does not speak. Emiliano slides
from his horse, throwing the reins to the sentry. He strides angrily
toward the shelter and parts the torn tent flap that covers the front.
Over his shoulder we see Eufemio lying down on the ground. He
is soddenly drunk. His head is on the shoulder of a woman, a
ragged woman, a dirty woman, and not a pretty woman. She shows
fear at the sight of the scowling Emiliano. He squats down. Eufemio
snores drunkenly and scratches his nose in his sleep.

EMILIANO (*Harshly*): Eufemio! (*There is no response.*) Eufemio!

     Eufemio nods, smiles, comes only half to life, then settles
back to sleep. The woman squirms. She would like to be someplace
else but is torn between fear of Emiliano and fear of moving her
arm from under the head of Eufemio.

EMILIANO (*Shouts*): Eufemio!

EUFEMIO (*Opens his eyes, smiles at his brother*): Emiliano! Glad to
     see you. Glad!

EMILIANO: Why didn't you attack? Those were your orders!

EUFEMIO: Got drunk. No good, drunk. I just got drunk.

EMILIANO: That is not permitted, and you know it.

EUFEMIO: I know. Did it anyway. (*He has charm.*) Sorry. Couldn't
     help it. I'm just tired.

EMILIANO (*His face softens. His love for his brother is beyond all
     reason and all discipline.*): I know, but I'm tired, too, Eufemio.

EUFEMIO (*He struggles up on one elbow. The woman tries to get out,
     but he casually pushes her back like a piece of furniture.*): I
     know that, Emiliano. You're more tired than that. You're even
     too tired to get drunk. Been that way for years. That's not
     good, Emiliano.

EMILIANO (*Suddenly and with passion*): That's it. Rest. Go with me,
     Eufemio. Let's go home for a day. (*And he adds with passion:*)
     I want to see Josefa.

EUFEMIO (*Sluggishly*): Sure, go home! Why not. Get a good sleep. (*His eyes clear.*) How did it go?

EMILIANO: All right. Fortunately we didn't need you. They are running now.

Eufemio gets to his feet. He uses the woman's throat under his hand to help himself up. Her eyes are very large, and she makes no protest.

EUFEMIO (*Unsteadily*): Let's go home now. Let's go home, Emiliano. Let's go home.

EMILIANO: For two days only.

EUFEMIO: For two minutes only. But let's go home now.

NOTE: I can't make it too vehement the quick change of pace of Eufemio. One moment he could be a complete brute beast and the next he could have great charm and gaiety. He was very brave and very cruel. In all the world he seems to have loved only his brother. He kept many women at once. (There will be a larger section on him a little later.) The next scene, like nearly all in the script, is a true one.

SCENE

The brothers are riding along a road through the mountains. Emiliano is speaking and Eufemio does not look at him.

EMILIANO: And the reports are bad, Eufemio. I don't like to tell you these things, but you should save your anger for our enemies. Last week you beat one of our own soldiers nearly to death. And he had done nothing. This week you mistreated the wife of another soldier, and the man deserted. Did you kill him, or did he desert?

EUFEMIO: I don't know. I was drunk. (*He is like a small boy confessing.*)

EMILIANO: You see, you were drunk. Yesterday, you were drunk.

And if we had not won the engagement it would have been your fault. I don't like to tell you these things, Eufemio, but you are mistreating our own people. I will have to ask you to leave us, my brother. You are doing harm to our cause. Our enemies say we are bandits, and you are giving them reason to say it.

EUFEMIO (*Hangs his head*): I won't do it anymore, Emiliano. I promise I won't.

EMILIANO: You have promised before.

EUFEMIO (*Hopefully*): I won the engagement of Tepoztlán by myself, I did.

EMILIANO (*Patiently*): By disobeying your orders. You ordered the charge when you were told to hold it up. You won it, but if you had not been lucky you would have lost all of your men.

EUFEMIO: I didn't think.

EMILIANO: You must either think and obey orders or not think and obey orders. You know, Eufemio, you may win battles, but every time you hurt our own people you lose more than a battle. And it is not only your loss, it is all of ours. All we have is love and trust of the people. If we should lose this we would have nothing to fight with. For they are our only weapons.

EUFEMIO: But I didn't think.

EMILIANO: Try to think. Will you?

EUFEMIO: I will.

Emiliano rides close to his brother, puts his arm around his shoulders and gives him a quick hug.

SCENE

We see a little rutted rough road. The fields on either side are neglected. To the left (and I will show you the exact place) are the ruins of a hacienda, the walls torn and blistered, and behind them a burned-out sugar mill, its brick smokestacks smashed and the whole thing blackened by fire. (These are still just the way they were left.)

Emiliano and Eufemio are riding down the road. The sun is blinding hot, a dreadfully hot light. Ahead we see a tiny village lying burning in the sun. There is one thing odd about this village—it is deserted. The two men are riding near to it.

EMILIANO: I will have clean clothes. I will sit and put my feet up, and I won't think of anything. Eufemio, I haven't seen Josefa in over three months.

EUFEMIO (*Coyly*): Maybe I still have a few friends too.

EMILIANO (*He reins in his horse and scans the village ahead. He has become nervous.*): Something is wrong!

EUFEMIO: Look at the sun. Everybody is asleep. Would you be out in this sun if you didn't have to? (*He yawns the midday yawn of Mexico.*)

EMILIANO: No. It's something else. I don't know what.

EUFEMIO: You think a trap?

EMILIANO (*Slowly*): No, no. (*He sniffs the air.*) I smell fire.

EUFEMIO: You always do.

EMILIANO (*Slips the carbine from its scabbard under his leg*): I'm nervous. I'm not, I'm not going in this way. (*To the side of the road there is a little clump of trees. Emiliano turns toward them.*)

EUFEMIO (*In excitement*): You mean you're going to leave your horse?

EMILIANO: Yes.

EUFEMIO (*Anxiously*): Then if it is a trap, how would you get away? On foot? Look, Emiliano, if you even think it is a trap, let me go in first.

EMILIANO (*Nods*): Well, no. No, but I want to see Josefa. (*He speaks as though he were punch-drunk.*)

EUFEMIO: Then let's go in on horseback. At least we could run for it.

Emiliano nods and turns back toward the road into the village. We see them moving up a little street, the characteristic village street of Mexico. It is brilliantly light where the sun strikes and a black shadow where it does not. Not a soul is in the street. The two horsemen cautiously move along, and we can tell from their posture that they are alert and worried. Then we see them come to a gap in the buildings. The house has been burned and its walls pulled down. A little lazy smoke rises from the ruins. Emiliano reins in his horse. His face is ravaged with weariness and sorrow. He simply looks at the ruins of the burned house. Eufemio starts to speak and then decides against it.

EMILIANO (*His voice is filled with tired sorrow.*): We thought we could rest, my brother, but there is no rest for us, maybe ever.

There is a little movement around a corner and a flash of white. Eufemio fires at it instantly with his rifle—a snap shot— and immediately after his shot an old, old woman bursts into view. This is really an ancient woman, as only these Indians can be. Her face is cross-hatched with tiny wrinkles, deep as cuts. Only by looking very closely can we see that this is the *curandera* who forecast Emiliano's birth, and who later would officiate at his burial. Both men lower their rifles. The *curandera* is incredibly ragged and dirty. Emiliano looks down toward her, but he does not speak. His eyes hold the question.

CURANDERA (*Her voice is a croak.*): A raid. They came and burned and left.

EMILIANO: When?

CURANDERA: Last night.

EMILIANO: Josefa?

CURANDERA: She got away.

EMILIANO: Where?

CURANDERA: I will show you. I took her there and came back. Help me up, my General.

Emiliano leans down and takes her wrist, and she clambers and scrambles up the side of the horse like an old blind monkey and takes her seat behind him.

SCENE: The two horsemen are moving up a dry creek between hills. The branches of trees whip at them. Only a tiny trickle of water runs in the creek and the banks are high on either side. The men do not speak. The horses' hooves sound loud on the water-washed stones of the creek bed. The *curandera* taps Emiliano on the shoulder.

CURANDERA: Here.

We see a pile of brush against the dirt bank of the creek. The *curandera* clambers down, helped by Emiliano. She goes to the pile of brush and pulls it aside, revealing a shallow little cave in the bank, the kind where coyotes whelp and wildcats spend the day. Josefa, hardly recognizable, is in the cave. She has a baby in her arms, and her clothing is torn. And her eyes are wild and weary. (We'll play this scene without words.)

Emiliano's face is noncommittal. He throws his leg over the horn and slides to the ground. He walks heavily to his wife and sits down beside her. He does not look at her, but past her. (Here we must show pain by an absence of expression.) We see his hand unclench, and the fingers move almost uncertainly to rest on her knee, which is covered by her dirty skirt.

Josefa looks down at the ground, and then her head comes gently down on his shoulder, and her face turns inward against his arm. We see his hand become clawlike on her knee.

Eufemio turns his horse and rides back in the direction from which he has come, and the *curandera* picks her way among the stones, following him like a dog.

SCENE

Against the preceding scene we cut to a court-martial. It is very informal. A table is set under a tree—a bare table, rough and crude. Behind this sits Emiliano, armed; at his right sits another rebel officer, and on his left, a man who keeps notes. In front of the table stand two guards and two prisoners. The guards are dressed in *calzones*, with crossed bandoliers on their chests. The prisoners, two men, one much older than the other—the first has gray hair, the second is hardly more than a boy. Standing in a half circle there is an audience of armed men.

EMILIANO (*His face is rocklike.*): What evidence have you against him?

GUARD: He was seen to meet with a Federal officer, to converse with him, and to return to our camp.

EMILIANO: Who saw him?

A crippled old man hobbles up, makes a silly salute.

MAN: I saw him, my General.

EMILIANO: You swear it?

MAN: On the sacred name of our Lady.

EMILIANO (*To the old prisoner*): Have you defense?

MAN (*Speaks in a hoarse whisper*): My brother-in-law.

EMILIANO: And what did you discuss?

MAN: I asked about my sister.

EMILIANO (*Sardonically*): She is well, I hope?

MAN: She is dead.

EMILIANO (*Stares at the man with dead eyes*): Suppose you are telling the truth. You go back to your company and no one is hurt. But suppose you are *not* telling the truth, and I lose a thousand men. (*He thinks for a moment.*) No, I cannot take the chance. (*His voice is harsh.*) Kill him!

From the circle of men a dozen step forward. There is no ceremony. They march the prisoner off the screen, and there is simply a series of random shots. It is a killing, not an execution. Emiliano looks very tired. He does not even look in the direction of the shots. But the circle of men do.

NOTE: A chance for good close-ups. At such a time some men giggle, some look away for a second, and some stare in fascination. There are many kinds of reactions.

Emiliano looks at the boy. When the shots were fired, his body froze for a moment, and his eyes closed.

STAFF OFFICER: In the next case, I want to ask clemency.

EMILIANO: The charge?

STAFF OFFICER: Looting.

EMILIANO: In a village?

STAFF OFFICER: Yes, sir.

EMILIANO: There is no clemency. We cannot steal from our own people. The sentence is death.

STAFF OFFICER: In this case, he stole food for his father.

EMILIANO: So he says.

STAFF OFFICER: I have seen the father. He is dying of starvation.

The prisoner's eyes flash to the Staff Officer. His tongue moistens his lips, and his lips snap shut to a line.

EMILIANO: There are no excuses for looting. The sentence is death.

The men move forward.

EMILIANO: He stands under the sentence.

Emiliano looks at the boy as though he were his own son. In his eyes there is an incredible and overwhelming sorrow. The men take the boy by the arm. His face is one huge appeal, and Emiliano's eyes waver before the look, and his will breaks. He cannot stand it any longer. And he shouts in a fury.

EMILIANO: Whip him! Whip him! I commute the sentence, but whip him, whip him almost to death! (*His voice is a cry of pain. He turns to the Staff Officer.*) I am sorry. I should not have let him go. I should not.

STAFF OFFICER: You should, sir.

EMILIANO: No. Now there will be more looting, and I will have to shoot men who might never have been tempted.

STAFF OFFICER: Will you rest now, sir?

EMILIANO (*Mumbles as though he had been drinking*): I have no time for rest. I have no time, not yet. No time.

NOTE: About this time Pancho Villa entered Mexico City from the north. The fight was finally forcing Huerta out; and again Zapata went to Mexico City. (It seems to me that this is a repetition of the first Capital scene. However, I submit this to the discretion of the director.) Villa had had the "Plan Agalla" read to him and approved of it. It is my private conviction that he did not even understand

it. I do not think that Villa was a great man at all. He was a good
guerrilla fighter, but he was finally bought off and accepted a huge
ranch in Sonora in payment for getting out of politics. There is,
however, a scene which on the judgment of the director I will write
or leave out.

SCENE

Villa and Zapata meet in the castle of Chapultepec. It is in the
same throne room where we have seen Zapata as a young delegate,
and now these two are the most powerful men in Mexico.

VILLA: Why don't you take over the presidency?

EMILIANO: No, I would not do that. It would be the denial of
everything I believe and the reenactment of everything I have
fought against.

VILLA (*Pointing to the presidential throne*): Sit in the chair and see
how it feels to you.

NOTE: Actually he said, "Put your ass down and let your bung
hole feel the high office."

EMILIANO: No, I do not even want to feel it.

VILLA (*Laughs*): Well, then, let my children, whoever they are, see
their father as President. (*He sits in the chair and is photographed there. That picture is in existence, with Zapata standing beside him. Zapata had no humor; no very great man has
ever had.*)

Later, in another scene, Villa and Zapata went to a house of
prostitution in Mexico City. The line of girls walked by.

VILLA: You should take that blonde there to Morelos with you.

EMILIANO: I have never been with a blonde. The *rancheras* have
been my companions.

VILLA: Well, you should try everything. (*The two men are drinking
quite heavily, for Emiliano, at least.*)

EMILIANO (*Shrugs his shoulders*): Why not? (*He speaks to the blonde,*

who is standing in front of him now.) Would you like to go
to Cuautla with me?

THE BLONDE (*Shrugs her shoulders exactly as Emiliano has, and in
the same tone says*): Why not? (*The men laugh.*)

VILLA: You see? Why not? Look, my friend, you work too hard.
You never laugh. You have no gaiety. That is not good. You
should take this piece of blonde laughter with you. I mean
it. It would be a rest for your weariness.

EMILIANO (*Quite seriously*): Perhaps you are right.

THE BLONDE: Can I buy some clothes first? I have nothing proper
to wear.

VILLA (*Scowls a little*): Maybe I was wrong. Blonde laughter here
is turning into a wife and a lady even quicker than most. They
all do, but some take longer, and then your laughter is gone.

EMILIANO (*Seriously*): No. I have said I will take her with me, and
I will.

VILLA: She will probably disapprove of you by tomorrow.

THE BLONDE (*Still holding to her original thought*): I didn't mean
anything, you know, fancy. But I've been sick and even the
things I have don't fit me. And you wouldn't want a frowsy
woman with you, would you? You'd want to be proud of my
looks, wouldn't you?

Emiliano nods solemnly, while Villa bursts into a roar of
sardonic laughter.

SCENE

Emiliano's headquarters at Cuautla. It is a large room where there
are a number of tables and benches. The outside door is open and
a blinding light comes in, so that the room is quite dusky by
contrast. The blonde is sitting at one of the tables eating her lunch.
And Villa was right. Her pinky finger is up, and she is a lady. At
the same time her eyes dwell on the young military secretary who
is entering some matters in a ledger at another table. Across the

table from her, Emiliano is seated. He is gloomy and suspicious. His eyes flash up and down, and he catches her each time she eyes the clerk provocatively. Emiliano's hands twist nervously and angrily in his lap. The clerk raises his eyes and looks back at the blonde, and she lets her eyes drop in invitation with what is called the "bedroom expression." Suddenly and without warning Emiliano leaps to his feet and whirls on the clerk.

EMILIANO: Get out!

CLERK (*Astonished*): Sir?

EMILIANO (*In a fury*): Get out, I said. You are relieved of your duty!

This is so unlike the Chief that the clerk can't believe his ears.

CLERK: But what, what have I done?

EMILIANO (*His fury is almost insane.*): Do you want to be shot? Get out before I have you shot!

The clerk gets up in fear and exits hurriedly, and his pen rolls slowly along the table and falls to the floor.

THE BLONDE (*Her voice is shrill and very wifelike.*): Now why did you do that? What's the matter with you lately? Nobody can get along with you. Even your friends tell me they can't get along with you. What's the matter with you? And that 'Tonio. You've always thought he was such a friend of yours, haven't you? Do you know what he said to me? He said, "Just wait until Emiliano is out of the way and—"

EMILIANO (*Shouts at her*): Shut up, you!

THE BLONDE: All right, if you don't want to know what kind of friends you have, the ones you really trust. Why your own brother—

EMILIANO (*Screams at her*): Shut up! Shut up! (*He raises his hand to slap her, then stops it in midair. He speaks with cold fury.*) Go to your room.

The blonde senses that this is as far as she can safely go. She rises and with an exaggerated ladylike hauteur she leaves the room. The door at the end of the room, on being opened, reveals stairs which the blonde climbs, and her behind wags with outrage. Emiliano puts his elbows on the table, and he beats the table slowly with his fist with a gesture of a man dealing with a woman. His eyes are sullen and angry. A man pauses in the doorway and looks left and up, and immediately his face breaks into an amused smile. Emiliano looks at him. Then offstage to the left we hear a burst of male laughter. Emiliano jumps up and goes to the door. We follow him. A group of soldiers are standing in the street looking up at the upstairs window. The blonde leans out the window exchanging jokes with them.

EMILIANO (*Shouts*): Clear the street! Quick! Come on, guards, clear the street!

The guards look up at the window and smile before they begin moving the men away. We cut to men nailing boards over the window. We cut to the bedroom door and hear the high, shrill, catlike voice of the blonde protesting, complaining. Through the closed door we hear the sound of a slap. Emiliano comes out, locks the door, goes down the stairs, and sits at the table, and again his closed fist pounds the table slowly, and from above we can hear the screams of rage from the outraged lady. Eufemio comes in, staggering a little, sits down by his brother. He hears the noise.

EUFEMIO: Why don't you turn her over to the soldiers? That would take the meanness out of her.

Emiliano does not answer.

EUFEMIO (*Continues*): You're too soft with her. Give me a stick and a key.

Emiliano still does not answer.

EUFEMIO: You're getting sick. She is making you crazy. Our Chief is gone. (*Earnestly*) Get rid of her, get rid of her.

There is a tantrum of screaming from overhead, feet beating on the floor, and a great crash. It is obvious that she is wrecking the room. Emiliano gets to his feet, his fists clench, and then he sits down again.

SCENE

The street is deserted except for our own group. There are four armed mounted horsemen. On the fifth horse sits the blonde. Her hands are tied in front of her and tied to the saddle horn. Her ankles are tied to the cinch. A handkerchief is in her mouth and held in by a strip of cloth tied behind her head. She still tries to talk and succeeds in getting out a series of growls. Eufemio stands in the doorway grinning.

EMILIANO (*Addressing the leader of the horsemen*): You are responsible for getting her to the Capital. I want her delivered to the house she came from. If she is mistreated I will hear about it. Do you understand?

SOLDIER: Yes, sir.

EMILIANO: And don't take the gag out, or she'll talk you into your own death. Now make it fast, and report back to me.

SOLDIER: Yes, sir.

The blonde tries to spit at Emiliano past the gag, and even with the gag in we can hear the shrillness of her voice. Her eyes are murderous. The troop rides away. Emiliano turns and stands in front of his brother.

EMILIANO: Eufemio, get a bottle. I'm going to get drunk.

NOTE: As time passed, Eufemio drank more and more, giving free rein to his desires, and the effects of the alcohol became increasingly and terrifyingly evident. At the same time, he gave less and less importance to the sufferings of those about him, and he delighted to make them suffer and to spill their blood. Within his own Zapatista camp he had made himself intolerable to his own men, because when he drank too much, which was almost daily, he was equally capable of acts of kindness and generosity, but was more commonly annoying everyone, injuring, striking, wounding, and even killing people.

When he was under the influence of alcohol, there was no woman who, to him, was worthy of respect. When the desire occurred to him, he would take possession of the woman who had provoked his desire, regardless of whether she was an honest woman, single or married, relative of an innocent civilian, or even related to one of his companions in arms. If he managed to excite the woman to the point where she would respond to his endearments, it was almost the same to him as if she had refused him. He possessed her at any rate.

He maintained many lovers simultaneously and had the curious custom of gathering them all together on the first day of the month, when that was possible, in the house of his favorite, where he would distribute his favors among them. This caprice naturally gave rise to a multitude of droll scenes and frequently violent quarrels among them.

Whenever he would leave his house, there was always a small group of women, children, and old folks waiting for him. The tall, slim figure of the guerrilla would appear in the doorway and immediately the anxious little group would fix their eyes upon him, trying to divine in what state of humor he might be. If they saw him smile, they precipitated themselves in greeting him and held out their hands in petition for help. And he would good-naturedly empty his pockets and divide the contents among them all, leaving himself without a penny. If, on the other hand, they saw that he was frowning in annoyance and contracted the slit of his mouth, they quickly turned away and fled, breaking up the group. But they were never so quick that he was not able to catch some of his importuners, and then he flung obscene words and injuries at them and lashed furiously at their backs with his horsewhip.

The same thing would occur in the plaza, where the sellers of refreshments would await his arrival. If they saw him approach calmly, they talked to him with affection and respect, and he would give them whatever money he was carrying. If they realized that he was approaching them in a state of drunkenness, they would flee in terror, abandoning their huge pots filled with all kinds of delightfully flavored drinks. When Eufemio would reach these vats, he would kick them over furiously and destroy them; then, next day he might well indemnify the claimant for her loss, with a good interest to boot, or he might just as well send her off with further insults and a whipping.

In battle, his soldiers had the utmost faith in him, because of his courage neighboring on daring, for the audacity of his decisions, and for the astuteness with which he planned ambuscades and small battles. But his ignorance and alcoholism caused him to commit so many arbitrary acts and injustices that he soon made himself hated by his troops who, like the peaceful civilians, began to tremble with fear before him and never dared to cross him in anything.

Eufemio began to annoy Emiliano so greatly with his excesses that one day Emiliano reprimanded him with much greater severity than usual. The older brother, highly displeased, told him that if he disturbed him it would be better if he left him altogether. Emiliano immediately took him at his word, saying that since it was impossible to correct him and he was bringing about a drop in the prestige of their cause, it would be better if he did leave general headquarters. Eufemio did as he asked, but without giving up his arms; he continued fighting as a guerrilla with a small group of his troops.

Eufemio was a true peasant, savage, aggressive, passionate, with some traces of generosity and many of cruelty. His lack of culture was absolute, but his wiliness was great. Intractable and disdainful of any discipline, he refused to go to school, for which reason he never learned to read or write as a child. It was not until he was a young man that he saw his first letters and learned how to write. This was due to the fact that he had then committed a murder and was captured and imprisoned in the jail at Cuautla. There he met Everardo Espinosa, owner of a mercantile establishment called "La Universal," a man who was well known and respected in that town and who was also a prisoner, but not for any dreadful crime. He was the victim of an unfortunate accident that in no way affected his honor, and he now took advantage of his imprisonment to aid his companions in captivity, who were for the most part destitute and ignorant. Espinosa made himself liked and respected by the delinquents, helping them with money, giving them advice, and teaching them to read and write. He was the one who at that time was able to teach Eufemio. Since Eufemio was now unoccupied, he allowed himself to be persuaded by the businessman, and he applied himself to his studies barely enough to learn half-way to read and write.

Eufemio had sudden ideas that scandalized everyone who heard them and which were, in reality, merely manifestations of his melancholy, infantile, and inconsiderate nature, which would cause him to execute some completely ingenuous act as well as one of extreme cruelty. Among these, a droll case is recalled: When the Zapatistas were encamped at San Angel, Eufemio and several of his men arrived on horseback at the Plaza of San Jacinto in the very moment that the electric tram was starting its return journey to Mexico City. In that instant, he had the bright idea of going to the city, but he pondered that it would take a long time to travel on horseback the ten or twelve kilometers between the place he was and the center of the city, a trip which could be made on the trolley car in half an hour. So he mounted the car, horse and all, followed by four of five of his men, provoking great consternation and fright among the passengers who had already installed themselves in their seats in the vehicle. The indignant motorman protested to Eufemio and demanded that he immediately leave the tram. On the spot, a .44 pistol flashed in Eufemio's hand and under this menace the poor employee drove the train to the Plaza de la Constitución, stopping at last before the doors of the National Palace itself. The motorman left the car quickly and asked for help. A picket of soldiers from the Palace guard approached and tried to apprehend the extraordinary passengers on the car, while a great number of curious passersby milled about trying to see what was going on. With the threatening attitude of the soldiers and the disdainful one of Eufemio and his men, the comedy might easily have become transformed into a tragedy. However, the Villista colonel who was then in charge of the Palace guard approached

the scene of the scandalous goings on, recognized the brother of
the Chief of the Army of the South, and ordered his men to let
him go in peace. The spectators of the scene were profoundly
disgusted but, on learning that the leader of the men was Eufemio
Zapata, whose reputation was only too well known and remembered,
they didn't dare to insist that the picturesque horseman be
punished.

Only half satisfied with his feat, the fumes of the alcohol now
inspired him with a still more daring idea—to install himself in
the ancient residence of the Chiefs of the Executive branch of the
government of the country. The colonel in charge of the district
tried to dissuade him, but Eufemio was insistent. Realizing that
rather than retreat, Eufemio would draw his pistol, and fearing the
consequences that might result if he were forced to fire upon the
southern general, he permitted him to enter the Palace and to
install himself at will in one of the bedrooms on the ground floor
of the old edifice, where Eufemio remained for several days.

On the day of his death, Eufemio, who had already had a few
drinks too many, entered the butcher shop of Señor Torres, his
friend, with whom he began to converse. A little girl, daughter of
the shopkeeper, entered the establishment, and Eufemio took her
in his arms, raised her to the level of his face, and kissed her. It
was strange to see a man like Eufemio, who had so often and in
so many unsavory ways kissed women, now kissing for the last
time in such an innocent manner. He continued to chat with the
butcher, at the same time taking from his belt a sharp dagger which
he slowly drove deep into a leg of lamb that was within his reach.

From the butcher shop, he went to the tavern "El Clarín de
los Gallos," where he remained, drinking many cups. Already
noticeably drunk, he started out into the street and approached
some stalls where cotton shirting was sold. He began to reproach
the merchants, telling them they demanded exaggerated prices for
their goods and then rebuking them as suspect of treason, since
the nature of their business permitted them to make frequent trips
to the factories of Puebla and Veracruz, within the territory oc-

cupied by the Carrancistas. He insulted one old man with particular hardness. The old man, who became indignant at this torrent of abuse, replied with great energy. This impelled Eufemio to bring out his machete and to wave it back and forth over the poor old man, striking him blow after blow. The old man was the father of one of Zapata's bravest officers, Sidronio Camacho.

Shortly after, Camacho, Jr., who was called "*el loco* Sidronio" (crazy Sidronio), heard about this occurrence, took his .30-.30 carbine in hand, and went in search of Eufemio, whom he found in the plaza. Camacho called him to account, and the two approached each other, while Eufemio made excuses and slipped his hand toward his pistol. Seeing this, Camacho started violently back from his opponent, in an effort to gain sufficient room to be able to move his rifle with liberty.

The first pistol shot that sounded came from the gun of Eufemio, but it did not find its mark. Camacho jumped toward the sidewalk, protecting himself behind a column, while Eufemio remained out in the open. Both contenders began to shoot and soon Camacho, who had remained more calm and was protected and better armed, overcame his enemy with a soft-nosed bullet from his rifle, which left a horrible wound in Eufemio's abdomen. Camacho approached the fallen man, realizing that he was already incapacitated for any further defense and was irremediably condemned to die. Eufemio also understood this, and thus asked his assailant to kill him at once so that he would not continue to suffer. But the avenger only replied:

"You have made many people suffer a great deal. Live a little longer, so that you also will learn what it is to suffer."

He dragged the wounded man along the ground despite his feeble protests and mounted him upon his horse. Then, climbing upon the haunches of the animal, he tied Eufemio to the saddle and set out precipitately from Cuautla, taking the road through a neighboring village and heading for the Carrancista lines. He was thinking of taking the corpse of the brother of his Chief to their enemies, which would assure him of a jubilant reception from the government forces and would enable him to elude the vengeance of Emiliano.

However, since Eufemio was constantly losing his balance, toppling from one side to another, Camacho realized that he could not advance except very gradually, which would give those who had witnessed his deed in Cuautla time to organize a party to pursue and catch up with him. He, therefore, abandoned his original idea, alighted from his horse, took down his victim and threw him face down into an anthill, in one last gesture of cruel and unsatisfied vengeance. He left the dying man thus exposed to the crawling ants whose bites would add a new torment to that which he was already suffering.

Shortly afterward, some women, led by Eufemio's favorite lover, before whose house he had fallen wounded, followed Camacho at a distance. This no man had made the slightest attempt to do, whether through the more probable consideration that the act had been fully justified, or through mere fear. The women soon reached the man who was now in his death throes, and tried to stanch the flow of his blood, improvising a bandage. They brought him back to Cuautla, to the house of his lover. Once in the city, they sent for a doctor, who did everything within his power to try to save his life, even though he knew it was useless, and he had to fail. At nine o'clock that same night, after horrible suffering, General Eufemio Zapata, brother of the great Chief of the Revolution of the South, breathed his last.

When Eufemio was killed, Emiliano was directing a campaign about fifty miles away. Messengers immediately rode at breakneck speed to inform him. The engagement was going on when they arrived. Emiliano, as usual, had found a position on a small hill where he could overlook the fighting.

SCENE

We see him looking down on the valley. But he is screened with
bushes so that he does not make a target of himself. In the wooded
valley below there is a great deal of firing with small arms, but no
soldiers are visible. There are some little clearings, and occasionally we see a man leap across a clearing and disappear again in
the undergrowth. A messenger rides near, dismounts and walks
up behind Emiliano.

MESSENGER: My General!

EMILIANO (*Does not look around*): In a moment, in a moment.

MESSENGER: I have bad news, sir.

EMILIANO: In a moment, in a moment. (*He is looking intently down
into the valley.*)

MESSENGER (*Doggedly*): Your brother has been killed, sir.

EMILIANO (*Curtly*): In a moment. (*We see his face as the information
gets into his head. We see his brain slowly take it up. We see
the face change, his shoulders slump a little; his eyes still
looking out on the valley become tragic and hopeless. And it
is possible to see such changes in a face and posture.*)

The messenger stands respectfully behind him, and we see
Emiliano reconquer himself, his face tighten up, lids drooping over
the eyes to conceal their pain, the shoulders straighten. Emiliano
turns slowly to the messenger and he speaks without emotion.

EMILIANO (*Slowly*): How was he killed?

MESSENGER: In a fight, sir, with one of our officers.

EMILIANO (*His Indian rage and sorrow break through. He is a cat
now.*): Where is that officer?

MESSENGER: He escaped to the enemy, sir. I guess he knew you
would kill him.

EMILIANO: Where is my brother?

MESSENGER: In Cuautla, sir. The people say he was wrong in the
fight.

EMILIANO: (*He speaks with overwhelming pity, to himself.*): In the
wrong. Yes, he was always in the wrong. (*It is a statement of*

love for his brother. He calls an aide to him and barks at him.)
You remember the plan and the action?

AIDE: Yes, sir.

EMILIANO: They are about ready to break. When they go, follow, but don't let the men disperse. Keep the troops together, pursue slowly, and don't let the enemy camp or sleep or in any way settle down to rest. Keep them moving.

AIDE: Yes, sir.

EMILIANO: I will be back when I can.

SCENE: We see Emiliano and three armed men riding hard. The Chief's face is set. His eyes look straight ahead. He is driving an exhausted horse to further exhaustion, which he rarely did.

ONE OF THE MEN (*Calls to him*): Sir. (*Emiliano looks around at him.*) Ahead is the cemetery we made for our fallen men, sir. Why don't you wait for us there? We will bring him to you.

EMILIANO (*Harshly*): He was not killed in battle; he cannot lie there. (*They ride on by the little cemetery.*)

SCENE: A street in front of Eufemio's house in Cuautla. (It is still in existence and can be used.) The street is crowded with people—silent men, women, and children. An old woman is weaving marigolds into a little frame on the front door. Marigolds are the flowers of the dead. We see Emiliano and his men ride into the street. The crowd separates as though a rope forced it apart. Emiliano rides woodenly to the door of the house. He dismounts, dropping his reins to the ground. Every man in the group takes off his hat and holds it over his chest. Emiliano says no word, and no one speaks to him. But an Indian picks up the ends of the bridle reins and holds them almost reverently against his chest. The old woman, who has been arranging the flowers, opens the door and stands back, and Emiliano walks through. His aides do not follow.

SCENE

Eufemio is laid out in the traditional Mexican manner. His body lies on two boards and is covered to the waist with a white cloth. His upper body is dressed in a silver-embroidered *charro* jacket. A crucifix is propped in his crossed hands, so that he seems to press it against his chest. A candle burns on either side of his head. A number of women, their heads covered with dark blue rebozos, stand about the room next to the wall. They are the same women who have brought Eufemio back from the anthill. When Emiliano comes in, they drift silently to the door and slip out, and close the door. But as the door is opened we see a crowd of people in the street, their heads bare and standing in complete silence.

NOTE: Mexican men do not cry in real stress. I have seen them cry for love or for some trouble which is not too deep; but when they are very deeply moved, their Indian blood takes over. Their eyes may be a little shiny, but tears do not flow.

Emiliano stands over his brother, looking down. His carbine is in his hand. His face is bleak. He stands for a long time looking down at his brother, and the curious, compelling love he has always had for him must be indicated without speech. His is a brooding inside sorrow, not one that has any possible escape. Finally he bends over and kisses the back of his brother's hand, as he always has done. Then he stands very straight and says: Adios. Adios, Eufemio. He turns and strides to the door, rushes to his horse and leaps into the saddle. The Indian hands him his reins. He wheels the horse. The people leap out of his way, for they know that he does not even see them. The women are creeping through the door into the house again. We see Emiliano, followed by his aides, ride rapidly down the street in the direction from which they came. Emiliano's shoulders are back, and he is on his way back to the fight.

NOTE: The plot and murder of Emiliano Zapata is pure melodrama. But it happened. It is a complicated and touchy affair, and it is one of the places where we might have trouble with censorship unless we handle it very carefully. For many people of importance, who are still in the government, were concerned in this dirty affair. For this reason I am going to simplify and to mention no names.

Since Colonel Guajardo was honored, paid, and reinstated for carrying out the murder, he became an honorable man. But in the encyclopedia *Historia de la Revolución*, which carries thousands of photographs, his is not included, as though even the government which employed and rewarded him was ashamed of him. There is some obscurity about his background, but from a number of sources this seems to be the story:

Carranza, realizing that he could not defeat or catch Zapata, was determined to have him murdered. Looking around for a tool, he hit on ex-Colonel Guajardo. This man had been cashiered from the army for forgery. Guajardo was approached by the high brass of the federal army and offered reinstatement, increase in rank, and a reward if he could carry out a plan that had been worked over by the military brass of the army. Simply, he was to "go over" to Zapata with his regiment and, once in the confidence of Zapata, to kill him.

It was a fairly dangerous mission, because no one knew what soldiers would really go over to Zapata. It happened all the time that Federal troops deserted to his cause. The matter had to be handled with great care because household servants, soldiers in the ranks, and poor people in general had the habit of communicating suspicious moves to Zapata.

Before he accomplished his mission Guajardo had to do very drastic things. He had to kill Federal troops, hang Federal officials, attack a Federal garrison with considerable losses on both sides. However, he had been given carte blanche. His end was to kill Zapata, and he could use any means he saw fit. It was a cloak-and-dagger matter, but it really happened, and it is documented.

As I have said, I am simplifying and using no names. I think this will get us by the censorship. Indeed I have been assured by an official in the censor's office that this method would go a long way in removing any tendency to interfere.

SCENE

We will use Carranza but will not use his name. He is to us a General of very high rank. Carranza wore a huge fan-shaped beard, by which he will be recognized whether he is named or not. In our scene, he is meeting with a staff of high officers, probably in the National Palace. The officers are in very formal uniforms, but their collars are open, and it is apparently toward the end of a long and tiring conference. We shall call Carranza simply The General. His staff will simply be made up of lesser generals and colonels.

THE GENERAL (*His hands are restless in his beard. He punishes it and then smooths it down, over and over again. He wears rather thick glasses.*): The man is a devil. He is not human. We defeat him, we destroy him, and he is back in another place with another army. And we cannot wear him out. Last week when we thought we were attacking him, he was attacking our garrison forty miles away. Gentlemen, this man must be removed; somehow, he must be removed.

A LEAN-FACED COLONEL (*Speaks very slowly and clearly*): My General, is the method of his removal of any importance?

THE GENERAL (*Smiles bitterly*): We have tried everything, as you well know. Ambush seems impossible. He has escaped every kind. Assassination is impossible. We cannot get near him. Surprise seems impossible. (*In despair*) Why, the hills and the trees and the rocks report to him. I am told he never sleeps twice in the same place. For that matter, he never seems to sleep at all.

LEAN-FACED COLONEL: And we are losing men, my General?

THE GENERAL: You know we are, hundreds, and not only men, weapons and towns. And worse than that, we are being laughed at. This little tiger is outfighting and outrunning us.

LEAN-FACED COLONEL: Then if the method were drastic it would still be considered worthwhile?

THE GENERAL: Drastic?

THE COLONEL: I mean, if a few more of our men were killed in accomplishing the death of this man, it might be considered that they died in action?

THE GENERAL: You have a plan?

THE COLONEL: I think I have, my General. Have I your permission to draw up my plan, make certain inquiries, and submit the whole to your judgment?

THE GENERAL (*He punishes his beard badly while he thinks.*): You have. But make your written plans very full. And let me warn you that if very many people know this plan, the little tiger will know it too. I don't know *how* he gets his information.

SCENE

We dissolve to one of the dirty, ill-lit doleful streets of Mexico City. It is in a bad district, and it is night. The terrible little bars are open. People are sleeping drunkenly in the streets. Out of little dim-lighted bars raucous music is coming. It is a ghostly time. Over the half-doors of some of the houses women are leaning out, and on the street corners the prostitutes are hustling wearily. The hungry dogs are feeding on every scrap of filth. It is the sad hilarity of 3 A.M. in the poor part of Mexico. We see the figure of our Colonel walking through this district. His military coat is buttoned high around his face; his cap is pulled down. He is solicited by the women who stand on the corners, and he does not even look around or answer them. When we have established the district, we see the Colonel turn into a dark doorway. We see him light a match to find a narrow stairway.

Now we see a poor, tawdry bedroom. Two figures are dimly

visible in a narrow bed. We hear a knock on the door, and then another. The man in the bed is aroused.

MAN: Who is it?

VOICE OUTSIDE: Eduardo.

MAN: What do you want?

EDUARDO: I want to see you. It's important.

The man in the bed lights a match and with it lights a candle. It is a poverty-stricken little room, but with some attempt at gaiety. There is a brilliant calendar on the wall, a wash basin, and pitcher on a chest. The bed is one of those curly brass horrors.

First the man covers the head of his companion with a blanket. Then he reaches under his pillow and takes out a pistol, looks at it in the candlelight and puts his hand holding it under the blanket. He has the lean and hungry look of a sick wolf.

MAN: Come in.

EDUARDO: The door is locked.

MAN: The door is never locked. It has no lock. Push it. (*The door squeaks open and the Colonel enters the room.*)

EDUARDO: I want to talk to you. (*And as he sees that there is someone else in the bed:*) This is private business.

MAN: What business, Eduardo? I have been punished. Do they want more?

EDUARDO: No. This is private business. Perhaps for you, good business. (*He points silently at the covered figure in the bed.*) Put on your clothes. I'll wait for you below.

MAN: Can't it wait until morning?

EDUARDO: It can't wait an instant. Come quickly. (*He goes.*)

SCENE

We see one of the small low-lit bars. At a table well away from the bar sit our Colonel Eduardo and the man who was in the bed. The second man shows in his clothing and in his face a life of despair. His once good clothing is battered, and his once good

face is battered too. He is unshaven. Here is an aristocrat gone to
pieces. The two men drink sparingly as they talk.

EDUARDO (*It is apparent that he has finished telling him.*): And there
   it is. There is only one thing more which I have not told you.

MAN: And what is that?

EDUARDO: That is for later. (*The man drains his drink and pours
   another; he looks at it gloomily. At length, he speaks:*)

MAN: You know my history, Eduardo—drink, gambling, forgery,
   cashiered from the army—a rascal going down the pig slide
   to death. (*He reaches out and touches the Colonel's sleeve.*)
   But Eduardo, I have never, never, thought of such a thing as
   this. Forgive me, Eduardo. I do not want to do it.

EDUARDO: Consider again. Reinstatement in your colonelcy and a
   reward. If you are successful, a raise in rank, a general. With
   one cut the black past is wiped out.

MAN: And a black present substituted.

EDUARDO: Consider again that these things will be in the service
   of your country.

MAN (*Shakes his head numbly, as though he wants to shake out a
   thought*): I cannot somehow think of murder as a service to
   my country.

EDUARDO: Is that for you to judge?

MAN: Yes, I think so. If I were angry, if he were my enemy, that
   would be different. But it seems to me, Eduardo, that murder
   to a gentleman is a very personal thing.

EDUARDO (*Sardonically*): Gentleman?

MAN: Yes. You would be surprised, but a little of that remains.
   My sins have been against myself so far. But this, no, Eduardo, forgive me if I thank you and ask your permission to
   refuse.

EDUARDO (*Studies him closely. He is as cruel and hard as steel. He
   is what is known as a man of the world. Now his voice turns
   silky.*): I have spoken first as a patriot, and second as your
   friend.

MAN: I know, Eduardo, and I thank you, but . . .

EDUARDO: Remember the sequence. I said there was one other thing. I am sorry for it. This plan will be carried out, if not by you, then by someone else. But you know this plan now . . . (*He lets his voice remain in the air. The man's eyes snap from his glass to the Colonel's eyes. He studies him very deeply, looks layers down into his eyes. The Colonel stares back at him. The man finally tosses his drink down.*)

MAN (*Speaks finally*): I see. (*He coughs as the hot liquor gags him. He comes out of his coughing spell. He reaches for a hand-kerchief; there is none. He wipes his eyes on his sleeve. He breathes deeply.*) I see. (*He pours his glass full from the bottle. His hand is not very steady. And he stares into his drink.*)

MAN: Do you think I might just be put in prison, where I could be of no danger?

EDUARDO (*Softly*): There are guards and wardens in prison. Men go in and out.

MAN: Yes. (*He speaks very slowly.*) Then, if I reduce it to its elements, it is this man's life or mine.

(*The Colonel does not speak, simply looks at him.*)

MAN: May I have an hour to decide?

EDUARDO: An hour? Yes, but not alone.

Now we see the man's face, his eyes inward, turning over the value of his own life.

NOTE: Since little seems to be known of the character of Guajardo, we can recreate him only from a very few suggestions. As a straight heavy he is not very interesting, but as a man surrounded and forced to murder he can be much more interesting. The circumstances are certainly plausible, indicated by some queer little bits of oblique evidence. The men in power were without morals. Besides, I like the idea of the rascal having compunction where the *gente decente* had none. I think we make the dramatic impact more sharp by making the heavy as much a victim as the victim.

However, this, like everything else in this script, is subject to discussion.

SCENE

It is a little hilltop overlooking a camp of guerrillas. The camp has very little equipment because Zapata's guerrillas carried very little equipment with them. Horses, guns and ammunition, and a little corn for food. Otherwise, they lived on the country. It is interesting that while all of the other armies, both Federal and Revolutionary, allowed women to accompany the men, Zapata never permitted women to follow his troops. It is true that he had women soldiers, but they were soldiers—not camp followers. It is likely that this was more military than moral; his men moved too fast to be encumbered.

Emiliano is seated under a little tree. He whips his leg with a quirt. Seated beside him is a humble-looking little man in thick glasses, dressed in clothing that would be worn by a schoolteacher of the period. This probably would be an ill-fitting business suit, a coat without lapels, and a round, small hat. The two are in conversation.

SCHOOLTEACHER: The message came through our usual sources. Naturally I took precautions. The Colonel says he wants to come over to our side.

EMILIANO: How many men has he?

SCHOOLTEACHER: A regiment.

EMILIANO: How equipped?

SCHOOLTEACHER: The best. New Mausers, machine guns, eight pieces of artillery, that new kind General Angeles invented —75 mm—and with ammunition.

EMILIANO: You looked into the Colonel's background? I have never heard of him.

SCHOOLTEACHER: Yes, I did. And here I recommend caution. He

has had some trouble and was removed from the army, and then he was brought back.

EMILIANO (*Laughs*): Do you think that I am a fool? They should know better.

SCHOOLTEACHER: I saw no reason why I should not ask him directly. He says he was falsely accused, that he hates his superiors, that he worked his way back so that when he came to you it would not be empty-handed.

EMILIANO: Do they think that I'm so stupid that I would let a regiment in arms come near me?

SCHOOLTEACHER: He had thought about that. He saw how you might think, and he suggested a test of his loyalty to you.

EMILIANO: And what test does he suggest?

SCHOOLTEACHER: He leaves it to you to suggest one.

EMILIANO (*Snaps his whip against his leg with little explosions while he thinks. Then he smiles.*): Well, let us start small things and work up to large. Then if he is lying, we will still be ahead. Let me see. Well, in the place he is occupying, the chief of police and the Federal liaison executed some of our people. Let the Colonel hang these men and have some of our people observe it so we will know.

SCHOOLTEACHER (*Stands up*): Yes, sir, my General. (*He is smiling too.*) And if he does that?

EMILIANO: In his garrison there is a squad which burned and raped in our territory, you know the ones?

SCHOOLTEACHER: Yes, sir.

EMILIANO: As a second test, let them be shot.

SCHOOLTEACHER: And if he does that?

EMILIANO: Then we will find other work for him, waiting. If he should follow these two orders, then let him openly declare for us and attack the Federal forces at Jonocatepec.

SCHOOLTEACHER: These are my orders?

EMILIANO: Those are your orders.

The next scenes will show the orders of Emiliano carried out by the Colonel and will be designed for their greatest effectiveness.

I suggest that the men be shot by indirection—the hanging of the two officials possibly conveyed by sound (not, for God's sake, with shadows on a wall). Perhaps the scene could be effective in this way:

SCENE: We see the two men bound, with ropes around their necks. (Mexican hangings are not done with a gallows or traps. A tree limb, a telegraph post, something of the sort. The man is drawn up and left to strangle.) I suggest that the scene be played on the Colonel's face and on the face of the schoolteacher, who watches. The schoolteacher watches, not the hanging, but the face of the Colonel. And I should like to convey the hopeless disgust of the Colonel for his job.)

SCENE: The execution of soldiers who have mistreated Zapatistas and their families. (There is a picture I will furnish of an execution, and its particular horror lies in the wall behind the man being shot. There are two man-shaped targets on either side of him, completely riddled with bullets, and the wall behind is pitted not only near the targets but as much as ten feet over and beyond. At twenty feet it is difficult to miss this far.) For this scene I suggest a little column of men, three abreast, waiting to be shot, three at a time. I would play this scene on the faces of the men left as each three are taken forward. And again I would go back to the Colonel and his observer, the schoolteacher, who will be standing nearby.

SCENE: A room with a table and benches, as usual. The schoolteacher is sitting beside the Colonel. The Colonel has been drinking, and continues to drink. He speaks with an attempt at jocularity.

COLONEL: Well, that should satisfy the General. When can I turn over my regiment?

SCHOOLTEACHER (*His eyes are baleful behind his thick-lensed glasses.*): The Chief requests that you now start in service to him. This is not so much a test as, well, you have a well-armed force and it is available, and we need it.

COLONEL (*His mouth is a little slack from drinking.*): And what are his orders?

SCHOOLTEACHER: You are to attack the garrison at Jonocatepec and destroy it.

COLONEL (*Laughs, uneasily*): How, how large is the garrison?

SCHOOLTEACHER: You should know.

COLONEL: Of course, of course. I don't know, but I can find out. When is the attack desired?

SCHOOLTEACHER: Immediately.

COLONEL: Tonight?

SCHOOLTEACHER: As soon as you can move effectively. (*His eyes never leave the Colonel's face.*)

SCENE: Now we see a full-scale attack by the regiment on the little town of Jonocatepec. It is a furious, full-scale attack, and there is no playacting in it. There is no quarter given. Indeed, at this period there rarely was. Prisoners were shot. In the shots of the Colonel, we see a man who is nearly mad with his mission. He can attack with even an increased ferocity because his feelings are so hurt, just as a basically moral man can be more degenerate than an amoral one. The town is taken and the defenders scattered or killed. The losses are heavy on both sides.

SCENE: The Colonel and the schoolteacher are walking through the shattered town. Dead men and animals are still in the streets.

SCHOOLTEACHER: You have the congratulations and thanks of the Chief. He asks you to come and eat with him.

COLONEL (*Excitedly*): He is here?

SCHOOLTEACHER: He is somewhere, not too far away. (*He feels that he's been too cold. He takes the Colonel's arm.*) It is a habit, you know, and one that you should learn. We never say where the Chief is to anyone. It has become a habit with us. You will learn it, I hope.

COLONEL (*He looks at the little man; his revulsion is in his face.*): I, I am not well. I think, if he will excuse me, I am not well. I cannot eat with him. I must lie down.

SCHOOLTEACHER: I will tell him.

COLONEL: He will come to the hacienda of Chinameca to receive the regiment and the supplies?

SCHOOLTEACHER: I cannot speak for him. The supplies are there?

COLONEL: All of them—guns, ammunition, horses, artillery.

SCHOOLTEACHER: I will tell him. Your permission, sir? (*He turns and walks away.*)

COLONEL (*Wanders along the street. His eyes are blank. He speaks very softly to himself*): Oh! But I couldn't *eat* with him.

NOTE: The above incident is taken from the account of General Castrajon, who says: "Zapata invited him to dinner, but Guajardo pretended to be ill and begged permission to be excused."

SCENE

A thatched shepherd's hut in the hills above Chinameca. It is more of a shelter than a house, three stone walls with a grass roof. It is evening. We see Josefa, a worn, tired, older woman now, with all the freshness and bloom gone from her. She is cooking on a tiny fire, patting out tortillas, like an Indian. The little pottery jars are being kept hot on the edge of the fire. She cooks the tortillas on a flat plate. Emiliano is sitting on the ground not far from her. The little glow of the fire lights his face.

NOTE: Toward the end of his life, his face became skull-like, and his eyes had a piercing, yet faraway look. For verification of this see photographs of him standing beside Villa in Chapultepec which show this same expression. His face had a luminous quality, as though the head were very thin and a light was inside. Zapata seems to have foreseen his own death, just as Lincoln did. Many speeches are imputed to him, and probably some of them he really said.

It is possible that the visit of the *curandera* to him the night before his death is folklore, but it is a story that is believed; although my use of the first *curandera* is an invention. However, it is told that he was visited by an old woman on this night—a witch.

Emiliano is speaking to someone beside him in the darkness, and only gradually do we see that it is the schoolteacher.

EMILIANO: He knows, of course, that his men must be drawn up outside the walls and without arms?

SCHOOLTEACHER: He was informed.

EMILIANO: You looked at him closely? How did he seem?

SCHOOLTEACHER: He looked ill, as he said he was.

EMILIANO (*He sighs very deeply.*): So, that is that.

SCHOOLTEACHER: You still suspect a trick?

EMILIANO: I always expect a trick. That is why I have lived as long as I have. I always give my enemy credit for being as intelligent as I am. If he is not, I have lost nothing; if he is, we are at least equal.

SCHOOLTEACHER: You have taken every precaution. But why do you go yourself? Why not send someone else?

EMILIANO: I do not know. I am drawn to go. My judgment in these things has usually been correct. And still, I feel a sadness.

JOSEFA: Will you eat now?

EMILIANO: Yes, Josefa. (*His voice is very gentle when he speaks to her.*)

She brings the pottery bowl with the covered tortillas and the little pitchers of sauce and meat to go in them.

JOSEFA: Will you take chocolate?

EMILIANO: Why, yes.

Josefa goes back to the fire. In another pitcher she beats the chocolate by whirling the little stick beater between her palms. From down the hill we hear a sentry's challenge. Emiliano looks. A soldier appears in the evening light. He approaches Emiliano.

SOLDIER: It is an old woman. She says she knows you.

EMILIANO: I know many old women.

SOLDIER: She says she helped at your birth.

EMILIANO (*His face lights up with one of his rare smiles.*): Why, of course. Let her come to me.

The soldier disappears in the darkness. In a moment, the *curandera* crawls like a big ant close to the fire. She is as wrinkled as smoked meat. Her skin is a mesh of wrinkles. All of her joints are crooked, so that she seems to crawl rather than to walk.

CURANDERA (*Speaks with excitement*): My Chief—they say you are going to meet a Colonel at Chinameca tomorrow.

EMILIANO (*In alarm*): Who says?

CURANDERA (*She squats down in front of him. Her head shakes in a kind of ancient palsy.*): I don't remember. Maybe I just thought it. Sometimes I know things. I foretold your birth, you know.

EMILIANO: Yes, I have heard.

CURANDERA: You are not to go there. You will be killed. Do you hear me? It is a trick. It is an ambush.

EMILIANO (*Quietly*): How do you know?

CURANDERA (*Her head shakes more and more, and her eyes are vague.*): I don't know. Maybe I just thought it, but I'm sure it is a trick.

EMILIANO (*Curtly, to shake her out of her maundering*): Tell me quickly. Do you know any fact?

CURANDERA: I just feel that you will be killed.

EMILIANO (*Now he speaks as much to the schoolteacher and to Josefa as to the* curandera. *Josefa stops whipping the chocolate to listen.*): I have taken every precaution. I have questioned everything. If I am wrong, I feel it must be that way.

CURANDERA: And if they kill you?

EMILIANO: There have been men who, dying, have become stronger. I can think of many of them—Benito Juárez, Abraham Lincoln, Jesus Christ . . . (*A silence falls on the little hut. Emiliano continues, almost as though he saw into a future.*) Perhaps it might be that way with me.

NOTE: He really said this, and mentioned those three names.

Emiliano very slowly makes a taco of a tortilla, pouring a little dark sauce into it, rolling it up, restraining the end away from him between his third and little finger. He bites into it, and stares straight ahead. Josefa brings him the little *jarro* of chocolate.

He takes it and, without thanks and still chewing, drinks some of it. It is apparent that he does not even know that he is eating.

CURANDERA (*Speaks eagerly*): Emiliano, do you still have the manito?

Still chewing, he opens his shirt and shows her the birthmark. She peers close with her old eyes until she sees it, and then her face breaks into a childish smile. She touches it with her finger.

CURANDERA: Of course! Why, there it is, and I was the first in all the world to see it.

EMILIANO (*Swallowing*): Is it any bigger?

CURANDERA: No, not bigger, nor not as bright. (*Then, as though a wind of fear blows on her, she cries:*) Emiliano! Do not go, do not go!

EMILIANO (*Impatiently*): Now that's enough. Let's have no more of it. Do you hear? Go away now. (*He buttons his shirt. He shivers.*)

CURANDERA (*She rises painfully to her feet, and she speaks with dignity.*): Good night, Josefa. Good night, Emiliano. Go with God. (*She goes off into the darkness.*)

SCHOOLTEACHER: Good night, sir.

The moon is rising over the mountain peaks to the east, the high jagged peaks of Morelos. It is a pale half moon.

JOSEFA (*Still squatting by her little fire*): Will you eat more?

EMILIANO: No.

JOSEFA: What are you looking at?

EMILIANO: The moon.

JOSEFA: Nothing more?

EMILIANO: Nothing more.

Josefa moves slowly to him and sits down beside him. His hand moves and touches her arm. Her whole body seems to snuggle, to fold, to flow toward him, yet does not touch him.

JOSEFA: A beautiful moon, Emiliano, beautiful! (*Her face loses some of its age and weariness, and her eyes light up.*) Emiliano, you know what it reminds me of? Do you remember . . .

EMILIANO (*In anguish*): Don't remember, don't remember, don't!

(*His voice is like a cry of pain.*) Just let your mind float . . .
(*And then more softly*) Let it float in nothing . . . (*More softly*)
in nothing.

Josefa is old again; the light has gone from her eyes. And
Emiliano is skull-faced, and his eyes are wet.

JOSEFA (*With a pleading tone*): Emiliano, will there ever be peace?
EMILIANO (*Nods as though hypnotized*): Yes, there will be peace.
(*Again his hand goes to her arm, and again, as we have seen
earlier, she puts her forehead down on his shoulder.*)

NOTE: Now that the trap is ready and baited, I submit to the
director that the murder move quickly, with an almost mechanical
feeling. He can use almost any kind of suspense he wants, but in
my opinion inevitability is more important than the suspense at
this point.

SCENE

We see the ancient hacienda of Chinameca, one of the oldest and
strongest in the country. It is a heavy-walled structure, built to
withstand siege. It has a huge, wooden double door which gives
entrance to a huge courtyard. There is no use describing it, because
it is still there. We see the disarmed regiment of Guajardo sitting,
standing, leaning, lying outside the wall. We move into the courtyard through the great door. The bait is at the far end of the
courtyard—the field guns, cases of ammunition, the stacked rifles
of the regiment. And in front of the pile of munitions, a little table
is set with white linen and silver. There are bottles of wine and
brandy on the table. It is a clean, inviting table.

We see the Colonel standing in the middle of the courtyard.
He is looking up the surrounding walls. We follow his eyes. About
twenty-five men with rifles are on the walls, on the roofs and in
the windows. They are watching the Colonel intently. He motions
with his hand, and they disappear from sight. This is the trap,

very carefully worked out and very carefully practiced. Each man is perfectly concealed. The Colonel raises his hand and they appear again, their rifles leveled.

There is the sound of a horse's hooves. The Colonel drops his hand. The men disappear. A lieutenant rides through the gate.

LIEUTENANT: Coming.

COLONEL: Very well. (*He walks out through the gate into the road.*)

Five mounted men are approaching. They ride near and salute the Colonel respectfully, and immediately go about their business. Two of them ride slowly past the regiment looking for arms. The other three ride in through the gate to the courtyard. The Colonel waits on foot in the road, and only his tense body and his hands show his anxiety. After a moment, the three men ride out of the gate, and the other two join them. Their leader waves his hat, and far down the road a man leaps up and waves his hat. It is a relay signal.

Now we see Emiliano riding at the head of a column of his men. He comes up to the Colonel and looks at his own men. The leader of the men gestures with his head to indicate that all is well inside. Emiliano dismounts and steps close to the Colonel. He opens his arms for the formal embrace. For a moment the Colonel cannot bring himself to accept this, but finally he does. The *abrazo* is completed. Emiliano turns and looks through the great door. He can see the stack of munitions. His eyes glow.

EMILIANO: Now here is a prize we need. (*He smiles at the Colonel.*)
 And not the least is that little white table there, and those little red bottles. You are very thoughtful, Colonel.

COLONEL: I am very happy that you are pleased, my General. Shall we go in? (*They turn and walk together to the door. They pause. The Colonel gestures that Emiliano should go first. He refuses.*)

EMILIANO: After all, it is your house.

COLONEL: But now it is yours.

EMILIANO (*Rubs his hands together*): Come, my friend, we shall not have ceremony. We shall go together. (*A bugler of the regiment blows a call. Emiliano pauses to listen. He speaks gaily.*) He is good, that one. (*He moves forward, the Colonel beside him. One, two, three, four, five steps.*)

Suddenly the Colonel flings up his hand and leaps back into the shelter of the thick gate. Emiliano stares around at him, and in that instant comes the volley. Emiliano is pounded with slugs, the racking pound of heavy lead on his body. He falls to the ground, and a second volley hammers his body. The Colonel cannot look at it; he turns and looks into the road.

Scene

A little ill-made obelisk in Cuautla. It is a sun-bitten, poor little thing. In our scene, a group of men in field clothes and women in the dark blue rebozos of the country are standing in front of the little monument. A cackling voice talks to them. Their faces are wooden. Seated on the ground is the *curandera*. She is very ancient now, ancient beyond belief, but there are many of her in Mexico.

CURANDERA (*Her voice cackles with laughter.*): And so he fooled them all. I saw the body. I looked close; there was no *manito* on the chest. It was not the tiger. It was not the beloved tiger. He fooled them all. (*A man breaks into a smile of pleasure. She continues:*) And do you want more proof? Well, are you whipped anymore? Are you held to the land with guns? Are you stripped and beaten? Is your land stolen?

OLD MAN (*Speaks very gravely*): No, what you say is true.

CURANDERA (*Triumphantly*): You see. There was no *manito*. If the little tiger was dead these things would still be true. But he is alive, and they are afraid of him.

YOUNG MAN: Where is he then?

CURANDERA (*She motions toward the hills.*): He is there. I have seen him. Why, you can hear his horse on the wind at night. You can hear his spurs in the summer rain. (*Her eyes roll back as they did when she was a young woman.*) He is there always. He fooled them, and they are afraid of him. We know that he is always near, our beloved tiger.

Now a man moves a little aside, and we see in heavy black letters at the base of the little monument, and we see for the only time in the whole film, Emiliano's last name:

ZAPATA

Part Two

VIVA ZAPATA!

The Screenplay

STEINBECK'S ZAPATA

Rebel Versus Revolutionary

An Introductory Essay by Robert E. Morsberger

In his studies of rebellion, Albert Camus makes an essential distinction between the rebel and the revolutionary. The rebel is an independent nonconformist protesting regimentation and oppression. He stands for freedom, and he is willing to die for it but reluctant to kill for it. If he backs the appeal to arms, he stops short of tyranny. The revolutionary, by contrast, speaks of liberty but establishes terror; in the name of equality and fraternity, he sets up the guillotine or the firing squad. For the sake of an abstract mankind, he finds it expedient to purge the unorthodox individual, to institutionalize terror, to enshrine dogma and dialectic. The rebel is like Socrates, Thoreau, or Martin Luther King, whereas the revolutionary is Saint-Just, Robespierre, Lenin, Stalin, and the enslaving liberators of the twentieth century. Camus states that "the great event of the twentieth century was the forsaking of the values of freedom by the revolutionary movement," which contended "that we needed justice first and that we could come to freedom later on, as if slaves could ever hope to achieve justice."[1] On the other hand, "The rebel undoubtedly demands a certain degree of freedom for himself; but in no case, if he is consistent, does he demand the right to destroy the existence and the freedom

---

[1] Albert Camus, *Resistance, Rebellion, and Death*, trans. Justin O'Brien (New York: Alfred A. Knopf, 1961), pp. 90–91.

of others. He humiliates no one. . . . He is not only the slave against the master, but also man against the world of master and slave."[2]

This distinction runs throughout the work of John Steinbeck and receives its most explicit treatment in his screenplay *Viva Zapata!*, which Elia Kazan made into one of the more successful movies of 1952. Unlike Steinbeck's earlier scripts for *Lifeboat* and *A Medal for Benny*, this was not a collaboration; Steinbeck alone wrote both the story and the script. He worked on *Zapata* from the fall of 1948 until May 1950, and then went on location during the filming. The finished film was very much Steinbeck's statement. It puts into final focus issues with which he had been concerned for the previous twenty years and clarifies the relationship of issues to individuals and leaders to people. The conflict between creative dissent and intolerant militancy has a timeless relevancy, and *Zapata* deserves a close analysis both as a social statement and a work of art.

As a study of leadership and insurrection, *Zapata* has roots in *In Dubious Battle*, *The Grapes of Wrath*, and *The Moon Is Down*. The protagonists of *In Dubious Battle* are Communists; but despite its sympathy for the strikers, the novel is profoundly critical of revolutionist tactics. Steinbeck commented that "Communists will hate it and the other side will too."[3] The battle is indeed dubious, for the means do not justify the end. Mac, the Communist organizer, is the professional and ruthless revolutionary to whom people are merely tools of guerrilla warfare. Zapata is given leadership by the already aroused people, but Mac is the manipulator who instigates a strike that he knows will fail and that is part of "the long view" toward a brave new world. For the cause, it does not matter which individuals suffer. To win the workers' confidence, Mac risks the

2 Camus, *The Rebel*, trans. Anthony Bower (New York: Alfred A. Knopf, Vintage Books, 1957), p. 284.

3 Peter Lisca, "John Steinbeck: A Literary Biography," *Steinbeck and His Critics*, E. W. Tedlock, Jr., and C. V. Wicker, eds. (Albuquerque: University of New Mexico Press, 1957), p. 10.

life of a woman in labor. He exploits the death of friends, for "We've got to use whatever material comes to us."[4] He hopes some of the strikers will be killed, for "If they knock off some of the tramps we have a public funeral; and after that, we get some real action"; and when he is told that innocent men may be shot, he replies, "In a war a general knows he's going to lose men."[5] Mac advises Jim Nolan, the Communist novice, "Don't you go liking people, Jim. We can't waste time liking people."[6]

Thus for the determined revolutionary, issues are more important than individuals. Jim Nolan is human enough at first, but he develops into such a True Believer that his "cold thought to fight madness" scares even Mac. When Mac smashes the face of a high-school boy, Jim says, "He's not a kid, he's an example . . . a danger to the cause," and beating him "was an operation, that's all."[7] Mac now feels that Jim is not human, but Jim insists that "sympathy is as bad as fear."[8] Like Ethan Brand, he has lost his hold on humanity and justifies torture in the name of human brotherhood.

Mac and Jim rarely discuss dialectic; they seem motivated less by party dogma than by a need for the transfiguring experience of revolution that Doc Burton calls "pure religious ecstasy."[9] The two Communists awaiting martyrdom in "Raid" have a similar emotion; but as Camus notes, "Politics is not religion, or if it is, then it is nothing but the Inquisition."[10]

In reaction to *In Dubious Battle* and *The Grapes of Wrath*, some right-wing critics of the time denounced Steinbeck as a rev-

---

4 John Steinbeck, *In Dubious Battle* (New York: Viking Compass Books, 1963), p. 53.

5 *Ibid.*, p. 305.

6 *Ibid.*, p. 103.

7 *Ibid.*, pp. 247–49.

8 *Ibid.*, p. 249.

9 *Ibid.*, p. 231.

10 Camus, *The Rebel*, p. 302.

olutionary, even as a Communist. It is no longer necessary to refute these charges; Steinbeck was never a Communist except in Mr. Hines's sense that "a Red is any son-of-a-bitch that wants thirty cents an hour when we're payin' twenty-five!"[11] In Russia, critics noted that *The Grapes of Wrath* did not follow the orthodox party line, but B. Balasov said the book has a "definite revolutionary direction."[12] Actually, as Chester E. Eisinger and others have pointed out, Steinbeck's migratory farm workers have their roots in Jeffersonian agrarianism. Far from wanting state collectivism, they long, like Lennie and George in *Of Mice and Men*, for a place of their own. Steinbeck was an ardent advocate of private property and wrote in *The Grapes of Wrath*, "If a man owns a little property, that property is him . . . and some way he's bigger because he owns it."[13]

Steinbeck predicted that if revolution should come, it would not be the work of professional agitators but would be an overflow of outrage in response to organized oppression. Under conditions of farm labor in California, "the dignity of the man is attacked. No trust is accorded them. They are surrounded as though it were suspected that they would break into revolt at any moment. It would seem that a surer method of forcing them to revolt could not be devised."[14] Steinbeck's solution was punishment of vigilante terrorism and encouragement for the agricultural workers to organize within a democratic framework.[15] Camus notes that "a change of regulations concerning property without a corresponding change of government is not a revolution but a reform,"[16] and this is what Steinbeck supported. But unless it came quickly, he predicted that

11 Steinbeck, *The Grapes of Wrath* (New York: The Viking Press, 1939), p. 407.

12 James W. Tuttleton, "Steinbeck in Russia: The Rhetoric of Praise and Blame," *Modern Fiction Studies*, 11 (Spring 1965), p. 80.

13 Steinbeck, *The Grapes of Wrath*, p. 50.

14 Steinbeck, *Their Blood Is Strong* (San Francisco: Simon J. Lubin Society of California, Inc., 1938), p. 13.

15 *Ibid.*, p. 29.

16 Camus, *The Rebel*, p. 106.

"from pain, hunger, and despair the whole mass of labor will revolt."[17]

Such a spontaneous uprising of the people occurs in *Viva Zapata!* Emiliano Zapata is not a conscious revolutionary but a natural leader of a justifiably rebellious peasantry. In the film, he first appears as a member of a delegation to the dictator Díaz. Like the dispossessed Okies of *The Grapes of Wrath*, the farmers complain that an anonymous "they" have taken the village land. The delegates claim ownership since before history—reinforced by papers from the Spanish crown and the Mexican republic. The question of ownership is recurrent and critical to Steinbeck. In *The Grapes of Wrath* and *Their Blood Is Strong*, he urges not collectivism but a fair redistribution of land among private holders. Later in *Viva Zapata!*, when Don Nacio, a landowner sympathetic to the peasants, entertains some large planters, he defends the Indian villagers' right to their land and urges the planters to "Give the land back. You don't need it. You have so much. . . . We're all in danger. If we don't give a little—we'll lose it all."[18] Don García replies indignantly that he paid for the land and therefore owns it, but Don Nacio insists that the Indians lived there for a thousand years, "since before the Conquest," and that such living makes them the true owners. His attitude, and that of the peasants, is like the tenant men in *The Grapes of Wrath* who say, "It's our land. We measured it and broke it up. We were born on it, and we got killed on it, died on it. Even if it's no good, it's still ours. That's what makes it ours—being born on it, working it, dying on it. That makes ownership, not a paper with numbers on it."[19]

Zapata's role is that of agrarian reformer, not a revolutionary remolder of society. When Díaz questions the delegation's ownership of the land, Zapata emerges as spokesman for the group. He speaks common sense and farmers' folkways, not dialectic, and

17 Steinbeck, *Their Blood Is Strong*, p. 30.

18 All quotations from *Viva Zapata!* are from Steinbeck's shooting final script, May 16, 1951.

19 Steinbeck, *The Grapes of Wrath*, p. 45.

tells Díaz that corn, not the courts, is essential to the farmers. When Díaz advises the men to check the boundaries but refuses them official permission to cross guarded fences to do so, Zapata replies that they will take his advice. We then see a close-up of Díaz's hand circling Zapata's name on the list of delegates.

Though he is more articulate than the others and takes more initiative, Zapata does not seek leadership; circumstances and the people thrust it upon him. Steinbeck shows the revolution beginning as at Concord and Lexington; the embattled farmers trying to survey their lands are attacked by *rurales*, who begin machine-gunning them. Zapata, who is mounted, lassoes the machine gun and enables most of the farmers to escape. Here and in later episodes, he has no plans but rather an impetuous reaction to tyrannic violence. But as the Mayor in *The Moon Is Down* tells Alex Morden, who hit and killed a Nazi overseer, "Your private anger was the beginning of a public anger."[20] Likewise Casy and Tom Joad at first have only a spontaneous and improvised response to episodes of outrage, but gradually they learn to make long-range plans.

Zapata meanwhile hides in the hills with a handful of followers. There he is sought out by Fernando Aguirre, who first appears as a young man with a typewriter, which he calls "the sword of the mind." Zapata at this point is still illiterate; he is no intellectual but is in tune with the ways of people and the land. One of the more moving scenes in the film is his urgent plea on his wedding night that his wife teach him to read. It is significant that he speaks Aztec as well as Spanish; this enables him both to get information from the peasants and to hear and empathize with their sufferings. Unlike this man of the people, Fernando has no background that we ever discover; we gradually learn that he is the revolutionary who will betray anyone for his own ends. Fernando comes as an emissary from Madero, "the leader of the fight against Díaz." Before agreeing to become an ally, Zapata sends his friend Pablo to Texas

---

20 Steinbeck, *The Moon Is Down* (New York: The Viking Press, 1942), p. 96.

to look in Madero's face and report what he sees; Zapata wants to evaluate a man, not an ideology.

While Pablo is away, Zapata receives a pardon from the charges that resulted when he attacked the *rurales* and is hired to appraise horses for his wealthy patron, Don Nacio. He begins courting the wealthy, aristocratic Josefa Espejo. Zapata now has a private life to lead and a promising future. But again, indignation intervenes. Camus notes that "rebellion does not arise only, and necessarily, among the oppressed, but . . . it can also be caused by the mere spectacle of oppression of which someone else is the victim. In such cases there is a feeling of identification with another individual."[21] Steinbeck composes such a scene very carefully. We first see eggs being beaten for rubbing down Arabian stallions. A hungry little girl dips her finger into the mixture and licks it. The mother, seeing Zapata observe this, slaps the child, who looks away in shame, and Zapata also looks away in shame. The manager says such people are lazy and orders servants to rub down the horses better. When the manager beats a starving boy whom he catches stealing food from the horses, Zapata can no longer stand by; he risks his job and his pardon by knocking the man down. Zapata's employer asks, "Are you responsible for everybody? You can't be the conscience of the whole world," but Zapata can only answer, "He was hungry." Yet Zapata does not want involvement; he longs for privacy, and so he apologizes to the manager. At this strategic moment, Pablo returns from Madero, accompanied by Fernando, who offers Zapata a command. Zapata's response is that he does not want to be a leader: "I don't want to be the conscience of the world. I don't want to be the conscience of anybody."

Yet he cannot be passive in the face of oppression. Later, when he encounters *rurales* dragging a prisoner by a noose, Zapata cuts the man loose and becomes an outlaw a second time. Like a migrant from *The Grapes of Wrath*, this man (significantly named

---

21 Camus, *The Rebel*, p. 16.

Innocente) had crawled through a fence at night to plant a little corn. Again, Zapata has no plan but improvises in reaction to events. Fernando, the revolutionary, however, has plans and he does not object to the sacrifice of the individual. Fernando smiles when Zapata rides off an outlaw. Zapata can serve the cause, and his private misfortune may be public good.

Camus observes that "when a movement of rebellion begins, suffering is seen as a collective experience"; the rebel "identifies himself with a natural community."[22] Likewise, Steinbeck notes in *Sea of Cortez*: "Non-teleological notion: that the people we call leaders are simply those who, at the given moment, are moving in the direction behind which will be found the greatest weight, and which represents a future mass movement."[23] This is what now happens to Zapata. When *rurales* capture him, the people accompany him in an increasingly massive procession until it is so large that it stops the column. The mere presence of this silent, spontaneous procession forces the captain to free the prisoner. The people bring Zapata's white horse and by this gesture make him their leader. Before, he had no followers, only a handful of friends; now he takes command. Fernando urges him to cut the telegraph wires, despite the captain's threat: "Don't touch that! This is rebellion!" In a fine dramatic pause, Zapata looks at his brother Eufemio, whose machete is raised; then he orders, "Cut it."

The film has been building symbolically to this moment. First, Zapata has overseen the cutting of the boundary wire. Next, he has cut the noose around Innocente's neck—but too late; the soldiers have dragged the man to his death, and Zapata concludes that he should have cut the rope first and then talked. After that, we see Zapata himself pulled by a halter. Thus, cutting the wire becomes a symbolic culmination, severing the bonds of oppression and signifying decisive action.

---

22 *Ibid.*, pp. 22, 16.

23 Steinbeck, *Sea of Cortez: A Leisurely Journal of Travel and Research*, in collaboration with Edward F. Ricketts (New York: The Viking Press, 1941), p. 138.

The film now presents a number of quick scenes of guerrilla warfare culminating in Díaz's defeat. Zapata says thankfully, "The fighting is over." This campaign has been like the first or real Russian Revolution, and fully half of the script deals with it. But instead of bringing peace and reform, the revolution is spoiled by the professionals, who inaugurate a series of betrayals. In a dramatically symbolic scene, Steinbeck shows Zapata first torn between the conflicting claims of power and the people. As the victorious Zapatistas are celebrating, Fernando arrives with a document from Madero designating Zapata "General of the Armies of the South." Brother Eufemio hands him a general's ornaments, while an Indian woman gratefully gives him "a dirty bouquet of live trussed chickens"; the last shot shows him standing with the chickens in one hand and the ornaments in the other. It is significant that Fernando is the emissary for power. Reveling in victory, the celebrants all get drunk except Fernando, who remains cold sober.

EUFEMIO: I know what's the matter with you. You are unhappy because the fighting is over.
FERNANDO (*muttering to himself*): Half victories! All this celebrating and nothing really won!
EUFEMIO (*embracing him*): I love you—but I don't like you. I've never liked you.
FERNANDO (*still going on*): There will have to be a lot more bloodshed.
EUFEMIO (*losing patience with him*): All right! There *will* be! But not tonight! (*gives him bottle*) Here—enjoy yourself! Be human!

It is never clear what Fernando wants or why he thinks there must be bloodshed, but he is intolerant of anything less than absolutism. He resembles Jim Nolan when the latter declares, "I'm stronger than you, Mac. I'm stronger than anything in the world, because I'm going in a straight line. You and all the rest have to think of women and tobacco and liquor and keeping warm and fed."[24]

Madero is now in charge. He is presented as a good man, mild and well-meaning, but bewildered. When Zapata presses him for immediate land reform, Madero insists that rebuilding must take time and be done carefully under the law. Zapata is impatient, though willing to give Madero a chance, but Fernando condemns the President as an enemy.

> PABLO: But you're his emissary, his officer, his friend. . . .
> FERNANDO: I'm a friend to no one—and to nothing except logic. . . . This is the time for killing!

For the True Believer, the revolutionary fanatic like Fernando, there can be no redemption without the shedding of blood. Camus notes that by contrast, "Authentic acts of rebellion will only consent to take up arms for institutions that limit violence, not for those which codify it."[25]

Fernando apparently wants a purge, and with some reason, for as the delegation departs, Huerta and a group of fellow generals enter and dominate Madero. Huerta advises him to shoot Zapata now, but Madero insists that he does not shoot his own people and that Zapata is an honest man. With true totalitarian logic, Huerta replies, "What has that got to do with it??!! A man can be honest and completely wrong!" From here on, Zapata's inevitable death is foreshadowed, and the film takes a tragic turn.

While the guerrillas are disarming under Madero's orders, Huerta and the regular army pull a coup and march against Morelos. Madero has been like Kerensky, insisting on a constitutional government; now the ruthless professionals take over. Madero falls into Huerta's hands and is murdered. The Zapatistas resume their guerrilla warfare against the new oppressor. Again Zapata is vic-

---

24 Steinbeck, *In Dubious Battle*, p. 249.

25 Camus, *The Rebel*, p. 292.

torious; but in the process, power inevitably involves him in evil. Camus asks "whether innocence, the moment it becomes involved in action, can avoid committing murder."[26] Zapata's forces are ambushed, and among the suspected traitors is Pablo, accused of meeting with Madero after Huerta betrayed the revolution. Pablo's defense is an eloquent plea for peace. Madero, he says, was trying to hold Huerta in check.

> PABLO: He was a good man, Emiliano. He wanted to build houses and plant fields. And he was right. If we could begin to build—even while the burning goes on. If we could plant while we destroy . . .

Fernando interrupts harshly, "You deserted our cause!"

> PABLO: Our cause was land—not a thought, but corn-planted earth to feed the families. And Liberty—not a word, but a man sitting safely in front of his house in the evening. And Peace—not a dream, but a time of rest and kindness. The question beats in my head, Emiliano. Can a good thing come from a bad act? Can peace come from so much killing? Can kindness finally come from so much violence? (*he now looks directly into* EMILIANO's *immobile eyes*) And can a man whose thoughts are born in anger and hatred, can such a man lead to peace? And govern in peace?

This point becomes the focus of the rest of the film, and it is an issue that concerned Steinbeck for a long time. Doc Burton, his spokesman in *In Dubious Battle*, tells Jim: "In my little experience the end is never very different in its nature from the means. Damn it, Jim, you can only build a violent thing with violence." When Jim insists, "All great things have violent beginnings," Doc replies:

---

26 *Ibid.*, p. 4.

"We fight ourselves and we can only win by killing every man."[27]

Eventually, Fernando helps to kill Zapata; but meanwhile his inflexible logic requires the death of Pablo, even though it was Fernando who first brought Pablo and Madero together. Now he tries to make even Zapata his tool. While Zapata himself is executing Pablo at the latter's request, a courier arrives and Fernando informs him, "General Zapata is busy." We hear the shot that kills Pablo; and Fernando then says, "General Zapata will see you now." Only once before had Emiliano been called "General Zapata," and that too was by Fernando. Otherwise, he had been simply a *campesino*, always approachable, as when a young boy, who like Zapata had lassoed a machine gun, demanded Zapata's white horse when offered a reward. Zapata's giving the horse to him foreshadows his renouncing power and returning it to the people. Now, setting up formal audiences and executive isolation, Fernando has become a barrier between Zapata and the people.

When some of the people turn against him, Zapata realizes that Pablo was right. Pablo, in his patience and wisdom, resembles Anselmo in *For Whom the Bell Tolls*; his friend the Soldadera, a Pilar-type woman warrior, tries to kill Zapata with Pablo's knife. The guards urge her death, but Zapata lets her go, insisting, "The killing must stop! Pablo said it. That's all I know how to do!" Whenever he has been tempted to act the tyrant, one of the people has reminded him of reality.

Zapata's refusal to take any rewards for himself leads to his death. Huerta is beaten, and Fernando and Villa propose Zapata for President. Though he refuses office, Zapata does take command in Mexico City, while Carranza and Obregón replace Huerta as the military opposition. An Old General proposes that Zapata form an alliance with these commanders "for the good of Mexico." Intervening, Fernando violently refuses, insisting, "The principle of successful rule is always the same. There can be no opposition. Of course, our ends are different." He advises Zapata to kill the

27 Steinbeck, *In Dubious Battle*, p. 230.

General; yet when Zapata relinquishes power, it is Fernando who joins Carranza and Obregón and gives the Old General the plan that betrays Zapata and leads to his death.

Again, it is a reminder from the people that recalls Zapata from power. A delegation from Morelos calls upon him to complain that his brother Eufemio has been taking their lands and women. Zapata at first equivocates, asks for time, then (in a re-enactment of the first audience with Díaz) circles the name of the spokesman for the group. Suddenly, with horror, he realizes what he is doing and what he is about to become. He rejoins his people, saying, "I'm going home. . . . I'm going home. There are some things I forgot."

> FERNANDO: So you're throwing it away. . . . I promise you you won't live long. . . . In the name of all *we* fought for, don't leave here!
> EMILIANO: In the name of all *I* fought for, I'm going. [editor's italics]
> FERNANDO: Thousands of men have died to give you power and you're throwing it away.
> EMILIANO: I'm taking it back where it belongs; to thousands of men.

When Fernando refuses to go with him, Zapata says, "Now I know you. No wife, no woman, no home, no field. You do not gamble, drink, no friends, no love. . . . You only destroy. . . . I guess that's your love. . . ."

In this context Zapata's love story is significant. The courtship and marriage of Zapata and Josefa (the only treatment of romantic love Steinbeck had so far written) is historically oversimplified but artistically valid. The real Zapata had dozens of women and numerous bastards. The screen Zapata is more saintly, but the love story humanizes him, adds a tragic dimension, and also enables Steinbeck to include some humor and folklore. In a picaresque episode, Zapata and Eufemio first approach Josefa and her aunt in church; the outlaw proposes while she is praying. Her father has predicted that Zapata's wife will become a peasant, and she rejects her suitor with the words: "I have no intention of ending up washing clothes in a ditch and patting tortillas like an Indian." Later, Zapata courts her more formally in a humorous scene with traditionally stilted proverbs; the tiger is momentarily tamed. The drama of their wedding night, when she starts teaching him to read while crowds celebrate outside, is moving; they are like earnest and innocent children with the book between them. Josefa does not appear again until near the end, when we see her washing in a stream with Indian women. "Her father's prediction has come true—she is practically indistinguishable from the others." But she is ennobled, not debased, by the change. Though she appears in only five comparatively brief scenes, the part is memorable, with humor, humanity, and pathos. The script conveys a sense of their whole life together, and her anguish on the eve of the fatal ambush is the climax of Zapata's sacrifice.

Once home, Zapata initiates a program of planting and building along with the fighting against Carranza and Obregón, and tells the people:

> About leaders. You've looked for leaders. For strong men without faults. There aren't any. These are only men like yourselves. . . . There's no leader but yourselves.

Thus when Fernando accomplishes Zapata's betrayal and murder, the people can go on.

In *The Moon Is Down*, the Nazi conquerors insist that Mayor Orden think for his people and keep them in order. Orden replies that his people "don't like to have others think for them" and that "authority is in the town," not in any individual.[28] Corell, the quisling traitor, tells the Nazis, "When we have killed the leaders,

---

28 Steinbeck, *The Moon Is Down*, pp. 36, 41.

the rebellion will be broken."[29] This issue had long been of concern to Steinbeck. Considering Steinbeck's self-reliant reformers, Frederic I. Carpenter asked in 1941, "What if this self-reliance lead to death? What if the individual is killed before the social group is saved?"[30] Though the Nazis do order the Mayor's death, Dr. Winter observes: "They think that just because they have only one leader and one head, we are all like that . . . but we are a free people; we have as many heads as we have people, and in a time of need leaders pop up among us like mushrooms."[31]

Zapata's wife, fearing a trap, asks, "If anything happens to you, what would become of these people? What would they have left?" His answer is, "Themselves."

> JOSEFA: With all the fighting and the death, what has changed?
> EMILIANO: *They've* changed. That is how things really change—slowly—through people. They don't need me any more.
> JOSEFA: They have to be led.
> EMILIANO: But by each other. A strong man makes a weak people. Strong people don't need a strong man.

A passage from *The Grapes of Wrath* anticipates the ending of *Zapata*. When Tom Joad leaves to become a rebel against oppression, Ma tells him, "They might kill ya."

> Tom laughed uneasily. "Well, maybe like Casy says, a fella ain't got a soul of his own, but on'y a piece of a big one—an' then—"
> "Then what, Tom?"

---

29 *Ibid.*, p. 171.

30 Frederic I. Carpenter, "The Philosophical Joads," *College English*, II (January 1941), p. 325.

31 Steinbeck, *The Moon Is Down*, p. 175.

"Then it don' matter. Then I'll be aroun' in the dark. Then I'll be ever'where—wherever you look."[32]

Perhaps the people don't need a leader, but they need a legend. When Zapata is shot to ribbons from ambush, some of the peasants emerge. The Soldadera, who had tried to kill Zapata, now composes his body, for his death is an atonement that makes him again one of her people. Lazaro, an old veteran who knew Zapata well, examines the body and spurns it, saying that such a shot-up corpse could be anybody. "I fought with him all these years. Do they think they can fool me? They can't kill him. . . ."

> YOUNG MAN (*agreeing*): They'll never get him. Can you capture a river? Can you kill the wind?
> LAZARO: No! He's not a river and he's not the wind! He's a man—and they still can't kill him! . . . He's in the mountains. You couldn't find him now. But if we ever need him again—he'll be back.

As they look up to the mountains, they see Zapata's white horse, which escaped and which is now walking toward the peak.

At first this may seem like a conventional Hollywood ending, but in fact it is historically and artistically appropriate. If Lazaro's name recalls Lazarus and thus links Zapata with Christ, there is a Mexican context for resurrection as well in the Montezuma myth that makes the slain emperor into a once and future king. Many of the people of Morelos did indeed refuse to believe that Zapata was dead; some insisted the corpse was not his, and others claimed to have seen his horse galloping into the southern mountains. In actuality, Zapata was not alone but accompanied by a bodyguard when he was killed, and his horse was not white but sorrel. The white horse comes from Diego Rivera's mural of Zapata. Thus slight

---

32 Steinbeck, *The Grapes of Wrath*, p. 572.

distortions of fact may come closer to the ultimate meaning of Zapata's death.

Some movie reviewers faulted the film for simplifying or distorting history, but the simplification is a virtue here. Steinbeck cuts through the complexities of campaigns and the incredible intricacies of political intrigues to get at what he sees as the essence of the events. The latter is what most bothered some reviewers. The movie had a mixed reception, praise going to the action sequences and to performances by Anthony Quinn (who won an Academy Award) as Eufemio, Joseph Wiseman as Fernando, and Harold Gordon as Madero, with divided opinion on the effectiveness of Jean Peters as Josefa and Marlon Brando as Zapata. *Newsweek*'s reviewer called the film a "sincere tribute" with "a careful and intelligent characterization"; *The Christian Century* found it "brilliant"; *Commonweal* termed it "a thoughtful film"; and the chief of the American History Division of the New York Public Library praised it as "exciting and impressive."[33] But *Holiday* complained of a "tedious and oratorical screenplay by John Steinbeck"; *Life* lamented Steinbeck's "mouthfuls of political platitudes"; *The New Yorker* found the film entertaining aside from "Mr. Steinbeck's murky views on revolution"; and *The New Republic* objected to "squelchy aphorisms of a kind we have had before from the Oakies [sic] of California and the doomed heroes of the Norwegian underground."[34]

Actually, resemblances to *The Grapes of Wrath* and *The Moon Is Down* reveal a continuity in Steinbeck's intellectual concerns, no more reprehensible than the reappearance of central themes in the work of Hawthorne and Henry James. A study of *Zapata* can enrich one's appreciation of the earlier books. The aphorisms occur

---

33 *Newsweek*, 34 (February 4, 1952), 78; *The Christian Century*, 69 (April 23, 1952), 510; Philip T. Hartung, *Commonweal*, 55 (February 29, 1952), 517; Gerold D. McDonald, *Library Journal*, 77 (February 15, 1952), p. 311.

34 *Holiday*, 11 (May 1952), 105; *Life*, 32 (February 25, 1952), 61; John McCarten, "Wool from the West," *The New Yorker*, 27 (February 16, 1952), 106; *The New Republic*, 126 (February 25, 1952), p. 21.

in an appropriate context of action, and they by no means constitute the greater part of the script. The philosophizing is dramatic as well as didactic. For instance, Zapata's statements that "there's no leader but yourselves" and that "a strong people is the only lasting strength" occur when the men of Morelos have asked him to punish his brother for stealing land and women. Zapata cannot kill his brother, but his speech (which also prophesies his own death) suggests what they must do. While he is still talking, Eufemio is killed in the hallway. Far from being sententious, Zapata's speech is tense with terror. When Hollis Alpert complained of so-called "stock phrases" like "A strong people does not need a strong man," Laura Z. Hobson asked Steinbeck about them, and he replied: "I interviewed every living person I could find in Mexico who had known or fought with Zapata. Again and again I heard those words or their first cousins." Against charges of bombast and cliché, he said, "Whenever a man disagrees with the ideas involved in a book, a play, or a movie, and cannot publicly admit his disagreement, he attacks on grounds of grammar or technique."[35]

Elia Kazan has explained some of the political pressures brought against the film. Noting that the Mexican revolution had other leaders besides Zapata, he claimed that he and Steinbeck were particularly fascinated by Zapata's renunciation of power in the moment of victory. "We felt this act of renunciation was the high point of our story and the key to Zapata himself." When they submitted the script for the opinion of some prominent Mexican film-makers, these men "attacked with sarcastic fury our emphasis on his refusal to take power." Kazan claims that he and Steinbeck felt such criticism came from Mexican Communists who wanted "to capitalize on the people's reverence for Zapata by working his figure into their propaganda. . . . Nearly two years later our guess was confirmed by a rabid attack on the picture in the *Daily Worker*, which parallels everything the two Mexicans argued, and which all but implies that John invented Zapata's renunciation of power.

---

35 Laura Z. Hobson, "Trade Winds," *The Saturday Review*, 35 (March 1, 1952), p. 6.

No Communist, no totalitarian, ever refused power. By showing that Zapata did this, we spoiled a poster figure that the Communists have been at some pains to create."[36] Curiously, some liberals then accused Steinbeck and Kazan of McCarthyism, while at the same time the far right denounced them for dealing with Zapata at all, since all rebels must be Communists. Kazan again replied, "There was, of course, no such thing as a Communist Party at the time and place where Zapata fought. . . . But there is such a thing as a Communist mentality. We created a figure of this complexion in Fernando," who "typifies the men who use the just grievances of the people for their own ends, who shift and twist their course, betray any friend or principle or promise to get power and keep it." Here then, is Camus's revolutionary, by contrast to Zapata the rebel, whom Kazan calls "a man of individual conscience."[37]

The controversy continued with a criticism of the film by Carleton Beals, an expert on Mexico and one-time instructor to Carranza, who claimed that Zapata's abdication of power was pure fiction. In fact, Zapata repeatedly insisted that he wanted to retire to private life.[38] He emphasized that he could not stand politicians and was afraid, as a politician himself, "of unwittingly betraying the trust his peers and their people had invested in him."[39] According to John Womack, Jr., Zapata did shun power "because it would complicate his original loyalties, but he never really had power to abdicate, or could have had it. Besides, he didn't want power. He wanted an end to harassment from outside, and local peace."[40] He never became President; but in December 1914, he gave up his military power and returned home, rejecting the Villa-Zapata coalition. This is the episode that Steinbeck dramatizes. In reply to Beals, Kazan defended Steinbeck's extensive research,

---

36 Elia Kazan, "Letters to the Editor," *The Saturday Review*, 35 (April 5, 1952), p. 22.

37 *Ibid.*

38 John Womack, Jr., *Zapata and the Mexican Revolution* (New York: Alfred A. Knopf, 1969), p. 128.

39 *Ibid.*, p. 205.

40 Womack, letter to Robert E. Morsberger, April 28, 1973.

which turned up numerous conflicting accounts of Zapata's mysterious departure from Mexico City. "John had to make choices and he made them with an eye to implementing his interpretation."[41] Likewise, Camus says of *The Rebel* that his book attempts to "present certain historical data and a working hypothesis. This hypothesis is not the only one possible; moreover, it is far from explaining everything. But it partly explains the direction in which our times are heading."[42]

Steinbeck's interpretation seems to have been reinforced by his earlier visit to Russia; the same year that he began his screenplay, he published *A Russian Journal*. In it he repeatedly condemned the concept of the strong man, objecting to the humorless museum mementos of Lenin and the ubiquitous iconography of Stalin. He recalled that he and photographer Robert Capa "tried to explain our fear of dictatorship, our fear of leaders with too much power, so that our government is designed to keep anyone from getting too much power, or having got it, from keeping it."[43] Steinbeck wanted to avoid political preconceptions and to see the Russian people. He found the Muscovites to be humorless under the weight of ideological dogma; and "after a while the lack of laughter gets under your skin" just as Fernando's sobriety annoyed Eufemio.[44] Eufemio's uninhibited zest resembled that of the Ukrainians and Georgians, with whom Steinbeck felt at home; like the Mexicans he enjoyed, the Georgians were "fiery, proud, fierce, and gay."[45] By contrast to the official Soviet "heroes of the world," Steinbeck admired the "little people who had been attacked and who had defended themselves successfully."[46]

The final rebel is the artist, in this case Steinbeck himself,

41 Kazan, "Letters to the Editor," *The Saturday Review*, 35 (May 24, 1952), pp. 25, 28.

42 Camus, *The Rebel*, p. 11.

43 Steinbeck, *A Russian Journal* (New York: The Viking Press, 1948), p. 57.

44 *Ibid.*, p. 44.

45 *Ibid.*, pp. 151–52.

46 *Ibid.*, pp. 134–35.

who noted in *A Russian Journal* that "although Stalin may say that the writer is the architect of the soul, in America the writer is not considered the architect of anything. . . . In nothing is the difference between the Americans and the Soviets so marked as in the attitude, not only toward writers, but of writers toward their system. For in the Soviet Union the writer's job is to encourage, to celebrate, to explain, and in every way to carry forward the Soviet system. Whereas in America, and in England, a good writer is the watchdog of society. His job is to satirize its silliness, to attack its injustices, to stigmatize its faults. And this is the reason that in America neither society nor government is very fond of writers."[47]

Viva Zapata!'s warnings against power apply equally to the extremists of left-wing revolution and right-wing reaction. The film not only interprets the past but foreshadows events that have since occurred. Philip T. Hartung judged that "few historical movies have stated so well the post-revolutionary problem or asked so disturbingly the questions that must be answered about all new leaders."[48] Far from being a digression into Hollywood, Steinbeck's script sums up issues that had long been central to his work. Steinbeck's continuing relevance may be seen in part by the fact that the California grape-pickers who once sang Woody Guthrie's "Tom Joad" now display posters of Emiliano Zapata.

R. M.

---

47 *Ibid.*, p. 164.

48 Hartung, *Commonweal, loc. cit.*

VIVA ZAPATA!

The Screenplay

by John Steinbeck

Under the main titles we see these shots:

(a) Long Shot—countryside.
> TWO MEN, *one on a* WHITE HORSE, *are riding fast and with intention toward* CAMERA. *Over their ride can be heard the* WAIL *of a* TRAIN WHISTLE, *which seems to increase the tempo of the ride.*

(b) Medium Shot—the Two Horsemen.
> *The* MAN ON THE WHITE HORSE *is in the lead. Both riders wear charro costume.*

(c) A Wayside Stop, or Water Tower—little more than a whistle stop, where the train stops to pick up passengers.
> *A number of white-clad* PEASANTS *are waiting expectantly. The* TWO HORSEMEN *ride into scene, and dismount.*

The Titles Stop.
OTHER HORSEMAN (*to the* MAN ON THE WHITE HORSE): You're wasting your time, my brother. Nothing will come of this—nothing at all.

> *Over scene comes the* SOUND *of the* TRAIN WHISTLE. *The* PEASANTS *and the* TWO HORSEMEN *look off toward the sound. The* MAN ON THE WHITE HORSE *turns back to his brother (the* OTHER HORSEMAN), *hands him the reins of the* WHITE HORSE, *and walks toward the group of waiting* PEASANTS.]

Fade out

Fade in:
Gate to Palace, Shooting toward Palace

> *The white-clad* PEASANTS *whom we saw waiting for the train are standing at the gate. Among them we recognize the* MAN ON THE WHITE HORSE. SOLDIERS *guard the gateway.*

Medium Shot—Group of Peasants at Gate

> ONE OF THE PEASANTS *produces a paper which is scrutinized by the* SOLDIERS, *who then proceed to search each member of the party for weapons. From one they take a knife, from another a gun, etc., and hand them to another* SOLDIER *who stands in the doorway of the guardhouse.*

Interior, Guardhouse

> *There are rows of nails on the wall. The* SOLDIER *in the doorway now turns, hangs the peasants' weapons on the nails—indicating that it is common practice to relieve callers of their weapons and retain them until they leave the palace. For the most part, the peasants' weapons consist of long, murderous-looking sheath knives.*

At the Gate

> *The* MAN ON THE WHITE HORSE *is standing before the* SOLDIER *who takes his weapon and hands it to the* SOLDIER *in the doorway. Immediately behind the* MAN ON THE WHITE HORSE *is a* SLIGHT MAN (PABLO), *who gives up his weapon—a short knife. The* SOLDIER *stares at the knife in disbelief.*

Insert—the Knife, a very inoffensive little weapon.

Back to Scene

> *The* SOLDIER, *with a grin, hands the knife back to* PABLO. *The* MAN ON THE WHITE HORSE *looks at the knife in amusement, and* SAYS *to* PABLO:

THE MAN ON THE WHITE HORSE: When are you going to get a *real* knife?

All the OTHER PEASANTS *smile.*

Now all the PEASANTS *have been searched, and passed. A* SOLDIER *gestures to them to follow him. As they start after him—*

Dissolve to:
Interior, Audience Room in Palace

An USHER, *in formal attire, admits the* PEASANTS, *then exits. An* ATTENDANT, *with a card and pencil, comes to them.*

ATTENDANT: Your names, please.

After they have given their names, the PEASANTS *look around the room. On one side there is a large throne-like chair. Prominently evident on one wall is a picture of* DÍAZ, *in all his glory. The* PEASANTS *group before this picture and all stare at it.*

VOICE (*offstage*): Good morning, my children.

Full Shot—The Audience Room

It is bare, with no chairs except one behind a big desk. The PEASANT DELEGATION, *standing before* DÍAZ's *picture, turns toward the* VOICE. *Standing in the doorway is* DÍAZ, *the President of Mexico. He looks at them briefly, then he moves briskly to his desk, and sits. The* ATTENDANT *gives him the card with the names of the delegation.* DÍAZ *studies it for a moment. Then:*

DÍAZ (*with a gesture*): Come closer, come closer.

They shuffle in toward his desk.

Medium Shot—Díaz and Delegation

DÍAZ: Now, then, my children . . . what's the problem you have brought me?

The DELEGATES *look at one another, hesitate as to who should speak first. (The* MAN ON THE WHITE HORSE *remains in the background.)*

DÍAZ: Well, one of you has to tell . . . you must have come for something.

LAZARO (*a* DELEGATE; *in simple agreement*): Yes, my President. We have come for something.

DÍAZ (*looking at* ANOTHER DELEGATE): Well, you—you tell me.

FIRST DELEGATE: You know that field, that field with the big white rock in the middle just south of Anencuilco. . . .

SECOND DELEGATE (*a prepared speech*): My President, our delegation—

PABLO (*interrupting with great violence*): They took our land away!

DÍAZ: Who took your land away . . . ? My children, when you make accusations, be certain that you have all your facts. Who took your land away?

DELEGATES (*together*): The big estate there! It's bigger than a kingdom! They have taken the green valley! They have left us only the rocky hillsides! There's a new fence—with barbed wire. We can't feed our cows.

FIRST DELEGATE: You know those three houses by the white rock? They burned those.

SECOND DELEGATE: They're planting sugar cane in our corn land.

DÍAZ: Can you prove you own this field?

LAZARO (*more calmly*): Our village has owned this land since before history. (*holding up worn leather case*) I have a paper from the Spanish crown. I have a paper from the Mexican republic.

DÍAZ: If this is true, you have no problem. (*pause*) My children, the courts will settle this. I will send you to my personal attorney. But before you see him, I urge you: Find the boundary stones. And check them against your grants and titles. Verify the boundaries. Facts—facts—

The DELEGATES *break into expressions of acquiescence and gratitude.*

DÍAZ (*continuing*): Now! I have many other matters to attend to. (*with a smile*) I have been your President for thirty-four years. It is not easy being President.

ELDERLY DELEGATE: Thank you, my President.

Wider Angle

> They all back away, leaving the MAN ON THE WHITE HORSE standing alone. He just stands there unmoving, looking at the PRESIDENT with calculating eyes. The OTHER DELEGATES, seeing that he has not moved, stop. When he SPEAKS, his face is expressionless but his VOICE is soft and pleasant.

THE MAN ON THE WHITE HORSE: We can't verify the boundaries, my President. The land is fenced, guarded by armed men. At this moment they're planting sugar cane in our corn fields.

DÍAZ (*starting to speak*): The courts—

> The MAN ON THE WHITE HORSE holds up his hand with instinctive authority.

THE MAN ON THE WHITE HORSE: With your permission—the courts! Do you know any land suit that's ever been won by country people?

DÍAZ: Has your land been taken?

THE MAN ON THE WHITE HORSE: My father's land, my President, was taken long ago.

> DÍAZ looks at him a moment. Then he turns and SPEAKS past him to the OTHER VILLAGERS.

DÍAZ: My children. I am your father, your protector, I am of your blood. Believe me these things take time, you must have patience.

THE MAN ON THE WHITE HORSE: My President, as you know we make our tortillas of corn, not patience. And patience will not cross an armed and guarded fence. To do as you suggest—to verify those boundaries—we need your authority to cross that fence. . . .

DÍAZ: I cannot possibly exercise such authority.

THE MAN ON THE WHITE HORSE: But you advised it. . . .

DÍAZ: I can only advise.

THE MAN ON THE WHITE HORSE: Then naturally, my President, we will do as you advise. Thank you, my President. (*he bows*) With your permission?

>And only as he turns is there the suggestion of a smile in his
>eyes. He starts for the door, the OTHER DELEGATES going along.

Close Shot—Díaz
>His face shows a suspicion that he has been had. Suddenly he
>calls out.

DÍAZ: You!

Medium Shot—Group at Door
>Just inside the exit door the MAN ON THE WHITE HORSE stops
>and half turns. There is a natural insolence about him.

THE MAN ON THE WHITE HORSE: Yes, my President?

DÍAZ'S VOICE: What's your name?

THE MAN ON THE WHITE HORSE: Zapata.

Another Angle—Including Díaz and Zapata

DÍAZ: What is it . . . ?

ZAPATA (*pronouncing it carefully*): Emiliano Zapata.

>DÍAZ *stares at him briefly, then, for his benefit he carefully*
>*writes on a pad, or card:*

Insert—Díaz's Hand, circling the name "Zapata" on the card which the At-
tendant gave him when he entered the room.

Back to Scene
>DÍAZ *looks up at* ZAPATA *to see if he notices the threat involved*
>*in the circled name.* ZAPATA *stares back at him. They look at*
>*each other for a moment, in a kind of combat; then* ZAPATA
>*turns, walks toward the* GROUP AT THE DOOR, *leaving* DÍAZ
>*looking after him.*

Lap Dissolve to:
Exterior, a Fenced Field in Morelos—near Agalla
>A large group of VILLAGERS, MEN, WOMEN, *and* CHILDREN,
>stand at the fence. Among them is a BOY who carries a picture
>of the Virgin of Guadalupe mounted on a stick. A VILLAGE

ELDER *holds in his hand the leather case we have established as containing the village titles and records. There is also a small* GROUP ON HORSEBACK, *among them* EMILIANO *and* EU-FEMIO ZAPATA.

Close Shot—Emiliano and Eufemio
EMILIANO (*to* EUFEMIO): Cut the fence.
EUFEMIO: Yes, my brother.

The People as they go through the fence.
Most of the WOMEN *remain outside. The* LEADERS *look for the first boundary marker.*

Close Shot—the Village Elder, holding the documents, and studying a map.
VILLAGE ELDER: The old boundary stone should be about here.

Wider Angle
An INDIAN *reaches down, picks up a piece of brick with mortar still clinging to its side.*
INDIAN: Here's a piece of it.
An OLD INDIAN *brings forth the picture of the Virgin of Guad-alupe, plants it in the ground. The* PEOPLE *pile stones about the picture. Suddenly over scene comes the* SOUND *of a* BUGLE *— a* SHRILL BLAST *which freezes the* PEOPLE *in the field. They stand rigid for a moment, then look off toward:*

Long Shot
FORTY MOUNTED RURALES *trot over a hill in the distance. Their* BUGLE BLOWS *again. They ride at full charge toward the* GROUP.

Full Shot—Inside the Fenced Field
EMILIANO *and* EUFEMIO *ride in*, YELLING: "Go!" "Run!" "Get out!" "Go through the fence!" *as they begin to herd the* PEOPLE *toward the hole in the fence. Suddenly there is a* BURST OF MACHINE-GUN FIRE.

Group at Hole in Fence

> *Struggling to get through the fence, are cut down by the* MACHINE-GUN FIRE.

Emiliano

> *He whirls about to locate the machine gun.*

The Machine Gun

> *It has been set up and is being worked by* FIVE MEN. WE ARE SHOOTING PAST *the* GUN CREW, OVER *the sights. Suddenly the* FEEDER *grasps the* GUNNER *by the arm and points. The* GUNNER *first looks and then swings his gun.* CAMERA SWINGS *too, and still over the sights we see* TWO HORSEMEN *coming zigzag at the machine gun. The* GUNNER FIRES.

Machine Gun and Crew

> *Now the* HORSEMEN (EMILIANO *and* EUFEMIO) *are on them.* EMILIANO *carries a* reata (*rope*) *and as his horse leaps the gun he drops the noose over the barrel.* WE STAY *with the* MACHINE-GUN CREW. *The noose tightens and the gun is yanked with great force out of their hands*

Long Shot—Rurales

> *The* RURALES *are riding over the* PEOPLE *who are trying to get through the hole in the fence. The* PEOPLE *are scattered, falling down, running, tripping, etc.*

Medium Shot—Captain of Rurales and Some of His Men

> *The* CAPTAIN *points toward* EMILIANO.

CAPTAIN: There he is! That's the one in our orders! That's Zapata! *They start toward him.*

Group of Rurales at Fence

> EMILIANO—*all alone—rides down on the* RURALES *and disappears into the melee. His* HORSEMEN, *seeing what he has done, charge in after him. There is a temporary diversion,*

during which a good number of VILLAGE PEOPLE *get through
the fence.*

Close Shot—Emiliano
Suddenly he leaps to the back of a RURALE'S HORSE, *holds the*
MAN's *arms, and drives his spurs into the* HORSE's *flanks.*

Wider Angle, as the frightened Horse bursts clear of the melee.
The RURALE *falls from the* HORSE. *In the background we see
the remnants of the* VILLAGERS *taking advantage of the mo-
mentary diversion* EMILIANO *has created, escaping through the
fence.*

*Medium Shot—Captain of Rurales as the Rurales surround him for further
orders.*
He points off *toward the fleeing* ZAPATA, *and orders his* MEN
after him. They whirl their HORSES, *ride off.*

Long Shot—Emiliano riding away.
He suddenly seems to vanish in a dense growth of chaparal
and mesquite. The moment he disappears, the RURALES RIDE
INTO THE SHOT. *They don't know where he has gone.*

*Medium Shot—Captain of Rurales as he hurriedly orders his men off in
different directions, to try to find Emiliano.*

Fade out

Fade in:
Long Shot—Precipitous and Savage Mountains—Day
Climbing up a steep footpath is a YOUNG MAN.

Close Shot—of the Young Man, Fernando Aguirre
He is dressed in rumpled city clothes. He is literally soaked
with sweat. He wears a high collar, and boots which come up
over his trouser legs. He carries his coat over one arm, a straw
hat, and a brief case in the other hand. Hanging from his belt

*is an 1892 American model typewriter. He is pooped. Suddenly
he stops, cups his hands, and* SHOUTS.

FERNANDO: Zapata. . . . Emiliano Zapata . . . !

Receiving no answer he trudges on.

A Cave Behind a Big Rock

*We go to a figure (*PABLO*), whom we should remember as one
of the* HORSEMEN *in the boundary-marking scene. . . . He has
just been awakened by the* SHOUT. *Nearby, the mouth of the
cave. In front of it is the* CARCASS *of a hung deer in the process
of being jerked, laid out on its own skin. Beside the cave* THREE
HORSES *are tied up short. One, a* STALLION, *is fighting its halter.*

A WOMAN OF THE COUNTRY, *still half girl, with a kind of
savage animal beauty, is crouched over the fire cooking strips
of venison. We will call her the* SOLDADERA.

A SHOT SOUNDS. . . . PABLO *gets heavily to his feet and
strolls to a big rock and looks around it.*

A Little Crevice Overlooking Trail—Emiliano and Eufemio lying there.

*Their clothes are ragged. They have the wary look of hunted
animals.* EUFEMIO *has just* FIRED *his rifle.* PABLO *comes into
scene.*

EUFEMIO (*looking down trail*): He's still coming.

EMILIANO: Who do you think he is?

PABLO: A stranger . . . look at his clothes.

EUFEMIO (*to* EMILIANO): Shall I kill him, little brother?

EMILIANO: Shoot in front of him again. . . .

PABLO: Careful. Don't hit him.

EUFEMIO: When I want to hit them, I hit them. When I want to
miss them, I miss them.

PABLO: A man has been known to die of a close miss.

EUFEMIO *carefully draws his carbine up and sights. . . .* SHOT
and WHINE *of a bullet.* FERNANDO *stops. Then holding up his
hat and brief case ahead of him in a gesture of peace, he
continues walking.*

Crevice—Emiliano, Eufemio, and Pablo

PABLO: He's crazy. It's not nice to kill crazy people.

EUFEMIO: Shall I try him again, a little closer? . . .

PABLO: A little closer! How can you come closer?

Close Shot—Fernando

FERNANDO: Zapata! Emiliano Zapata!

Crevice—Emiliano, Eufemio, and Pablo

PABLO: Maybe he has a message. . . .

EUFEMIO: Maybe it's a trap. Why don't we kill him? It's so much
easier instead of so much worry. Besides, what does it cost?
One little bullet.

EMILIANO: No.

He stands up and faces the approaching FERNANDO.

EMILIANO (*calling to him*): What do you want?

Wider Angle—Crevice, as Fernando comes in to them.

EUFEMIO *covers him with his gun.* FERNANDO *turns to* PABLO,
holds out his hand.

FERNANDO (*introducing himself*): Fernando Aguirre.

PABLO (*taking his hand*): Pablo Gómez.

FERNANDO: I'm looking for Emiliano Zapata.

EUFEMIO (*answering for* PABLO): He's not here!

FERNANDO: His friends sent me.

EUFEMIO: Who are his friends?

FERNANDO: The people of the village.

EUFEMIO: He's not here!

EMILIANO *gestures to* EUFEMIO *to search* FERNANDO. *He goes
over his pockets, and legs of trousers.*

FERNANDO: I have no weapons.

EUFEMIO (*points to typewriter*): What's this?

PABLO: It's a writing machine.

FERNANDO: Yes—the sword of the mind.

EUFEMIO: I thought you had no weapons.

EUFEMIO *lifts it as though to smash it on a rock.*

FERNANDO (*suddenly, with great violence*): Don't you dare break that! (EUFEMIO *pauses*) Don't you dare. Put it down!!!

EUFEMIO *looks at his brother.* FERNANDO *has ferocity.* EMILIANO *respects this.*

EMILIANO: Put it down.

FERNANDO (*with sudden anger*): You're Emiliano Zapata. I have news of Madero, the leader of the fight against Díaz. Give me some water.

EMILIANO: Why do you come to me?

FERNANDO (*fiercely*): Give me some water!! I want to talk to you.

EMILIANO *turns, starts off toward their camp.*

Exterior, Camp—near Cave

The FOUR MEN *come in.* EMILIANO *hands* FERNANDO *a gourd of water, then crosses over to his* STALLION. PABLO *crouches at the fire near the* SOLDADERA. *He holds out his hand. She puts a piece of meat in it. He drops it because it is hot, and shakes his fingers. The* SOLDADERA *picks up the meat, dusts it off, blows on it, and puts it back in his hand.* FERNANDO *drinks from the gourd.*

Close Shot—Eufemio, watching Fernando.

Close Shot—Pablo, watching Fernando.

Close Shot—Emiliano pretending to be engrossed in his Horse, but at the same time stealing glances at Fernando.

Medium Shot, taking in all Four Men.

FERNANDO *finishes drinking, looks at the other* THREE MEN, *who quickly drop their eyes.*

FERNANDO (*to* EMILIANO): I want to talk to you.

EMILIANO (*from the side of the* STALLION): Talk.

FERNANDO: I want you to listen.

EMILIANO: Talk.

FERNANDO *picks up his brief case and goes over to* EMILIANO.

Eufemio, Pablo, and the Soldadera at the fire.
> *As they talk, they watch* FERNANDO *and* EMILIANO, *who are about twenty feet away.*

EUFEMIO (*worried*): It's so much harder to kill a man after you once talk to him. Even a few words.

PABLO: Shsh! Listen.

Fernando and Emiliano
> FERNANDO *takes out a packet of clippings, selects one which has on it a photograph of* MADERO. *He starts reading from it.*

FERNANDO: "The despotism of Porfirio Díaz is unbearable. For more than thirty-four years he has ruled with the hand of a ruthless tyrant."
> EMILIANO *takes the newspaper from him and studies* MADERO's *picture.*

Insert—Newspaper Clipping, showing picture of Madero. Back to Scene
> EMILIANO *looks intently at the picture. A* COYOTE HOWLS; *the* WHITE STALLION *is restive.*

EMILIANO (*gently, to the* HORSE): Steady. Pretty soon now, Blanco.

FERNANDO: Listen—(*reads from another newspaper*) "The true meaning of democracy has long been forgotten in Mexico. Elections are a farce. The people have no voice in the Government. The control of the country is in the hands of one man and those he has appointed to carry out his orders."

PABLO'S VOICE (*calling across*): Who wrote that?

FERNANDO: Francisco Madero.

EMILIANO (*still studying the photograph*): I like his face.
> *He folds the newspaper clipping and puts it into his pocket.*

FERNANDO (*reading*): "If we are to bring back to Mexico the freedom that goes with democracy we must unite to drive this tyrant from office. We will blow the little flames into one great fire!"

Close Shot—Eufemio and Pablo at the Fire
EUFEMIO (*to* PABLO): Who is Madero?

Close Shot—Fernando

> *He turns toward them as he overhears* EUFEMIO'*s question.*

FERNANDO: Leader of the fight against Díaz.

Wide Angle—Group

> FERNANDO *walks over to the fire, to* EUFEMIO *and* PABLO.

PABLO: Where is he?

FERNANDO: Right now he's in a part of the United States. Texas.

EUFEMIO: A fine place to lead a fight against Díaz!

FERNANDO (*fiercely*): From Texas he's been making preparations.
Now he's ready to move. He's sending out many people like
me to spread the word and search out leaders in other parts
of Mexico. (*looks toward* EMILIANO) I was sent to the State of
Morelos.

Emiliano

> *He's been listening intently, but now he covers up by busying
himself with his* WHITE STALLION.

EMILIANO: I don't like to tie him close. But the smell of a mare
came in on the wind this morning. He's restless. So am I.

Full Shot—Featuring Fernando

> *He reacts to the speech, and looks at* EMILIANO *penetratingly.
Then:*

FERNANDO: The people in your town told me—

EUFEMIO (*interrupting*): Don't believe what people tell you. Eat!!!

> *The* SOLDADERA *takes a piece of the venison from the fire, blows
on it, hands it to* FERNANDO. *Now* PABLO *moves toward* EMI-
LIANO *with affected casualness. . . .*

PABLO: Let me see that split hoof. . . .

Pablo and Emiliano bending over the HORSE'*s hoof.*

EMILIANO (*eagerly*): Madero!

PABLO: Yes. You remember I once read about him to you from the
newspaper. . . .

EMILIANO (*with the sudden violence of frustration*): You promised to teach me to read!!

PABLO (*placatingly*): I will. . . . I will. . . . Let's ask this man more about Madero. Maybe he's got a letter.

EMILIANO: Anybody can write a letter, even you. . . . I'd like to look at Madero's eyes. . . .

PABLO: Then go—go to wherever he is and talk to him. . . .

EMILIANO: No, I can't. Not now.

PABLO: Why not? (*no answer.* PABLO *speaks a little bitterly*) I know why. . . .

EMILIANO (*bending close to him*): I want you to go to Madero and look in his face and tell me what you see. . . .

PABLO: Me! He's in Texas. . . .

EMILIANO: Well, go to Texas.

PABLO: How far is it?

EMILIANO: Who knows? Go and see.

He takes out the newspaper clipping and looks at it again.

PABLO: I've never been out of our state. . . .

EMILIANO: Now you will be. . . . I can't go now. I want you to go. Look at Madero and see whether we can trust him. . . . A picture is only a picture.

PABLO: When do you want me to go?

EMILIANO: Now. . . . When else?

PABLO *still hesitates.*

EMILIANO: Now!! Cinch up.

Wider Angle as Pablo Mounts.

EMILIANO *goes to the fire . . . takes hunks of cooked meat and stuffs them in* PABLO's *saddlebag.*

Close Shot—Emiliano and Pablo

EMILIANO (*whispering*): If you like what you see in his face, tell him we recognize him as the leader of the Revolution. Tell him about our troubles here.

Full Shot

> PABLO *kicks his* HORSE *and rides off.* EMILIANO *goes to the fire and picks up a piece of meat and chews, thinking.*

FERNANDO: Where did he go?

EMILIANO: I don't know. He didn't say.

> *Suddenly he turns to his* HORSE, *quickly mounts, and rides away in an opposite direction.*

FERNANDO (*amazed*): Now *he's* going! Where's he going?

EUFEMIO (*same tone as* EMILIANO): I don't know—he didn't say!

FERNANDO: What's the matter with him?

EUFEMIO (*turning toward his* HORSE): A woman. What else? (*he mounts the* HORSE)

FERNANDO: Where are *you* going?

EUFEMIO (*shrugging*): What else?!

> *He turns his* HORSE, *starts after* EMILIANO.

FERNANDO (CALLING AFTER *him, indicating the* SOLDADERA): What about her?

Close Shot—Eufemio

> *He* CALLS *back over his shoulder.*

EUFEMIO: She'll take care of herself. . . .

> *He disappears.*

Close-up—Fernando

> *looking off after* EUFEMIO. *He takes out his handkerchief, mops his brow.*

FERNANDO (*to the* SOLDADERA): This is all very confusing.

Wider Angle

> *He turns toward her and stops suddenly as he sees she is not there. He looks around for her—sees:*

Long Shot

> *of the* SOLDADERA, *disappearing down the trail.*

Close-up—Fernando

>   *He lets out an exasperated sigh, picks up his typewriter, prepares
>   to leave.*

Dissolve to:
Exterior, Street in Agalla—Night

>   TWO WOMEN, *black shawls concealing their heads and lower
>   faces, hurry down the narrow street. They pass a* POLICEMAN.

POLICEMAN: Good evening, Señora Espejo; good evening, Señorita. . . .

>   *He moves on. As he passes a corner, around the building appear*
>   EMILIANO *and* EUFEMIO, *looking after him. They don't want
>   the* POLICEMAN *to see them. They look down the street after the*
>   TWO WOMEN. *Then covering their noses with their serapes, they
>   move cautiously after the* WOMEN.

Exterior, the Church

>   *as* JOSEFA ESPEJO *and her* AUNT *enter. As the door closes behind
>   them,* EMILIANO *and* EUFEMIO *come into scene, quickly enter
>   the church.*

Interior, Church

>   *It is provincial and rather dark and deserted. The* TWO WOMEN
>   *make their duties, and sit down.*

Rear of Church

>   EMILIANO *and* EUFEMIO *have entered, and stand looking off
>   toward the* WOMEN. *They, too, make their duties, then start
>   past the screen which is around the fount. As they do,* EMILIANO
>   *taps* EUFEMIO *on the shoulder, points to the rifle he is carrying.
>   Both men stand their rifles in the corner. Then they separate,
>   one going down one aisle, the other, the other.*

Josefa and Her Aunt, Seated in Church

> EMILIANO *moves in beside* JOSEFA, EUFEMIO *on the other side of the* AUNT. *Simultaneously they are beside the women.*

Close Shot—Group

EMILIANO (*to* JOSEFA): I must talk to you. . . .

> *The* AUNT *turns her head, with an* EXCLAMATION—*and instantly finds her arms pinned to her side and her mouth covered by* EUFEMIO'*s hand.* JOSEFA *looks at her* AUNT, *sees she is held tightly by* EUFEMIO, *then turns to* EMILIANO.

JOSEFA: The Rurales are after you!

EMILIANO: I know, Josefa, I have risked my life to come here. . . . When may I call on your father?

JOSEFA: What for?

EMILIANO: To beg his permission to ask for your hand.

JOSEFA: Oh no! Don't do it!

EMILIANO: Why not?

JOSEFA: Don't do it.

EMILIANO: What's wrong with me?

JOSEFA: That's not it. What would be wrong with me if I married you?

EMILIANO: What do you mean?

JOSEFA: I have no intention of ending up washing clothes in a ditch and patting tortillas like an Indian.

EMILIANO: Who says that?

JOSEFA: Sh! My father.

EMILIANO (*his* VOICE RISING *steadily and fiercely to a crescendo*): My mother was a Salazar! Zapatas were chieftains here when *your* grandfather lived in a cave!

JOSEFA: Shsh! We're in church. Well, you're not chieftains *now*! You have no money, no land. Without luck you'll probably be in jail by tomorrow.

EMILIANO: It happens I have been offered an important position by Don Nacio de la Torre y Mier.

JOSEFA (*her* VOICE RISING): Don Nacio de la Torre does not employ fugitives from the law!

EMILIANO: If I accept his offer, he will have the charges against me dismissed!

JOSEFA: Why in the world would Don Nacio need anyone like *you*?? Why??

EMILIANO: Apparently you have not heard that I am the best judge of horses in the country. You are the only one who has not heard this. I worked for him for years. I bought every horse in his stable for him. When I have not helped Don Nacio buy his horses, it is later discovered that they have—(*almost* SHOUTING)—five legs!

EUFEMIO, *who has been listening with interest, has let his hand slip from the* AUNT'*s mouth.*

AUNT: What a conceited monkey!

EUFEMIO'*s hand comes back to place.*

JOSEFA: Well, I notice you haven't accepted this offer. And now if you'll allow my aunt to breathe we'll continue our devotions. . . . (*there's a pause*)

EMILIANO: Then I will have to take you by force—

JOSEFA: By force? I would not prevent you. I would go with you because I couldn't prevent you. . . . But sooner or later you will go to sleep. . . .

EMILIANO: What's that got to do with it?

JOSEFA (*takes a steel pin from her hair—holds it up in front of his eyes and repeats*): Sooner or later you will go to sleep. . . .

EMILIANO: You'd never do that. A respectable girl like you.

JOSEFA: Yes I would! Because I *am* a respectable girl. A respectable girl wants to live a safe life—Protected! Uneventful! Without surprises! And preferably with a rich man.

EMILIANO (*really deeply shocked*): You don't mean that . . . !

JOSEFA: I do. Come back when you can offer me that. (*turns to* AUNT) He's going to let you go now. Don't scream. The police are after him. . . . (*now to* EUFEMIO) Let her go. . . . (EUFEMIO *doesn't*)

EMILIANO (*abruptly*): Let her go. . . . (EUFEMIO *does so*) I'll be back. Don't think I won't be back.

The TWO MEN *rise, quickly and quietly slip away from the* WOMEN, *go to the rear door of the church.* JOSEFA *and her* AUNT *look at each other. Suddenly and unexpectedly, and even to her own considerable surprise the* AUNT *says:*

AUNT: I like him.

JOSEFA (*shocked, surprised*): You do?

AUNT: I mean—he's a terrible man . . . a fugitive—a criminal!

JOSEFA: I like him too. . . .

Dissolve to:
Exterior, Large Courtyard

walled on three sides. Along one side, watching, are some poverty-stricken PEOPLE. *The fourth side is the entrance to a magnificent stable. In the center of the courtyard,* FIVE ARABIAN HORSES *are being led in a circle. Each* HORSE *is led by an* INDIAN, *and as they lead the* HORSES, *they* TALK SOFTLY *among themselves in the Aztec language. The* HORSES *are being shown off to* DON NACIO DE LA TORRE, *who is seated in a chair. Beside him stands* THE MANAGER *and slightly behind him on the other side is* EMILIANO.

[*Medium Shot—Don Nacio, Emiliano, and Manager*

THE MANAGER: Directly from Arabia, pure blood line. I don't know why my master is willing to sell them, Don Nacio.

DON NACIO: I think they're beautiful. (*turns to* EMILIANO; *in a* WHISPER) I don't trust his master. Do you trust the horses?

EMILIANO *has been listening to the* TALK *of the* INDIANS *who lead the* HORSES. *His attention is pulled back.*

EMILIANO: They're all right.

DON NACIO (*preparing to get up*): Well . . . if you think so. (*turns to* MANAGER) My major-domo has the best eye for a horse in the south of Mexico.

EMILIANO *puts his hand on* DON NACIO'S *arm.*

EMILIANO: Where are the others?

THE MANAGER: What others?

EMILIANO: Weren't there ten in the shipment from Arabia?

THE MANAGER (*stumbling*): Oh, I didn't think you'd want to see them, Don Nacio.

DON NACIO: Oh, but we do!

THE MANAGER: Besides, they're not for sale.

DON NACIO: We'll look at them.

THE MANAGER: Certainly . . . this way. (*he starts out*)

DON NACIO (WHISPERING *to* EMILIANO): How did you know there were ten?

EMILIANO: The Indians. They were talking in their own tongue.

As they start after THE MANAGER, EMILIANO SPEAKS *to the* IN-DIANS *in the Aztec language. They* LAUGH.

DON NACIO: I forgot you knew Aztec. Our Spanish is fine in the cities, but in the country I've often wished I could understand the Indians.

The INDIANS LAUGH *again to themselves.* DON NACIO *looks at* EMILIANO.

DON NACIO: I must say you look very well. You take naturally to being a gentleman.]

Close Shot—Bowl, showing hands breaking eggs in the bowl.

Another hand puts a sponge into the egg mixture and the CAMERA RISES *with the sponge and we see an* INDIAN *sponging the eggs into the coat of a* HORSE *tied to the outside of a box stall.* CAMERA PULLS BACK *and we see that we are in the magnificent stables. The floor is cobbled in tiny stones set in designs, black and red. Along one wall are luxurious carriages. To the rear are box stalls. The building is of stone, the stalls and mangers of marble. A stream of clear, fresh water runs in a trench down the middle.*

Into the scene walk THE MANAGER, DON NACIO *and* EMI-LIANO. *The first two are looking at the* HORSE, *which is being*

polished. A LITTLE GIRL, *sitting beside the* WOMAN *who is breaking the eggs, with a quick thievish gesture, dips her finger into
the mixture and puts it into her mouth. Her* MOTHER, *seeing
that* EMILIANO *has noticed this, slaps her hand. The* LITTLE
GIRL *puts down her head in shame.* EMILIANO *also looks away
in shame.*

THE MANAGER (*to the* INDIAN *who is wielding the sponge*): Rub it in
. . . rub it harder. (*to* DON NACIO) They're so lazy. . . .
Luncheon is ready now. (*he moves toward the door*)

EMILIANO (*gesturing toward the* HORSE *being sponged; softly to*
DON NACIO): That's the best of the lot. Let's look at the
others.

THE MANAGER: So lazy! If they're not stealing, they're asleep. If
they are awake, they're drunk.

DON NACIO (*loudly*): Let's look at the others!

THE MANAGER (*loud*): But luncheon is served!

DON NACIO (*loud and strong*): It can wait!

DON NACIO *and* EMILIANO, *trailed by* THE MANAGER, *walk down
the line of box stalls,* CAMERA MOVING *with them.* EMILIANO
pauses and looks into a box stall. THE OTHERS *walk on a few
paces, then turn and look back at* EMILIANO. *They step back
to him, look in through the bars of the stall.*

Close Shot—Manger

A LITTLE BOY *is shrinking into the hay at the bottom of the
manger, attempting to hide. He's been caught in the act of
stealing the* HORSES' *food. His hand and mouth are caked with
mash.* THE MANAGER *reaches in, grabs the* BOY, *yanks him out
of the manger.*

Group Shot at Manger

DON NACIO: What is it?

THE MANAGER: Stealing! You see? You can't turn your back on
them! Even the *horses'* food!

He slashes at the BOY *with his quirt. The second time he raises his hand,* EMILIANO *grabs his wrist.*

EMILIANO: Stop it.

THE MANAGER: They steal everything!

He tears his wrist loose and slashes again at the CHILD. EMILIANO *reverses his* charro *whip and knocks* THE MANAGER *to the floor. He means to kill him! As he raises the* charro *whip again,* DON NACIO *throws himself at him and knocks him off balance.*

DON NACIO: Stop it! . . . Emiliano . . . stop it!

He forces EMILIANO *outside.*

Exterior, the Stable

EMILIANO *is standing still, trembling.* DON NACIO *paces around him.*

DON NACIO: When I had the charges against you dismissed you promised—

EMILIANO: I know.

DON NACIO: It wasn't easy.

EMILIANO: I know.

DON NACIO: I don't want to regret it. Emiliano, I told you. Violence is no good.

EMILIANO (*suddenly reverting*): Then why does *he* use it?

DON NACIO (*stopping him with his arm*): You're full of anger.

EMILIANO: That boy was hungry.

DON NACIO: Calm down, calm down! (*lighting a cigar*) Look, Emiliano. . . . You're a clever man and an able man. You might even be an important man, have money and property, be respected. That's what you told me you wanted. . . . Do you want it or don't you?

EMILIANO (*quietly*): He was hungry.

DON NACIO: Are you responsible for everybody? You can't be the conscience of the whole world.

Wider Angle

     taking in a ragged group of INDIANS *watching the* TWO MEN.
     They've seen and understood. One of them makes a joke in his
     own language and the rest burst into LAUGHTER. EMILIANO
     LAUGHS *too, in spite of himself. The air is cleared.*

EMILIANO (*to* DON NACIO): Have you another cigar?

DON NACIO: The most civilized thing about you is your taste
     for good cigars. (*the* INDIANS LAUGH *again*) What was the
     joke?

EMILIANO: Just Indian talk. . . . They're just Indians.

     He bursts out LAUGHING *again.*

DON NACIO: I'm going to prescribe for you. You need that wife.
     Have you ever spoken to Josefa's father?

EMILIANO: No.

DON NACIO: Why not?

EMILIANO: I don't like him and he doesn't like me.

DON NACIO: In the world of business, few people like each other,
     but they have to get along—or there wouldn't be any business.
     . . . Emiliano, look, now you have a position—clothes—go
     to Señor Espejo—tell him I'm your patron. Make your peace
     with him. (*warningly*) And don't forget that the President has
     drawn a circle around your name. You must behave. (*he points
     to* THE MANAGER *standing at a distance*) Now you'd better start
     practicing. Go over and apologize to him.

     EMILIANO *hesitates, then turns and stalks toward* THE MANAGER.
     THE MANAGER *moves away.*

EMILIANO (*shouting after him*): I apologize!

THE MANAGER (*from a safe distance*): Accepted, accepted.

EMILIANO (*turning to* DON NACIO): Was that all right . . . ?

     DON NACIO LAUGHS. *Then stops as he notices that* EMILIANO *is
     suddenly intent on something. He turns and looks and sees
     among the* INDIANS *in the background behind him a* STRANGER
     who walks toward* EMILIANO. *It is* PABLO.

DON NACIO: Do you know him?

EMILIANO: Yes. He's a friend. He's been away.

Without another word he leaves DON NACIO *and walks toward* PABLO.

Close Shot—Pablo and Emiliano

PABLO *is dressed as usual, in a worn brown* charro *costume, except that, at the throat, instead of a scarf or string tie, he wears a celluloid collar and a bright necktie.*

EMILIANO (*pointing to collar and tie*): What's that . . . ?

PABLO (*simply*): Texas!

EMILIANO LAUGHS. *They embrace warmly. . . . Suddenly he sees something.*

FERNANDO *is standing, as if waiting, at one side. He looks at* EMILIANO. *Smiles.*

Dissolve to:

Long Shot—Road—Day

The road leads up to a ford of a small stream. FOUR HORSEMEN *ride up and dismount, to let their* HORSES *drink in a stream. It's apparent from the dust on their mounts and themselves that they are on a journey.*

Medium Shot—The Four Men: Pablo, Emiliano, Eufemio, and Fernando

FERNANDO *squats in the sand beside the river, picks up a stick and idly draws what might be a half-imagined map in the sand.*

PABLO: He's not a tall man, has a brown beard, soft voice . . . and his hands—

EUFEMIO (*breaking in*): Doesn't sound like a fighter.

PABLO: Well no . . . he's quiet—(EMILIANO *seems abstracted*)

FERNANDO: He's firm and he's brave! —I know he's brave!

PABLO: We spoke of you, Emiliano.

FERNANDO: He wants a message from you. . . . (EMILIANO *does not answer*) One strong push from the north or south and Díaz will

drop like an old bull with a sword under his shoulder . . .
the time has come!

EMILIANO *has raised his* HORSE's *front foot and is pulling off
a loose shoe.* EMILIANO SPEAKS *soothingly to the* HORSE.

EMILIANO: Steady, Blanco . . . steady. . . .

EUFEMIO: I don't understand it. How can this Madero stay in the
United States? Why don't they lock him up?

FERNANDO: Up there they protect political refugees—

EUFEMIO: Why?

PABLO (*groping for an explanation*): Well—up there they are a
democracy.

EMILIANO: We're a democracy, too, and look what's happened.

PABLO (*earnestly*): Yes, I know, but up there it—it's different—

FERNANDO (*cutting him very short*): I will explain it. There the
Government governs, but with the consent of the people. The
people have a voice.

PABLO: That's right.

FERNANDO (*continuing*): They have a President, too, but he governs
with the consent of the people. Here we have a President,
but no consent. Who asked us if we wanted Díaz for thirty-
four years?

EUFEMIO: Nobody ever asked me nothing.

Suddenly EMILIANO *turns around from his* HORSE *and looks
sharply at* FERNANDO.

EMILIANO: And you—how are *you* in this?

PABLO: Madero sent him with me.

FERNANDO (*to* EMILIANO—*very tough*): He wants a message from
you. I am waiting to hear what to tell him.

EMILIANO (*equally tough*): He wants a leader here. It's not me.

He mounts his HORSE. PABLO *looks at him, shocked.*

FERNANDO: You don't believe in him?

EMILIANO: Yes.

FERNANDO: So?

EMILIANO: Tell him to get another man.

FERNANDO: As you wish.

EMILIANO: I have private affairs. Besides, I don't want to be the conscience of the world. I don't want to be the conscience of anybody.

They glare at each other murderously.

FERNANDO (*tight-lipped*): As you wish.

EMILIANO *turns his* HORSE *and starts across the ford.* EUFEMIO *splashes into the river, comes abreast of* EMILIANO, *grabs his bridle.*

Emiliano and Eufemio

EUFEMIO (*with great violence*): Why do you want her? Emiliano, I took a very good look—by daylight! Not only isn't she pretty, she's stringy! There's nothing on her! Take a good close look. Why I know twins over in Cuautla, both of them ten times as good and they aren't pretty either. And with money, too! And you can have either one! Or both!

EMILIANO *doesn't answer.* EUFEMIO *releases the* HORSE—EMILIANO *crosses the stream.*

Dissolve to:

Long Shot—Piece of the Road Ahead

Two mounted RURALES, *leading a* PRISONER.

Medium Shot—Group

There is a noose about the PRISONER's *neck, the other end tied to the saddle horn of one of the* RURALES. *The* PRISONER *is the* OLD INDIAN *who was in the boundary-marking scene,* MEMBER *also of the* DELEGATION *who called on* DÍAZ. *He has no hat now and is dressed in the ragged white field clothes characteristic of the district. His hands are tied behind him. His face is parched with dirt and sun. There are whip marks on his face. About twenty feet behind him trudges* HIS WIFE, *carrying a big bundle.*

Wider Angle

 as EMILIANO, EUFEMIO, *and* PABLO *ride up alongside, pass the*
WOMAN *and ride even with the* PRISONER. *They pull their* HORSES
down to a walk.

EMILIANO: Why, it's Innocente! What's the matter?

Close Shot—Emiliano and the Prisoner

 INNOCENTE *looks up. His mouth is dry; he licks his lips, attempts
to speak, and then looks down at the road. Suddenly the rope
around his neck is jerked.*

FIRST RURALE'S VOICE: Get away from the prisoner!

EMILIANO (*ignoring* RURALE): Innocente, what are they taking you
in for?

 INNOCENTE *is silent.*

EMILIANO: Innocente?

 INNOCENTE *doesn't even look up.*

Wider Angle

 as PABLO *and* EUFEMIO *ride up beside* EMILIANO.

PABLO: He can't talk, Emiliano. He's thirsty.

 EUFEMIO *reaches for the gourd of water which he carries.*

Another Angle—Including Mounted Rurales

 EMILIANO *rides up alongside the* RURALES.

EMILIANO: What did he do?

FIRST RURALE: They're all crazy. They're the craziest people I ever
saw.

EMILIANO (*persistently*): But what did he do?

SECOND RURALE: Who knows. . . . They're always doing something.

EMILIANO: What are you going to do with him?

 The RURALES *look at him as if to say*: "How dumb can you
get!"

EMILIANO: Let him go.

 They look back at the PRISONER.

The Prisoner
> EUFEMIO *rides in beside him, holds the water gourd to his mouth, trying to give him a drink.*

Full Shot—Group
> *Without explanation, or a word, the* RURALE *jerks the* OLD MAN *off his feet and the water gourd flies from* EUFEMIO'S *hand and breaks on the road. The* OLD MAN *is flat, face downward on the road.*

Another Angle—Favoring Emiliano
> *He whips out his machete; the* RURALE *ducks and whirls his* HORSE *to escape. The* SECOND RURALE *follows him.*

The Prisoner
> *He has partially risen to his feet; now, since he is tied to the saddle of the fleeing* RURALE, *he is again thrown flat, and is dragged along the road.*

Exterior, Road—Moving Shot
> *as* EMILIANO *pursues the fleeing* RURALES. *He closes the distance between them, and slashes at the rope which ties the* PRISONER.

Close Shot—Prisoner
> *As the rope is cut, the* PRISONER *is released, and rolls clear.*

The Two Rurales
> *flee into the field of cane alongside the road, and disappear from view.*

Emiliano
> *He whirls around, starts back to* GROUP *around the* PRISONER.

Exterior, Road—Group Around Innocente's Body
> INNOCENTE'S WIFE *is beside him . . . turning him over. He is dead. The* PEOPLE *of the fields appear from the cane. They*

surround the body. EMILIANO *rides in, dismounts.* FERNANDO
rides in to the GROUP.

WIFE (*to the body*): I told you and I warned you. You couldn't get
it through your head. The land isn't ours any more. Even after
they killed Plutarco, you went in at night to plant the field.

Close Shot—Emiliano and Fernando

FERNANDO: You should have cut the rope, without talking.

EMILIANO: It was my fault. I should have cut the rope and then
talked.

Wider Angle—Group

WIFE (*accusingly to the corpse*): You're headstrong, that's what you
are. You always have been. You're stubborn.

EUFEMIO *and* PABLO *come near to* EMILIANO. *Other* INDIANS,
among them LAZARO, *have appeared from nowhere.*

EMILIANO (*to* EUFEMIO *and* PABLO): He's dead.

WIFE (*still to the corpse*): You crawled through the fence at night
to plant the corn.

AN INDIAN: My father does the same thing. . . .

WIFE (*still scolding the corpse*): Stubborn—that's what you are. . . .

LAZARO (*defending the body gently*): No . . . not stubborn . . . the
field is like a wife . . . live with it all your life, it's hard to
learn that she isn't yours. (*gesturing toward* EMILIANO) *He*
understands.

WIFE (*turns to* EMILIANO, *apologetically*): I'm sorry we caused you
trouble. . . .

ANOTHER INDIAN: Now they'll be after you. . . .

LAZARO: You can hide in my house. . . .

ANOTHER INDIAN: I'll take care of your horse. . . .

EMILIANO *removes his hat, leans down toward the body.*

EMILIANO: I'm sorry, Innocente. . . .

He turns, quickly mounts his HORSE, *and rides off in fury.*

Fernando and Pablo stand looking after him. Fernando smiles.

Dissolve to:
Interior, Small Half-Warehouse, Half-Office

> *The business place of* SEÑOR ESPEJO, *which is one section of the* ESPEJO *home. Packages and bales of soaps, candles and basic hardware which* ESPEJO *imports and sells.* SEÑOR ESPEJO *sits behind his desk,* EMILIANO *stands before it.*

EMILIANO: Don Nacio is my patron. He has assured me that I will be a man of substance. On this basis I presume to sue for your daughter's hand.

> SEÑOR ESPEJO *rises, and as he speaks he casually walks to the door which separates the living quarters from the business quarters of his establishment and opens it a few inches. The opened door discloses for the audience (but not for* EMILIANO) *the figures of* JOSEFA, *her* MOTHER, *and her* AUNT, *sitting primly, each with her embroidery frame. They lean forward, listening, but pretending not to.*

SEÑOR ESPEJO *to* EMILIANO (*as he is opening the door*): My friend, do not think I am insensible of the honor you do me in offering to take my daughter off my hands. But I do not need to give the problem a great deal of thought before I answer with a permanent and unchanging NO! The answer is no. . . .

EMILIANO: What's the matter with me?

SEÑOR ESPEJO (*returning to his desk, seating himself*): There is a proverb: "Though we are all made of the same clay, a jug is not a vase."

EMILIANO: What's the matter with me?

SEÑOR ESPEJO: I hoped you would not ask that again, but since you have, allow me to say that you are a rancher without land, a gentleman without money, a man of substance without substance!

> *He looks toward the door to the living quarters.*

Interior, Living Quarters

> *The embroidering has stopped. The* WOMEN *are listening.* JO-SEFA *leans forward, intently listening.*

Espejo and Emiliano

SEÑOR ESPEJO *is* SPEAKING *now especially for his* WOMEN.

SEÑOR ESPEJO: A fighter, a drinker, a brawler; these things you are. I have nothing against you personally. I can see where in some quarters you might be considered desirable. But my daughter! I have no intention whatsoever of one day finding her squatting on the bare earth, patting tortillas like a common Indian.

There is silence for a moment. Then EMILIANO *strikes the desk with his hand. The papers jump out of their pigeonholes.* SEÑOR ESPEJO *leaps back with fear. A nineteenth-century Shepherdess of cheap plaster falls and crashes.*

EMILIANO: Don't be afraid, little man. (EMILIANO *crosses to the door of the living quarters*)

SEÑOR ESPEJO: What are you doing?

EMILIANO: Find her a merchant—a musty, moth-eaten man like yourself.

He has said this in the direction of the door. Now he opens it wide, revealing the WOMEN *listening. The* OLDER WOMEN *are terribly frightened.* JOSEFA *is rather pleased, smiling. . . .*

EMILIANO: Let her be queen of the warehouses and mistress of the receipt books!

He turns toward the front door and steps through into the street. . . .

Exterior, Espejo's Office

As EMILIANO *exits, he is pinned down by both arms. Many* RURALES *hold him. They are taking no chances with* EMILIANO. *Among the large force of* MEN *are the* TWO RURALES *whom* EMILIANO *met on the road with the* PRISONER. *Expertly the* MEN *begin to bind* EMILIANO'S *arms behind him.*

Full Shot—Village Square

At this moment a little crowd of PEOPLE *come slowly across the square, carrying a body on a rude litter made of two poles and* a serape. *They see that* EMILIANO *is being arrested and know it is because of what he tried to do for them.*

Exterior, Square

The RURALES *lead* EMILIANO *away. The* PEOPLE *watch. Then they all turn and look toward* ESPEJO's *store.*

Close Shot—Señor Espejo standing in his doorway. He becomes aware of the Indians. He turns, enters his store, closes the door.

The Street

About a dozen RURALES *now surround* EMILIANO, *whose hands are tied behind him.* FEATURE *this tying.*

Pablo and Eufemio watching—then they ride off.

Group Shot of people watching. They know what is intended for Emiliano. Beginning of the summoning of the People.

Emiliano and Rurales

Twelve RURALES, *six on either side of* EMILIANO. *His hands are tied behind him; he is on foot, and he is led by the neck by a rope which the* OFFICER *riding ahead of him holds.*

Close Shot—Emiliano

as his eyes quickly search the CROWD. *There is a change of expression as he sees—*

Eufemio, Pablo, and Fernando

among the CROWD. *They stare back at* EMILIANO.

Close Shot—Emiliano

He looks away from EUFEMIO, PABLO, *and* FERNANDO, *stares straight ahead.*

Full Shot—Procession

as it starts down the street, EMILIANO *walking between the* TWO COLUMNS OF RURALES.

Quick Dissolve to:
Exterior, Road Past the Original Field

> The PROCESSION *on the move. In the distance, ahead of the* PROCESSION, *a few* COUNTRY PEOPLE *are casually walking along.*

Exterior, Cane Field

> *A* GROUP OF COUNTRY PEOPLE *moving secretly through the cane.*

Exterior, Road—Near a Corner

> The PROCESSION *rounds a corner and ahead of them are trudging a large* GROUP OF COUNTRY PEOPLE.

Close Shot—Captain of Rurales

> *He sees the* COUNTRY PEOPLE; *then he turns and looks back.*

What He Sees

> GROUP OF COUNTRY PEOPLE *following, very casually.*

Close Shot—Captain, frowning.

Dissolve to:
Road Through Hilly Country

> The PROCESSION *moves along.* SHOOTING ACROSS THE COLUMN *we see a mass of* PEOPLE *moving down a hill.*

Close Shot—Rurales, apprehensive.

Close Shot—Captain, very apprehensive.

Full Shot—Procession

> *now surrounded on all sides by* PEOPLE *pressing on them. Movement is becoming very difficult. The* COUNTRY PEOPLE *look straight ahead as they trudge along.*

Close-up—Emiliano, in midst of Procession.

The Procession

> We are SHOOTING DOWN *on them. As they move along* CAMERA RISES, *and we see ahead a line of* MOUNTED AND ARMED MEN *blocking the road.*

Medium, Shot—Mounted Men

> EUFEMIO, PABLO, *and* FERNANDO *prominent among them.* EUFEMIO *holds the reins of* EMILIANO'S WHITE HORSE.

Close Shot—Captain

> He looks at the MOUNTED MEN, *then turns in the saddle and looks back at* EMILIANO.

Close Shot—Emiliano

> He stares back, without expression.

The Procession

> The CAPTAIN *holds up his hand and the* PROCESSION *stops a few feet from the* MOUNTED MEN. EMILIANO *looks up a little sardonically. The* CAPTAIN *rises in his stirrups, and* YELLS *to the* MOUNTED MEN:

CAPTAIN: Clear the way!

> *No movement. No answer.*

Close Shot—Captain

CAPTAIN (*a little hysterically*): This man is a criminal! You are making yourselves liable for his crime!

Group Shot—Mounted Men

> No movement at all. No answer. They stare back impassively.

Close Shot—Captain

> He looks toward the MOUNTED MEN, *then looks around at the* COUNTRY PEOPLE, *who surround the* COLUMN.

CAPTAIN: What are you trying to do?

Medium Shot—Group of Indians

LAZARO: We are here, my Captain, with your permission, to see that the prisoner does not try to escape. For if he did try, you would be forced to shoot him in the back. Is it not so, my Captain?

Captain—and Column, Including Emiliano

After a pause, the CAPTAIN *CRIES:*

CAPTAIN: You're defying the law!

LAZARO: No, helping the law, with your permission—Guarding the prisoner!

OTHERS CHIME IN. *There is another pause. Then the* CAPTAIN *turns his* HORSE, *goes back a few paces to* EMILIANO, *takes out a knife and cuts the ropes which bind his hands.* EMILIANO *looks up at him without expression.*

Full Shot

as EMILIANO *walks from the midst of the* COLUMNS *to the* GROUP OF MOUNTED MEN, *takes the reins of his* HORSE *from* EUFEMIO.

Group Shot—Mounted Men and Emiliano

He stands beside his HORSE, *puts his hand between the cinch and the belly.*

EMILIANO (*to the* HORSE): Blanco! The cinch is too loose!

He tightens the cinch and mounts. PABLO *hands him his hat.*

Group Shot—Captain and Rurales

The CAPTAIN *is livid at this defiance.*

Group Shot—Country People

Looking toward EMILIANO *in a new way. Somehow through this incident he has become the leader of these* PEOPLE.

Emiliano, Eufemio, Pablo, Fernando, and the Mounted Men

EMILIANO (*to* EUFEMIO, *with wonder—looking off toward the* PEO-PLE): How did they all get here?

EUFEMIO (*with a smile and a shrug*): Who knows . . . ? Let's
go. . . .

FERNANDO: Zapata!—the wire—

EMILIANO: What do you mean?

FERNANDO: The telegraph wire. Cut it before he uses it—

Wider Angle
> *as* EUFEMIO *rides to the lowest place in the telegraph wire loop
> and reaches up with his machete.*

Close Shot—Captain as he sees what Eufemio is about to do.
CAPTAIN: Don't touch that! This is rebellion!

Eufemio
> *standing high in his stirrups, machete raised. He pauses, looks
> at* EMILIANO.

Close Shot—Emiliano
> *He looks back at* EUFEMIO.
EMILIANO: Cut it.

Eufemio
> *He brings his machete down on the wire. The wires spring
> apart.*

Emiliano and Mounted Men
> *As* EUFEMIO *rides back to them. They whirl, ride away.*

Full Shot—Road
> *The* COUNTRY PEOPLE *suddenly and silently melt away. The
> twelve* RURALES *are on a deserted road. They look at each other
> . . . and then around at the deserted country.*

Fade out

Fade in
A Pavilion in a Garden of a Hacienda—Evening
> This is the home of DON NACIO. *Lanterns provide illumination.*
> *Flowers, shrubs,* SINGING *birds in gilt cages.* STRINGS PLAYING
> *a waltz,* SOFTLY. *On a tiled roof, directly above the* ORCHESTRA,
> *concealed by the leaves of a banana tree,* TWO LITTLE INDIAN
> BOYS *watch.*

Full Shot—Dinner Table
> INDIANS, *dressed in the white clothes of the period, and under*
> *the direction of a French* MAJOR-DOMO, *serve the* GUESTS. *This*
> *is a dinner party given by* DON NACIO *for two of his neighbor*
> hacendados. *One of them,* GENERAL FUENTES, *wears the full-*
> *dress uniform of a Mexican general, with decorations that*
> *include the Iron Cross. The other man is* DON GARCÍA. *Their*
> WIVES *are rather dumpy, food stultified, and overdressed. They*
> *sit like bug-eating plants. At the opposite end of the table from*
> DON NACIO *is a* WOMAN *who is ravishingly beautiful.* DON NACIO,
> *it will appear, is somewhat drunk.*

Medium Shot—Group at Table
DON NACIO (*speaking very earnestly, and with difficulty*): Gentlemen,
    my family has been here three hundred years. I know the
    facts. These fields *do* belong to the Indian villages since before
    the Conquest!
DON GARCÍA: I paid for the land! I put the money in the hands of
    one who sits next to President Díaz himself!
GENERAL FUENTES: I remember very well a similar incident.
DON NACIO (*earnestly*): Give the land back. You don't need it. You
    have so much. . . .
DON GARCÍA: Don Nacio, you're drunk . . . or indisposed.
DON NACIO: I'm drunk—with wine and with worry. We're all in
    danger. If we don't give a little—we'll lose it all. . . . (*repeating*

with new conviction) The village people have been on that land for a thousand years. They own it.

DON GARCÍA: I paid for it! *I* own it!

DON NACIO (*suddenly turning to one of the waiters*—MANUEL): Isn't that right, Manuel? A thousand years?

MANUEL: Yes, Don Nacio.

DON NACIO: Manuel is from Anencuilco. . . . You don't know these Indians—they're fierce people.

MANUEL: Yes, Don Nacio. . . .

DON NACIO: They will fight for their fields.

GENERAL FUENTES: With what? With what will they fight? As a military man, I'm curious. . . .

DON GARCÍA (*suddenly exploding with rage*): Don't you think *I'll* fight? Don't you?

His WIFE *calms him. She gives him a pill. He takes it.*

GENERAL FUENTES: It seems ridiculous to ruin this beautiful dinner with politics. . . . (*referring to* DON NACIO'*s* LADY) Don Nacio, why do you raise sugar when you have such sweets already at your table. . . .

DON GARCÍA: Sugar! You know I am not an absentee farmer. I am a scientist. I know land. And this land was made for sugar . . . made by God himself. I say so in all reverence: for sugar. . . . Not corn!

DON NACIO: But they eat corn.

DON GARCÍA (*to his* WIFE, *who is trying to get his attention*): What?

GARCÍA'S WIFE: The cream, dear.

DON GARCÍA: What?

GARCÍA'S WIFE: The cream . . . only the cream, if you please.

DON GARCÍA (*loudly*): Yes, of course, the cream . . . (*does not pass it*) We will transform this land from a corn-ridden desert to a paradise. These animals can't be expected to understand the science of agriculture. Don't misconstrue me. The Indian is my neighbor. I *like* the Indians, and they *love* me. (*to his* WIFE) Don't they?

GARCÍA'S WIFE (*chewing*): They adore you.

DON NACIO: They eat corn!

DON GARCÍA: Sugar cane. The money from sugar will reach everywhere. I foresee a land of happy families. You'll see the whole population rising.

DON NACIO (*apparently he has given up*): I think they've risen.

Full Shot—Pavilion

> *From out of the undergrowth and the beautifully landscaped garden,* WHITE FIGURES *silently arising all around the pavilion on which the dinner is being served. They are expressionless, silent, stolid. They hold machetes. Among them stands* EMILIANO. *The* GUESTS *look around.*

DON GARCÍA: What is it? Who are they?

DON NACIO: Some of your neighbors. They love you.

> PABLO *comes forward, dressed in white field clothes, holding his hat over his breast humbly. . . .*

Medium Shot—at Table

PABLO (*to* DON NACIO): Emiliano Zapata wants to know, have you reached a conclusion. . . . He can't wait longer.

> DON GARCÍA *and* GENERAL FUENTES *look at* DON NACIO *for an explanation.*

DON NACIO (*turning to other* MEN): Emiliano Zapata came to me this morning. He asked my help in restoring the village lands, before the country burns up with fighting. The most I could offer him was to call you gentlemen together and beg you to stop this tragedy.

GENERAL FUENTES: The Army will stop this tragedy! They're on the way.

DON NACIO (*again trying desperately to make them understand*): He came this afternoon—oh, I told you that. He wanted help, he wanted money, he wanted food, he wanted some weapons from my little armory. Why am I drunk? I couldn't give him help. I knew he was right, but I didn't have the courage to help him.

PABLO: Excuse me, sir, but—

EMILIANO'S VOICE (*silencing him*): Pablo—

DON NACIO (*to* EMILIANO): The Army. Did you hear, Emiliano? I didn't send for them.

Close Shot—Emiliano

EMILIANO: Good-bye, Don Nacio.

He turns, walks away.

Full Shot—Dinner Table

> GENERAL FUENTES *takes a pistol from his holster and points from the waist at* EMILIANO'*s back.* DON NACIO *grabs his wrist.* MANUEL, *the Indian servant, sees this; he removes his coat, puts it on a chair and follows* EMILIANO.

GENERAL FUENTES (*to* DON NACIO): By saving him you may have killed a thousand men. You may have killed yourself.

> DON NACIO *goes to the edge of the platform, stands there, looking off into the darkness.*

Close Shot—Don García

DON GARCÍA (*suddenly horror-stricken*): If there's fighting, who'll harvest the sugar cane??!!

Full Shot—Group—Favoring Don Nacio

> *Over scene comes the* SOUND *of* TWO MEASURED THUMPS *and a* SMALL CRASH *of shattering wood. The* GUESTS *react in alarm. A smile appears on* DON NACIO'*s face, rueful and proud.*

DON NACIO: If you don't give a little, they'll take it all.

> *Now there is a* GREAT CRASH, *and splintering of wood.*

DON GARCÍA (*alarmed*): What's that?

DON NACIO: My armory. *Now* they have weapons.

> *They all stare at one another. As* DON NACIO *starts to pour himself a drink—*

Dissolve to:
Exterior, a Road—a Brilliant Moonlit Night
> A platoon of mounted FEDERAL SOLDIERS *on the march. We*
> HEAR *a series of* SHORT COYOTE BARKS. *The road at one point*
> *is flanked by trees, whose branches overhang and meet. As they*
> *enter the arch of branches—*

Close Shot—Man Behind Rock—Side of Road
> *He raises his head, cups his hand around his mouth and gives*
> *a* FULL COYOTE HOWL.

Close Shot—Two Officers, at Head of Procession
ONE OFFICER (*to the* OTHER): What was that?
OTHER OFFICER: Coyote.
> *The* FIRST OFFICER *nods, trying to dismiss his fears. But he*
> *looks around apprehensively.*

Head-on Shot—Procession
> *at it enters the arch of trees. The* COYOTE HOWL ECHOES *through*
> *the valley. At this signal,* FIGURES *drop from the branches*
> *onto the mounted* FEDERALS. *Instantly the orderly* COLUMN *has*
> *become a plunging, struggling, tangling mass of* MEN *and*
> HORSES.

Dissolve to:
Close Shot—Emiliano on Horseback looking off into the trees.

Wider Angle
> *Out from under the trees appears a* PROCESSION OF INDIANS,
> *leading the* HORSES *of the troops loaded with the equipment,*
> *clothing, arms, even the shoes of the now extinct soldiers. Some*
> INDIANS *with armloads of rifles.* EUFEMIO *is directing the* MEN.
> *He rides over to* EMILIANO.

Two Shot—Emiliano and Eufemio
EUFEMIO: Wait till you see some of the horses!
EMILIANO: How about bullets?
EUFEMIO: No pack animals, but wonderful horses! What horses!

Wider Angle

> *A circle of* ZAPATISTAS, *all carrying various pieces of captured equipment, surround* EMILIANO. *Some hold their prizes in the air.*

EMILIANO: But bullets—we need ammunition—what good are horses? How can we fight without bullets and ammunition?

> *Suddenly he spins his horse around with a violent angry gesture and rides away. The* OTHERS *follow.*

Dissolve to:

A Deep Gulch, as Seen from a Spot High Above

> *A railroad track runs through the gulch. A train of boxcars, with* TROOPS *on top, is entering the gulch.*

Medium Shot—a Little Gasoline Handcar, its whole front loaded with dynamite, is racing along the railroad track.

Long Shot—Shooting from Above the Gulch

> *Now we see that the handcar is speeding toward the oncoming train. It hits. There is a* TREMENDOUS EXPLOSION.

Full Shot

> *From all sides of the gulch come* WHITE-CLAD FIGURES; *they swarm over the train like bees.*

Moving Shot—at Train

> *Along the string of boxcars come* EMILIANO, *and* PABLO, *preceded by* MEN *who are breaking open the car doors. They stop at a door. The* MEN *who have opened it look out.*

EMILIANO: What is it?

A ZAPATISTA: Canned beef.

> *The* GROUP *moves on to the next car, pause.*

EMILIANO: What is it?

A ZAPATISTA: Uniforms and blankets.

> *The* GROUP *moves on to the next car, pause.*

EMILIANO: What is it?

ZAPATISTA: A piano . . . some furniture—

> *There is a* SUDDEN SHOUT *from up ahead.* EMILIANO *and his entourage run forward, up to a boxcar that has a door thrown open.* EUFEMIO *is standing at the door of a boxcar which has been fixed up as a kind of traveling ladies' apartment. Inside there are* THREE GIRLS, *frightened to death, and an old tough-looking* WOMAN, *probably a procurer of some kind, who stares defiantly at the* MEN. EMILIANO *looks at them for a moment. Then there is* ANOTHER SHOUT *from up ahead.* EMILIANO *moves up to another car.*

EMILIANO: Ammunition?

> *A* ZAPATISTA *comes to the door of the boxcar.*

ZAPATISTA: No . . . but powder and dynamite.

EMILIANO: How much?

ZAPATISTA: Half a car. . . .

EMILIANO: No ammunition?

ZAPATISTA: No. . . .

EMILIANO (*after a pause*): We won't wait any longer! We'll use what we have.

Dissolve to:

The Tower of the Citadel in a Garrison Town—the Hour Before Dawn

> *In the foreground a machine gun, pointing at the plaza. We see an empty plaza with a small bandstand in the middle.* MACHINE GUNNERS *are anxiously looking over the parapet. An* OFFICER (CAPTAIN) *approaches. The scene that follows should be shot entirely from the viewpoint of these* MEN.

CAPTAIN: Anything moving?

FIRST SOLDIER: A few women.

SECOND SOLDIER: I liked it better when they were shooting.

CAPTAIN: Maybe Zapata ran out of ammunition.

SECOND SOLDIER: I wouldn't depend on that.

FIRST SOLDIER: I think they've gone away. . . . Look there, sir,

some market women. If there's a market, they must have gone
away.

SECOND SOLDIER: With these Indians I don't trust the women any
more than the men. . . .

CAPTAIN: But there hasn't been a sign of them since yesterday
noon. I'm going to send out some scouts. (*looks over the parapet
and* CALLS *down to the* WOMEN) What are you doing down
there?

The Gate—Shooting Down from the Tower

> The WOMEN *stop in front of the gate and look up.* (*Among the*
> WOMEN *is the* SOLDADERA.)

CAPTAIN: What are you doing down there?

SOLDADERA: Going to market, sir.

CAPTAIN: Get away from the gate. . . .

SOLDADERA: Would you like to buy some eggs, sir?

CAPTAIN: Get away from the gate!

Medium Shot—Old Women at Gate

> The SOLDADERA *speaks rapidly in the Indian language to the
> other* WOMEN. *They pile their baskets in a cluster against the
> gate.*

CAPTAIN'S VOICE: Get away from the gate or we'll shoot you!

> The SOLDADERA *gives a short sharp order and the* WOMEN *scuttle
> away like chickens in all directions.*

Exterior, Tower of the Citadel

> The CAPTAIN *turns to* ONE OF HIS MEN.

CAPTAIN: Go down and get those baskets—quick!

> The MAN *exits quickly.*

Street in Town

> A *wild-looking* WOMAN *comes out of a side street, carrying a
> torch. The* SOUND *of a* MACHINE GUN *comes over. The* WOMAN

falls. Immediately she pulls herself up, starts to crawl, still carrying the torch. With a final effort she reaches her goal— a powder train which has been laid in the plaza. She sets the torch to the powder train. Another BURST OF MACHINE-GUN FIRE *hits her, kills her.*

Exterior, Plaza

The powder train runs quickly across the plaza, toward the CAMERA. *There is a huge* EXPLOSION *right in the face of the* CAMERA.

Series of Quick Shots

of MEN *pouring out of doors, racing around street corners.*

Full Shot—Plaza

Through the smoke and debris we see a charge of masses of SHOUTING MEN. *Some on foot, some on horseback. At the height of the charge—*

Dissolve to:
The Tower of the Citadel—Day

The machine gun is gone. Bodies of the MACHINE GUNNERS *and of* ZAPATISTAS *lying about. The* CAMERA MOVES OVER *to the parapet,* SHOOTS DOWN *on the plaza. Now it is full of* ZAPATISTA TROOPS, *camped on their equipment.*

Full Shot—Plaza

The MEN *who won the victory are lying about on their serapes, resting, eating, and generally celebrating.* WOMEN *and* CHIL-DREN *are clustered around them.*

The Bandstand

PEOPLE *crowd around the bandstand, looking up at:*

Emiliano seated at a carved state table.

> *The table is littered with gifts: fruits, piles of flowers, chickens, a small trussed pig.* EMILIANO *sits in a state chair at one end of the table, holding court, administering justice, giving rewards. Behind him an* OLD INDIAN WOMAN *is cooking tortillas and passing them to the young and lovely* JUANA (*a girl we have not seen before*), *who makes the tacos as she knows* EMILIANO *likes them and hands them to him, one at a time, as the scene progresses.* EUFEMIO *and* PABLO *are nearby.*

Angle at the Table

> *A* WOMAN *comes up with a bouquet of flowers.*

WOMAN: A present for you, my chief.

EMILIANO (*taking them*): Thank you.

> *He puts them on the table. The* WOMAN *moves away.* JUANA *hands him a glass of pulque. Her warm eyes tell us how much this man means to her.*

Another Angle at the Table

> *Another* WOMAN *approaches, looks intently at* EMILIANO.

EMILIANO: Yes?

WOMAN (*peering into his face as though to memorize it*): I want to see you close up.

> *She steps aside as a tough, grizzly* GUERRILLA FIGHTER *comes up, pulling a reluctant* LITTLE BOY *by the arm.*

Three Shot—Emiliano, Guerrilla Fighter (Eduardo), and Little Boy

EDUARDO: Emiliano, remember that machine gun that flanked us from the hill. . . .

EMILIANO: Yes?

EDUARDO (*almost incredulously*): This boy and his brother crept out in the dark. They lassoed that gun and pulled it right out of the gunner's hands. Look at the size of him!

EMILIANO (*to* BOY): Did you do that?

The LITTLE BOY *drops his head.*

EDUARDO: Sure he did. (*he* SHOUTS) Bring the machine gun!

EMILIANO: Leave the gun. . . . (*to the* BOY) Did you do that?

LITTLE BOY (*forcing the words out*): Yes, my chief.

EMILIANO: Where's your brother?

EDUARDO: He was killed. . . .

EMILIANO: You should have a reward. . . . (*pointing*) Want that pig?

The LITTLE BOY *looks at the pig, then slowly his eyes move around and he looks past* EMILIANO. EMILIANO *follows his gaze, and sees:*

His Own Horse held by a Soldier.

Back to Scene

EMILIANO: Not my horse? (LITTLE BOY *frowns. It's a problem. Then he nods*) That's a good horse.

LITTLE BOY WHISPERS *something.* EDUARDO *bends over then straightens up and says:*

EDUARDO: He says that's why he wants it.

EMILIANO (*to the* BOY): Take it!

The LITTLE BOY *turns and scuttles away.* EMILIANO *rises, stands looking down into the plaza, munching on a tortilla which* JUANA *hands him.*

Exterior, Plaza—near Bandstand

The LITTLE BOY *rushes in to* EMILIANO'S HORSE, *attempts to take the reins from the* SOLDIER. *The* SOLDIER *looks up at* EMILIANO.

Angle at Bandstand—Emiliano

looking down at the GROUP. *He nods to the* SOLDIER.

Group at Horse

The SOLDIER *helps the* LITTLE BOY *into the saddle. He turns, smiles up at* EMILIANO, *rides out of the square.*

Close Shot—Emiliano, back to Camera, looking off at the disappearing Horse. He turns, stops suddenly.

Wider Angle

> EMILIANO *is face to face with* SEÑOR ESPEJO, *dressed in his best. Standing immediately behind him is a tough* ZAPATISTA *with a bandaged head. This is* LAZARO, *who has now become a toughened guerrilla fighter.*

EMILIANO (*with a certain anticipated pleasure*): What did he *do*?

LAZARO: I don't know.

SEÑOR ESPEJO: Don Emiliano, my friend, I wish to present representatives of our great liberator, Francisco Madero.

EMILIANO: What!!!???

Full Shot—Group on Bandstand

SEÑOR ESPEJO: Gentlemen—here he is—

> *He turns, looks toward* THREE OFFICERS *in the uniform of the North.* FERNANDO *is with them.*

SEÑOR ESPEJO:—Don Emiliano Zapata, one of my oldest acquaintances.

FERNANDO (*with irony*): We know each other. My congratulations, General Zapata.

> EUFEMIO, *who has come up beside* EMILIANO, *reaches across him to make a taco, looks up to* EMILIANO.

EMILIANO: General?

> FERNANDO *puts a sealed document on the table.* EUFEMIO *bends over. Some chili from his taco falls on the paper.* EMILIANO *picks it up and wipes it on his sleeve.*

EMILIANO: Pablo. . . . (PABLO *comes up*) Read it.

Two Shot—Emiliano and Pablo

> PABLO *opens paper and reads it to himself. Looks at* ZAPATA.

EMILIANO: Well, read it.

PABLO (*reads*): "To Emiliano Zapata. I, Francisco Madero, acting on the authority given me by the forces of triumphant liberation, create you General of the Armies of the South. . . .

May the day soon come when I embrace you in triumph! Long
live Mexico!" (*impressed*) And he signed it with his own hand.
EMILIANO *snatches the paper and inspects it. He looks up with
childlike pleasure.* . . .

Group Shot

EUFEMIO (*to* EMILIANO): Now you'll have to wear those things a
general wears.
*He pulls a general's cap ornament out of his pocket and throws
it on the table.* EMILIANO *picks it up.*

SEÑOR ESPEJO (*coming forward*): I and my family will be very happy
if you will honor us with—

EMILIANO (*paying no attention to him—to* EUFEMIO, *indicating the
cap ornament*): Where did you get it?

EUFEMIO: Off a general. . . .

SEÑOR ESPEJO (*trying again*): I and my family—

AN INDIAN WOMAN (*pushing* ESPEJO *aside*): A present, my general. . . .
*She thrusts a large dirty bouquet of live trussed chickens into
his hands.* . . . EMILIANO *holds in one hand the chickens, in
the other, the general's ornaments.*

Dissolve to:
The Town Square—Night
Little fires with the "JUANS" (*cf. our GIs*) *squatting around, fed
by their* WOMEN *who cook at the little fires.* PANORAMIC SHOT
to a MAN *and a* WOMAN *by a little fire and it is* EMILIANO. *He
has a serape around his shoulders, like all the other* INDIANS.
To the right and slightly behind him is a pretty INDIAN GIRL
*cooking the tortillas and wrapping each one around bits of
meat.*

Close Shot—Emiliano and Juana
ZAPATA, *thinking deeply while he eats. As he finishes one taco,
he reaches out his hand, without looking at the* GIRL. *She puts*

a cup of pulque in his hand, he swallows it, hands it back, still without looking at her. She puts another taco in his hand. He never looks at her.

JUANA: Eat.

EMILIANO: No.

JUANA: Had enough?

EMILIANO: Yes.

JUANA puts the chili and meat in her basket and covers it with a cloth. Then she comes and sits on the ground close to him and embraces his leg in a gesture of the nakedest kind of love. She looks up at him, her eyes full of desire. He looks at her. It is very hard now to say what he has to say, but he does.

EMILIANO: You will have to go now, Juana. I don't need you any more.

She doesn't move. He touches her with affection.

EMILIANO: I will give you a cornfield. You will never go hungry.

Meekly JUANA arranges her rebozo over her face in a very modest way, picks up her basket of food, and moves off.

Juana—Moving Shot

She walks among the fires. She looks at various GROUPS OF SOLDIERS being fed by WOMEN and at length comes to a VERY YOUNG SOLDIER, sitting on the ground. She looks at him a moment, and he looks back at her, expressionless. Then without a word she squats down, fans up her little charcoal fire, and begins to pat out a tortilla. He looks at her. He leans back, smiles.

Dissolve to:

Exterior, Espejo Home—Late Afternoon

PABLO is looking through a barred window into a room where we see EMILIANO with THREE WOMEN. The CAMERA travels along to a second window, where EUFEMIO and FERNANDO are looking in.

EMILIANO ZAPATA (Marlon Brando) as a delegate to PORFIRIO DIAZ

FERNANDO (Joseph Wiseman) finds ZAPATA at his mountain camp

ZAPATA talks to JOSEFA ESPEJO (Jean Peters) in church

ZAPATA is taken prisoner after an act of defiance

A procession of the people, prepared to free the captured ZAPATA

ZAPATISTAS surrendering their weapons after defeating DIAZ

ZAPATA circles the name of a rebellious
charro as FERNANDO watches
(above right)

ZAPATA talks to the men of Morelos
while his brother is being killed
(right)

Zapata with captured government soldiers

Josefa tries to prevent Zapata from meeting with Guajardo

LAZARO (Will Kuluva) and others examine ZAPATA'S body

EUFEMIO (*disapprovingly*): What a waste of time. He should have stolen her if he wanted her.

FERNANDO: This way he gets her father's money, too.

A couple of GIRLS *stroll by, and as he speaks* EUFEMIO *turns to look after them.*

EUFEMIO: But is it worth this?? While he's still after this one, I've loved with all my heart one hundred women I never want to see again. (*he shakes his head in bewilderment*) It escapes me.

Interior, Espejo Home

The stiff parlor of the ESPEJO *home. Small, uncomfortable chairs; heavy framed pictures, religious figures.* EMILIANO *and* JOSEFA *sit in the center of the room. On* JOSEFA's *right, her* MOTHER; *on* EMILIANO's *left,* JOSEFA's *middle-aged* AUNT. *Both are embroidering—in background is seen* SEÑOR ESPEJO. JO- SEFA *is dressed in an all-covering dress that comes to the floor.* EMILIANO *is wearing his brilliant* charro *costume. His hat and carbine on the floor beside him.* EMILIANO *and* JOSEFA *look at each other and then at their flanking* FEMALE GUARDS. EMILIANO *tries to break the silence.*

EMILIANO: Did you think of me . . . ?

The CHAPERONS *stop their work, and straighten up. Their disapproval is clearly conveyed.*

JOSEFA: It is said that a warrior's shield is his sweetheart's heart.

EMILIANO: Uh?

JOSEFA *has spoken in the customary manner of a courtship, i.e., through the traditional "saying."* EMILIANO *for a moment doesn't "get" it.*

JOSEFA (*admiring his gorgeous* charro *outfit*): We have a proverb: A man well dressed is a man well thought of.

EMILIANO (*now getting it*): A monkey in silk is still a monkey. (JOSEFA *beams approvingly*) But when love—(*he indicates himself*)—and beauty—(*indicates* JOSEFA)—come in the house, throw out the lamps.

Exterior, House—Fernando and Eufemio

FERNANDO: Listen to that!

EUFEMIO (*spitting*): Makes me sick! But that! The way these people go about getting married!

He swivels his head around to look at a PASSING GIRL. *She smiles.*

EUFEMIO (*to* FERNANDO): Excuse me.

He takes off after the GIRL.

Interior, Parlor

JOSEFA: Do you believe the saying: An egg unbroke, a horse unrode, a girl unwed?

EMILIANO: I believe that man is fire and woman fuel. (*looks at her closely*) She who is born beautiful is born married. . . .

JOSEFA *flutters. She leans toward him. Then constrains herself, fans her face and bosom violently. The* WOMEN *unconsciously pick this up and all begin to fan themselves. It is hot and the formal clothes are no help. . . .* EMILIANO *looks around.*

Interior, Parlor—Shooting toward Windows

The windows are jammed with SPECTATORS, *all watching.*

EMILIANO: Get away from those windows—let a little air through.

He sees his WHITE HORSE, *with the* LITTLE BOY *sitting on its back. They are watching the courtship.*

EMILIANO: Get that horse out of here. . . . (*muttering to himself*) Best horse I ever had . . . that's rubbing my nose in it.

Again he looks toward the windows, which are absolutely jammed with SPECTATORS: SOLDIERS, CHILDREN, WOMEN, *all of whom watch without expression.*

Medium Shot—Emiliano, Josefa, Mother, and Aunt

EMILIANO: Josefa, let's go for a walk. There might be a breeze in the park.

Of course this is not allowed until after the wedding. The THREE WOMEN *stiffen. The* MOTHER *and* AUNT MURMUR, *incredulously,*

"A walk?!" "Alone?" EMILIANO *looks from one to the other and realizes he is quite out of step. He looks at* JOSEFA, SIGHS.

EMILIANO: A whipped dog is a wiser dog.

JOSEFA (*coming to his rescue*): Do you think that three women and a goose make a market? (*she looks at him waiting*)

Slowly he rises and takes a traditional position. The women lean forward. He speaks with measured significance.

EMILIANO: I think that love cannot be bought except with love. (*with faces of the* WOMEN—*very much as if they were kicking in a horse*—*encouraging him. He proceeds*) And he who has a good wife—(*bows, puts his hand over his heart*)—wears heaven in his hat.

It is over. He has proposed. The WOMEN SIGH *with relief, settle back.*

Close Shot—Eufemio—at Window

He disgustedly pulls his hat down over his eyes. Then he looks up quickly as the sound of EXCITED VOICES *comes over. He moves away from the window.*

Interior, Parlor—the Three Women and Emiliano

MOTHER: After love, food. A cup of chocolate?

Over scene we hear the SOUND OF EXCITED VOICES *getting closer.*

EMILIANO: A starved body has a skinny soul.

They all look at him with admiration; they COO *the Mexican equivalent of* "Isn't that sweet."

Another Angle, Shooting toward Window

PABLO *suddenly appears in the window.*

PABLO: Emiliano—

EMILIANO: Go away. (*to* AUNT) The pediment of the heart . . . (*with a bow*) . . . is the stomach. . . .

The MAIDEN AUNT *melts,* GIGGLES.

MOTHER: Alicia Candelaria, will you bring chocolate?

PABLO: Emiliano—

EMILIANO: Go away!

PABLO: Emiliano, Díaz has run away; he's left the country!

> *As if on cue,* FIRING BREAKS OUT *in the streets,* HIGH LAUGHTER, CATCALLS, *more* SHOTS. *Everybody is* FIRING *his rifle in the air. All hell breaks loose outside.*

Two Shot—Emiliano and Josefa

> *His face is suffused with triumph and pleasure. He throws himself at* JOSEFA *and takes her in his arms.*

EMILIANO: Josefa, Josefa . . . the fighting is over . . . the fighting is over! (*he's about to kiss her*)

MOTHER'S VOICE: Josefa. (*sharply*) Josefa!

JOSEFA (*to her* MOTHER): Mama! Quiet! (*looking at* EMILIANO's *face raptly*) The fighting is over. . . .

> *She kisses him.* EMILIANO's *arms go around her tightly, and they stand there, locked in embrace. The* MOTHER *opens her mouth to protest, but nothing comes out. She looks at the* AUNT, *who is fanning herself as she watches* EMILIANO *and* JOSEFA.

Medium Shot at Windows

> *Rejoicing faces of* WOMEN, MEN, *and* CHILDREN *are poked in through the windows,* CHEERING *happily.*

Dissolve to:

Exterior, the Church

> *The door opens and out comes* SEÑOR ESPEJO, *dressed to the teeth, followed by the* WEDDING PROCESSION. *He has taken it on himself to clear a passage through the* CROWD OF ZAPATISTA FIGHTERS *and* VILLAGE PEOPLE *for the bride and groom,* EMILIANO *and* JOSEFA. *The* PROCESSION *passes through a double line of* GUERRILLA FIGHTERS *in white field clothes who present arms in a highly irregular salute. . . . As the* WEDDING PARTY *passes, the* MEN *behind break ranks and follow. . . .*

Dissolve to:
Interior, Room—Large Brass Bed
>*All alone lies* JOSEFA *in her nightgown.* RIFLE FIRE OUTSIDE.
>JOSEFA *awakes. She is alone in bed.* ANOTHER COUPLE OF SHOTS.
>*She looks around . . . hears* EMILIANO'S LAUGHTER.

JOSEFA: Emiliano . . . ?
>EMILIANO *at the window is* LAUGHING, *looking out.*

EMILIANO: It's almost morning. They never get tired. . . .
>JOSEFA *gets out of bed and goes over to the window . . . and looks down.*

Exterior, Courtyard from Their Angle—Night
>*The ruins of the feast tables, wine, spilled food all over every-thing and a gallant little band of* DRUNKS, *among them* EU-FEMIO, FERNANDO, PABLO, *still holding forth.*

Emiliano and Josefa at the Window
JOSEFA: Come back to bed, Emiliano. . . .

Group at Table in Courtyard
>*In the midst of throwing his head back to* SING LOUDER, EUFEMIO *sees them in the window. He stops in his song.*

EUFEMIO: Emiliano, my brother. Josefa, my sister!
>*Full of love for everybody he turns to an old and ugly battle-scarred* VETERAN, *sitting next to him.*

EUFEMIO: My darling friend. (*weeps*) We're getting old. (*a closer look*) We're getting *very* old.
>*The* OLD WARRIOR *bends over on the table and he too cries.*
>EUFEMIO *looks for new fields to love. Next to him, cold sober, is* FERNANDO.

EUFEMIO: I know what's the matter with you. You are unhappy because the fighting is over.

FERNANDO (*muttering to himself*): Half victories! All this celebrating and nothing really won!

EUFEMIO (*embracing him*): I love you—but I don't like you. I've never liked you.

FERNANDO (*still going on*): There will have to be a lot more blood shed.

EUFEMIO (*losing patience with him*): All right! There *will* be! But not tonight! (*gives him bottle*) Here—enjoy yourself! Be human!

Interior, Bedroom

JOSEFA *goes back to bed. She* CALLS SOFTLY.

JOSEFA: Emiliano!

He goes to the bed and sits on the edge.

JOSEFA: You're restless. (*no answer*) Are you unhappy?

EMILIANO: No! Go to sleep.

JOSEFA: Can't you sleep?

EMILIANO: Pretty soon.

JOSEFA: What are you thinking?

EMILIANO: I'm not thinking anything.

JOSEFA: You are too. I know all about it. I've been married to hundreds of generals. Emiliano!

Suddenly she throws a pillow at him. This brings him around.

EMILIANO: Yes.

JOSEFA: What are you worried about? We'll find a good piece of land somewhere and we'll settle down. You'll raise horses and you'll raise melons, and you'll raise me.

EMILIANO: And I will buy you two new dresses—both beautiful. (*he kisses her*) Go to sleep now.

JOSEFA: I don't want to sleep! (*suddenly, serious*) Emiliano, the fighting *is* over?

EMILIANO: Yes. Madero is in the Capital. Tomorrow, I'll go see him. It's over.

JOSEFA: Can I go with you?

EMILIANO: No.

JOSEFA (*quickly, without transition*): Do you think we'll have children?

EMILIANO (*just as quickly*): Of course.

JOSEFA: We'll name them all Francisco after Madero because he brought peace.

EMILIANO *is pacing the floor like a polar bear in a cage.*

JOSEFA: Emiliano? (*no answer*) Is it something about me?

EMILIANO *goes over to her tenderly.*

EMILIANO: No, no Josefa . . . don't think that.

JOSEFA (*no longer playing*): Then I want you to tell me. . . .

EMILIANO: I'll see Madero and the men around him. . . .

JOSEFA: You're not telling me.

EMILIANO (*continuing*): Men from the schools, lawyers, strangers . . . educated men . . .

JOSEFA: Emiliano, you're not telling me.

EMILIANO: A horse and a rifle won't help me there!

Suddenly he looks keenly at her. He goes closer to her, whispers in her ear, as if ashamed of himself.

EMILIANO (*whispering*): I can't read.

She looks at him with understanding and love.

EMILIANO (*continuing*): Teach me.

JOSEFA: Of course. . . .

EMILIANO (*with growing excitement*): Teach me now. Get a book. . . . Now!

Noise of a drunken party outside. . . . EMILIANO *goes to the window and leans out.*

EMILIANO: Go away! Get out! Can't you let a man sleep on his wedding night?

He turns back to the bed. JOSEFA *has a large open book in front of her.* EMILIANO *sits down beside her. They look like two children. . . .*

EMILIANO: Begin!!

Dissolve to:
Full Shot—Interior, a Government Office in Mexico City

It is in a state of confusion. MEN *are moving filing cabinets. There is the characteristic constant repair that is invariable in Mexico; this always involves* HAMMERING. *On one side a* WORK-

MAN *is measuring a pane for replacement, and we see that there is a bullet hole in the glass. We discover* FRANCISCO MADERO *pointing to a large map on the floor, around which stand* EMILIANO *and* FERNANDO.

MADERO: Díaz was rottener than we knew. When Huerta pushed from the north, with Pancho Villa's help . . . and you, General, from the south, why, Díaz crumbled.

EMILIANO (*very humbly*): If you will forgive me, sir, when will the village lands be given back? The country people are asking.

MADERO: Now we must build—slowly and carefully!

EMILIANO: Thank you. . . . But the country people want to know—

MADERO: They will get their land, but under the law. This is a delicate matter. It must be studied.

EMILIANO: What is there to study?

MADERO: The lands must be given back under the law so that there will be no injustice. And speaking of lands, let me show you this. (*he turns to his desk, riffles through a number of maps, pulls out one and lays it on top*) You see here, where these two streams meet? The land is very rich here, rich and level and well watered . . . and I'm told it has a good house on it. . . . Do you know what this is, General?

EMILIANO: No, sir. . . .

MADERO: This is your ranch and no one deserves it more than you.

EMILIANO: *My* ranch?

MADERO: Yes. It is a fine old custom to reward victorious generals . . .

Suddenly with a tremendous violence EMILIANO BANGS *his gun on the floor. . . .*

EMILIANO: I did not fight for a ranch!

MADERO (*quickly*): I don't think you know what I meant.

EMILIANO (*topping him*) I know what you meant. . . .

Now he tries hard to get control of himself. Then he SPEAKS *. . . with difficulty.*

EMILIANO: Pardon me, sir. . . . But the land I fought for was not for myself!

MADERO: But General—

EMILIANO: What are you going to do about the land I did fight for?

MADERO: General . . . General . . . that will be taken care of, believe me, in good time.

EMILIANO: *Now* is a good time!

MADERO: General Zapata, sit down.

EMILIANO: I'm not tired.

MADERO: This is a constitutional government, there is only one way to do these—(*there is a tremendous* HAMMERING) I can't think! I can't think here! This confusion! Get out . . . get out!
He goes to the MAN *fixing a window and drags him to the door, herds the* OTHERS *out . . . stops a* MAN *with a paper. . . .*

MADERO: Give me these. I'll sign these now. Don't let anybody else in. . . .

Another Part of the Room—Eufemio and Pablo
EMILIANO, *followed by* FERNANDO, *walks toward them.*

EMILIANO: This mouse in the black suit talks too much like Díaz.

PABLO: No, he's right. This is peace. We must work by law now.

FERNANDO: Law? Laws don't govern. Men do. And the same men who governed before are here now, in that room. They have his ear—it's obvious. They must be cleaned out. . . .

EMILIANO: First, I want the land given back . . .

FERNANDO: And if Madero doesn't do it—

EMILIANO: Yes?

FERNANDO: Then he is an enemy, too.

PABLO: But you're his emissary, his officer, his friend. . . .

FERNANDO: I'm a friend to no one—and to nothing except logic. . . . This is the time for killing!

EMILIANO: Peace is very difficult.

During the foregoing EUFEMIO *has turned aside, is standing by the map on the desk.* EMILIANO *steps over to him.*

EMILIANO (*to* EUFEMIO): What do you think?

EUFEMIO (*sotto voce*): That's a nice piece of land he offered you. . . . What's the harm? You've never taken anything. And what have you got? Nothing!

Wider Angle

The room has grown quiet. . . . MADERO *comes toward them.*

MADERO: Now it's quiet. (*sinks wearily in his chair*) General Zapata—do you trust me?

Close Shot—Emiliano, silent.

Fernando and Pablo looking at Emiliano.

Eufemio, staring at his brother.

Group Shot—around Madero

MADERO: You must trust me! I promise you that my first preoccupation is with the land, but in a way that is permanent. But, before we can do anything by law, we must have law. We cannot have an armed and angry nation. . . . It is time, General, to stack our arms . . . in fact, that is the first step. . . . That is my first request of you. . . . Stack your arms and disband your army.

EMILIANO: And who'll enforce the laws when we have them?

MADERO: The regular army. The police!

EMILIANO: But they're the ones we just fought and beat!

Now EMILIANO *picks up his rifle, advances slowly toward* MADERO.

EMILIANO: Give me your watch!

MADERO: What?

EMILIANO: Give me your watch.

This is an order. Fiercely given and meant. MADERO *slowly*

removes his watch from his breast pocket and holds it out.
EMILIANO *takes it, looks at it.*

EMILIANO: It's a beautiful watch . . . expensive. . . . (*now quickly*)
Now, take my rifle.

He reverses his gun and offers it. MADERO *does not take it.*
ZAPATA *lays the gun on the desk, with the barrel pointing
toward his own chest.*

EMILIANO: Now . . . you can take your watch back. . . . but without
that—(*he points to the gun*) Could you?

MADERO (*chuckling*): You draw a strong moral . . .

EMILIANO: You ask us to disarm . . . are you sure we could get
our land back, or keep it, if we disarm?

MADERO: It's not that simple, there's the matter of time.

EMILIANO: Time . . . yes, time . . . time is one thing for a lawmaker,
but to a farmer there is a time to plant and a time to harvest.
. . . You cannot plant in harvest time.

MADERO: General Zapata, do you trust me?

EMILIANO: Just the way my people trust me. I trust you and they
trust me as long as we keep our promises. (*reaches for his
gun*) Not a moment longer.

He thinks a moment, turns, and starts toward the door. FER-
NANDO, PABLO, *and* EUFEMIO *follow.*

MADERO: Where are you going?

EMILIANO: I'm going home.

MADERO: What will you do there?

EMILIANO: I'll wait. But not for long!

The door closes on THE FOUR.

Another Door to the Room

It opens and there enters a MAN *we have not seen before. He
is* VICTORIANO HUERTA, *one of* MADERO's *generals from the
north. A hard, cruel, ambitious man. An aide now steps in
behind him.* HUERTA *starts forward.*

Angle at Madero's Desk, as Huerta enters, followed by several tough, hardened Generals. As the scene progresses, they gradually step in near to Madero, so that they seem to be surrounding him.

HUERTA: Kill that Zapata now. Save time, lives, perhaps your own.

MADERO: Were you listening, General Huerta?

HUERTA: I advise you to shoot Zapata now.

MADERO: I don't shoot my own people.

HUERTA: You'll learn . . . or you won't learn. . . .

MADERO: He's a fine man.

HUERTA: What does that mean?

MADERO: I mean he's an honest man.

HUERTA: What has that got to do with it??!! A man can be honest and completely wrong!

MADERO: I trust him.

HUERTA: To do what? I feel it is essential that I take my troops down to Morelos and help him decide to disarm.

There is a KNOCK *on the door, then the door opens. It is* PABLO. *He sees who's there.*

PABLO: Oh. . . .

MADERO: Come in. . . .

Angle at Door

PABLO *looks at* HUERTA *uncertainly. . . . He hesitates, still by the door.* MADERO *crosses over to him warmly. . . .*

PABLO (*to* MADERO): I thought—

HUERTA: You can speak freely.

MADERO: I want to speak to General Zapata again. . . . Ask him to come back, will you?

PABLO: He won't come back. He's stubborn, you know . . . but if you could come down to Morelos, he's different there. You know, his whole life has been fighting. (*sotto voce*) He can hardly read. (*urgently*) He needs you. He may not know it yet, but he needs you to help him. And he can learn . . . he wants to . . . and, if you'll excuse me, you need him too.

MADERO *thinks for a moment; then looks at* PABLO.

MADERO: I will come. . . .

PABLO: Thank you. (*bows, then formally*) With your permission, sir
. . .(*to* HUERTA) Excuse the interruption, please.

This means: "May I leave now?" MADERO *answers by stepping
over to* PABLO *and embracing him.*

MADERO: Tell him I will come. . . .

PABLO *exits.* . . . MADERO *turns back to* HUERTA.

MADERO (*to* HUERTA): I will do it *without* troops. . . . Troops are
not necessary . . . these are fine men. . . .

MADERO *turns to exit, pauses.*

MADERO: You know, General Huerta, there *is* such a thing as an
honest man. . . .

MADERO *smiles and exits.*

Close Shot—Huerta and Aide

HUERTA *whoops.*

HUERTA: What a fool! Oh, the odor of goodness! Give me a
drink. . . .

The AIDE *gets out a bottle.* . . .

HUERTA: We'll never get any place as long as Zapata is alive. He
believes in what he's fighting for. . . .

AIDE: So does Madero, General. . . .

HUERTA: Oh, I know, but he's a mouse . . . he can be handled.
. . . Zapata's a tiger . . . you have to kill a tiger!

CAMERA MOVES DOWNWARD, *and we see that* HUERTA *is standing on the map, his feet firmly planted on the State of Morelos.*

Dissolve to:
Exterior, the Plaza of a Town

In front of a table where there are CLERKS, *slowly passes a line
of* ZAPATISTA FIGHTERS *surrendering their guns. As the weapons
are surrendered, the name of each owner is written in a book
and on a tag tied to the gun. The line stretches all the way
across the plaza.*

Medium Shot—Group at Table

> As each man surrenders his weapon it is thrown into a farm cart. Behind the table stand EMILIANO, MADERO, PABLO, and EUFEMIO. (*The* SOLDADERA *is in the background.*)

MADERO: You see, they feel all right about giving up their arms now that I have explained it to them.

PABLO: He explained it very well, didn't he, Emiliano?

> EMILIANO *is silent.* MADERO *watches him.*

MADERO: They've accepted it. Have you?

EMILIANO: I've been fighting so long. I don't understand peace.

MADERO: Peace is the hard problem. Many men have been honest in war. . . . I often wonder how a man can stay honest under the pressure of peace. . . .

> A MAN *in the line who is just about to give up his rifle holds it up.* . . .

MAN: Let us keep these.

MADERO (*turns*): What do you mean?

EUFEMIO: He means, so he can shoot you if you turn crooked!

> *He suddenly bursts into crude* LAUGHTER *and goes off. The* MAN *hands over his rifle and moves along.* MADERO *looks at* EMILIANO *and they* LAUGH, *too.* . . .

EMILIANO (*he points to a grizzled* OLD MAN *who is next in line*): He doesn't look like much, but he's one of the best fighters we had. Aren't you, Apolonio?

APOLONIO: No.

> *He gives up his rifle and moves on. They all* LAUGH.

EMILIANO (*to* MADERO): Did I tell you about the little boy who got my horse?

MADERO: Yes, you did. Where is he? I'd like to meet him.

EMILIANO (*throwing it away*): He's dead. (*thinks a second, then:*) We were never able to find the horse.

Another Angle

> EMILIANO *indicates a* WOMAN *who is bringing three rifles. Nods at her with his head.*

MADERO: That woman has three rifles!

EMILIANO: Lost a husband and two sons—killed.

The WOMAN *deposits the guns.* MADERO's *eyes fill with tears. He moves toward the* WOMAN, *reaching in his pockets for something to give her. All he can find is his watch. He hands it to her. She puts her hand under her apron.*

MADERO: Take it!

WOMAN: Oh, no, it is too valuable.

MADERO *takes her hand and puts the watch in the palm and closes the fingers over it and* SAYS, HARSHLY:

MADERO: As valuable as your sons?

CAMERA MOVES INTO CLOSE SHOT *of* EMILIANO *and* PABLO. *We see that* EMILIANO *likes and believes in* MADERO. PABLO *sees this and is glad.*

Wider Angle

FERNANDO, *followed by* EUFEMIO, *comes into the scene, and gestures to* EMILIANO.

FERNANDO (*anxiously*): Emiliano, come here!

EMILIANO: What do you want?

FERNANDO (*changes his mind. Speaks sullenly, gesturing toward* MADERO): Ask *him!*

EMILIANO: Use respect!

MADERO (*with a gesture of helplessness*): What is it . . . ?

EUFEMIO: General Huerta's forces are coming through the pass!

FERNANDO (*to* MADERO): Pretend you don't know it!

MADERO: Oh, no, they're not—no, they can't!

EMILIANO (*to* FERNANDO): How do you know?

FERNANDO *points to three dusty and perspiring* SCOUTS *who are drinking water thirstily.*

EUFEMIO: The Scouts! Three regiments with artillery.

EMILIANO: Who posted Scouts?

FERNANDO: I did.

EMILIANO: You?

FERNANDO (*indicating* MADERO): I don't trust him. And I'm right! Look at him!

MADERO *is bewildered. The* OTHERS *stare at him. A* CITIZEN, *unaware of what is happening, approaches* MADERO.

CITIZEN (*to* MADERO): I want to shake the hand of our Liberator. I can tell my children.

Automatically, MADERO *extends his hand.*

MADERO (*as though to himself*): Troops are coming, Huerta has disobeyed orders. . . .

CITIZEN: What—what do you say, sir?

MADERO: Thank you very much. (*the* CITIZEN *goes*) I'll have to go and stop them. Huerta wouldn't dare.

He rises, walks away a few steps, hesitates—confused and bewildered.

FERNANDO (*to* EMILIANO): Don't let him get away!

PABLO: You *must* trust Madero, Emiliano! He can bring us peace.

FERNANDO (*interrupting*): Peace! . . . Three regiments coming down on us! Peace! You ugly little ape, you fool!

PABLO *goes for his knife and for* FERNANDO's *neck. . . . A knife has suddenly appeared in the hands of the* SOLDADERA.

EMILIANO: Pablo! Stop it! Put that knife away! Fernando, send cavalry to engage—see to the outposts. . . .

FERNANDO: Yes, General. . . . (*starts away, stops—to* MADERO) Go on back to Mexico City. . . . Huerta is a strong man . . . he'll gobble you up. . . .

EMILIANO *interrupts violently.*

EMILIANO: Fernando!

FERNANDO *exits. . . .*

EMILIANO: Pablo! The snipers. Flank the road. . . .

EUFEMIO (*sotto voce, indicating* MADERO): Might be a good idea to finish him off! What do you say?

Before EMILIANO *can reply,* MADERO *comes back to him.*

MADERO: Emiliano, believe in me! I will stop the troops.

EMILIANO: I hope so. . . . But if you can't, I will! (*to* EUFEMIO)
Come on.
They exit.

Another Angle
EMILIANO *is issuing orders. The line reverses. Guns are issued.
An electric quality comes into the square like a storm breaking.*
HORSES *and* RIDERS *move about with great speed.*

Medium Shot—Madero and Pablo (*the Soldadera in the background*).
MADERO *nervously wipes his forehead.* PABLO *looks at him
sympathetically.*
MADERO: General Huerta must have misunderstood.
PABLO: I'll talk to Emiliano. I'll bring you two together again. . . .
He hurries off, followed by the SOLDADERA. MADERO *still stands
there, confused and bewildered.*

Dissolve to:
*Long Shot—Mounted Federal Scout, coming down a road which leads to a
river.*

*Medium Shot—the Scout as he stops at the edge of the river, looks carefully
in all directions; then he turns in his saddle, signals in the direction of a
heavily wooded area.*

Long Shot—Shooting toward the Wooded Area
A mounted FEDERAL COLUMN *emerges from the woods, comes
toward the river.*

Full Shot of the Column Crossing the River.
As they are in the middle of the stream, suddenly they are
FIRED UPON. *There is a wild thrashing about of the frightened*
HORSES. *The* FEDERALES *look around, trying to find out where
the firing is coming from.*

Another Angle around the River.

> *From the tall grass the figures of the* ZAPATISTAS *rise, continue* FIRING. *At the height of this battle, we* CUT TO:

Close Shot—Emiliano

> *on horseback, his field glasses held to his eyes, watching the battle. He lowers the glasses, and a look of satisfaction comes over his face. The way he planned it, that way it worked!*

Dissolve to:

A Small Room in the National Palace—Mexico City

> *It is sparsely but adequately furnished.* TWO SOLDIERS *stand at the door guarding it. At a bare table sits* MADERO, *staring straight ahead. He's in a highly nervous state . . . almost hysteria.*

> *There's a* KNOCK *at the door. The* TWO SOLDIERS *open it a slit, and then, seeing who it is, open it wide. An immaculately dressed* SENIOR OFFICER *enters.* MADERO *almost runs to him.*

MADERO: Did you see him? Did you see Huerta?

OFFICER: Yes, my President. . . .

MADERO: How does he explain this? Why am I a prisoner here?

OFFICER (*suavely*): You're no longer a prisoner, my President.

MADERO: But they won't let me leave! I've been in this room for days!

OFFICER: Of course. He's guarding you for your safety. You have enemies outside.

MADERO: What enemies?

OFFICER: Zapata, Pancho Villa, they've all turned against you. But don't worry. General Huerta loves you. He will protect you. You must agree—here you have been safe.

MADERO: Why doesn't he give me safe conduct to the Port? When is he going to let me see him?

OFFICER: Tonight. He asked me to take you to him.

> *Frantically* MADERO *runs to a mirror. We watch him* CLOSE UP *as he ties his cravat, straightens his worn hair. . . .*

Dissolve to:
A Military Car with a Driver

> *In the back seat,* HUERTA *and an* AIDE, *smoking cigars.* HUERTA
> *looks at a watch.*

HUERTA: They are late.

> *A* SOLDIER *runs up to the car.*

SOLDIER: They're coming. . . .

> HUERTA *throws away his cigar. Looks out the window of the*
> *car.*

An Open Car Drives into View, Its Lights Dimmed

> *In the back seat between* TWO OFFICERS *sits* MADERO. *His face*
> *is full of anticipation. The car stops;* MADERO *looks around*
> *questioningly at an* OFFICER.

OFFICER: Get out.

MADERO: Is he here?

OFFICER: Get out.

> MADERO *raises his head and sees the wall of the penitentiary,*
> *before which the scene is being played.*
>
> *Suddenly the whole plot and all knowledge of it crash in*
> *on his mind.*

Close-up—Madero.

> *He knows he's doomed.*

Wider Angle

> *Suddenly the* TWO OFFICERS *give him a boost.* MADERO *seems*
> *to accept his fate. Almost aloofly he steps from the car.* TWO
> SOLDIERS *appear from the darkness, take him by the arms and*
> *conduct him almost gently in front of the car. They leave him.*
> *Suddenly the full headlights turn on him. They blind him. He*
> *looks around, for where to go. . . . Takes a few tentative steps*
> *. . . turns back toward the car and starts to* SPEAK. . . .

MADERO: My friend, what—

> *The* EXTRA LOUD HORN *of the car* SOUNDS, *drowning out his*

VOICE. MADERO *turns away hopelessly, his body waits for the bullets he knows are coming.*

Huerta's Car

HUERTA *is listening tensely. . . . There is a* VOLLEY OF SHOTS *offscreen. The* SOUND *of the automobile* HORN DIES OUT. *The open car, in which* MADERO *came, crosses behind.*

HUERTA (*to his* AIDE): So much for the mouse. Now we'll go for the TIGER.

He takes a fresh cigar, bites off the end of it.

Dissolve to:

Zapata's Headquarters—the Courtyard of a Ruined Hacienda

A court-martial is taking place. ZAPATA, *looking much older and much more worn, is sitting at a table. Behind him stands* FERNANDO, *who looks fiercer and meaner. All around in a great circle stand the* MEN *of his army listening. They are really battle-worn. A high wind is blowing.* EUFEMIO *is conducting the court-martial.*

Medium Shot—at Table

ZAPATA *looks at a* GUARDED MAN, *who stands in front of the table.*

CLERK OF THE COURT: Consorting with the enemy. He was seen talking to an officer of Huerta's army.

EUFEMIO (*leaning toward* PRISONER): We were ambushed. We *know* that now! What have you got to say for yourself?

PRISONER (*with a certain amount of arrogance*): Why shouldn't I talk to him? He was my brother-in-law. He brought me a message from my wife.

EUFEMIO: How did he know where to find you?

PRISONER (*pause—he is trapped*): I sent word.

EUFEMIO (*rising*): You sent word and we were ambushed!

PRISONER (*again defensive*): I haven't seen my wife in two years!

EUFEMIO (*to* GUARDS): Shoot him!

EMILIANO: Wait a minute.

> *An electric pause, as they all look toward him. The* PRISONER's *face lights up with hope.*

EMILIANO (*to* PRISONER): Look behind you.

Long Shot

> *What he sees: A* LONG LINE *of white-clad* ZAPATISTAS, *each carrying the body of a* DEAD ZAPATISTA *up a hill* (*moving away from the* CAMERA) *and disappearing over the brow of the hill.* ANOTHER LINE *comes back, moving toward us.*

Back to Scene

ZAPATA: Two hundred and forty-four fighting men. We planned a surprise. Huerta was ready for us. (*he* SPEAKS *to* ALL THE MEN) When they killed Madero, we had to start all over again. We lost many men. It was necessary. But *this* was useless. Two hundred and forty-four good farmers, your relatives, with victory in their mouths, will never chew it. (*to the* PRISONER, *with sudden violence*) Now do you see why we have *hard* discipline? You told your wife where we would be—and—(*he turns to* EUFEMIO) Shoot him.

> *The* PRISONER *is led away.* EMILIANO *looks up and sees a group of* FEDERAL SOLDIERS *under guard.*

CAPTAIN OF THE GUARD: Thirty-two deserters, my General. They want to come over to us. . . .

EMILIANO (*he has said this many times recently, there have been many* DESERTERS *brought to him*): If you want to fight for your land and your liberty, you're welcome. You'll be watched. There's no mercy for traitors. None! It's easier to come over to us now that we are winning, isn't it? (*to* FERNANDO) Take care of them.

> FERNANDO *gestures to another* MAN, *who comes forward and escorts the* DESERTERS *away.*

EMILIANO (*to* EUFEMIO): Go on.

EUFEMIO (*to* CLERK): Next!

A PRISONER *is brought forward.*

CLERK: This one broke our law against looting.

EMILIANO (*rising, to* EUFEMIO): I'll sleep a little.

He takes from EUFEMIO *a bottle of strong liquor (which* EUFEMIO *has been liberally using). He goes off,* FERNANDO *follows him.*

Moving Shot—Emiliano and Fernando

FERNANDO *watches him.*

FERNANDO: Putting it off?

They go up to a door opening in the thick wall and enter. CAMERA STOPS *on the* SOLDADERA, *who is squatting against the wall on the side of the door. Her face, as ever, is expressionless. By now she is really worn. Much time and misery have passed. In her* rebozo, *slung over one shoulder, lies an* INFANT. *She pays no attention to it. . . . She is making tortillas. She doesn't look up as the* MEN *go by.*

Small Dark Room

PABLO *is sitting on a bench with a* GUARD *on either side of him. He looks up as* EMILIANO *and* FERNANDO *enter.* EMILIANO *takes a seat, avoids* PABLO's *glance.*

PABLO: You look tired, Emiliano.

EMILIANO *doesn't answer.* FERNANDO *takes charge.*

FERNANDO: He met with the enemy: I have witnesses!

In the scene that follows, FERNANDO ADDRESSES PABLO, *but* PABLO *never talks to* FERNANDO *nor looks at him. He* SPEAKS *to* EMILIANO.

PABLO: You don't need witnesses, Emiliano. Just ask me. It's true I met Madero before he was killed.

FERNANDO: You met him many times!

PABLO: Many times, Emiliano.

FERNANDO: Even after Madero had signed orders to destroy us!

PABLO: That was at the end, Emiliano. Madero wasn't himself. He was trying to hold Huerta in check. Then Huerta killed him. He was a good man, Emiliano. He wanted to build houses and plant fields. And he was right. If we could begin to build—even while the burning goes on. If we could plant while we destroy . . .

FERNANDO: This is your defense?

SOUND *of execution offstage.*

PABLO: You and Villa will beat Huerta, soon! But then, there will be other Huertas, always other Huertas! Killing only makes new enemies, Emiliano. . . .

FERNANDO: You deserted our cause!

PABLO: Our cause was land—not a thought, but corn-planted earth to feed the families. And Liberty—not a word, but a man sitting safely in front of his house in the evening. And Peace—not a dream, but a time of rest and kindness. The question beats in my head, Emiliano. Can a good thing come from a bad act? Can peace come from so much killing? Can kindness finally come from so much violence? (*he looks now directly into* EMILIANO's *immobile eyes*) And can a man whose thoughts are born in anger and hatred, can such a man lead to peace? And govern in peace? I don't know, Emiliano. You must have thought of it. Do you know? Do you know?

Silence. EMILIANO *does not answer. A pause . . . offscreen— a* FUSILLADE *is* HEARD. *The* EXECUTION SQUAD. FERNANDO *looks at* EMILIANO.

FERNANDO (*slowly*): Two hundred and forty-four of our fighting men were killed this morning. We planned to surprise the enemy. They surprised us!

Pause.

Close Shot—Emiliano and Pablo

PABLO (*sensing what is happening behind* EMILIANO's *mask*): Emiliano, we've been friends since we guarded the corn against the blackbirds.

EMILIANO (*slowly*): You knew our rule against consorting with the enemy?

PABLO: Yes, my General.

EMILIANO: And yet you ignored it?

PABLO: Yes, my General.

FERNANDO'S VOICE: Shall I call the squad?

PABLO (*with pleading in his eyes*): Emiliano, not strangers. Do it yourself. Do it yourself!

> FERNANDO *gets up, silently, and goes outside.*

Full Shot—Room

> FERNANDO *gestures to the* TWO GUARDS, *who leave.* FERNANDO *follows.* EMILIANO *and* PABLO *are alone.*

Exterior, Small Dark Room

> FERNANDO *comes out, closes the door.*

Close-up—Soldadera

> *She looks up at him for a moment.*

Back to Scene

> FERNANDO *stands just outside the door to the small dark room. A* COURIER, *guarded, comes up.*

COURIER (*to* FERNANDO): Where's General Zapata? I have a message of great importance from General Villa.

FERNANDO: General Zapata is busy.

> *From inside comes the* SOUND *of* A SHOT. *The* SOLDADERA *dumps the charcoal from her brazier; she stands up and, gathering her food, walks away.*

FERNANDO (*to* COURIER): General Zapata will see you now.

Fade out

Fade in:

Emiliano's and Josefa's Home—Night—Josefa and Señor Espejo

> *It is poor. Against one wall is the brass marriage bed. A small altar is against another wall. In the center of the room is a table and two primitive chairs. A candle burns on the table. On one side of the table* JOSEFA *is working . . . on the other*

the FATHER *gulps beans and lectures her, gesturing with his spoon for emphasis. At the same time he is reading a newspaper.*

SEÑOR ESPEJO: Tell me: Why is he a general at all? What has he got from it? Look at you. Look at that dress! Is this a general's house? Pancho Villa knows what to do with his opportunities. Look how *he* dresses!

Insert—the Newspaper

A picture of PANCHO VILLA *in full-dress uniform in shiny boots.*

Back to Scene

SEÑOR ESPEJO (*mouth full of beans, to* JOSEFA, *who has looked over at him*): Don't argue with me! I know. Being a general is a business opportunity, and he's not taking advantage of it. He could take half the state and everyone would respect him for it, and he won't touch it. . . . (*with sudden violence*) I give up on him! Never had any faith in him . . .(*suddenly*) What's that? Do you hear horses . . . ?

The door opens and EMILIANO *walks right in. . . . Outside, his* ESCORT *can be* HEARD *dismounting, tying* HORSES, *etc.* JOSEFA *gets up and goes to him. He strokes her hair . . . her cheeks. She sees something desperate in his face.*

JOSEFA: Are you hurt?

EMILIANO: No.

JOSEFA: How did you get through the lines?

EMILIANO: There are no lines. Huerta's army is beaten. Villa has entered Mexico City. . . . I'll meet him there.

JOSEFA is helping him take off his equipment. . . .

SEÑOR ESPEJO: Congratulations, my General!!

ZAPATA just looks at him. He seems deeply bitter. JOSEFA *sees this. . . .*

JOSEFA: Are you sick?

EMILIANO: No . . . tired. . . . Tired. . . .

JOSEFA: But something's wrong . . . ?

EMILIANO: No. We've won. Nothing's wrong. I need sleep. . . . Let me sleep. . . .

SEÑOR ESPEJO: Before you go to Mexico City—my son—I'd like to have a talk with you. . . .

JOSEFA: Father . . . !

SEÑOR ESPEJO: About business conditions.

> JOSEFA *takes her* FATHER *by the elbow and leads him toward the door.* . . .

JOSEFA: Father. . . .

Close Shot—at Door

SEÑOR ESPEJO (*whispering in the doorway*): Don't let him miss this chance. He can be President. Villa's not so smart. . . . When he gets rested I want to have a practical talk with him.

> *She puts him out the door. Just as she's closing it:*

SEÑOR ESPEJO: He needs some practical advice.

Interior, Room

> *She crosses over to* EMILIANO, *who is lying down on the bed in exhaustion.* . . . *He smiles at her.*

EMILIANO: Why is it that since your father has come to adore me I can't stand him? When he had no use for me I rather respected him.

JOSEFA: You can *still* respect him.

> *She kisses him.*

Dissolve to:
Exterior, Their House—Night—Late

> *The* GUARDS' *campfire.* . . . *They are asleep.* SOUND *of* DOGS BARKING. ONE *of the* GUARDS *lifts up out of his sleep, looks around, sees and senses nothing, then drops down into sleep again. The silhouetted figure of a* WOMAN *is seen crossing towards the hut of the* ZAPATAS.

Interior, Hut, lit only by a votive candle.

> The door to the outside is stealthily opened and the figure of a WOMAN steals in, closing the door. We cannot see her for a moment, then suddenly she is very close to us. We see who it is: PABLO's SOLDADERA. We PAN her over to where ZAPATA is sleeping. JOSEFA awakens, sees the CREEPING FIGURE. She leaps toward her. The SOLDADERA lunges, her knife striking JOSEFA's hand.

Wider Angle

> JOSEFA is upon her. EMILIANO has just rolled over to avoid her blade. The GUARDS rush in and hold her. Lights are lit. EMILIANO sees who it is. He stares at her. She at him.

EMILIANO: You! What is this?

SOLDADERA: Go ahead and shoot me!

EMILIANO (*to* GUARDS): Take her out. . . .

> The GUARDS take her out. She does not struggle.

Medium Shot—Emiliano and Josefa

> EMILIANO stands dazed. JOSEFA looks at a cut on her hand. EMILIANO notices.

EMILIANO: She cut you. Let me see.

JOSEFA: It isn't deep.

> EMILIANO pulls his neck scarf off, wraps her hand. Suddenly something seems to quit in him. He collapses in complete despair.

JOSEFA: Emiliano. . . .

> She takes his head in her hands. He is crying from exhaustion and bewilderment and pain.

EMILIANO: My own people. She's from my village.

JOSEFA: She tried to kill you.

EMILIANO: Pablo—Pablo— I've known her since—before Pablo. . . .

JOSEFA: Lie down and sleep. . . .

> He pulls himself away from her and walks toward the door

as if listening for a shot. Then walks back toward JOSEFA. . . .

JOSEFA: Lie down, you must sleep.

EMILIANO (*shouts*): It must stop! The killing must stop! Pablo said it. That's all I know how to do!

Exterior, Hut

The campfire has been built up. A GUARD *is taking out his pistol to shoot the* SOLDADERA, *who is on her knees. Many half-dressed* ZAPATISTAS *have come out of the barracks nearby and watch.*

EMILIANO'S VOICE: Get away from her.

She stays on her knees as EMILIANO *enters. He crouches beside her and puts his arm around her.*

Close Shot—Emiliano and the Soldadera

EMILIANO: Look at me!

He turns her around and forces her to look at him.

SOLDADERA (*expressionless*): He was your friend.

EMILIANO (*a* VIOLENT CRY *of pain*): I *had* to kill him!

The SOLDADERA *snarls like a cat.*

EMILIANO: He was a traitor.

SOLDADERA: He was your friend.

EMILIANO: There were reasons.

SOLDADERA: No reason!

She spits in his face. He doesn't move.

Wider Angle

EMILIANO *walks away from her. He is close to* ONE *of the* GUARDS, *the one who holds the pistol.*

GUARD: My General. She's crazy. Dangerous and crazy. I will shoot her.

EMILIANO: Let her go.

GUARD: Think, my General, she's dangerous!

EMILIANO: Let her go.

GUARD (*walks up to the* SOLDADERA): Go on. . . . (*she looks at him*)
   Go on!
   She gets up, looks in EMILIANO's *face and walks off . . . no
   expression on her face. A* GUARD *picks up the* SOLDADERA's
   knife, which has been lying on the ground. He holds it out to
   EMILIANO, SAYING, "Here's her knife. . . ."*

Close-up—Emiliano, holding the knife.
   We see that it is the little knife which belonged to PABLO. *There
   are tears in his eyes as he looks at the knife which belonged
   to his friend.*

Dissolve to:
Full Shot—Interior, Throne Room at Chapultepec
   A large gathering of ROUGH FIGHTING MEN *from* VILLA's *army
   and* ZAPATA's.

Close Shot—Photographer
   *He has his camera ready and is waiting for them to get set,
   so he can take a picture.*

Villa and Emiliano
   EMILIANO *and* VILLA *embrace each other formally.* VILLA *invites*
   EMILIANO *to sit in the presidential seat.* EMILIANO *refuses, and
   invites* VILLA *to sit there. There is a slight argument.* VILLA
   shrugs, sits in the presidential throne. ZAPATA *sits beside him.
   The* OTHERS *range themselves about.* VILLA *pushes* ZAPATA *a
   little aside because his hat is obscuring* VILLA's *face.* ZAPATA
   takes his hat off. They all LAUGH. *There is a flash of powder.
   . . . A* CHEER! *Then* PANDEMONIUM. . . .

Close Shot—Villa and Emiliano
   VILLA *leans toward* EMILIANO *and says in a* HOARSE WHISPER:
VILLA: Let's get out of here!

They get up together and start to sneak out. Throughout this scene an ARMY BAND PLAYS *a wild victory march.*

Dissolve to:
Long Shot—a Wooded Area Surrounding a Lake

In the foreground are TWO GUARDS; *one is replacing another. Behind them we see a small lake with beautiful overgrowing trees. In the middle of the lake is a small island . . . and in the clearing on the island are* TWO FIGURES. VILLA *sits on the ground, leaning against a tree.* ZAPATA *is standing, leaning, practically lying against an upright tree. He is very relaxed. At various points around the pond are other* SENTINELS, *like those in the foreground of our scene. Behind them are a circle of* PEOPLE *in white, drawn there out of curiosity or anxiety and concern.*

FIRST GUARD (*who is replacing the* SECOND GUARD): All right, I'll stand now. (*confidentially*) What are they doing?

SECOND GUARD: Still talking. Deciding the fate of Mexico. Let them take their time. It's important!

Medium Shot—Villa and Zapata

We see also another FIGURE *close by—a* LITTLE URCHIN GIRL *with her little charcoal brazier. She is silent in the background. She is making tortillas.* (FERNANDO *is there, too, but not immediately seen.*)

VILLA: Why don't you come up to my country for a visit? It's not as green as yours but it is interesting. You'd like it.

EMILIANO: What do you do there?

VILLA: Hunting and women.

EMILIANO: What is there to hunt?

VILLA: Women.

EMILIANO LAUGHS. *He has "bought"* VILLA. . . . VILLA *eats what the* LITTLE GIRL *has offered him. He doesn't laugh. He means it.*

VILLA (*to the* LITTLE GIRL): These are good. (*to* EMILIANO) We have some wild pigs up there, not big, but they're tough. Run in packs. Eat a man right off a horse. The women are little pigs, too. Not so pretty, but they're nice. (*He eats*) They make them better in the north. I mean these—(*he holds up a tamale*) Pretty good. . . .

Overcome with good feeling he reaches into his pocket and pulls out a medal, with ribbon, holds it up to the LITTLE GIRL, *admires it with her, and then hands it to her.*

VILLA: Here. Wear it with pride. It once hung on the chest of a former President of Mexico.

EMILIANO LAUGHS *again. This time* VILLA *joins him.*

Close Shot—Little Girl
as she gravely pins the medal to her chest.

Group Shot
EMILIANO *and* VILLA LAUGH TOGETHER *as they watch the* LITTLE GIRL. *They like each other.*

Wider Angle as Fernando steps forward to the Group.

FERNANDO: Gentlemen, it's past three.

VILLA: You're right, we should be asleep!

FERNANDO: We have a great deal to discuss.

VILLA: What do you think we're doing?

FERNANDO: Political matters.

VILLA (*looks at* FERNANDO *and* BELCHES): I eat too much. . . . I don't have anything to discuss. I've made up my mind. I'm going home. I have a nice ranch up there now. I got something out of the fighting. I'm going to be president of that ranch. In the morning I'll hear roosters instead of bugles. . . . You know, somebody took a shot at me this morning . . . somebody I didn't even know.

FERNANDO: What do you propose?

VILLA (*to* EMILIANO, *ignoring* FERNANDO): I've been fighting too long. Lost my appetite for it.

EMILIANO: You mean—you're going home?

VILLA: I'm sick of it. We beat one of them and two more jump up. I used to think it would work.

FERNANDO: What about Mexico?

VILLA: I figured it out. Only one man I trust. (*to* EMILIANO) Can you read?

EMILIANO (*with a look of pride*): Yes.

VILLA: You're the President.

EMILIANO (*Violently*): No!

VILLA (*sleepily*): Yes, you are. I just appointed you. Sleep on it. You'll see I'm right. (*covers his head and sleeps.* FERNANDO *and* EMILIANO *look at each other.* VILLA *uncovers his head*) There's no one else. Do I look like a president? (*covers his head*)

FERNANDO (*to* EMILIANO): He's right. About himself and about you. There *is* no one else!

Close Shot—Emiliano
> *An absolutely Indian look. . . .*

Dissolve to:
Interior, Government office
> EMILIANO ZAPATA *is holding audience.* FERNANDO *stands slightly behind him, his hands full of papers. A* SECRETARY *is in front of the desk. Along the side of the wall sit various* MEN *of different classes: an* OLD GENERAL, *a* FOREIGN DIPLOMAT, *a* CHARRO, *a* DELEGATION *of country people. They are all waiting for an audience with* EMILIANO ZAPATA.

Medium Shot—Emiliano and Staff
> *The* SECRETARY *is* READING.

SECRETARY: Acting on the report that there have been gatherings of disgruntled officers in Sautillo, Colonel Chávez, on your orders, my President, moved in with a troop of cavalry after nightfall. The names of the deceased officers are appended, my President.

EMILIANO: General. I am not President.

FERNANDO: All killed?

SECRETARY: All.

FERNANDO: Telegraph congratulations to Colonel Chávez. (*turns to the* OLD GENERAL, *and beckons him*) Can we have your report on the enemy?

The OLD GENERAL *comes forward.* . . .

OLD GENERAL: General Carranza is still at Veracruz. His forces are intact.

FERNANDO: And General Obregón?

OLD GENERAL: Obregón is dug in at Puebla. He would be hard to dislodge. He's a fine officer. (*he turns to* EMILIANO) May I speak, my General?

FERNANDO: Your report is finished.

ZAPATA: Speak.

OLD GENERAL: I don't want to support men who have been against you. But Carranza and Obregón are strong, clever, resourceful, and really *quite honest*. Good officers, as you know. Would it seem presumptuous, my General, to suggest that you consider an alliance with them, for the good of Mexico?

FERNANDO (*violently*): For the good of Mexico! Madero made an alliance with Huerta for the good of Mexico and Huerta killed him! There are no good alliances! We hunt them down and kill them or they hunt us down and kill us. Díaz did not make alliances and he ruled for thirty-five years.

OLD GENERAL: But Díaz was a dictator.

FERNANDO: The principle of successful rule is always the same. There can be no opposition. Of course, our ends are different.

The OLD GENERAL *hesitates. He knows he is taking his life in his hands.* . . . *Then he* SPEAKS *to* ZAPATA.

OLD GENERAL: I don't believe that. . . . Do you, my General?

ZAPATA *does not answer him. He is looking straight ahead.*

Close Shot—Old General

OLD GENERAL: I am old and I may be foolish. I have killed so many men who differed with me. I've forgotten why, except that they opposed. And I've forgotten why that, too. You know how time goes . . . and always there were just as many left who opposed. My friends, somewhere, sometime, we must start building for peace. As an old soldier I have learned that there are times when you *must* fight. But unless the purpose is peace, the road is endless, the journey empty.

Close-up—Fernando
His eyes are blazing with hostility.

Close Shot—Emiliano's Staff
They drop their eyes before the OLD GENERAL's *stare.*

Close-up—Emiliano
He is looking straight ahead as if he didn't see the OLD GENERAL.

Group Shot
OLD GENERAL (*to* EMILIANO): With your permission, my General. . . .
EMILIANO *has been looking at him sharply. Now he nods. The* OLD GENERAL *starts out.*

Two Shot—Emiliano and Fernando
FERNANDO (*to* EMILIANO *in a* WHISPER): That man is dangerous!
EMILIANO: General. . . .

Close Shot—Old General—at Door
The OLD GENERAL *stops just at the exit door. . . .*
EMILIANO'S VOICE: Thank you.

The OLD GENERAL *smiles a rather sad smile, bows, and goes out.*

Group Shot—Around Emiliano
> EMILIANO *is affected by the* OLD GENERAL's *smile.*

FERNANDO (*briskly*): What next?

SECRETARY: A delegation from Morelos with a petition, my—my General. Here's the list of names. (*hands him list*)
> EMILIANO *glances at the names. . . .*

EMILIANO: Why, I know some of these . . .
> *He looks up. For the first time his eyes light up as the* DELE-GATION *enters.*

EMILIANO: Carlito—Pepe—and you, Lazaro, what are you doing here? What do you want . . . ? What can I do for you?

Delegation Just Inside Door of Room
> *A young, dark* CHARRO *stands in their midst. He has an insolence about him—just as* EMILIANO *had in the scene with* DÍAZ *at the opening of this screenplay.*

LAZARO (*to* EMILIANO): We have a complaint against your brother.

Close-up—Emiliano
> *He freezes; his eyes lower.*

Medium Shot—Delegation at Door all trying to voice the complaint.

VOICES: Your brother moved into the hacienda at Agalla. . . . He took the land you just distributed. . . . He's living there. . . . He kicked us out. . . . He killed a man who wouldn't go. . . .

Close Shot—Emiliano, looking off toward the Delegation.

EMILIANO: Is this true?

AN OLD INDIAN'S VOICE: Yes, my General.

EMILIANO (*stalling*): Well, we'll have to do something about that. We'll need a little time. . . .

Wider Angle

> The young CHARRO *comes close to* EMILIANO *and* SPEAKS *for the first time. What follows should be reminiscent of the opening scenes of this screenplay.*

CHARRO: These men haven't *got* time!

EMILIANO: But—

CHARRO (*holding up his hand for silence*): They plowed the land. And they've got it half sowed.

EMILIANO: Did you have any land there . . . ?

CHARRO (*insolently*): No.

EMILIANO: Then what are you doing here?

CHARRO: These are my neighbors. I can read and write. I wrote the letter for the appointment.

EMILIANO: Neighbors. . . . My brother is a general. He became a general by fighting for many years and killing many of your enemies. Let's not forget that now. (*he turns away from the* CHARRO, *speaks past him to the* DELEGATION) You can trust me. I'm one of you, I was—

CHARRO (*continuing*): Since you are, you ought to know that the land can't wait. The furrows are open. The seeds not planted. Stomachs can't wait either.

EMILIANO (*with sudden anger*): What's your name . . . ?

CHARRO: Hernandez. H-E-R—

EMILIANO: I have it.

Insert—Emiliano's Hand

> On the list of names he is slowly circling a name . . . exactly as DÍAZ did his early in our story.

Close Shot—Emiliano

> Suddenly an electric shock goes through him. He stares at the paper. His hand is still making a little circle above the paper. He holds the pencil up . . . point in the air . . . suddenly his thumb moves in a spasm, and the pencil breaks. He drops the

pencil . . . picks up the paper with a gesture of violence and crunches it . . . and drops it on the floor.

Wider Angle—Taking in Delegation

EMILIANO *is like a man in a trance. Slowly he crosses to the* CHARRO. *The* INDIANS *pull back, but the* CHARRO *stands his ground with a little fear in his eyes. There's a feeling of coming murder in the room. When he gets to the* CHARRO, ZAPATA *raises his hand very slowly, and with tenderness, puts it on the* CHARRO'*s shoulder. Then he looks blindly around the room, sees his hat on an ornate hatrack. He goes to it, and puts it on.*

Two Shot—Emiliano and Fernando

FERNANDO: Where are you going?

EMILIANO: I'm going home. . . . I'm going home. There are some things I forgot.

FERNANDO: So you're throwing it away. Leave tonight and your enemies will be here tomorrow—in this room—at that desk! They won't walk away. They'll hunt you down . . . and you'll get your rest in the sun with the flies in your face. I promise you you won't live long.

EMILIANO: I won't live long anyway. . . .

FERNANDO: Zapata—in the name of all we fought for, don't leave here!

EMILIANO: In the name of all I fought for, I'm going.

FERNANDO: If you leave now—I won't go with you. . . .

EMILIANO: I don't expect you to. . . .

FERNANDO: Thousands of men have died to give you power and you're throwing it away.

EMILIANO: I'm taking it back where it belongs; to thousands of men.

FERNANDO: I won't go with you.

EMILIANO: I don't want you.

He turns abruptly, stares at FERNANDO.

EMILIANO: Now I know you. No wife, no woman, no home, no field. You do not gamble, drink, no friends, no love. . . . You only destroy. . . . I guess that's your love. . . . And I'll tell you what you will do now! You will go to Obregón or Carranza! You will never change!

Wider Angle as Emiliano turns toward the Delegation.
EMILIANO: Come on—!
He walks out the door with the DELEGATION *striding behind him. . . .*

Dissolve to:
Interior, Corridor in a Semi-Ruined Hacienda
It is the corridor which leads to the great central hall or drawing room.

Exactly in the same tempo, EMILIANO *and the* DELEGATION *are striding through a corridor.*

Interior, the Central Hall
It is a mess. CAMERA PANS *around room to disclose: windows are broken; a little charcoal fire burns in the middle of a parqueted hall; a* VERY OLD INDIAN WOMAN *is cooking; pigs and chickens wander about the room, over the Oriental rugs and upholstered chairs; in a great chair sits a blowsy, blondined* WOMAN, *slightly fat and unattractive, very drunk and asleep with her mouth open. . . .* CAMERA STOPS *on* EUFEMIO, *lying on a couch. He is up on one elbow, a wine glass in his hand. He is drunk and dangerous. Balefully he watches his* BROTHER *and the* DELEGATION *approach and stop in front of him. His hand rests lightly on the butt of a gun in his holster.* EMILIANO *stops in front of him.*

Medium Shot—Emiliano and Eufemio
EUFEMIO: Brother, be careful what you say to me!
EMILIANO: Eufemio, did you take land away from these people?

EUFEMIO: I took what I wanted.

> *An* INDIAN WOMAN *behind* EUFEMIO *moves.*

EMILIANO: Eufemio, I . . .

EUFEMIO: I took their wives, too.

> *He looks directly at a* MAN *who stands behind* EMILIANO.

Close Shot—the Man

> *We recognize him as a* MEMBER *of the* DELEGATION. *He is looking at the* WOMAN *behind* EUFEMIO. *Murder is in the air.*

Close Shot—the Woman, her eyes filled with shame and fear.

Group Shot around Eufemio and Emiliano

EMILIANO (*with sudden terrific violence*): What kind of an animal are you?

EUFEMIO (*stopping him*): Animal? I'm a man! Not a freak like my brother.

EMILIANO: Get out of here. . . .

EUFEMIO: I fought as long and as hard as you did. Every day you fought, I fought. I'm a general. Here's my pay—(*turning his pocket inside out*)—a little dust. I can't buy a bottle of tequila. We beat Díaz. He's living in a palace in Paris. I've got a hut. We beat Huerta. He's a rich man in the United States. I have to beg pennies in my home village from people who never fired a gun! Well now, since I'm a general I'm going to act like a general. I'll take what I want. Let no one try and stop me. (*he turns and addresses the* WOMAN *behind him very directly*) Come on.

Close-up—the Woman

> *A quick glance off at her* HUSBAND.

Close-up—the Husband

> *His eyes glued on his* WIFE.

Group Shot

EUFEMIO *exits*, THE WOMAN *following. When they have gone*
EMILIANO *turns, looks at the* HUSBAND. *He drops his eyes.* EM-
ILIANO *looks at the* MEN *around him. He* SPEAKS, *in an at-
mosphere charged with murder. He is talking about the land,
but he's also referring to the* WOMAN.

EMILIANO: This land is yours. But you'll have to protect it. It won't
be yours long if you don't protect it. And if necessary, with
your lives. And your children with their lives. Don't discount
your enemies. They'll be back. But if your house is burned,
build it again. If your corn is destroyed, replant. If your
children die, bear more. And if they drive us out of the valleys
we will live on the sides of the mountains. But we will live.
(*now he looks at the* HUSBAND *for a sentence or two*) About
leaders. You've looked for leaders. For strong men without
faults. There aren't any. There are only men like yourselves.
They change. They desert. They die. There's no leader but
yourselves.

During the last couple of sentences the HUSBAND *has moved
toward the head of the passage.*

Head of Passage

The HUSBAND *is there. Coming out of the room at the end of
the passage is* EUFEMIO, *loaded down with his equipment. He
stands in the doorway to the room and he sees the* HUSBAND,
glares at him, then turns toward the room and SAYS, *"Come
on, Chola."*

Group Shot around Emiliano

EMILIANO: I will die, but before I do I must teach you that a strong
people is the only lasting strength.

Over scene comes the SOUND *of a tremendous* OUTBREAK OF
SHOOTING.

In the Hallway

> EUFEMIO *and the* HUSBAND *just stand* BLASTING *away at each other. The* HUSBAND *has a shotgun. The* WOMAN *is lying on the floor between them. The* HUSBAND *keels over.*

Wider Angle—Hallway

> *As* EMILIANO *runs in,* EUFEMIO *staggers out the door, falls outside the house.*

Exterior, House

> EUFEMIO *is lying on the ground dead.* EMILIANO *comes to him. Tears fill his eyes. He is immobilized. A* MAN *comes up, stands beside him.*

MAN: They are both dead.

> *It is as though* EMILIANO *has lost power of listening. Anyway, he knew it. More* PEOPLE *crowd around him.*

AN OFFICER (*looking down at* EUFEMIO's *body*): When he served the cause, he served it well.

> EMILIANO *does not answer because he can't.*

ANOTHER AIDE: He was a general. What he said was true. He fought every day we fought. We'll bury him as a general.

EMILIANO (*coming out of it, only enough to answer*): Not in the military cemetery. He didn't die in battle. I'll take him home with me.

Dissolve to:

Long Shot—a Tiny Village

> *A road goes through it. A column of* FEDERAL CAVALRY *suddenly rides into the village. As though on order they quickly dismount and go about searching the village.*

Closer Shot

> *The* SOLDIERS *apparently find the village completely deserted.*

Exterior, One of the Huts

A SOLDIER *goes in to search the hut. The* C.O. *and a* JUNIOR OFFICER *meet in front of the hut.*

JUNIOR OFFICER: The village is deserted. There isn't a soul here.

They turn toward the door of the hut as a YELP OF PAIN *comes from within. The* SOLDIER *who went in to search now comes out, shaking his hand and grimacing with pain.*

THE SOLDIER: There are still coals in the ashes. (*holding out a tortilla*) The food is still warm.

The C.O. *takes the tortilla, eats it.*

C.O.: They can't be very far away.

A VOICE CALLS *from offstage and they all turn.*

VOICE (*offstage*): We found one. . . .

Another Angle—Exterior of Hut

TWO SOLDIERS *are holding by the elbows an* OLD, OLD MAN (LAZARO) *and dragging him toward the hut. The* OLD MAN *has a crutch composed of a stick and a half-moonlike piece of branch. The* SOLDIERS *hang onto him as though he were dangerous.*

LAZARO (*sarcastically*): I surrender, my General. But I hate to tell you—when you've caught me, you've caught nothing.

C.O.: Where are the people? Where is Zapata?

LAZARO, *with a vague circular gesture of the hand, points to the surrounding hills vaguely. . . .*

LAZARO: Up there. . . .

C.O.: When did they go . . . ?

LAZARO: Just before you came. . . .

There's a tiny pause.

LAZARO: Why don't you go up after them . . . ?

With a quick brutality, the JUNIOR OFFICER *smacks the* OLD MAN *on the face and knocks him down.*

LAZARO: I remember you went up after some last week.

The JUNIOR OFFICER *knocks him down again. The* OLD MAN, *with a kind of frightening smile,* SPEAKS *with almost a sense of pity. . . .*

LAZARO: My son, I'm too old to be afraid.

JUNIOR OFFICER (*to the* C.O.): Your orders, sir.

C.O.: Orders? How can you fight an enemy you can't see???

LAZARO: You can't. . . .

C.O. (*coldly—he's done it many times before*): Burn the village.
MEN *come toward the* CAMERA *with burning torches.*

Dissolve to:
Interior, a Government office

 A different GROUP OF MEN. *The leader is a* NEW GENERAL. *All
the* MEN *are in uniform. Among them is the* OLD GENERAL *we
saw in the scene with* EMILIANO *in this room.*

NEW GENERAL: Always the same report! Always the same—

YOUNG OFFICER: Sir, how can you fight an enemy you can't see?

NEW GENERAL: You're looking for an army to fight. There is no
army. Every man, woman, and child in the State of Morelos
is Zapata's army. There is only one way. Wipe them out, all
of them.

YOUNG OFFICER: Excuse me, sir. We can't find anybody to wipe
out. We go there. The corn is growing; there is a fire in the
hearth . . . and no one! We burn the house—we destroy the
corn—we go back there. A new shelter! The corn is growing
again. And the people—like a different race! They aren't
afraid of anything!

OLD GENERAL (*with the subtlest irony . . . the faintest smile*):
Gentlemen—this is not a man . . . it's an idea and it's
spreading. . . .

 A HARSH VOICE *breaks in:*

VOICE: It's a *man!*

Close Shot—Fernando in uniform.

FERNANDO: It's Zapata! Cut off the head of this snake and the body
will die!

Wider Angle—Fernando and Group

OLD GENERAL: Ideas are harder to kill than snakes. How do you
kill an idea?

FERNANDO: Kill Zapata and your problem is solved.

YOUNG OFFICER: But how? We surrounded his village; he was there; he got away. Then we surrounded his house; he was there; he got away.

With a contemptuous look at all of them, FERNANDO *goes to the door and opens it.*

FERNANDO: Come in, Colonel.

An unshaven, disheveled derelict of a MAN *comes through the door. . . .*

FERNANDO: Sit down, Colonel.

The DERELICT *looks around the room. His eyes are uneasy, wary, glazed. He sits.*

Two Shot—Fernando and Guajardo

FERNANDO: Have you considered my proposition?

GUAJARDO: I was a soldier . . . I have never done anything like that.

FERNANDO (*interrupting*): Since you were a soldier, then you know that the object of war is to win.

GUAJARDO: I'll think about it. I'll answer tomorrow.

His eyes go to a bottle of liquor on the table.

FERNANDO: Answer *now*!

GUAJARDO (*his hand shakes—his eyes on the liquor*): May I have a drink . . . ?

FERNANDO: After you decide. . . .

Wider Angle—Favoring Guajardo

GUAJARDO: If I should refuse to carry out what you—It would be dangerous because I know your plan. . . . (*pause*) I would be put in protective custody. (*pause*) It is logical that I would try to escape, and I would be killed in the attempt. In effect, I have no choice!

FERNANDO: You are very intelligent! (*to* ANOTHER MAN) Give the Colonel a drink.

Dissolve to:
A Stream—Indian Women Washing—Among Them Josefa
> JOSEFA *is finishing. Her* FATHER's *prediction has come true—*
> *she is practically indistinguishable from the* OTHERS. *Just now*
> *she is listening to the* WOMEN TALKING.

FIRST WOMAN: I heard them talking . . . they said something about
> new rifles. They are very happy.

SECOND WOMAN (*to* JOSEFA): What is it, Josefa?

JOSEFA (*gathering up her things, preparing to go*): What?

SECOND WOMAN: What is going on about ammunition, rifles?

A Close Shot—Josefa
> *She is very worried.*

JOSEFA: I don't know. Emiliano doesn't tell me. . . .

Full Shot—Group of Women as Josefa leaves.

Quick Dissolve to:
Exterior, Hill—Moonlight
> THREE HORSES *coming up the hill.*

Interior, Zapata's Hut
> EMILIANO *and* JOSEFA *in bed. Their eyes are open, staring*
> *straight up. Over the shot the* SOUND OF RIDING.

Very Close Shot, the eyes of Emiliano and Josefa.

Medium Shot
> ZAPATA *has moved down toward the end of the bed. He grabs*
> *his pants, and settles back, putting them on. As he moves back*
> *the* CAMERA PANS *to include* JOSEFA *coming toward him with*
> *his carbine. She is covered with a* rebozo, *and that's all. But*
> *it covers practically all of her. They have been sleeping naked.*
> SOUND OF KNOCKING *outside.*

Another Angle
> ZAPATA *takes the gun and goes toward the door. He opens it*
> *a crack, revealing the* CHARRO. *He goes outside.*

Exterior, Hut

FOUR *perspiring* MEN *waiting.* EMILIANO *comes out.*

EMILIANO: Well?

CHARRO: We saw the supplies. The guns are new. Some never fired. Machine guns, too.

EMILIANO: Ammunition?

CHARRO: A mountain of it.

The door behind them opens, and JOSEFA, *staying well screened behind the door, hands out water. The* MEN *drink as they* TALK.

EMILIANO: You saw the ammunition?

CHARRO: Yes.

EMILIANO (*thoughtfully*): This could give us a year and in a year we'd be ready for anything.

Interior, Hut

JOSEFA *listening. The* VOICES *come over her.*

EMILIANO'S VOICE: Why does he want to join us?

CHARRO'S VOICE: He says he was stripped of his rank for nothing. He wants revenge.

EMILIANO'S VOICE: Stripped of his rank, and now he's suddenly a colonel with a first-class regiment. Sounds like a trap.

CHARRO'S VOICE: Yes.

EMILIANO'S VOICE: But it's also strange enough to be true.

CHARRO'S VOICE: Yes.

Exterior, Hut

EMILIANO: How is he going to prove good faith?

CHARRO: He executed Juan Calsado, the Chief of Police who killed so many of our people. Further proof he leaves to you.

EMILIANO: Does he? Come back at sunset ready to ride. I'll think out some proofs by then. . . .

He starts into the house.

Interior, Hut

EMILIANO *comes by the door. We get a glimpse of* JOSEFA— *enough to note that she has been there all the time. The* CAMERA

FOLLOWS EMILIANO, *who goes and throws himself on the bed.*
JOSEFA *still stands by the door. The* HORSEMEN *can be* HEARD
going off.

JOSEFA: What has happened?

EMILIANO: Something! Nothing!

JOSEFA: Emiliano, I want to know.

EMILIANO: What?

JOSEFA: What is happening?

EMILIANO: Are the hens beginning to crow?

JOSEFA *goes over to the bed and lies on it with* EMILIANO. *They
are outside the covers. He is lying on his back. She is very
tender and loving. Toward the end of the following* SPEECH *she
begins to make love to him, kissing him with a wild but helpless
love.*

JOSEFA: Emiliano, every night I have the same thought. My heart
says, now you have your husband for the first time, alone
sometimes, without fighting, running, hiding. But my heart
also says you will be dead soon and I have never known you
in peace.

EMILIANO: Josefa, enough! I'm trying to make a plan. . . . We're
getting the ammunition we need.

JOSEFA: I don't want to hear.

EMILIANO: Josefa. . . .

JOSEFA (*suddenly, full of the harshest bitterness*): My father told me!
"You'll squat over the grinding stone," he said. "You'll
beat your clothes clean on a river stone. You'll walk behind him on the trail and he will only speak to give you
orders." And I said, "I love him and I will have him."
(*pauses*) And now you do not talk to me, and one day you will
be gone and a stranger will come to the door and tell me you
are dead. This is what is left for me. . . . This is what is left
for me. . . .

EMILIANO, *feeling her great pain, now* SPEAKS. *With difficulty.*

EMILIANO: A Federal colonel is giving his regiment and equipment
to us.

JOSEFA: A trick?

EMILIANO: I always suspect a trick. I wouldn't be alive now, if I didn't.

JOSEFA: This is an easy way to kill you.

EMILIANO: I haven't even decided to meet with him yet.

JOSEFA: Don't go, Emiliano.

EMILIANO: We need the ammunition.

JOSEFA: I have a feeling. Don't go!

EMILIANO: That's enough now. I'll make up my mind.

JOSEFA: Emiliano. . . .

EMILIANO: Josefa, enough! I haven't decided. . . .

JOSEFA: Do you *want* to die?

EMILIANO: I must do what's needed. (*looks at her*) It will be all right. If I go down, I'll buy you two new dresses, both beautiful.

But he, himself, is now troubled. He can't look at her, moves away. . . . Then turns and SAYS,

EMILIANO: I must do what's needed.

JOSEFA: I won't speak again. I won't speak again. . . .

He takes her in his arms.

Dissolve to:
A Field of Battle—a Tent—Fires Burning—Executions

GUAJARDO *is pouring himself a drink. He throws it down. Now another.* CHARRO *enters.*

GUAJARDO: Well? Did you see them?

CHARRO: Yes. They are the ones who burned our home village.

GUAJARDO: Were they dead enough for you?

CHARRO: Just as dead as they deserved!

Food is brought to GUAJARDO. *He sits.*

GUAJARDO: Is he satisfied?

CHARRO: With this. Yes.

GUAJARDO: Then what?

CHARRO: He orders you to attack the garrison at Jonocatepec and to destroy it.

GUAJARDO: How large is the garrison?

CHARRO: You should know.

GUAJARDO: Of course. I'll find out. (*he can't eat*) When do I attack?

CHARRO: Now.

GUAJARDO: Tonight?

CHARRO: As soon as you can. Tonight, if you can.
> *He starts out.*

GUAJARDO: Will this be the last test?

CHARRO (*at the door*): After you've done it, you'll find out.
> *He exits.* GUAJARDO *pushes the food away. Pours himself a drink.*

Dissolve:
In Front of Emiliano and Josefa's Hut—Evening
> EMILIANO *is standing, leaning against the wall. He seems to be waiting.* JOSEFA *is sitting on a low bench.*

EMILIANO: Look how the little clouds go across the face of the moon . . . the moon is racing. Time races, too. . . .

JOSEFA: It reminds me—

EMILIANO: Don't remember anything. Let your mind float. Everything is in the future.

JOSEFA (*at his feet*): You've made up your mind. . . .

EMILIANO: Shshsh!

JOSEFA (*bitterly, in a burst*): I don't speak for myself now. But, if anything happens to you, what would become of these people?

EMILIANO: What?

JOSEFA: What would they have left?

EMILIANO: Themselves.

JOSEFA: With all the fighting and death, what has changed?

EMILIANO: *They've* changed. That is how things really change— slowly—through people. (*with a faraway look*) They don't need me any more. (LAUGHS)

JOSEFA: They have to be led.

EMILIANO: But by each other. A strong man makes a weak people. Strong people don't need a strong man.

Wider Angle

> *There is a sudden entry of* HORSEMEN. CHARRO *on a* HORSE *comes right up to* EMILIANO. *In the background a movement of* HORSES *continues. . . .*

Emiliano and Josefa as Charro enters to them.

EMILIANO (*to* CHARRO): Well?

CHARRO: Jonocatepec is destroyed. Its garrison dead.

EMILIANO: You saw it?

CHARRO: The garrison is destroyed.

EMILIANO: The supplies?

CHARRO: Stacked and waiting. I saw them.

EMILIANO: What do you think?

CHARRO: He has passed every test.

EMILIANO: Then . . .

> *He shrugs. Looks down at* JOSEFA. *She does not move.*

CHARRO: When will you go?

EMILIANO: Tonight. It's safer at night. We will leave now. (*he* CALLS) Otillano!

> *A* HORSE *is brought up.* EMILIANO *looks at* JOSEFA. *She looks at him. She has never moved from her first position. Her face is full of pain. She is bitterly and completely opposed to what he is doing.*

EMILIANO: Charro—suppose something happened to me?

CHARRO: What?

EMILIANO: Someday I'll die.

CHARRO: Someday you'll die . . . and then . . . well, we wouldn't be much if— I mean, we'll get along.

EMILIANO: But look at us. They have pushed us up to the very edge of the world.

CHARRO: But we're still here. And someday we'll go down into the valleys again. Until then, we know how to survive.

> EMILIANO *turns and looks at* JOSEFA. *Her face is expressionless. He smiles. She looks at him expressionless. She hasn't moved*

from her crouch at his feet. He mounts, turns his HORSE, *and trots it slowly away.*

Close Shot—Josefa
 Suddenly JOSEFA *is crying. Then she* SCREAMS *in terror.*

Wider Angle
 EMILIANO *stops his* HORSE *and turns and rides back to her. He leans down from the saddle and cups her chin in his hand and lifts her face up.*
EMILIANO: Josefa. Don't worry, I'll be back. And this time I'll bring you two new dresses, both beautiful.
 He straightens and lifts his reins. She leaps and takes hold of his bridle.
JOSEFA (*screaming*): Don't go! Don't go! I beg you, 'Miliano, don't go! Send someone else!
 The HORSE *rears in fright.* EMILIANO *has trouble controlling him.* JOSEFA *hangs on, crying hysterically. Finally* EMILIANO *leans forward and forcibly opens her hands. He wheels his* HORSE *and rides off. Other* INDIAN WOMEN *come up and comfort her.*

Dissolve to:
Long Shot—the Old Semi-Ruined Hacienda at Chinameca
 It is surrounded by a high wall. A large double gate opens into the central courtyard. Out of the gate ride FIVE MOUNTED ZAPATISTAS. *They have just completed their reconnaissance of the courtyard.* ONE *of them rides a little down the road, away from the hacienda, stands in his stirrups, and waves his hat in signal. . . .*

The Road
 EMILIANO *and some* ATTENDANTS *come rapidly into sight. They ride toward us. . . . Along the edge of the road are stands of*

rifles, cases of ammunition, machine guns, four pieces of artillery.

Close Shot—Emiliano
> *He looks admiringly at the materiel as he rides.*

Full Shot
> EMILIANO *rides in front of the gate and he looks into the court-yard. . . . Inside the courtyard, we can see* COLONEL GUAJARDO *. . . now cleanly dressed and in full regimentals. Behind him and at the side, stands* ZAPATA's WHITE HORSE, BLANCO, *with a beautiful new saddle and bridle.*

Close Shot—Emiliano
> *He has seen the* HORSE. *He leaps from his* HORSE *and runs in. . . .*

Emiliano and Blanco
> *There is a love scene. The* HORSE *knows him, nuzzles him.* EMILIANO *looks at* GUAJARDO.

EMILIANO: Where did you get him?

GUAJARDO: A Federal officer had him. . . . He's yours.
> EMILIANO *buries his head in the* HORSE's *mane, rubs his forehead on the neck. . . .*

Another Angle
> *While* ZAPATA *is occupied with the* HORSE *. . . we can see past them,* GUAJARDO *slowly, slowly backing away. . . .*

EMILIANO: Blanco! (*to* HORSE) Look at you! Where have you been! You've got old!

Guajardo—Foreground—Past Him We See
> EMILIANO *and the* HORSE. *. . .* GUAJARDO *has reached a recess in the wall a few feet from* EMILIANO *and the* HORSE.

Close Shot—Emiliano and the Horse
> BLANCO *suddenly raises his head* SNORTING. . . .

Guajardo
> *He raises his arm . . . ending in a salute.*

Emiliano
> *He looks up and around.*

The Parapets, suddenly lined with Armed Men.

Long Shot
> EMILIANO *is all alone in the middle of the courtyard. . . .*
> > *A* FUSILLADE *from the parapets.*
> > *The* HORSE *rears, bolts. . . .*

Emiliano
> *He has been knocked down by the very weight of the lead being poured into him. But he's still* FIRING. . . .

Parapets
> *Another* VOLLEY. . . .

Close-up—Guajardo's Face.

Emiliano, dying.
> *Instinctively he still* FIRES. *Then his hand is still. . . . He lies there without moving. A silence. Then he twitches. Instantly there is another* VOLLEY. . . . *Now he is dead. . . .*

Dissolve to:
Long Shot—the Courtyard Later—the Sun Is Setting
> *The courtyard is empty, except for the form of* ZAPATA's *body, covered by a serape, in the center. The paving around the body is chipped with bullets. In the far background the* WHITE HORSE *can be seen standing motionless.* ARMED GUARDS *in the shadows.*

Enter, at an opposite gate of the courtyard, FERNANDO *and the* OLD GENERAL, *attended.*

As they enter the gate, the HORSE *raises his head and* SNORTS.

FERNANDO *and the* OLD GENERAL *walk up to the body. As they walk:*

OLD GENERAL: That's a beautiful horse.

FERNANDO *leans down to uncover the body.*

FERNANDO: You can have him now.

As he throws the serape off, the HORSE *first shies and then bolts full tilt out the gateway of the courtyard.*

FERNANDO: Catch that horse. Shoot him! Shoot him!

He seems hysterical. . . .

OLD GENERAL (*in horror*): Shoot him. . . .

FERNANDO (*recovering and explaining not quite convincingly*): These people are very superstitious. . . .

Men run out the gate. . . . FERNANDO *and the* OLD GENERAL *look at the body.*

FERNANDO: He's dead.

OLD GENERAL: They shot him to ribbons. They must have been terribly afraid of him. (*half-hidden admiration*) The tiger is dead.

FERNANDO: And that's the end of that.

OLD GENERAL: I don't know . . . sometimes a dead man can be a terrible enemy.

FERNANDO *stares at him a moment, uncomprehending. . . . Then he gets the* OLD GENERAL*'s point. . . . He explodes with real rage.*

FERNANDO: Expose his body in the plaza so they can see it! So they can *all* see that he's dead!

Dissolve to:
Long Shot—Plaza at Roma

About a DOZEN HORSEMEN *of the Federal cavalry ride into the plaza. The plaza seems deserted in the brilliant sunlight. Un-*

ceremoniously, ONE OF THE RIDERS *dumps a body on the cistern head which is the center of the plaza. Then they ride off.*

Medium Shot—Side of the Plaza

> *The figure of a* WOMAN *is seen stepping from the shadow where she cannot be identified, into the light where it is seen that she is the* SOLDADERA. *She looks much older than when we last saw her. She starts toward the body.*

Full Shot—Plaza

> *From the shadows at the sides of the plaza a number of* MEN, *young and old, cross toward the body. They do not come slowly, but quickly, lithely, like angry cats.*

Medium Shot Around the Body

> *The* SOLDADERA *has composed the body. The group of* MEN *look at it curiously. An old scarred, beat-up veteran of the wars,* LAZARO, *steps up and leans down over the body. His attitude is not funereal. He has come to find out something. He examines the body for a moment, the* OTHER MEN *watching him curiously; then he turns away and spits on the ground in a gesture of contempt.*

LAZARO: Who do they think they're fooling? Shot up that way! Could be anybody!

A YOUNG MAN: He fooled them again!

ANOTHER MAN: Are you sure?

LAZARO: I rode with him. I fought with him all these years. Do they think they can fool me? They can't kill him. . . .

YOUNG MAN (*agreeing*): They'll never get him. Can you capture a river? Can you kill the wind?

LAZARO (*violently disagreeing with* YOUNG MAN): No! He's not a river and he's not the wind! He's a man—and they still can't kill him!

> *During this some* WOMEN *have come forward, bringing flowers which they put around the body.*

A MAN (*looking around—with a sense of awe*): Then where is he . . . ?

LAZARO: He's in the mountains. You couldn't find him now. But if we ever need him again—he'll be back.

YOUNG MAN (*with a secret kind of smile*): Yes . . . he's in the mountains. . . .

They're all looking up. . . .

Exterior, a Mountain Slope
Over a rise of MUSIC *we see* BLANCO, *the* WHITE HORSE, *walking up the slope toward the peak. He's all alone, grazing peacefully. . . .*

Fade out

The End

APPENDIX

A Note on the Script

Many screenplays are a collaboration between the initial author and the director; some American directors like John Huston, Sam Peckinpah, and Stanley Kubrick often receive credit as co-author of their films. But *Viva Zapata!* is Steinbeck's script. Elia Kazan states: "John and I consulted on the structure and continuity of the script. He wrote it. I made cuts as I shot. But the body of the film, the preponderance of it, is a faithful rendering of John's script. No actor rewrote it. I don't go for that. Zanuck did not rewrite it. He made a few suggestions, several of which we incorporated. But nothing of any moment. The significant changes in the shooting and editing had to do with placing the scenes in locations which we didn't have in mind when we wrote the script. And cuts, cuts, cuts. When a picture tells it, you cut the words. But all John's important words and thoughts are faithfully in the film."[1]

As with most movies, there are a number of changes between

---

1 Elia Kazan, letter to Robert E. Morsberger, March 29, 1973.

the shooting final and the dialogue and details that are ultimately fixed on the sound track. Most of the changes, as Kazan indicates, are cuts, sometimes of a few words or lines, occasionally of an entire scene or sequence. The most notable cuts are the deletion of the opening title scene of the horsemen and train, a long discussion between Don Nacio and other aristocrats about land ownership, an ambush of a column of horsemen, a conversation between Josefa and her father, in which he complains of Zapata's failure to seize business opportunities, an attempt by the Soldadera to kill Zapata with Pablo's knife, a dialogue between the Charro and Guajardo just before Zapata's assassination, and the entire role of Juana, a camp follower in love with Zapata, who may have been his mistress. Though some of these scenes elaborate on Steinbeck's political philosophy, most of them are expendable; their omission makes the script more taut. Other changes involve reassigning dialogue from one member of a group to another or rearranging some of the word order of a speech. Occasionally, the changes in phrasing sharpen the focus or characterization. For instance, in the audience with Díaz, the shooting final has Lazaro say, "I have a paper from the Spanish crown. I have a paper from the Mexican republic." On the sound track, he says, "We have a paper from the Spanish crown. We have a paper from the Mexican republic." Thus he speaks not for personal gain but for his village. At the end of his first meeting with Zapata, Fernando in the shooting final says, "This is all very confusing." The revision to "This is all very disorganized" is much more in character for his role of the efficient, relentless ideologue. In the shooting final, Zapata tells Josefa he wants to call on her father "To beg his permission to ask for your hand." The revision, "To ask permission for your hand," is not only more concise, but more in character, since Zapata is not one to beg for anything.

Occasionally, the film makes an addition to the shooting final. The most notable of these is the conclusion to the wedding night, when Zapata persuades Josefa to teach him to read. The shooting final calls for a dissolve after he says, "Begin!!" The film continues, to have her read the opening passage of Genesis, "In the beginning, God created the heaven and the earth," after which she says each phrase slowly for Zapata to repeat.

Elia Kazan says that these changes "seem hardly more than an 'easing' of a certain stiffness or artificiality (conscious and for a purpose) in John's dialogue. They were done on the set and without John's consultation."[2]

It might be argued that since the sound-track dialogue is all that the audience hears, that should be the definitive version. But for readers interested in John Steinbeck's writing, his entire shooting final should be available, even if bits of it were cut or changed in production. After all, very few stage versions use the entire text of a published play. From Shakespeare to Shaw to Tennessee Williams, plays are invariably cut and sometimes even rewritten for performance. The elaborate screen device for *The Glass Menagerie* is never used in production but is always included in the published text. In editing *Twenty Best Film Plays*, John Gassner published complete shooting scripts, despite cuts by the director or the film editor, arguing that "no one reading *Hamlet* is unhappy because the published text does not conform to the abbreviations and modifications employed by David Garrick or Sir Harry Irving in their respective productions of the play."[3] However, there can be a number of different stage interpretations from an original text, whereas the movie is fixed in one version. Therefore, in this edition, Steinbeck's shooting final is presented complete with only major cuts for the film indicated by square brackets. The directions for action and camera in the shooting final are Steinbeck's and were not necessarily followed in the filming. Elia Kazan writes that "all shooting script directions have to be adjusted with every day's

---

2 Kazan, letter to Morsberger, August 7, 1973.

3 John Gassner, "The Screenplay as Literature," *Twenty Best Film Plays*, John Gassner and Dudley Nichols, eds. (New York: Crown, 1943), ix–x.

work. They are not intended by John or any other decent author to be followed rigidly. I didn't. Stage directions are trivia. The words, the spirit, the big images, the theme are the thing."[4]

R. M.

4 Kazan to Morsberger, March 29, 1973.

Credits

VIVA ZAPATA!

Twentieth Century-Fox, 1952

Director	*Elia Kazan*
Producer	*Darryl F. Zanuck*
Screenplay	*John Steinbeck*
Director of Photography	*Joe MacDonald, A.S.C.*
Art Direction	*Lyle Wheeler, Leland Fuller*
Set Decorations	*Thomas Little,*
	Claude Carpenter
Musical Score	*Alex North*
Musical Direction	*Alfred Newman*
Film Editor	*Barbara McLean, A.C.E.*
Wardrobe Direction	*Charles Le Maire*
Costume Designer	*Travilla*
Makeup Artist	*Ben Nye*
Special Photographic Effects	*Fred Sersen*
Sound	*W. D. Flick, Roger Heman*
Time: 113 minutes	

Cast

Emiliano Zapata	*Marlon Brando*
Josefa	*Jean Peters*
Eufemio	*Anthony Quinn*
Fernando	*Joseph Wiseman*
Don Nacio	*Arnold Moss*
Pancho Villa	*Alan Reed*
Soldadera	*Margo*
Pablo	*Lou Gilbert*
Madero	*Harold Gordon*
Señora Espejo	*Mildred Dunnock*
Huerta	*Frank Silvera*
Aunt	*Nina Varela*
Señor Espejo	*Florenz Ames*
Díaz	*Fay Roope*
Don García	*Harry Kingston*
Lazaro	*Will Kuluva*
Zapatista	*Bernie Gozier*
Colonel Guajardo	*Frank De Kova*
General Fuentes	*Joseph Granby*
Fuentes's Wife	*Fernanda Elizcu*
Innocente	*Pedro Regas*
Old General	*Richard Garrick*
Officer	*Ross Bagdasarian*
Husband	*Leonard George*
Captain	*Abner Biberman*
Commanding Officer	*Philip Van Zandt*
García's Wife	*Lisa Fusaro*
Nacio's Wife	*Belle Mitchell*
Soldier	*Henry Silva*
Eduardo	*Guy Thomajan*
Rurale	*George J. Lewis*
Soldiers	*Salvador Baguez,*
	Peter Mamakos
Manager	*Ric Roman*
Senior Officer	*Henry Gorden*
New General	*Nester Paiva*
Captain of Rurales	*Robert Filmer*
Wife	*Julia Montoya*

Steinbeck's Screenplays
and Productions

Among modern American authors, John Steinbeck has had the greatest success in the movies, both with adaptations of his novels to the screen and as a screenwriter himself. William Faulkner supported himself for years by writing screenplays, but few of them are distinguished and all are collaborations; with a few exceptions, film versions of his own fiction have been travesties. Hemingway had power at the box office, but the movies often exploited him as if he were a pulp writer of sensational sex and violence. His only writing directly for the screen was the rather formless narrative for the documentary *The Spanish Earth*. F. Scott Fitzgerald complained that Hollywood invariably mangled any screenwriting that he was proud of. But most Steinbeck films have been both artistic and commercial successes, and a number of them have become screen classics. Steinbeck movies received twenty-five Academy Award nominations and won four of them, and Steinbeck himself was nominated three times for screenwriting.

Steinbeck's films fall into four categories: those adapted by others from his work, those he adapted himself from his fiction, those based upon unpublished stories that he wrote for the screen, and his original screenplays.

The best adaptations of Steinbeck novels for the movies were the first two, *Of Mice and Men* (1939) and *The Grapes of Wrath* (1940), directed, respectively, by Lewis Milestone and John Ford. Steinbeck had no direct hand in these productions; the screenplays, by Eugene Solow and Nunnally Johnson, preserved much dialogue verbatim from the novels but sometimes softened Steinbeck's harsh details and then-censorable language. George Bluestone and Warren French have shown how the script for *The Grapes of Wrath* blunted the novel's detailed attacks on specific oppressors and how, by rearranging sequences, it gave the film an upbeat ending that took away the necessity for social and political action. Even so, both films created a visual and dramatic record of the Depression that is historically valuable and transcends the period in a timeless account of man's inhumanity to man, the American loneliness, and the dream of a place of one's own. Both have become part of American folklore. Musically, *Of Mice and Men* offered a distinctive score by Aaron Copland, and *The Grapes of Wrath* prompted Woody Guthrie to write the ballad "Tom Joad."

Since Steinbeck himself was a playwright whose stage version of *Of Mice and Men* won the New York Drama Critics' Circle Award, it would have seemed natural for him to adapt his own work for the screen. Nowadays writers often do so. But in the 1930s and 1940s, few novelists of note worked on film versions of their own books. Instead, they were usually put to hack work on other people's projects. Therefore, despite the commercial success of *The Grapes of Wrath*, Steinbeck did not pursue Hollywood's big money.

Instead, he wrote a script for *The Forgotten Village*, a semi-documentary film about science versus superstition in a small Mexican mountain village. For this project he teamed up with director-producer Herbert Kline, to whom he wrote, "Zanuck is offering me five thousand a week to write a Hollywood movie, but I like your offer better, Herb—to write with no pay on a film I really want to do in Mexico."[1] Steinbeck's long-standing interest

---

[1] Herbert Kline, "On John Steinbeck," *Steinbeck Quarterly* 4 (Summer 1971), pp. 82–83.

in Mexico had been whetted the year before by his trip with marine biologist Edward F. Ricketts into the Gulf of California and by their collaboration on a documentary study, *Sea of Cortez*. Now he joined Kline on location and spent months in Mexico becoming familiar with details of village life and with the efforts of the Mexican Rural Medical Service to overcome the hostility of *curanderos*, or herbalist healers, and the Indians' fatalism toward disease. Steinbeck explained that his screenplay was "a very elastic story" that was actually a question, to which he found the answers when "the crew moved into the village, made friends, talked, and listened."[2] Since the filmmakers planned to use illiterate Indians who knew no English and in some cases not even Spanish, Steinbeck could not write a conventional scenario with dialogue. Instead the villagers spoke naturally among themselves in their own language while enacting Steinbeck's story. In many cases Kline was able to capture the details of village life as they happened. Steinbeck's screenplay is entirely a narration, spoken by Burgess Meredith.

The Forgotten Village won numerous prizes as a feature documentary but played only in small independent art theaters because the major studios then controlled most distribution through block booking. Like *Viva Zapata!*, *The Forgotten Village* shows Steinbeck's concern for the Mexican peasants and his desire to improve their condition. His protagonist, an Indian boy named Juan Diego, is driven away from his village after he brings in doctors who inoculate the children and disinfect poisoned wells to fight a cholera epidemic. The superstitious villages consider inoculation a form of diabolism and would rather have their children die and go to heaven, but Juan Diego saves his afflicted sister. Banished, he goes to the city to become a physician and eventually returns to enlighten his people. The film itself helped bring enlightenment, for a Mexican villager some years later told Kline, "Jefe, the children do not die here anymore."

---

2 John Steinbeck, *The Forgotten Village* (New York: The Viking Press, 1941), p. 5.

Steinbeck was not personally involved in the next two films made from his fiction. In 1942 M-G-M made a sentimentalized version of *Tortilla Flat* that was notable mainly for the performance of Frank Morgan as the Pirate, for which he received an Academy Award nomination as best supporting actor. A year later Twentieth Century-Fox made a competent low-budget movie of *The Moon Is Down*, about the growth of a resistance movement after the Nazi invasion of Norway, with a screenplay by Nunnally Johnson. Steinbeck's stage version had enjoyed only a nine-week run in New York, so when Johnson asked Steinbeck for suggestions on the screenplay, the author replied, "Tamper with it." Johnson followed Steinbeck's plot and dialogue carefully but opened up the action and dramatized episodes that were only offstage in the novel and play. Accordingly, most reviewers found the film more effective than its source in dramatizing German brutality and the growing fury and resistance of the villagers. Steinbeck himself acknowledged, "There is no question that pictures are a better medium for this story than the stage ever was. It was impossible to bring the whole countryside and the feeling of it onto the stage, with the result that the audience saw only one side of the picture."[3]

When *The Moon Is Down* was first published as a novel, some critics and readers condemned it for being "soft" on Nazism by daring to portray the German invaders as human beings who could be lonely and homesick as well as brutal. The novel is clearly anti-Nazi, however, and the movie version won better acceptance, but the controversy was revived with Steinbeck's next war film. In 1944 Twentieth Century-Fox released a picture billed as "Alfred Hitchcock's Production of *Lifeboat* by John Steinbeck." Actually the scenario was by Jo Swerling, who had written *The Westerner*, *Pride of the Yankees*, and other Gary Cooper films for Samuel Goldwyn. Planning a film about the Merchant Marine, Hitchcock said that he'd originally assigned Steinbeck to the screenplay but considered his treatment incomplete. He had MacKinlay Kantor work on it

3 "Brighter Moon," *Newsweek* 21 (April 5, 1943), p. 86.

briefly but did not like the results, so he then turned the project over to Swerling. Finding the narrative still rather shapeless, he then went over it himself.[4] The unpublished Steinbeck treatment is a novella in which, as in *The Wayward Bus*, Steinbeck isolates a group of representative figures and lets them interact. All the action is confined to a ship's launch containing the survivors of an Allied freighter sunk by a German submarine, plus the commander of the submarine, which was also destroyed in the encounter. The lifeboat becomes a microcosm, and the film an allegory of the war, with the democratic nations adrift at sea.

The controversy arose over the contrast between the Nazi and the democratic survivors. The latter are usually divided and ineffectual, while the sub commander, with single-minded purpose, is so resourceful and confident that the others often turn to him for leadership. Hostile critics accused Steinbeck of perpetrating the myth of the Aryan superman, even though the Nazi is actually treacherous, sinister, and murderous. When the others discover how he has betrayed them, they turn on him in a hysterical rage, beat him savagely, and drown him. This nautical lynching resembles the mob violence of *In Dubious Battle* and "The Vigilante." But *In Dubious Battle* also contains the line "There's a hunger in men to work together," and the democratic survivors do learn some teamwork and generally grow in sympathy and humanity.

Hitchcock interpreted Steinbeck's allegory to mean that, "while the democracies were completely disorganized, all of the Germans were clearly headed in the same direction. So here was a statement telling the democracies to put their differences aside temporarily and to gather their forces to concentrate on the common enemy, whose strength was precisely derived from a spirit of unity and of determination."[5]

Expertly directed by Hitchcock, with outstanding perfor-

---

4 François Truffaut, *Hitchcock*, with the collaboration of Helen G. Scott (New York: Simon and Schuster, 1967), p. 113.

5 *Ibid.*

mances by Tallulah Bankhead, William Bendix, and Walter Slezak, *Lifeboat* was a popular success. *Time* found it "remarkably
intelligent" and called it "an adroit allegory of world shipwreck."[6]
Other reviewers considered it thoughtful and exciting, but others
complained that the seeming realism was actually bland and su-
perficial, while James Agee judged the allegory clever but con-
trived.

Though Steinbeck received an Academy Award nomination
for the best original story, he was so unhappy with Swerling's
reworking of his material that he tried in vain to have his name
removed from the finished film. He objected to the way in which
Swerling had removed his gritty realism and replaced it with slick
and implausible details. In Steinbeck's treatment, for example, the
survivors swim through an oil slick to the lifeboat, whereas Swerling
has Connie Porter (Tallulah Bankhead) already seated in the lifeboat, fashionably dressed in dry clothing, with a neat hairdo and
no evidence that she has ever been in the ocean. She has salvaged
a typewriter and a camera, with which she is photographing the
disaster. While men are drowning all around her, she complains
of a broken fingernail and a run in her stocking. Steinbeck's Nazi
is not the superman Swerling makes him, nor does he row a ship's
launch alone, a patent impossibility. Steinbeck found particularly
offensive the way Swerling changed his black sailor: A sensitive
classic musician named Joe, whom Steinbeck calls the bravest man
aboard, became a stereotypical 1940s Hollywood black called
Charcoal, who is a thief.

Nevertheless, for Steinbeck studies, *Lifeboat* is notable for its
use of allegory (as in *The Grapes of Wrath*, *The Wayward Bus*, and
East of Eden) and for such recurring Steinbeck themes as the group
man, the stripping away of civilized surfaces, the brutality of people
carried away by mass violence, and the nature of leadership. The
finished film is more an ingenious entertainment than a serious

---

6 *Time* 43 (January 31, 1944), p. 94.

study of these themes, but most of the veneer was provided by
Swerling and Hitchcock.

Steinbeck was not yet ready to undertake an entire screenplay,
however. His third World War II movie, *A Medal for Benny*, has
a screenplay by Frank Butler based on an unpublished story by
Steinbeck and Jack Wagner; the screenplay was published in *Best
Film Plays*, 1945, edited by John Gassner and Dudley Nichols.
Benny, the title character, is a brawling paisano like Danny and
Pilon in *Tortilla Flat*. He never appears in the picture, for the
police have run him out of his small California town and he has
joined the army. The girl he left behind, Lolita Sierra (Dorothy
Lamour), is wooed in his absence by a likable ne'er-do-well, Joe
Morales (Arturo De Cordova), who is certain that he is a better
man than the legendary Benny. Benny is, in fact, a heel whom
Lolita never really loved. But just as she agrees to marry Joe, a
message comes that Benny has been killed in action and is to
receive a posthumous Congressional Medal of Honor. Ignorant of
Lolita's true feelings, the community expects her to spend the rest
of her life in heartbroken bereavement as a tribute to the hero.

The town officials meanwhile plan to exploit the medal for its
full publicity and profit. When they realize that Benny is a Chicano
from the wrong side of the tracks, they temporarily move his father
from his shack into a new house in order to impress the celebrities
at the award ceremony. But when Charley Martini, the father,
realizes how he is being used, he returns home in disgust, and the
medal is awarded among the scruffy children, scratching chickens,
and careless surroundings of his old neighborhood. The hitherto
comic Charley now takes on dignity as he asserts that a hero can
come from any kind of background and not just from the Establishment. At the end Joe goes off to war, but it is now clear that
Lolita is his girl and will be waiting for him.

A Medal for Benny succeeds admirably on its modest terms
and was considered one of the best films of 1945. J. Carrol Naish
was nominated for an Academy Award as best supporting actor for

his performance as Charley, and Steinbeck and Jack Wagner received nominations for the best original story. Bosley Crowther wrote, "Particular merit is here given to Mr. Steinbeck because the spirit of the work is so richly consistent with the spirit of all his 'paisano' yarns."[7]

Steinbeck was now ready to undertake a full screenplay, though not yet completely on his own. His next film was an adaptation of his novella *The Pearl*. This parable of a poor Mexican fisherman who learns that wealth brings corruption and death was not promising material for Hollywood, so Steinbeck teamed up with a Mexican company to make the film in Mexico, with Mexican performers acting in English. Released by RKO in 1948, *The Pearl* was the first Mexican movie to be widely distributed in the United States.

Steinbeck wrote the screenplay in collaboration with director Emilio Fernandez and Jack Wagner, co-author of the story *A Medal for Benny*. The adaptation is faithful to Steinbeck's plot but alters some significant details. In a comparison of the film and the book, Charles R. Metzger notes that Kino's brother Juan Tomás and the priest are omitted, the great machete with which Kino defends himself is left out, and a drinking sequence and an extravagant fiesta are added. Metzger argues that these changes weaken the novella's symbolism and diffuse its themes, but he concludes that the film still retains most of Steinbeck's *exemplum* of corruption and survival.[8] The main liabilities of the production are that the leads were too glamorous, while the supporting players came out of central casting and the costumes out of a well-laundered studio wardrobe. *The Pearl* lacks the authentic poverty and weather-worn faces of *The Forgotten Village*, but this is the fault of the director, not of Steinbeck. To compensate, *The Pearl* has superb photography of Baja California mountains and seascapes and beautifully com-

---

7 Bosley Crowther, "Review of *A Medal for Benny*," *The New York Times*, May 24, 1945, p. 15:2.

8 Charles R. Metzger, "The Film Version of Steinbeck's *The Pearl*," *Steinbeck Quarterly* 4 (Summer, 1971), pp. 88–92.

posed shots that John McCarten compared to the murals of Orozco, who had illustrated the book. In its depiction of Mexican peasant life and its attack on the exploitation of the poor by the unjustly wealthy, *The Pearl* has affinities with *Viva Zapata!* Steinbeck, in fact, began his research on Zapata at this time.

Meanwhile, Steinbeck wrote a screenplay for Republic's 1949 production of *The Red Pony*. Consisting of four loosely connected short stories, *The Red Pony* lacks a strong central narrative. However, there had been a number of successful movies in the 1940s featuring a child and an animal—the *Lassie* series, *My Friend Flicka*, *National Velvet*, and *The Yearling*—and Republic seemed to think that *The Red Pony* could repeat the formula. But Steinbeck's episodes lack sentimental appeal. Essentially grim, they focus on Jody Tiflin's painful initiation into an understanding of suffering, death, and the difficulties of adulthood, with a psychological and biological realism that is far from the usual Hollywood pastoral romance.

Blending these stories into a commercially popular picture was a considerable challenge. Steinbeck wrote the screenplay himself, the only time he had the sole responsibility for adapting one of his books. Combining "The Gift," "The Leader of the People," and part of "The Promise," in that order, with a more affirmative ending, Steinbeck produced a loose, leisurely narrative that some reviewers found unexciting. Perhaps because the boy in M-G-M's 1946 movie of *The Yearling* is also named Jody, Steinbeck changed Jody Tiflin's name to Tom. For no particular reason, he altered the parents' names from Carl and Ruth Tiflin to Fred and Alice. Considering the problems of adaptation, the screenplay is quite competent. Lewis Milestone, who had made *Of Mice and Men*, did a routine job of direction with somewhat miscast players (Myrna Loy as the mother, Shepperd Strudwick as the father, Louis Calhern as the grandfather, young Robert Mitchum as Billy Buck, and Peter Miles as the boy). In the long run, the most memorable feature of the film is the vigorous score by Aaron Copland.

Steinbeck's only completely original screenplay with dialogue is *Viva Zapata!*, unquestionably his finest work in the genre. The Mexican revolution was so complex that it would be impossible for any film to reproduce it in close detail—even in a production as long as *Nicholas and Alexandra* on the Russian revolution. Steinbeck made no attempt to do so. The structure of *Viva Zapata!* is like Shakespeare's chronicle histories: episodic yet tightly coherent, with a few skirmishes to sketch in an entire war. His screenplay is not so much history as folklore, parable, and poetry. The actual events in the film cover a period of ten years, from 1909 to 1919. Though Steinbeck's Zapatistas speak of long and arduous campaigning, there is no sense of such a long period, and none of the film's characters age perceptibly. The oppression of the Morelos peasant farmers by the deliberate action of the planters' plutocracy recalls *The Grapes of Wrath*; but Steinbeck eliminated the wealth of historical detail on social and economic conditions that make up much of his original treatment in *Zapata, the Little Tiger*. Instead he brings the broad historical background to life with a few incisive scenes: the audience with Díaz, soldiers gunning down peasants trying to establish boundaries, the murder of Innocente, the arrest of Zapata. The exposition is dramatic rather than documentary; the actors and the audience are involved more than they are informed. In the film we never learn the background of Madero—a schoolteacher who campaigned for president against Díaz; we first hear of him via Fernando, when Madero is already in exile in Texas. But Steinbeck's portrait of him matches historian John Womack's account of Madero's "characteristic innocence . . . touching gentleness, concern, and sincerity."[9]

In the film Zapata's patron, Don Nacio de la Torre, gets him pardoned for his early acts of rebellion. In actuality, Ignacio de la Torre y Mier was Díaz's son-in-law. Instead of getting Zapata pardoned, he got him discharged from the army, into which he had been drafted in 1910; in return, Zapata worked "as chief groom

---

9 John Womack, Jr., *Zapata and the Mexican Revolution* (New York: Alfred A. Knopf, 1969), p. 57.

in his Mexico City stables."[10] Later, in active opposition to Díaz, Zapata sent Pablo Torres Burgos to Texas to discover if Madero was sincere. But this Pablo, who became a Zapatista commander, otherwise had nothing in common with the peasant Pablo Gómez in the film; and Zapata never killed him or any other Pablo. The entire relationship is Steinbeck's fiction.

After Díaz had abdicated and sailed to Paris in May 1911, Zapata demanded agrarian reform and Madero stalled, as in the film; but the movie considerably oversimplifies Huerta's treachery during the disarming of Morelos. In fact there were several episodes in which the Zapatistas began to disarm, were betrayed, and fought back. When Huerta invaded Morelos in August 1911, it was with Madero's backing. But two episodes in the film at this point correspond in detail to the facts. On one occasion, Zapata did use Madero's watch to argue against disarming, insisting, "Look, Señor Madero, if I take advantage of the fact that I'm armed and take away your watch and keep it, and after a while we meet, both of us armed the same, would you have a right to demand that I give it back?" "Certainly," said Madero. "Well," argued Zapata, "that's exactly what has happened to us in Morelos, where a few planters have taken over by force the villagers' lands. My soldiers—the armed farmers and all the people in the villages—demand that I tell you, with full respect, that they want the restitution of their lands to be got under way right now."[11] Madero then promised to visit Morelos and inspect conditions there for himself.

Likewise, as in the film, Eufemio wanted to shoot Madero when Huerta's troops began maneuvers while Zapata was again disbanding his men. Madero insisted that there was a misunderstanding. In the film Madero is sincere, but in fact he kept betraying Zapata, had his government outlaw him, and sent Huerta to capture him. By then José Maria Lozano, in Congress, said, "Emiliano

10 Ibid., p. 60.

11 Ibid., p. 96.

Zapata is no longer a man, he is a symbol. He could turn himself in tomorrow . . . but the rabble [following him] . . . would not surrender."[12]

Madero became president of Mexico in 1911 and was murdered in 1913; Huerta fled the country in July 1914. Five more years would pass before Zapata's death, but this period is greatly condensed in the film, which never attempts to explain Carranza and Obregón. In part, this condensation may be due to Steinbeck's use of Edgcumb Pinchon's *Zapata the Unconquerable* as a source, for Pinchon spent 306 of his 332 pages leading up to Zapata's meeting with Villa in 1914.

Steinbeck's screenplay omits many historic characters and stresses instead fictitious ones like Fernando, Pablo Gómez, Lazaro, the Soldadera, and the Charro whose actions reenact Zapata's. John Womack, Jr., writes that the filmmakers "included in their simplification some factual details that complicated the superhumanly heroic image of Zapata that then prevailed—like his marriage to the daughter of a hostile local rancher, his difficulties with her, etc.—details which were then practically unknown; in introducing them, they made the character much more true to life and interesting."[13] In August 1911 Zapata married Josefa Espejo, the daughter of an Agalla livestock dealer who had died in 1909. Zapata had been courting her since before the revolution, so it's possible that her father had earlier opposed the match, but the film keeps him alive after the marriage, to complain about his son-in-law's failure to secure power and wealth. The film omits the fact that Josefa bore two children who died in infancy, and it makes no mention of Zapata's bastards, some of them born after his marriage. The shooting final ambiguously includes a camp follower named Juana, who adores Zapata; this role, however, was cut from the final film.

Though the movie alters some details of Zapata's death, it is

---

12 *Ibid.*, p. 123.

13 *Ibid.*, p. 420.

dramatically true. The suspicions of Zapata's lieutenants and Josefa's forebodings and despair create a sense of fated inevitability, so that the audience feels as if Zapata is riding into martyrdom. The historic Zapata was murdered on April 10, 1919, betrayed by Jesús Guajardo; the fact that the Judas in the case is named Jesus adds a macabre irony to the film. Historically, Guajardo had given Zapata a sorrel horse the day before; Zapata was riding it when he entered the hacienda with ten followers, three of whom were killed with him. The film achieves greater tension by having Zapata alone, reunited with his lost white stallion. During this sequence there is utter silence, except for the nervous sounds of the horse, while the camera repeatedly focuses on three old men withered like mummies, waiting, and on four old women in black fingering their prayer beads, the shadow of a cross on the wall. Then, as in the ending of *Butch Cassidy and the Sundance Kid* seventeen years later, we see the killing from the rooftops, filled with soldiers who cut down Zapata with a rain of bullets. Afterward, in both film and fact, Guajardo had Zapata's body dumped on the pavement of the main plaza of Cuautla. John Womack's account of the aftermath closely parallels Steinbeck's ending: "Many would not believe Zapata was dead. Odd stories began to circulate. One went that Zapata was too smart for the trap, and had dispatched a subordinate who resembled him to the final meeting. Anyway, it went on, the corpse on display was not Zapata's. . . . In a few days the Chief would reappear as always. Then stranger reports were passed on. The horse he rode the day he died, the sorrel Guajardo had given him—it had been seen galloping riderless through the hills. People who saw it said it was white now. And someone thought he had glimpsed Zapata himself on it, heading hard into the Guerrero mountains to the south."[14]

Some simplification of Zapata and the Mexican revolution was inevitable. Certainly, Steinbeck's treatment is as historically and dramatically legitimate as Robert Bolt's for the Academy Award—

14 *Ibid.*, p. 330.

winning *Lawrence of Arabia*. In *Zapata and the Mexican Revolution*, John Womack calls *Viva Zapata!* "a distinguished achievement" but notes that "in telescoping the whole revolution into one dramatic episode, the movie distorts certain events and characters."[15] Womack thinks that these indefensible distortions include "the presentation of Zapata as illiterate, which he was not, and the presentation of his brother as a lush, which he was not." (Womack does record, however, that Eufemio became notorious for alcoholic excesses just before his death.) Womack also challenges the role of Fernando, observing that "intellectuals had very little part in determining Zapatista policy, or in determining anything about the Mexican revolution as a whole. Most of them despaired of the revolution and left for other parts, or did what their *jefes* told them." But Fernando is not especially intellectual; like the lieutenant in Graham Greene's *The Power and the Glory*, his role is that of the ruthless revolutionary determined to destroy all opposition. "Still," concludes Womack, "what rings longest in my mind from the movie is Zapata's integrity, his suspicion of all outsiders, his absolute sense of responsibility to his local people, a sense which I think Marlon Brando captured precisely."[16]

Much of the artistic success of *Viva Zapata!* goes to director Elia Kazan. Though the screenplay is the essential framework, without which there is no drama, screenplays alone are comparatively stark. A stage play depends more exclusively on dialogue and therefore seems more complete to the reader, whereas a movie may convey much of its impact through wordless action, visual details, and musical effects. In this sense, *Viva Zapata!* may be the most cinematic of all Kazan's films. He had previously distinguished himself as a director of stage plays (*Death of a Salesman*) and of their screen versions (*A Streetcar Named Desire*). Earlier films like *Boomerang* and *Gentleman's Agreement* had relied more on character and dialogue than on action. But in *Viva Zapata!*

---

15 *Ibid.*, p. 420.

16 John Womack, Jr., letter to Robert E. Morsberger, April 28, 1973.

Kazan made full use of the movie medium to reinforce Steinbeck's ideas and symbols. The action sequences are brisk and graphic. The settings (location shots in Roma, Texas, and other sets constructed in California at the Fox Studios or on the Fox Ranch) convey authentic local color; and Joe MacDonald's photography brings out the beauty, alternately austere and ornate, of the Mexican villages, palaces, and countryside. One of the most moving sequences in the film—the procession of villagers and farmers who free Zapata from the *rurales*—is entirely a combination of visual composition and music. Kazan also got the most out of his cast. The main shortcoming of the performances is the mixture of accents. Brando, Anthony Quinn, and some others undertook Mexican accents, while others portrayed Mexicans with a flat middle-American speech. Most of the supporting players were relatively little known, but all are impressive. Madero, Huerta, and Villa in the film look exactly like photographs of their historic counterparts.

Viva Zapata! received five nominations for Academy Awards for 1952 but won only one, for best supporting actor (Quinn). Steinbeck personally received nominations for story and screenplay, but the award went to *The Lavender Hill Mob*. Alex North's musical score lost to Dimitri Tiomkin's for *High Noon*. For black-and-white art and set decoration, *Viva Zapata!* was beaten by *The Bad and the Beautiful*.

Despite the film's recognition, Steinbeck felt that it had not been adequately promoted or properly appreciated. On March 1, 1963, he wrote to Kazan proposing that they try to get *Viva Zapata!* rereleased with better studio support, so that it might find a fuller audience. He argued that the film "never got off the ground" in the United States because "the studio was scared of it—at least unsure—and that communicated." Steinbeck claimed that Communist pressure kept the picture from being allowed any scope in Mexico and South America, and that for the same reason "it was never shown in Russia or the satellites." The film never mentions Communism, and it is never specified that Fernando is a Communist; nevertheless, the thesis that relentless totalitarians betray revolution for dictatorship seemed to be borne out by too many examples from recent history. In fact, in 1963 Steinbeck suggested that he and Kazan could rework the film to "point up the parallel with Cuba." "In Europe," on the other hand, "where people knew about revolutions, there were not these problems." Ever since the publication of *In Dubious Battle*, the Communists had joined with the radical right in denouncing Steinbeck; and Kazan noted that "at the end of his life they were calling him a 'jackal' and a 'running dog' and all those other absurd epithets they use."[17]

In addition, Steinbeck suggested to Kazan that the film had "spread too far—tried to take in too much. It became more biography than the story of a revolt. It was obscure in time and purpose. It needed clarification." He therefore proposed reworking the picture by doing some cutting, editing, and tightening (but suggested no particular details) and by adding a commentary. No reshooting would be required. "I would like to write the commentary and perhaps read it," he said. "It's not that I would do it well but that I would do it better than anyone else because I know best what it wants to say." Steinbeck wished the title to be changed "to the one I wanted from the beginning, *Zapata Vive*." He argued that the film came out ahead of its time and that in the early 1960s the theme "that revolutions get taken over by the wrong people after they are accomplished" might find more responsive audiences. "We would sharpen and clarify the tendency of the revolt to go Fascist as it has all over the world." With proper State Department support, possible sponsorship by the U.S. Information Agency, and perhaps even the backing of President Kennedy, "it would be a public service." Steinbeck proposed that he and Kazan should ask "not for money but for participation."

Considering the conduct of foreign affairs since 1964 and the debacle of our war in Southeast Asia, Steinbeck's proposals seem overly optimistic, but that is a hindsight not so obvious in 1963. Kazan concurs that he and Steinbeck did try to persuade Spyros

---

17 Elia Kazan, letter to Robert E. Morsberger, August 7, 1973.

Skouras at Fox into reworking and releasing the film, but the studio refused to spend any more money on it. Probably this is just as well. *Viva Zapata!* succeeds better through dramatic action than didacticism, and a propagandistic commentary might destroy the film's lyricism and reduce it to a semidocumentary. It has eventually found its audience, in rerelease at individual theaters, frequent showing on television, and on videotape. Films Incorporated promoted *Viva Zapata!* as one of its first twelve films excerpted for the study of film technique in colleges and universities.

Kazan and Steinbeck were particularly committed to *Viva Zapata!* Kazan wrote that he was fond and proud of it, and he thought the title role "was the most difficult job Brando ever attempted and one of his most subtle portraits."[18]

He and Steinbeck were so pleased with their collaboration that "we were eager to do another film after this one. I suggested we do the last ninety odd pages of *East of Eden* and John gave me the boom."[19] Since Steinbeck was writing another book at the time, Kazan suggested that Paul Osborn do the screenplay, and Steinbeck agreed. Osborn was a playwright who'd written *On Borrowed Time* and *Mornings at Seven* and adapted John Hersey's *A Bell for Adano* and J. P. Marquand's *Point of No Return* for the stage. Beginning at approximately Chapter 37 in Part Four of the novel and eliminating the Chinese philosopher-servant Lee, Osborn expanded the conflict between Cal and Aron Trask for Aron's girl Abra and for the affection of their father, Adam. The film's Cal is a more brooding, violent, and self-destructive young man than Steinbeck's character; as played by James Dean, he became the symbol of rejected and rebellious youth. (Kazan had wanted Brando for the role, but the star was unavailable.) After Dean's death in a car accident, *East of Eden* became a part of the James Dean cult that generated a chapter in John Dos Passos's *Midcentury*.

The team of Steinbeck and Kazan had a considerable success,

---

18 Kazan, letter to Morsberger, March 29, 1973.

19 *Ibid.*

both critically and financially, with *East of Eden*. Academy Award nominations went to Kazan for best director, Paul Osborn for his screenplay, James Dean for best actor, and Jo Van Fleet (who won) for best supporting actress.

Two years later, Twentieth Century-Fox brought out a routine movie version of *The Wayward Bus* as a vehicle for Jayne Mansfield. William Saroyan did an initial script that followed the book carefully, but his screenplay was rejected in favor of a slick adaptation by Ivan Moffat that glamorized the characters and simplified the story. Some reviewers blamed Steinbeck for weaknesses that are in the film version but not in the novel. For twenty-five years, it was the last commercial Steinbeck film.

During that interval, Barnaby Conrad wrote and produced a feature-length film of *Flight*, expanded from the short story in *The Long Valley*. The low-budget amateur production has considerable verisimilitude and was well received in London and at the Edinburgh Film Festival, but it was never released commercially in the United States. Steinbeck liked the picture and proposed that Conrad add an introductory narration written and spoken by Steinbeck. Conrad did so, and this introduction is Steinbeck's final writing for the movies.

Meanwhile, television presented feature-length remakes of *The Red Pony* in 1973 (with Maureen O'Hara as the mother and Henry Fonda playing a composite of the father and Billy Buck), *Of Mice and Men* (twice: in 1968, with George Segal and Nicol Williamson as George and Lennie, and in 1981 with Robert Blake and Randy Quaid), and *East of Eden* in 1980. The latter, a four-hour miniseries with an all-star cast headed by Timothy Bottoms as Adam Trask and Jane Seymour as Cathy/Kate, attempted to present the entire novel, though there were some inevitable cuts. In 1983 *The Winter of Our Discontent* was telecast with Donald Sutherland and Teri Garr as Ethan Allen Hawley and his wife and Tuesday Weld as Margie Young-Hunt.

The first new commercial motion picture based on Steinbeck's fiction since 1957 was the 1982 production of *Cannery Row*, adapted and directed by David Ward, best known for his Academy Award–winning screenplay for *The Sting*. A Steinbeck fan, Ward had wanted to film *Cannery Row* for years but was frustrated by the novel's episodic nature. He was at first unaware of the sequel, *Sweet Thursday*, but when he finally discovered and read it, he located his dramatic and narrative center in the love story between Doc and Suzy, a hooker at the Bear Flag. Combining the two novels, Ward came up with a script that the president of Orion Films told him was "the best script I've ever read" before declining it. Conferring with Paul Newman, whom he wanted to play Doc, Ward did several rewrites to build up Doc's part and get inside his mind, only to have Newman drop out. Unfortunately, in trying to give Doc the background that Newman thought was missing in the novels, Ward came up with a gimmick to make Doc a man of mystery. Concluding that Doc is the only character who does not have to be in Cannery Row, Ward asked why he chose to live there, aside from the presence of tide pools. By way of an answer he fabricated a mysterious past in which Doc had been a major-league baseball pitcher nicknamed "Eddie the Blur" who had caused brain damage to a batter by hitting him with a fastball and had then dropped out, concealed his past, and taken a new identity. Gradually uncovering this mystery, Suzy discovers in it the reason that Doc fears intimacy. But this concocted subplot is false to Steinbeck's Doc, who is not hiding a secret past, and it detracts from the main story.

Ward insisted on directing the film himself but found that the studios were reluctant to gamble with a first-time director. Ward was about to give up when Nick Nolte, a long-time Steinbeck enthusiast, announced that he was eager to play Doc. A deal was struck with M-G-M, and filming got underway, with Debra Winger as Suzy, M. Emmet Walsh as Mack, Audra Lindley as Fauna, and John Huston providing a voice-over as the narrator. Photographed by Sven Nykvist, scored by Jack Nitzsche, and played to the hilt by a raffish cast, *Cannery Row* was made with loving care, and much of it works; the frog hunt is a comic masterpiece. However, critical reaction was mixed, and the film was a commercial failure. One reason may have been that in combining *Cannery Row* with *Sweet Thursday*, Ward left out what Steinbeck called the poison in his "cream puff." In any case, the romantic charm of poverty has worn off, if it ever did exist, and Steinbeck's view is somewhat dated as well as sentimental; nowadays there is nothing comic about being unemployed and homeless.

Since most of Steinbeck's novels have been filmed, the next step was to film his short stories. Several episodes from *The Pastures of Heaven* were televised in the early 1950s. Steinbeck's adaptation of several of the stories in *The Red Pony* was not altogether successful, and Barnaby Conrad's expansion of "Flight" into a feature-length film sometimes seemed padded. Commercial films of short stories often follow the Conrad route and add material (for example several versions of Hemingway's "The Killers" and Roger Corman's productions of Poe stories), usually departing drastically from the original. Another commercial approach has been to film at their proper length an omnibus package of several stories by the same author, such as Somerset Maugham's *Quartet, Trio* and *Encore* and *O. Henry's Full House*, five stories that were introduced by none other than John Steinbeck. The other route is to film stories noncommercially for educational use. Such versions are too often dryly academic and obviously low budget. But a low-budget film need not be either dry or amateur, as demonstrated by films of two stories from *The Long Valley*. In 1989 Pyramid Films made 16mm versions of "The Chrysanthemums" and "The Raid" that were released on videotape in July 1990. Not only were they filmed at their proper length (22:28 minutes and 24:18 minutes, respectively), but as scripted by Steve Rosen and Terri Debonno—who also served as directors, producers, and editors—they used Steinbeck's dialogue verbatim and followed in careful detail his narrative and descriptive passages as if they were directions for the production. Rosen said he was not interpreting the stories, just translating them to the screen. The translation works remarkably well, for these stories are written primarily in dialogue. With only three speaking characters in "The Chrysanthemums" and chiefly two in "The Raid," supported by several others with a few lines each, the stories lend themselves admirably to low-budget productions that do not look cheap. Making the most of location filming, artful photography, and competent but unknown casts, the short films render Steinbeck's stories effectively. Following "The Chrysanthemums" is a short subject, "Behind the Camera," about the making of the film, an apologia for producing quality films on a low budget. In 1991 Pyramid released a third Steinbeck story on film: "Molly Morgan," from *The Pastures of Heaven*. At thirty-two minutes running time, it too uses all of Steinbeck's dialogue. All three films are available from Mac and Ava Motion Picture Productions, 602 Lighthouse Avenue, Monterey, California 93940.

Steinbeck continues to be potent on film. In 1991 PBS telecast the Steppenwolf Theatre production of *The Grapes of Wrath* to great acclaim. With dialogue almost entirely by Steinbeck, Frank Galati's stage version had won a Tony Award for the best play of 1990, and it was equally powerful on screen. A new film of *Of Mice and Men*—with a screenplay by Horton Foote and directed by Gary Sinise, who also plays George, with John Malkovich as Lennie—was released in the fall of 1992. And there has been talk of a film version of *In Dubious Battle*. With classic Steinbeck films enjoying theatrical revival and continued life on television and videotape and with new productions underway, Steinbeck's work remains vital and compelling.

R. M.

Steinbeck's Films

Here is a complete list of films written by John Steinbeck for the screen or adapted by Steinbeck and others from his fiction. It also includes the one film narrated by Steinbeck. The films are listed in chronological order, with the major credits.

Of Mice and Men

Screenplay by Eugene Solow, adapted from the John Steinbeck play. Directed and produced by Lewis Milestone. Musical score by Aaron Copland. A Hal Roach presentation. United Artists, 1939.

George	Burgess Meredith	Candy	Roman Bohnen
Lennie	Lon Chaney, Jr.	Whit	Noah Beery, Jr.
Mae	Betty Field	Jackson	Oscar O'Shea
Slim	Charles Bickford	Carlson	Granville Bates
Curley	Bob Steele	Crooks	Leigh Whipper

The Grapes of Wrath

Screenplay by Nunnally Johnson, adapted from the novel by John Steinbeck. Musical score by Alfred Newman. Directed by John Ford. Photography by Gregg Toland. Produced by Darryl F. Zanuck. Twentieth Century-Fox, 1940.

Tom Joad   *Henry Fonda*
Ma Joad   *Jane Darwell*
Casy   *John Carradine*
Grampa   *Charley Grapewin*
Rosasharn   *Dorris Bowdon*
Pa Joad   *Russell Simpson*

Al   *O. Z. Whitehead*
Muley   *John Qualen*
Noah   *Frank Sully*
Uncle John   *Frank Darien*
Winfield   *Darryl Hickman*
Ruth Joad   *Shirley Mills*

The Forgotten Village

Story and screenplay by John Steinbeck. Music by Hanns Eisler. Photography by Alexander Hackensmid. Narrated by Burgess Meredith. Produced and directed by Herbert Kline. An Arthur Mayer–Joseph Burstyn release, 1941.

Tortilla Flat

Screenplay by John Lee Mahin and Benjamin Glazer, based on the novel by John Steinbeck. Directed by Victor Fleming. Produced by Sam Zimbalist. M-G-M, 1942.

Pilon   *Spencer Tracy*
Danny   *John Garfield*
Dolores (Sweets) Ramirez   *Hedy Lamarr*

The Pirate   *Frank Morgan*
Pablo   *Akim Tamiroff*

The Moon Is Down

Screenplay by Nunnally Johnson, based on the novel by John Steinbeck. Directed by Irving Pichel. Produced by Nunnally Johnson. Twentieth Century Fox, 1943.

Colonel Lanser   *Sir Cedric Hardwicke*
Mayor Orden   *Henry Travers*
Dr. Winter   *Lee J. Cobb*
Molly Morden   *Dorris Bowdon*

Madama Orden   *Margaret Wycherly*
Lt. Tonder   *Peter Van Eyck*
Peder   *Irving Pichel*
George Corell   *E. J. Ballantine*

Lifeboat

Screenplay by Jo Swerling, from a story by John Steinbeck. Directed by Alfred Hitchcock. Produced by Kenneth MacGowan. Twentieth Century-Fox, 1944.

Connie Porter   *Tallulah*
  Bankhead
Gus   *William Bendix*
The German   *Walter Slezak*
Alice Mackenzie   *Mary Anderson*

Rittenhouse   *Henry Hull*
Kovac   *John Hodiak*
Stanley Garrett   *Hume Cronyn*
Joe   *Canada Lee*

A Medal for Benny

Screenplay by Frank Butler, from a story by John Steinbeck and Jack Wagner. Directed by Irving Pichel. Produced by Paul Jones. Paramount, 1945.

Lolita Sierra   *Dorothy Lamour*
Joe Morales   *Arturo De Cordova*

Charley Martini   *J. Carrol Naish*
Raphael Catalina   *Mikhail Rasummy*

The Pearl

Screenplay by John Steinbeck, Emilio Fernandez, and Jack Wagner. Directed by Emilio Fernandez. Produced by Oscar Danugers. RKO, 1948.

Kimo   *Pedro Armendariz*
Juana   *Maria Elena Marques*

The Red Pony

Screenplay by John Steinbeck. Music by Aaron Copland. Directed and produced by Lewis Milestone. Republic, 1949.

Alice Tiflin   *Myrna Loy*
Billy Buck   *Robert Mitchum*
Grandfather   *Louis Calhern*
Fred Tiflin   *Shepperd Strudwick*

Tom [Jody]   *Peter Miles*
Teacher   *Margaret Hamilton*
Beau   *Beau Bridges*

Viva Zapata!

Screenplay by John Steinbeck. Directed by Elia Kazan. Produced by Darryl F. Zanuck. Twentieth Century-Fox, 1952.

Emiliano Zapata   *Marlon Brando*
Josefa   *Jean Peters*
Eufemio   *Anthony Quinn*
Fernando   *Joseph Wiseman*
Don Nacio   *Arnold Moss*
Soldadera   *Margo*

Pancho Villa   *Alan Reed*
Madero   *Harold Gordon*
Pablo   *Lou Gilbert*
Señora Espejo   *Mildred Dunnock*
Huerta   *Frank Silvera*

O. Henry's Full House, based on five stories: "The Cop and the Anthem," "The Clarion Call," "The Last Leaf," "The Gift of the Magi," "The Ransom of Red Chief." Narrated by John Steinbeck. Twentieth Century-Fox, 1952.

East of Eden

Screenplay by Paul Osborn, based on the novel by John Steinbeck. Music by Victor Young. Directed by Elia Kazan. Warner Bros., 1955.

Abra   *Julie Harris*
Carl Trask   *James Dean*
Adam Trask   *Raymond Massey*
Aron Trask   *Richard Davalos*
Kate   *Jo Van Fleet*

Sam   *Burl Ives*
Will   *Albert Dekker*
Ann   *Lois Smith*

The Wayward Bus

Screenplay by Ivan Moffat, based on the novel by John Steinbeck. Produced by Charles Brackett. Twentieth Century-Fox, 1957.

Johnny Chicoy   *Rick Jason*
Alice Chicoy   *Joan Collins*
Camille   *Jayne Mansfield*
Ernest Horton   *Dan Dailey*
Norma   *Betty Lou Keim*

Mildred Pritchard   *Dolores Michaels*
Pritchard   *Larry Keating*
Morse   *Robert Bray*
Mrs. Pritchard   *Kathryn Givney*

Flight

Screenplay by Barnaby Conrad, adapted from the short story by John Steinbeck. Produced by Barnaby Conrad. Music written and played by Laurindo Almeida. Directed by Louis Bispo.

Cannery Row

Screenplay by David Ward, based on the novel by John Steinbeck. Directed by David Ward. Produced by Michael Phillips. M-G-M, 1982.

Doc   *Nick Nolte*   Fauna   *Audra Lindley*
Suzy   *Debra Winger*   Hazel   *Frank McRae*
Mack   *M. Emmet Walsh*

The Chrysanthemums

Written, directed, produced and edited by Steven Rosen and Terri Debonno, from the story by John Steinbeck. Pyramid Films, 1990.

Elisa   *Nina Capriela*   The Tinker   *Michael Halton*
Henry   *Paul Henri*

Raid

Written, directed, produced and edited by Steven Rosen and Terri Debonno, from the story by John Steinbeck. Pyramid Films, 1990.

Root   *Matthew Flint*
Dick   *John Rousseau*

Molly Morgan

Written, directed, produced and edited by Steven Rosen and Terri Debonno, from John Steinbeck's story in *The Pastures of Heaven*. Pyramid Films, 1991.

Molly Morgan   *Teressa McKillop*   Mrs. Whiteside   *Louise*
Molly Morgan as a child   *Eunice*   *Nachman*
   Clay   Bill   *Norman Stottmeister*
Molly's father   *Jeffrey Heyer*   Bert Munroe   *Dennis McIntyre*
Mr. Whiteside   *Rollie Dick*

Bibliography

Benson, Jackson J. *The True Adventures of John Steinbeck, Writer*. New York: The Viking Press, 1984.

Bluestone, George. *Novels into Film*. Baltimore: Johns Hopkins Press, 1957; Berkeley and Los Angeles: University of California Press, 1966. Includes a detailed study of the film version of *The Grapes of Wrath*.

Bogdanovich, Peter. *John Ford*. Berkeley and Los Angeles: University of California Press, 1968. Contains a discussion with the director about the film of *The Grapes of Wrath*.

Camus, Albert. *The Rebel*, trans. Anthony Bower. New York: Alfred A. Knopf, Vintage Books, 1957. The classic study of rebellion and revolution.

———. *Resistance, Rebellion, and Death*, trans. Justin O'Brien. New York: Alfred A. Knopf, 1961.

Ciment, Michel. *Kazan on Kazan*. New York: The Viking Press, 1974.

Crowther, Bosley. "Review of 'A Medal for Benny,'" *The New York Times*, May 24, 1945, p. 15:2.

Everson, William K. *The Films of Hal Roach*. Greenwich, Connecticut: Museum of Modern Art, New York, 1971. Discusses the filming of *Of Mice and Men*.

French, Warren. *Filmguide to The Grapes of Wrath*. Bloomington: Indiana University Press, 1973.

Gassner, John, and Dudley Nichols, eds. *Best Film Plays, 1945*. New York: Crown, 1947. Contains Frank Butler's screenplay of *A Medal for Benny*.

———. "The Screenplay as Literature," *Twenty Best Film Plays*. New York:

Crown, 1943. The volume contains Nunnally Johnson's screenplay of *The Grapes of Wrath*.

Gussow, Mel. *Don't Say Yes Until I Finish Talking: A Biography of Darryl F. Zanuck*. Garden City, New York: Doubleday, 1971. Discusses the Twentieth Century-Fox production of *The Grapes of Wrath*.

Hobson, Laura Z. "Trade Winds," *The Saturday Review*, 35 (March 1, 1952), 6. Discusses controversial reactions to *Viva Zapata!*

Kazan, Elia. "Letters to the Editor," *The Saturday Review*, 35 (April 5, 1952), 22; (May 24, 1952), 25, 28. The director's reply to criticisms of *Viva Zapata!*

————. *Elia Kazan: A Life*. New York: Alfred A. Knopf, 1988.

Kline, Herbert. " 'The Forgotten Village,' An Account of Film Making in Mexico," *Theatre Arts*, 25 (May 1941), 336–343.

————. "On John Steinbeck," *Steinbeck Quarterly*, 4 (Summer 1971), 80–88. Recollections by the director of filming *The Forgotten Village*.

Lisca, Peter. "John Steinbeck: A Literary Biography," *Steinbeck and His Critics*, E. W. Tedlock, Jr. and C. V. Wicker, eds. Albuquerque: University of New Mexico Press, 1957.

Metzger, Charles R. "The Film Version of Steinbeck's *The Pearl*," *Steinbeck Quarterly*, 4 (Summer 1971), 88–92.

Morsberger, Robert E. "Adrift in Steinbeck's Lifeboat," *Literature/Film Quarterly*, 4 (Fall 1976), 325–338.

————. "*Cannery Row* Revisited," *Steinbeck Quarterly*, 16 (Summer–Fall 1983), 89–95.

————. " 'The Chrysanthemums' and 'The Raid' on Film, 1990," *Steinbeck Quarterly*, 24 (Summer–Fall 1991), 125–130.

————. "*Viva Zapata!*": *A Study Guide to Steinbeck* (Part II). Metuchen, New Jersey, and London: The Scarecrow Press, 1979.

Pinchon, Edgcumb. *Zapata, the Unconquerable*. New York: Doubleday, Doran, 1941.

Schickel, Richard. *Brando: A Life in Our Times*. New York: Atheneum, 1991. Contains a discussion of the filming of *Viva Zapata!*

Steinbeck, Elaine and Robert Wallsten, eds. *Steinbeck: A Life in Letters*. New York: The Viking Press, 1975.

Steinbeck, John. *The Forgotten Village*. New York: The Viking Press, 1941.

————. *The Grapes of Wrath*. New York: The Viking Press, 1939.

————. *In Dubious Battle*. New York: The Viking Press, Compass Books, 1963.

————. *The Moon Is Down*. New York: The Viking Press, 1942.

————. *A Russian Journal*. New York: The Viking Press, 1948.

————. *Sea of Cortez: A Leisurely Journal of Travel and Research* (in col-

laboration with Edward F. Ricketts). New York: The Viking Press, 1941.
————. *Their Blood Is Strong*. San Francisco: Simon J. Lubin Society of California, Inc., 1938.

Truffaut, François. *Hitchcock*, with the collaboration of Helen G. Scott. New York: Simon and Schuster, 1967. Discusses the making of *Lifeboat*.

Tuttleton, James W. "Steinbeck in Russia: The Rhetoric of Praise and Blame," *Modern Fiction Studies*, 11 (Spring 1965), 80.

Womack, John Jr. *Zapata and the Mexican Revolution*. New York: Alfred A. Knopf, 1969.

REVIEWS OF *Viva Zapata!*:

The Christian Century, 69 (April 23, 1952), 510.

Hartung, Philip T. *Commonweal*, 55 (February 29, 1952), 517.

Holiday, 11 (May 1952), 105.

Life, 32 (February 25, 1952), 61.

McCarten, John. "Wool from the West," *The New Yorker*, 27 (February 16, 1952), 106.

McDonald, Gerold D. *Library Journal*, 77 (February 15, 1952), 311.

The New Republic, 126 (February 25, 1952), 21.

Newsweek, 34 (February 4, 1952), 78.

FOR THE BEST IN PAPERBACKS, LOOK FOR THE

In every corner of the world, on every subject under the sun, Penguin represents quality and variety—the very best in publishing today.

For complete information about books available from Penguin—including Puffins, Penguin Classics, and Arkana—and how to order them, write to us at the appropriate address below. Please note that for copyright reasons the selection of books varies from country to country.

In the United Kingdom: Please write to *Dept. JC, Penguin Books Ltd, FREEPOST, West Drayton, Middlesex UB7 0BR.*

If you have any difficulty in obtaining a title, please send your order with the correct money, plus ten percent for postage and packaging, to *P.O. Box No. 11, West Drayton, Middlesex UB7 0BR*

In the United States: Please write to *Consumer Sales, Penguin USA, P.O. Box 999, Dept. 17109, Bergenfield, New Jersey 07621-0120.* VISA and MasterCard holders call 1-800-253-6476 to order all Penguin titles

In Canada: Please write to *Penguin Books Canada Ltd, 10 Alcorn Avenue, Suite 300, Toronto, Ontario M4V 3B2*

In Australia: Please write to *Penguin Books Australia Ltd, P.O. Box 257, Ringwood, Victoria 3134*

In New Zealand: Please write to *Penguin Books (NZ) Ltd, Private Bag 102902, North Shore Mail Centre, Auckland 10*

In India: Please write to *Penguin Books India Pvt Ltd, 706 Eros Apartments, 56 Nehru Place, New Delhi 110 019*

In the Netherlands: Please write to *Penguin Books Netherlands bv, Postbus 3507, NL-1001 AH Amsterdam*

In Germany: Please write to *Penguin Books Deutschland GmbH, Metzlerstrasse 26, 60594 Frankfurt am Main*

In Spain: Please write to *Penguin Books S.A., Bravo Murillo 19, 1° B, 28015 Madrid*

In Italy: Please write to *Penguin Italia s.r.l., Via Felice Casati 20, I-20124 Milano*

In France: Please write to *Penguin France S.A., 17 rue Lejeune, F-31000 Toulouse*

In Japan: Please write to *Penguin Books Japan, Ishikiribashi Building, 2-5-4, Suido, Bunkyo-ku, Tokyo 112*

In Greece: Please write to *Penguin Hellas Ltd, Dimocritou 3, GR-106 71 Athens*

In South Africa: Please write to *Longman Penguin Southern Africa (Pty) Ltd, Private Bag X08, Bertsham 2013*